DANGEROUS ANGEL

by

Deborah Martin

A TOPAZ BOOK

TOPAZ
Published by the Penguin Group
Penguin Books USA Inc., 375 Hudson Street,
New York, New York 10014, U.S.A.
Penguin Books Ltd, 27 Wrights Lane,
London W8 5TZ, England
Penguin Books Australia Ltd, Ringwood,
Victoria, Australia
Penguin Books Canada Ltd, 10 Alcorn Avenue,
Toronto, Ontario, Canada M4V 3B2
Penguin Books (N.Z.) Ltd, 182–190 Wairau Road,
Auckland 10, New Zealand

Penguin Books Ltd, Registered Offices:
Harmondsworth, Middlesex, England

First published by Topaz, an imprint of Dutton Signet,
a division of Penguin Books USA Inc.

First Printing, September, 1994
10 9 8 7 6 5 4 3 2

Printed in Canada

PROOF POSITIVE

"There is one way you could prove how much you care about my feelings," Cordelia told the duke.

Sebastian hesitated, almost afraid to know. "What is that?"

Her eyes darkened as her voice dropped to a throaty murmur. "You could make love to me."

"Is that all you want of me? A stallion to assuage your maidenly curiosity? I'm sure you can find any number of men to give you that."

"I don't want another man," she said. "I want you."

Something snapped in him then. With a groan, he dragged her body to his, crushing his mouth against hers. As his steely arm imprisoned her waist, he invaded her mouth, plundering it until she clung to him breathlessly.

Then he drew back. "Bloody hell, it strikes the soul from my body every time I realize I can never have you."

Sucking in a ragged breath, she said, "You can have me for tonight, Sebastian."

And this night would have to last forever. . . .

ANNOUNCING THE

TOPAZ FREQUENT READERS CLUB
COMMEMORATING TOPAZ'S
1 YEAR ANNIVERSARY!

THE MORE YOU BUY, THE MORE YOU GET

Redeem coupons found here and in the back of all new Topaz titles for FREE Topaz gifts:

Send in:

 2 coupons for a free TOPAZ novel (choose from the list below);

- ☐ **THE KISSING BANDIT**, Margaret Brownley
- ☐ **BY LOVE UNVEILED**, Deborah Martin
- ☐ **TOUCH THE DAWN**, Chelley Kitzmiller
- ☐ **WILD EMBRACE**, Cassie Edwards

 4 coupons for an "I Love the Topaz Man" on-board sign

 6 coupons for a TOPAZ compact mirror

 8 coupons for a Topaz Man T-shirt

Just fill out this certificate and send with original sales receipts to:

TOPAZ FREQUENT READERS CLUB-1ST ANNIVERSARY
Penguin USA • Mass Market Promotion; Dept. H.U.G.
375 Hudson St., NY, NY 10014

Name_____

Address_____

City_____State_____Zip_____

Offer expires 1/31 1995

This certificate must accompany your request. No duplicates accepted. Void where prohibited, taxed or restricted. Allow 4-6 weeks for receipt of merchandise. Offer good only in U.S., its territories, and Canada.

To all my writing buddies—Rexanne Becnel, Pamela Caldwell, Barbara Colley, Marie Goodwin, and Dr. Emily Toth. Thanks for listening.

To Dr. Roseanne Osborne and Dr. Anita Tully, my two wonderful English professors, who encouraged me to write.

And to my beautiful son Nicholas—I give you all my love and all the music it takes to pierce your silent world.

Chapter One

And if I fail ever to honour thee,
Let this heavenly light I see,
Be as dark as hell to me.
—John Dowland,
"Rest Awhile, You Cruel Cares"

March 1743, Cumberland County, England

"Come, heavy slee-ee-eep . . . the image of troo-oo-oo death . . . an' clo-o-ose up these my weary . . . weepin' eyes . . ."

Cordelia Shalstone clapped her hands over her ears as the toneless singing rose in the vicarage's upper rooms. Thank heavens no one had called for the vicar this afternoon, for how could she explain Father's drunken moaning of a heart-wrenching madrigal?

Of course she could always remind them what this dreadful day signified—the three-year anniversary of Mother's death. Faced with that reminder, any of the villagers would be as understanding as always about Father's grief.

Still, Father had been caterwauling since noon, and despite her own grief, she had work to do. There was Father's sermon to write for tomorrow . . . accounts to balance . . . Sunday dinner to plan. . . . Not to mention that Mrs. Weston was due to deliver her fifth child any day now, and Cordelia had promised to sit beside her during the birthing. Cordelia could easily find herself pulled from a warm bed tonight and sent out into the cold.

Please, Father, be quiet, she pleaded silently. *For once, let it rest.*

As if he'd heard her, the sound abruptly ended. A few seconds of silence passed. She removed a hand from one ear and cocked her head, listening. Stumbling steps echoed overhead, followed by a muffled groan and the creak of the oak bed.

. More silence, blessed silence. She removed her other hand and laid it on her father's massive oak desk before her. His even, heavy snore greeted her ears, and she sighed. With Father asleep, the vicarage at Belham would be as quiet as the church during sheep-shearing time, and she'd have at least two or three steady hours in which to work.

Cordelia stared mournfully at the chaotic jumble atop the desk. She should work on Father's sermon first. She really should. Nonetheless, despite her resolve, her gaze turned to the pages of her latest composition partially hidden beneath the heavy Bible at her elbow.

A loud snort echoed from the room above before her father lapsed back into snoring. That decided her. She'd not get another chance to work peacefully on her music until Monday, and the sermon, after all, could be jotted down in the morning before the service.

With that decided, she tipped up the Bible and pulled out the sheets of choral music, dislodging a few letters from her music publisher in London. No, *Father's* music publisher in London. It grew harder each day to remember that it was Father's signature on the letters that accompanied her music to London; it was *his* name Lord Kent knew and respected. After all, no respectable publisher would seriously consider the music of a woman. If it weren't for the money her chorales brought them, money they needed to maintain an adequate household, she'd balk at such a deception.

She sighed, then pushed the letters aside and spread her choral music out across the desk so she could study the carefully penned notes. It took a few moments to gain that treasured space of concentration where she could blot out the world, but soon she succeeded in immersing herself in the music. Before long, she was analyzing the contrapuntal, trying to figure out how to alter the tenor and alto lines so they weren't the same for two measures.

She wrinkled her nose. Perhaps if she moved the tenor in the second note of the first measure . . . but then there would be almost an octave leap and that would severely tax the talents of Belham's small church choir. . . .

"Miss?"

At the sound of the strident voice, Cordelia glanced up to see their servant, Prudence, standing in the doorway.

Quickly Cordelia slid the piece of music under the letters and met the servant's harsh stare. "Don't tell me. Mrs. Weston's time has come."

Hearing Cordelia's too sharp tone, Prudence drew her mouth into a tight, disapproving knot. Prudence's advanced age and lack of family were the only things keeping her employed in the vicarage household. Cordelia's mother had hired Prudence in haste and repented at leisure, but had been too kind-hearted to dismiss the bitter old woman. Now, as with nearly everything else, Cordelia followed in her mother's footsteps.

Prudence tilted her chin to peer down her nose at Cordelia, whose cap was askew and gown mussed. "I'm unaware of Mrs. Weston's condition. However, there is a man waiting for you in the parlor." Prudence said "a man" in the same tone of voice she reserved for "a serpent" or "a piece of offal."

"A man?"

"He claims to be a lord, miss."

With difficulty, Cordelia suppressed a smile. Naturally, Prudence would suspect any man in Belham "claiming" to be a peer. Belham's only nobleman, the earl who provided her father with his living, was an elderly recluse. The rest of the peerage ignored the hills of Belham in north England, preferring to tour the lake region to the west. Thus Belham remained a quiet town, where sheep grazed contentedly while their owners bickered over whose wool had the softest texture.

No wonder Prudence was suspicious. Cordelia, on the other hand, couldn't help a surge of excitement. "What does he want?"

Impossible as it seemed, Prudence's mouth drew even tighter. "He claims he came from London to see the vicar."

"Oh, dear." Father was at his worst this afternoon, and if she wanted to preserve his reputation, she daren't disturb him, not even for a lord. "Did he give his name?"

"Lord Waverley. Never heard of him myself."

Cordelia paled. Lord Waverley? Here? Could it be? She stared at Lord Kent's letters. Lord Kent had a brother, a titled older brother who had become the Duke of Waverley only a few years before.

Her heart began to pound. Surely it wasn't possible. Honorine, her mother's girlhood friend, had mentioned in one of her numerous gossipy letters that Lord Waverley resided in India. So he couldn't be in Belham, could he?

Then again, Lord Kent did have a brother who was Duke of Waverley, so who else could it be? She knew no peers other than their local earl.

She strained to remember what Honorine had written about the man. Honorine had been awed that the vicar knew the brother of a duke. But hadn't there been something else, too? Hadn't Honorine mentioned something about his dealings with the East India Company? Yes. Honorine had said the duke was "in trade," to which he'd been driven because his father had died heavily in debt, leaving his heir with siblings to provide for.

Shaking her head, Cordelia rose and absently smoothed her skirts. None of that explained why he was here. It must involve the music his brother published for her. But how?

"Shall I tell this man that the master is unwell, and ask him to return tomorrow?" Prudence asked.

It was their standard excuse, but she doubted it would suffice today. "Nay, I'll speak with his lordship," she said distractedly as she left the room.

Another woman would have pinched her cheeks and worried about the worn spots on her slippers. Another woman would have tucked in the few wisps of curls sticking out in all directions from beneath her cap.

Not Cordelia. Although the thought of Lord Waverley waiting in her parlor both intrigued and disturbed her, she paid scant heed to her appearance. Like her father, she had too many other things to worry about. Some vague inner voice cautioned that her linsey-woolsey gown was too simple for receiving a duke and her apron and fingers too ink-stained, but she ignored it, as always.

The sight of her visitor through the parlor's open door, however, stopped her short. She might ignore her own appearance, but she certainly couldn't help noticing his.

She surveyed him unobserved as he stood with his profile to her, leafing through the pieces of music scattered haphazardly atop her prized harpsichord. So this was Lord Waverley. Merciful heavens, he wasn't at all what she'd expected. She'd thought he'd be older, much older. Yet his lean, well-muscled figure and unlined face bespoke a man thirty years old at most.

Surely this wasn't the same Lord Waverley Honorine had spoken of—the captain of industry. This man had the dashing air of a rakehell.

Then she cocked her head and revised that opinion. He wasn't actually handsome. Boldly cut, almost wolf-like, cheeks defined a fierce face, and not a speck of fashionable powder dulled his tanned skin. Not to mention that his concentrated scowl made him look untouchable, which wasn't at all proper for a charming rake.

There was also his lack of a wig. Everyone wore a wig these days, even her father. She thought it a silly fashion. Why should one shave off a perfectly good head of hair only to cover it with something resembling a rat's coat?

Lord Waverley's chestnut hair was drawn back into a simple queue at his neck. But just as she was admiring the way his natural hair glinted with fiery highlights in the late afternoon sun coming through the room's one window, he turned and spotted her. Interest flickered in his eyes.

Embarrassed to be caught peeping at him through the door, she strode into the room and held out her hand. "Lord Waverley, I am Miss Shalstone."

He took her hand, brushed his lips over the knuckles, and released it with an easy courtesy. "You're the lady of the vicarage?"

His voice came as an unexpected pleasure, the rich rumble of a baritone when she'd thought from his lean figure that he'd be a tenor.

"Yes. I'm the vicar's daughter." She summoned forth a calm she didn't feel. "Prudence tells me you wish to see my father."

Lord Waverley nodded, then arched a brow. "I assume he isn't available, since you're here and he's not."

His astuteness flustered her. "I-I'm afraid you're right. Father is . . . ill this evening and unable to accept callers. Perhaps I can help you?"

"Thank you, but I'm afraid only your father can help me. I'm sure he'll speak to me despite his illness. Tell him I've come on behalf of Lord Richard Kent. My brother."

So it really was the Duke of Waverley, she thought, her stomach knotting. She decided to get right to the point. "Lord Kent publishes . . . er . . . Father's music. I assume that's what you've come about."

Lord Waverley surveyed her with an aggravated air, then tossed his head as if to dismiss her. "I'd prefer to discuss this with your father, so if you'll call him—"

"Father is ill. When he's ill, I administer his affairs. I assure you, I know everything about Father's music and his dealings with your brother." She fought the urge to be sarcastic. *"Everything."*

A leaden silence weighted the air. At last the duke quipped, "Do you write his music, too?"

She paled. He had no idea how close to the truth he'd come. "Your Grace, why must you see Father tonight?"

Dark gold eyes glinted with the force of a temper carefully held in check. Their odd color reminded her of the eyes of a beast she'd once seen in the forest, savage and unrelenting. And like the beast's, they studied her as if gauging her weaknesses.

Suddenly his unsettling gaze shifted to the harpsichord. He gestured to it with a nonchalant flick of one finger. "Do you play?"

The question caught her offguard. "Why . . . of course."

"Of course?"

"The harpsichord is mine," she said in a fit of daring, gesturing to the instrument before she caught herself and folded her hands together. Father always accused her of talking with her hands.

"I see. And where is your father's instrument?"

Her lips tightened. "Your Grace, I don't wish to be rude, but I must return to my duties. Would you please tell me why you've come to see Father?"

The duke rubbed the edge of his jaw. "I can see you're going to be stubborn about this."

"Yes, I am."

He glared at her, then sighed. "All right. As you've surmised, I've come about his music. I'm sure you know that my brother admires your father's music a great deal."

She stared at him bewildered. The duke had come all

this way to pay a compliment? "Lord Kent has said as much in his letters."

"Has he?" Lord Waverley regarded her more thoughtfully. "Well, it seems your father has gained another admirer, a man you might have heard of." He paused. "George Frideric Handel."

Suddenly the room seemed sucked dry of all sound. The pace of Cordelia's heart quickened even as disbelief swamped her. George Frideric Handel. Merely one of the greatest composers in London. Last year's Dublin performances of his new oratorio, *The Messiah,* had been discussed from farm to town. Honorine had said the music rivaled that of the angels.

And Handel admired *her* music? How could that be?

"I see you've heard of Handel," Lord Waverley interrupted her thoughts.

She could only nod. Heard of Handel? Who hadn't?

"Richard's been actively attempting to acquire Handel's music for publication. But as you may know, Handel is loyal to a publisher named John Walsh, and thus has ignored Richard's overtures. Until recently."

"Recently?" What had all of this to do with her?

"Apparently, Handel bought a few of the chorales that Richard had published anonymously at your father's request. Handel made a bargain with my brother. Handel would give him an oratorio to publish if Richard would introduce him to his 'best composer,' the writer of the chorales."

Suddenly everything fell into place. She'd completely forgotten about the letters Lord Kent had sent a few months ago, inviting Father to visit London at Lord Kent's expense. Those letters hadn't mentioned Handel, however. Her replies had insisted such a visit would be impossible. The vicar couldn't handle the travel. Besides, she'd written, he wished to keep his identity secret, for it wasn't seemly that a vicar should write church music for money.

Her response had been a temporary measure at best, but when Lord Kent had dropped the subject after a few letters, she'd considered it successful. His recent letters hadn't mentioned a visit.

If she'd known the source of his desire for the visit, however, she'd have realized he wouldn't give up. Not with Handel's music as the reward for perseverance.

Merciful heavens, what was she to do? It thrilled her to think that a composer of any significance wanted to meet *her,* to speak with *her,* but it was utterly impossible.

For one thing, it wasn't actually *she* whom Lord Kent wanted to present to Handel; it was her father. Even if she could admit to being the composer, Lord Kent would never introduce her to Handel. His letters had often stated that women were incapable of composing. In fact, when she'd timidly suggested he consider a chorale by the vicar's daughter, he'd politely refused, stating that women were better suited for domestic duties. Even if she told the truth, he'd never believe her, and that would be the end of any meeting with Handel.

At any rate, Handel himself undoubtedly had the same bias. She could almost guess what the composer's reaction would be if she were allowed to meet him. He'd laugh her from the room. What's more, she'd make a fool of herself and her father before her publisher, and that would be the end of the music that had become her whole life.

The duke broke into her thoughts again. "Now you see why I must speak to your father in person."

"You've come to invite him to go with you and meet Handel," she said dully.

"Yes. My brother won't reveal your father's name without his permission. I've come to obtain that permission and take your father to London. I wish to leave immediately, if possible."

She wrung her hands and whirled away from him to pace the small room. "But it's not possible!"

"What's not possible? That we leave immediately? That I meet your father? I don't see why my request should be such—"

"It's not possible for Father to meet Handel." She drew a deep, steadying breath. She mustn't show her agitation. "I . . . er . . . Father explained that in his letters." She faced him, affecting a dignity she didn't feel, although her heart bled at the thought of having to relinquish such an opportunity.

"You must tell Lord Kent that the composer of those chorales can't travel and in any case wishes to maintain his anonymity and privacy." She forced a steely edge into her voice. "Tell him it can't be done."

His granite, implacable expression bespoke a man who didn't accept defeat. "Believe me, Miss Shalstone, that isn't possible either. I didn't journey to this deserted portion of England in search of some vicar with dubious musical talent without good reason." He hesitated, drawing himself up into ramrod straightness, every inch the duke.

He seemed to debate whether to say more. Then he took a deep breath. "Richard's publishing company is failing."

If he'd wanted to stun her completely, he'd certainly succeeded. She stepped back, her hand rising to cover her heart. "What do you mean?"

Glancing away from her, he stiffened. She could tell he chafed under the necessity of revealing so much to a stranger. "I mean, it's on the verge of being eaten alive by its creditors."

She thought of Lord Kent's amiable letters and grimaced. "I see. How is he taking it?"

"How is he taking it?" Lord Waverley laughed harshly. "He's not eating or sleeping and he wanders the house like a wraith. That's how he's taking it."

She gazed at his stark expression and felt instant pity.

"One of my sisters summoned me back when things began going sour. She thought I could help. I'd assumed that she exaggerated the situation, but I was due for a visit anyway—" A muscle high in his cheek tightened. "When I saw him, I couldn't believe it. He's thin to the point of emaciation. He has creditors beating at his doors, he won't take money from me, and he's letting the situation drain him body and soul."

"I'm sorry." Inadequate words, but what else could she say?

In any case, he ignored them. "Unfortunately, Richard isn't a strong man. As a child, he had an illness that partially impaired his legs. When he took over the company our father had acquired and built it into something substantial, it became his salvation. It kept him from feeling useless and unwanted. Then when it started to fail, he deteriorated. Now when we try to coax him to take better care of himself, he says he has nothing to live for anyway."

His gaze swung back to hers, angry and resentful. "Nothing to live for! What about three sisters who rely on him totally?"

"I don't see how a visit from my father would prevent all this. I mean, if it's money he needs—"

"It's more than a matter of money or I could save him." He glanced away from her. "A year ago he unknowingly published a manuscript that had apparently been stolen from a composer with powerful patrons. The man condemned Richard publicly for it, and now Richard's reputation as a publisher is damaged. No musician will buy his publications because they think he's untrustworthy, and decent composers won't publish with him because no one buys the music. It's a vicious circle he can't escape."

"Surely if he explained—"

"He did. He explained. To everyone who would listen. No one believed him." He sighed. "To be honest, I didn't tell you the whole story about Handel. Handel only suggested this meeting after Richard went to him for help, hoping that if he could convince Handel of his innocence, Handel would back his company. To his credit, Handel did sympathize with his situation. That's when he brought up Richard's publications of your father's music."

He shot her an enigmatic look. "Of course, since your father insisted on having his works published anonymously, Handel was curious to know who'd written them ... curious and suspicious because Richard already had a reputation for stealing musicians' works. Handel agreed to champion Richard's company and give him an oratorio to publish ... if he could speak with the 'brilliant composer of these chorales' in person and hear him testify that the music was his own. That's why this visit is so crucial."

"You think Father's visit would ensure Handel's aid and thus reverse the downward turn of Lord Kent's business," she said flatly.

"Yes. Without it, I fear his business will end."

Her mind reeled at that awful thought. The kind sentiments of Lord Kent's letters, the broad encouragement he'd always given her, or rather, Father—all of it gone. She couldn't bear to think of him suffering through such failure, for she'd come to respect him despite his opinions of women musicians.

A sudden guilt choked her. She'd deceived him. Even his "best composer" was a fraud. What would knowing the truth do to him? He expected a vicar, a man whose request for anonymity was odd, but characteristic of his self-effacing profession.

If he learned the truth. . . .

The thought brought her up short. Lord Kent mustn't learn the truth. It was impossible.

The duke scowled. "I tell you, Miss Shalstone, I won't have my only brother waste away when the solution to his problem is at hand. I spend much of my time abroad, and he is the only one to care for my sisters in my absence. Moreover, I can't bear the thought—"

He broke off, and she ached for him. Her refusal was forcing him to bare his soul to a stranger, something to which the duke was undoubtedly unaccustomed.

Lord Waverley leveled her with a gaze so determined it frightened her. "No matter what it takes, I'll make certain Handel meets your father, by God! And you'll not put me off by telling me nonsense about his not being able to travel!"

He obviously meant it. But she couldn't help him. He must be made to understand that. Unfortunately, the only way to convince him would be to tell him the truth. Surely once he heard the truth, he'd understand why he must find another way to help his brother.

She sighed. "We have a problem—"

"No problem," he snapped and stepped closer, impatience in his face. "Merely take me to the composer of the chorales—your father—and the problem is solved."

She faced him with trepidation. "The problem is, my father is *not* the composer of the chorales."

That set him back a moment, but not for long. "Then who is? Some country curate of your father's acquaintance? The church choirmaster? A laborer even? It doesn't matter. As long as this person will announce to Handel that Richard is his publisher, I'm sure Handel will be appeased, for he doesn't know your father's identity anyway. So tell me who wrote the bloody things, and I'll be on my way!"

It was time for the truth. "I'm afraid, Your Grace, that *I* wrote 'the bloody things.' "

He opened his mouth, and for a moment she thought he'd shout at her. His face went through such contortions of disbelief that she was insulted. Then he did something absolutely unexpected.

He threw back his head and laughed, not a few polite titters, but a full-out laugh with decidedly cynical overtones. His laughter cut her to the quick, even if it was understandable.

With remnants of his laughter still in his voice, he muttered, "How droll. You wrote them, did you?" His expression tightened, and the humor disappeared from his drawn features as instantly as it had come. "I take it you're an admirer of Handel yourself and wish to see him in person. Fine. You may accompany us. You don't have to lie to receive an invitation."

Lie? He dared to accuse her of lying? "It's the truth. I wrote every one of the chorales Lord Kent published."

"Indeed." His voice lowered. "I suggest you take me to see the vicar now. This has been amusing, but I don't have time to waste on jests."

"This is *not* a jest. I tell you, I wrote those chorales!"

"My brother insists that the letters he received came from a vicar." His eyes raked her body with an insolence that made her color. "You don't look like a jowly, stern-faced old cleric."

She'd expected him not to believe her, but did he have to be so detestably insulting? "No, I don't think I'm jowly. Not that I've noticed, at any rate. Stern-faced?" She raised one eyebrow as she glanced pointedly at the mirror hanging over the mantel. "Perhaps on occasion. As for being old, I don't believe three-and-twenty is a decrepit age, no matter what society may say."

"My point is, you're not the vicar," he gritted out.

"Nonetheless, I wrote that music."

"For God's sake, you're a woman!"

Anger swelled within her. She glanced down at her body, at her modest breasts and slender waist, then flashed him an expression of mock surprise. "Fie upon it, I believe you're right! Fancy that, I'm a woman! All this time I'd thought I was a toad!" She met his seething gaze. "You have this incredible talent for stating the obvious."

He closed his eyes as an expression of utter frustration crossed his face. "Miss Shalstone, if you don't call your father down here this minute and stop playing games with me, I shall tread upstairs myself and find him."

Sudden alarm beat through her. She couldn't allow this man to see Father this evening. It was absolutely unacceptable. "There's no need to be rude. Father is resting, and I'll not have him disturbed. If you wish to return—"

"I bloody well want to see your father now!" he shouted. Then apparently realizing he was losing control, he lowered his voice to a threatening murmur. "I won't be thwarted in this."

An unholy gleam lit her face. "Your Grace is becoming overly excited."

Apparently that wiped all consideration for her right out of his mind. "Devil take you, Miss Shalstone, you haven't begun to see 'overly excited'—"

"What's all the fuss about?" a voice came from the stairs.

With a groan, Cordelia shut her eyes and pressed one hand to her temple. Merciful heavens, it was Father. She should have known he'd hear the noise, but did he have to appear now?

She faced the door as her father stepped gingerly into the room, looking for all the world like Lord Waverley's imagined vicar. He was indeed jowly, and at the moment, stern-faced. Certainly, the word "old" fit him these days, for he'd aged ten years in the three since her mother had died.

In other respects, however, he resembled a publican more than a vicar, with his wig askew, his clothes rumpled, and his bleary eyes unfocused.

"Can't a man have some peace around here?" he said peevishly as his gaze finally settled on her.

"Good evening, Father." Her voice was more clipped than usual. "I'm so glad you're here. Your publisher's brother has come to call."

She ignored the duke and his probable expression of delight at this turn of events.

"My publisher?" Her father rubbed his reddened nose, then wiped his hand on his sleeve.

At least his words weren't slurred. She could be thankful for that. She softened her voice. "Yes, Father. Don't you remember? Lord Kent in London. He publishes the music."

Her father thought a moment, scratching at his head and completely dislodging his wig, which tumbled to the floor unnoticed. Then he harrumphed. "Oh, yes, yes. The music. I forgot." He turned to the duke. "You've come about the music?"

"I have."

Waving his hand dismissively, her father frowned. "Then talk to my daughter. I don't do a thing with it but sign my name to the letters, y'know." He stared about him, confused. "Otherwise, people wouldn't approve."

"Of what, sir?" Lord Waverley asked, clearly growing more irritated by the moment.

"Of women and music. I mean, writing it. I mean, of Cordelia writing it. People frown on that kind of thing. Don't see why, though." He grew glassy-eyed. "My wife was an angel on the spinet. Aye, a perfect angel. An' if she could play music, then certainly—"

"You're saying your daughter actually writes the chorales my brother publishes?"

At his incredulous tone, Cordelia snapped her head around. If condescension were considered a virtuous trait among the nobility, she thought, Lord Waverley had virtue to spare.

Her father pulled on his ear. "We-ell, yes. 'Course she does. *I* couldn't. Can't hold a tune to save m'life. It's a bunch of jumble to me. Choirmaster says she writes a good hymn, though. Who'm I to judge otherwise?"

At least Father had the good grace to defend her. Instinctively, she stepped toward him, linking her hand in the crook of his bent arm. He patted her fingers with a vague smile.

She flashed the duke a triumphant look, but he seemed not to notice. He'd gone very still, and his gaze fixed on her father's face. "Do you mean to say everyone knows the music isn't yours? And they allow this . . . this duplicity to continue? They perform your daughter's music without a thought?"

Her father's hand tightened on her arm. So far he'd held himself together admirably well, but the increasing lean of his body told her he wouldn't last much longer. She led him to one of their damask-covered chairs.

As he plopped down heavily in it, she hastened to answer the duke's question, a hint of irony in her tone. "Are you crediting our fair town with being more discriminating than London musicians?"

He winced at the reminder that, by his own admission, Handel and his brother thought a great deal of her compositions.

She sniffed. "Our parishioners are happy to get what music they can. They don't question who produces it."

A slash of a frown crossed the duke's brow. "Then they're a bloody meek lot. But it's not your townspeople who concern me." He faced her father. "You, sir, should never have allowed your daughter to deceive my brother. Why would you let your daughter draw you about by the nose and make a fool of you?"

"Make a fool of him!" Cordelia exploded. "You have no idea—"

" 'Tis all right, Cordelia," her father interrupted. An oddly lucid expression passed over his face. "The gentleman merely worries about me. I can see that." He lifted his unsteady gaze to the duke. "What did you want again?"

Lord Waverley uttered a low curse of the sort Cordelia would have expected from a tavern boy and not a gentleman. Then again, what did she know of gentlemen?

She did know the situation had gotten out of hand. Father was cracking his knuckles as he did whenever he was agitated. Any minute now he'd begin to babble, and then the duke would think them both even more mad than he undoubtedly already did.

She placed a reassuring hand on her father's shoulder. "His lordship has come about the music. It's nothing to concern yourself with, as I'm sure he now realizes." She got a snort from the duke for that. "I'll take care of it, so why don't you return to bed, since you're ... ah ... not feeling well this evening. You need your rest if you're to deliver your sermon in the morning."

Her father stood, rocking a bit before he settled on his feet. "Yes, yes. There's that. I'm not feeling well, y'know," he added with a conspiratorial nod to the duke. Then to her horror, he began searching in his waistcoat. "Aye, not well at all. Where's my medication? It's here somewhere. I know it." He patted his breast pocket, growing more perturbed each moment.

She could see the wine flask poking out of his coat pocket, and with what she hoped was a surreptitious movement, she whisked it into her apron pocket. "Come now, Father, I'm sure you left it upstairs. Let's go see."

At that precise moment, her father careened, then crumpled to the floor in a heap of squat legs and flailing arms. As she watched in helpless horror, tears splashed down his wan cheeks.

"Cordelia, I've forgot what I came down for. And I can't find my medication. Where's my medication?"

Cordelia fought the abject humiliation settling into her gut like sour milk. She couldn't bear to look at the duke. Ducking her head, she knelt to catch her father beneath his arms. "It's all right, Father. We'll find it. Try to stand. Come on."

Then before she could protest, Lord Waverley bent and easily lifted her father. Murmuring, "I'll help," he clasped her father about the waist and urged him toward the stairs.

Shame flooded her. She followed close behind. "Please, there's no need—"

He stopped, then fixed her with a steady gaze. He seemed to see into her heart, to uncloak all the secret longings, the bitter secrets. "Ah, but there is. A man in your father's ... ah ... condition can be difficult to handle."

Of all the blessed things.... The duke had guessed the truth, despite her attempts to hide it. Of course, how could he not? Father's breath reeked of wine, and his red nose practically glowed in the semidarkness of the hall.

As usual, her father went into a panic when he thought she'd left him. "Cordelia, love, where are you?" He pushed the duke aside and whirled around, almost toppling himself to the floor once more.

"I'm right here, Father." She caught him by the arm and shot the duke a helpless glance. "I have to help him now, Lord Waverley. When he's . . . ill like this, I have to help him." She couldn't bear to say aloud what the duke must be thinking. Her father leaned heavily against her with the sigh of a contented child as she continued, "Besides, there's the sermon to prepare for tomorrow—"

"Are you planning to write that too?" the duke bit out.

She ignored his question. "It'll take me some time to calm him, so I'm afraid I must go up, or he'll thrash about, running into things while he looks for me and for his . . . his medication."

Lord Waverley frowned. "Our discussion isn't over, Miss Shalstone. We must still speak about the meeting with Handel."

She stopped short, scarcely noticing her father's weight against her left side. Surely Lord Waverley couldn't mean to continue with his mission. She'd told him the truth about who'd written the music, and her father had confirmed it. Didn't he believe her? Did he still think he could arrange this meeting?

Apparently so. Well, he could try all he liked, she thought, but his efforts were pointless. His condescension about her abilities were only a taste of what she'd get in London, and she didn't intend to have more such disdain forced down her throat.

Suddenly her father slumped against her and she nearly buckled under the weight. The duke quickly slid his arm around her father's ribs, relieving her of the burden, and without a word began to climb the steps.

Grateful for the help, she mounted the stairs with him and her stumbling father. But when they reached the top, she attempted to take him from the duke.

"Let me help you get him into bed," Lord Waverley said, still supporting all of her father's weight with his broad shoulder.

"No!" She fought the panic in her voice. "No. I'd rather deal with him myself." She couldn't bear for Lord Waverley to see her father blubbering and babbling as she urged him to sleep. Her eyes pleaded with the duke's. "Go now. Please."

He regarded her solemnly for a moment. "I'll go," he said at last. "But I'll return tomorrow."

She nodded, knowing she wouldn't be able to persuade him otherwise. "Come after the morning services." She paused, thinking quickly. "Come for dinner at two. Father and I will both be better able to talk then." And dealing with the duke would be much easier in a pleasant social setting, surrounded by her father, the choirmaster, and the other friends who generally came to dinner on the Sabbath.

Lord Waverley frowned, which made him appear even more wolfish. "As you wish." His reproving gaze settled briefly on her. "But I think I'll ensure that your father can handle tomorrow's discussion."

To her astonishment, he thrust his arm around her father and snatched the flask of wine right out of her apron, pocketing it neatly in his coat.

As she stared at him wide-eyed, mortified to the depths of her soul, he murmured, "Your father will have to survive without his 'medication' tonight, Miss Shalstone. For I fully intend to have a conversation with him on the morrow."

When he released her father and strode down the stairs with such arrogant confidence, she groaned aloud. Did he truly think she'd have returned the flask to Father? Merciful heavens, she spent half her days emptying the flasks she found hidden throughout the house, yet they always reappeared, mysteriously filled again.

No matter what she did, no matter how well she locked the cellar, Father always got his liquor. Either he was coercing a villager into buying it for him or secretly buying it himself somewhere. She'd been unable to determine who his source was, but if she ever found the monster, she'd tear the man's eyes out. Plugging it at the source seemed her only hope, since Father seemed incapable of stopping, no matter how she begged.

So his lordship thought it was as easy as confiscating a flask, did he? She could almost laugh at his naiveté.

With a bitter sigh, she opened the door to her father's bedchamber and half carried, half dragged her father to his bed.

He fell heavily on it. "Where's my medication?"

"No more medication, Father. It's time for you to rest."

With a pained sigh, he laid his shaved head on the pillow. His eyes slid closed, but he grumbled, "She's left me, you know. Left me all alone. So unfair. 'Tis unfair, isn't it?"

There was no need to ask who "she" was. Privately, Cordelia thought it more than unfair, but she merely said in even tones, "Mother's with God now. It does no good to question God's will."

He nodded, his eyes still closed. She stared at him. He never failed to squeeze her heart. Yet how much longer could she take his place before someone complained to a high church authority? How much longer could she hide his obsession with drink? She didn't know. She only knew she must protect him as long as possible and hold his place for the day when he relinquished his grief and took up his duties once more. To keep him safe, she'd do anything he asked of her.

Lately, however, she'd begun wishing he didn't ask

quite so much. Lately, she'd begun wishing he were more than half a father and half a man.

Angry at herself for the thought, she reached down and stroked the gray stubble that frosted his fleshy cheek.

He stirred slightly. "I wish Florinda hadn't gone, Cordelia. How I wish she hadn't gone."

Something blocked Cordelia's throat, making it difficult for her to answer. Then she swallowed hard. "I wish she hadn't, too, Father."

Because when Cordelia's mother had died, she'd also taken away Cordelia's father. The trouble was, Cordelia didn't know anymore how to get him back.

Chapter Two

Hark! did you ever hear so sweet a singing?
They sing young Love to waken.
The nymphs unto the woods their Queen are bringing.
There was a note well taken!
                                    —Ellis Gibbons,
                                      "Long Live Fair Oriana"

It was odd to sit in an inn with a mug of ale before him when he had half a flask of wine in his pocket, but Sebastian Kent was used to being odd. He'd made a profession of it. After all, a duke wasn't supposed to "peddle spices" in India nor, for that matter, travel about a godforsaken wasteland in northern England on a foolish quest.

He thought of Richard, pale and distracted, roaming the house aimlessly on his crutches, and Sebastian's stomach twisted into knots. This was his last resort for rousing Richard from his despair after numerous failed attempts.

Settling deeper into his seat, Sebastian peered into the mug of ale and groaned. So here he sat in the midst of nowhere, trying to deal with a drunken vicar and his impertinent daughter.

Impertinent *pretty* daughter, Sebastian amended, thinking of Miss Shalstone's trim, neat figure and saucy, kissable mouth.

Kissable mouth? Sweet mother of God, where were his brains tonight? The past week of travel had obviously unsettled him, or he wouldn't be regarding a vicar's daughter with abject lust.

He'd been too long away from Judith, that was the trouble. He hesitated, thinking of his fiancée, who, until this trip, had been his constant companion since his return to England. Nay, he hadn't been away from her long enough. Unfortunately, absence had not made "the heart grow fonder." No matter how many times he thought of Judith's petal-fine skin, soft blond curls, and buxom figure, he couldn't drum up enthusiasm for their wedding.

Yet she suited him in most ways. Her easy amiability and proper demeanor would make her a perfect duchess. What's more, unlike the unruly vicar's daughter, Judith didn't cause trouble. Not for nothing had she earned the nickname, "The Biddable Judith."

Never had she raised her voice to him, never had she questioned his decisions regarding their engagement or future marriage. Granted, sometimes he felt as if he dealt with a chameleon who changed her colors to suit his every mood. Sometimes he wished she'd state her own opinions. But when he pressed her, she always insisted that she agreed with him totally, which made it nearly impossible to discuss anything with her.

Not so with the vicar's daughter. Devil take it, here the chit was again, popping into his every thought. He leaned forward to rest an arm on the table, his brow knit in a scowl. Too bad the vicar's daughter wasn't the horse-faced spinster he'd expected. When his brother had mentioned the vicar's daughter, Sebastian hadn't envisioned a pert, young slip of a woman with winsome brown eyes, soft and sweet as a bowl of chocolate.

He shook his head. From the moment he'd seen her in that tiny parlor with its dresser displaying Staffordshire china and its samplers of Biblical exhortations, he'd known she didn't belong there. She wasn't a timid country maiden.

But she wasn't haughty either. No, Miss Shalstone was far more dangerous. Imagine: a woman with not only talent and intelligence, but an affectionate temperament and endearing good looks to match. Now *that* was a woman who'd draw her husband about by the nose. Look at the way she led her father about.

Which reminded him, he'd wanted to ask the innkeeper about the strange pair. He raised his hand and motioned Mr. Gilwell over. Tomorrow when he visited the vicarage again, he must be better prepared. Today had been a fiasco he didn't want repeated. Still, how could he have expected a woman who was a bloody virtuoso, and her father either an idiot or a drunk?

"Yes, Your Grace?" the innkeeper asked in an obsequious manner. People had bowed and scraped from the moment Sebastian arrived in Belham. It was becoming almost ludicrous the way men bent in half and women swept the floor with their skirts every time Sebastian glanced their way.

He smiled tightly, trying to put the innkeeper at ease. "Thanks for the fine ale. It's the best I've had in days."

The man beamed his delight. "I'm sure as Your Grace generally gets better in London, so's I know we appreciate the kind words. I'll pass them on to me wife. She brews it special herself."

"And a wonderful alewife she is," he said and meant it. "By the way, I wonder if you might give me information about someone in Belham."

"Oh, certainly, Your Grace. Anything you need to know." He bent forward and flashed a sly smile. "I'm the one as hears all the gossip 'round here. I can tell you sumpthin' on everyone."

"Good, then perhaps you can tell me about the vicar."

The innkeeper straightened so quickly he nearly fell over. "Our vicar?"

"Aye."

Mr. Gilwell swallowed and rubbed his thick hands on his apron. "Not meanin' to meddle, Your Grace, but what would you be wantin' with information about Vicar Shalstone?"

The wary, near hostile tone of the innkeeper's voice took Sebastian aback. "I merely wish to know what he's like."

"Why? Is it to know if we're happy with him? Because we're happy, delighted to have him. Don't want him to leave." Then a look of confusion spread over his face. "Then again, he ain't the best vicar in the world. I mean he's got his problems. If you're searchin' for a vicar, you'd probably want to search elsewhere."

It took a second for Sebastian to realize the source of the man's concern. "I'm not here to steal your vicar, if that's what you're worried about."

The man let his guard down a little. He looked Sebastian over suspiciously. "Then why're you askin' about him?"

"This afternoon I went to visit him, but his daughter cut short the visit. She insisted he was ill."

Up went the man's guard again. He eyed Sebastian with concern. "Er, well, Reverend Shalstone has his bad days, y'know, like the rest of us."

Sebastian clamped down on the desire to ask if the vicar's "bad days" were the result of illness or simple drunkenness. Mr. Gilwell was nervous enough as it was.

He took another tack. "Is he often ill?"

Mr. Gilwell rubbed his hands more fiercely against his apron. "Often? How do you mean, often?"

Frustrated by the man's defensiveness, Sebastian gestured to the seat opposite him. "Please sit down."

The innkeeper sat on the very edge of the chair, his eyes wide and worried.

Sebastian leaned forward. "Let me be frank, Mr. Gilwell. I'm concerned about your vicar's health. You can be honest with me. How ill is your vicar? Do you think, for example, he's capable of traveling?"

The innkeeper started up from the table, knocking over Sebastian's mug in the process. Ale spilled into Sebastian's lap.

With a sharp cry of distress, the innkeeper rushed to dab at Sebastian's breeches with his apron. "Beggin' your pardon, Your Grace, but I didn't mean to—"

"Don't worry about it." Sebastian stayed the man's

hand. "Sit down. Please. I've spilt worse things than ale on my clothes in India."

But the innkeeper continued to hover over him. " 'Tis a clumsy oaf I am. I can't believe—"

"No, no, it's my fault. I had no idea that mentioning the vicar's illness would upset you."

The innkeeper went still as stone, then dropped abruptly into the chair again.

"Is he so very ill then?" Sebastian asked.

"You're not here to run him off, are you?" the man asked anxiously.

"Run him off?"

"Aye. All this talk of travelin'—you're not here on behalf of some high churchman from London, are you? I mean, you're not here to turn him out of his post, I hope." His tone turned pleading. "Because we got to have our vicar, Your Grace. 'Tis the only one we've had in a hundred years, ever since the last one were killed by a mob of Papists. Belham's got a reputation, y'know, and besides that, we're a small town and a wee bit provincial, if you hadn't noticed. Takes a long time to get here from London, but then you must've noticed *that*. And we got the Scots only a few miles from us, the murthering Scots."

Sebastian suppressed the wry retort that rose to his lips.

"Your Grace, we got to keep our vicar."

"I see." Sebastian surveyed the innkeeper curiously. "To be honest, sir, you don't seem the kind of man to be overly concerned with religion. Why are you so attached to the vicar?"

Mr. Gilwell colored, but leaned forward to rest two beefy arms on the table. "I understand how you mightn't see the importance of it, bein' as you're in London where there's churchmen to spare. But here . . ." He waved his hand back at the kitchen door, through which three buxom women had been coming and going all evening. "Here we got a need for one. I got three daughters 'bout nearin' the age to marry.

What do I do 'bout a weddin' without my vicar? I got to send all the way to Kensingham for one, that's what. Then there's the seein' to the sick and the poor and—"

"Your vicar does all that?" Sebastian thought of the broken man he'd seen that afternoon.

The man shrugged. "He sees that it gets done if he can't do it hisself."

"You mean, his daughter does it."

Mr. Gilwell looked startled, then gave a noncommittal grunt. "As I say, it gets done."

"Do you mean to tell me that Miss Shalstone does all her father's work?"

"Nay, not all of it." Absently he scratched at a scab on his arm. "He preaches—good sermons, too, without that hellfire business the Enthusiasts fancy. An' he performs baptisms and weddin's and such."

"But his daughter does anything he doesn't absolutely have to do."

The innkeeper shifted uncomfortably in his chair. "Sort of. Let's just say, she gets things done, like her mother before her."

"You mean, he's always been this way?"

"Nay, I didn't mean to say that. Before his wife died, the vicar was a right good one for preachin' and givin' good advice to the men about their souls and preparin' the brides. But he couldn't do it all hisself, y'know, and his wife saw to it that the poor were well-served and the women well-cared for. They made a pow'rful team, they did. Then she died. After that . . . well, after that, his mind . . . it sort of went, y'know."

He didn't know at all. "His mind went? Are you saying he's mad?"

"Not mad. He just ain't always up to doin' his duties. Y'see, his grief took over and he got real sick for a time. And now—"

"Now he drinks," Sebastian stated flatly.

"I didn't say that, did I?"

"No, but it's obvious the man has a problem with

spirits. I could tell he was drunk from the moment I met him."

The innkeeper stiffened, his porcine belly shaking with indignation. "Begging y'r pardon, but ye'd best not say that to anyone else in this town. The man's sufferin' from 'is grief, an' we allow for that, s'long as the work gets done."

"You mean, you cover up for him and let his daughter do his duties."

"S'long as the work gets done," the innkeeper repeated stubbornly.

Sebastian sighed. His question remained unanswered. Did the vicar suffer from an illness brought on by his sorrow, or was he an irresponsible drunk? And could the bloody man travel, for God's sake?

Sebastian altered the line of his questioning. "What about the vicar's daughter?"

Settling back against the chair, Mr. Gilwell crossed his arms over his chest. "Cordelia, you mean?"

Cordelia. Ah, yes, that had been her name. How appropriate, he thought, although Shakespeare had probably envisioned a milder sort of faithful daughter when he'd written *King Lear*. "Yes. Tell me about Miss Shalstone."

"I already told you. She does what things the vicar can't."

"Obviously." He thought of how she'd evaded his statement when he'd asked if she wrote her father's sermons, too. "But why does she live with him? She's of marriageable age. Has she no suitors? When I met her, she seemed perfectly capable of attracting a husband." *More than capable,* he silently amended.

"Well, now, that's been a problem. Y'see, she's had a few suitors, perfectly respectable ones, but she's refused them all. Can't leave her father, she says."

That explained a lot, he thought. Why she dabbled in music, why she became so defensive of her father ... why she had that odd, haunted look in her eyes. His own mother had worn that look in the last months before her death. She, too, had lived with a wastrel.

He shook his head. But a vicar! It didn't make sense. He might have understood it of a nobleman, but not a vicar. His father, for example, had only been one in an illustrious line that had drained the family's fortune. The process had finally ended when Sebastian had parlayed his father's holdings in the East into a trading network that was slowly paying off the family debts.

Unfortunately, that same network suffered at present without Sebastian's attention and would continue to suffer until he took care of this problem with Richard. But to take care of Richard's problem, he had to have this vicar, who apparently was drinking himself into oblivion.

Sebastian brought himself up short. He was jumping to conclusions again, assuming from very little evidence that the vicar drank heavily. Then Sebastian thought of Reverend Shalstone's near desperation in his search for his "medication." No, he felt certain his hunch was right. The rest of the townspeople might consider the man ill, but Sebastian knew a drunk when he saw one.

The trouble was, Sebastian needed a vicar—a sober vicar—to present to his brother and to Handel. And at the moment, it didn't appear as if he'd get one.

The next morning, Sebastian arrived early at Belham's small church, impatient to finish his business and be on his way. His coach, which had followed him at a slower pace from London while he rode ahead on horseback to set up his meeting with the Shalstones, would be here by tomorrow at the latest, and he wished to leave as soon after it arrived as possible. A pity he had to sit through a long church service before he could speak to the vicar, but Sebastian was prepared to do what was necessary.

As soon as he entered, he was given a special seat in a pew near the front. It was apparently the pew for the vicar's family, although at the moment only the sour old woman he'd met the day before and another servant occupied it.

After he took his seat, he spotted Cordelia at the front, speaking in hushed tones to the choirmaster, who was preparing to climb into the gallery where the choir awaited him. Sebastian grinned when he noticed how expressively she used her hands. The woman seemed always to be waving them about to emphasize some point or another.

She looked quite different from the day before—her gown of yellow silk with the décolletage modestly covered by a long lace scarf made her appear more the lady than yesterday. Once again, she wore her hair covered, this time by a day cap and straw hat.

To his chagrin, he found himself wondering what the hair beneath was like. He knew the color—a nice shade too dark for blond, yet too light for brown. But how did she wear it? In the short, girlish curls so often worn by women at court these days or had she let it grow long, tying it up in a bun that she let down at night?

The thought of her letting down a mantle of rich fawn hair made all the muscles of his stomach tighten ... . and some other muscles over which he should have better control.

As he scowled at his uncharacteristic lack of self-discipline and his peculiar attraction to a vicar's daughter, she looked up and her eyes met his.

To his surprise, even delight, she blushed and ducked her head. He bit back a smile. Had she read his lascivious thoughts? Bloody hell, the woman did everything else. It wouldn't surprise him if she read minds, too.

He watched as she joined them in the vicar's pew, sitting on the other side of the two servants from him so he couldn't see her without leaning forward. A pity, he thought. Sitting beside her might have livened what promised to be a dull hour.

Shifting his seat on the uncomfortable pew, he glanced around the church, which was illuminated in a multitude of colors by the sun streaming through its stained-glass windows. He hadn't entered a church in years, not since his mother's funeral.

He'd been quite young then, but even at eight, he'd felt an overwhelming sense of loss, a pain so acute he'd never been able to assuage it completely. He still remembered his mother's soft pink cheek, which she'd lain often against his . . . the way her fingers were always plucking at his clothing and smoothing his hair . . . her timid smile when his father entered the house, a smile that never faltered, even when the man was roaring drunk.

He'd missed his father's funeral two years ago. He'd been in India, shoring up the family fortune. He could imagine, however, what it had been like: his uncles trying to find something nice to say for the eulogy, his grandmother standing thin-lipped and sour, and his sisters confused about whether to be sad.

At least they'd had Richard.

The pain of impending loss bit into him. He scarcely noticed as the choir sang a familiar opening hymn. His sisters wouldn't have Richard much longer, not unless Sebastian could do something about it. The future of the entire family depended on Sebastian's success.

But what if he failed? He already had to deal with the possibility of Cordelia's being the real composer. What if he couldn't untangle this knotty situation? What if he couldn't convince her to help him?

He shook his head. No, he wouldn't let her dissuade him from his purpose. No vicar's daughter would prevent him from saving Richard.

A layman went to the pulpit to read a scripture, and Sebastian listened with half an ear to the words about the shepherd who left his ninety-nine sheep to search for one lost lamb. Sebastian watched the faces around him as the scriptures, read in a halting, coarse voice, filled the church. The mention of sheep perked up most of the parishioners, but all too soon they lost interest.

Then the choirmaster stood again and the room's atmosphere altered instantly. Sebastian could sense the change in the charged air, could see it in the expectant expressions of the mob-capped servant girls and laborers around him.

Caught up in the spirit of anticipation, he was nonetheless unprepared for the sounds that greeted his ears as the choir began to sing. It wasn't the imperfect voices that captured his attention, nor the energy they brought to their singing. It was the music and the lyrics of a hymn utterly unlike anything he'd heard before. The words—about loss and acceptance and faith—had a poignancy that seeped into one's blood like sweet wine. Totally lacking were the images of judgment and a warlike God. In their place were gardens and precious walks and forgiveness.

And the music. He found himself straining to hear every subtle drop of the lilting, vocal nectar spilling from behind the altar. He tore his gaze from the choir only a moment, and that was to lean forward and glance at Cordelia.

What he saw made him wonder. Her head dipped ever so slightly to every note, her fingers tapped a silent rhythm on her skirt, and her face wore a pleased, joyous expression. She seemed to know every nuance of the music, yet he didn't recognize it himself. Admittedly, his knowledge of church music was sketchy, but he and Richard had both been taught by a meticulous music tutor who'd given them a passing familiarity with the work of noteworthy musicians. He could swear this particular piece hadn't been written by any of those.

He forced himself to resist the pull of the music so he could better observe those around him. Some sat with eyes closed, their lips moving to the words as if they'd heard them before. Others smiled beatifically, nodding their approval at every swell of sound. When

Sebastian shifted his gaze to the choirmaster, he noticed the man casting glances over his shoulder to where Cordelia sat, as if seeking her direction.

Her music? he wondered. There was nothing pretty or facile about it, yet he could see how a woman might have written it. If it was hers, it gave the lie to all his brother had told him about women writing music. If it was hers, it was the purest he'd ever heard.

If it was hers, Handel had good cause to admire it.

He settled back against the pew once more, his expression thoughtful. He found it incredible that she'd written the music Handel admired. But since she obviously had, she ought to be the one to speak to the composer. Unfortunately, that was impossible. Richard would never introduce her to Handel. His bias against women musicians ran too deep and was too personal. Besides, Richard had to prove he was reliable, and how could he if he produced such an unlikely composer for Handel's approval?

A pity, Sebastian thought. It would have to be the vicar or none. Now how was Sebastian to manage that when the vicar obviously hadn't written the music?

The hymn ended amid satisfied sighs. Then the choir sat down, and the vicar approached the pulpit. Sebastian scrutinized him for signs of yesterday's dissolution, but found none. The man did have his red nose, but his eyes were clear and his posture erect. He looked like a typical vicar, except perhaps younger than Sebastian had at first thought.

Reverend Shalstone laid some papers on the pulpit, then peered at them before speaking with a sonorous voice. His sermon concerned the text that had been read earlier. The sermon itself was neither dull nor riveting, but merely competent. Then again, Sebastian wasn't predisposed to enjoy such stuff and nonsense, so how could he judge it?

He could, however, judge the delivery, which gave him a glimpse into what had no doubt made Reverend Shalstone a wonderful vicar before his wife died. The man had a truly dramatic voice, a way of weighting simple words with profound meaning. Sebastian found himself listening attentively through the vicar's recitation of the symbolism of the sheep, despite the dull text.

"Like the ninety-nine, we are admonished to understand God's concern with the one lost lamb," Reverend Shalstone said in ringing tones. He paused, peering at his notes, and continued with deep meaning, "Here you should read to them the scripture beginning—"

The vicar stopped short, realizing his mistake. Sebastian suppressed a chuckle, and noticed he wasn't the only one struggling not to laugh. Bloody hell, so he'd been right about Cordelia's writing the old man's sermons.

In the midst of the long silence could be heard muffled titters and a strangled cough or two. As the vicar harrumphed and searched for his place, Sebastian noted the indulgent faces of his fellow listeners. Clearly this wasn't uncommon. No doubt the vicar's sermons kept the parishioners awake, if only so they could catch his mistakes.

The vicar recovered quickly. "Can't read my notes, y'know," he muttered, before resuming the sermon as if nothing had happened.

After the third time the vicar's resounding delivery faltered in confusion over his text, Sebastian leaned forward to look at Cordelia. She stared straight ahead, her hands folded demurely in her lap and a brittle smile on her face. He kept his eyes trained on her until she looked his way. Her smile faded and she glared at him, her lower lip trembling. Then she faced forward once more, squared her shoulders, and ever so slowly flattened herself against the back of the pew so his view of her was once again blocked.

He relaxed against the pew with a smile. Clearly all was not well at the vicarage. The vicar couldn't or wouldn't perform his duties, Cordelia was apparently doing everything to hide his incompetence, and not a soul in town was willing to change this peculiar state of affairs.

Perhaps he could use that fact to his advantage. His plans had been permanently altered yesterday when Cordelia had revealed that she'd written the pieces, but that didn't mean he had to give up. Not at all. There had to be a way out of this muddle, and he intended to find it this afternoon.

No doubt dinner at the vicarage would be like it was at every clergyman's house on Sunday afternoon—filled with guests or parishioners. Cordelia had invited him for two o'clock. He'd show up at one. He wouldn't allow the woman to thwart him by surrounding herself with people. He had no time to waste. One way or the other, he'd gain Cordelia's cooperation. And the vicar's, of course, although the old man would no doubt do as his daughter urged.

The creases in Sebastian's brow deepened as he thought about what he could use to tempt the vicar's daughter. Cordelia was clearly not pleased with her current situation. Perhaps he could offer her a different one.

But how could she ensure that Richard got Handel's support? As the beginnings of a plan swirled in his brain, a self-satisfied smile spread over his face. The vicar's daughter excelled at masquerading as her father, didn't she? Well, perhaps it was time for the vicar to masquerade as his daughter.

Chapter Three

Better a thousand times to die,
Than for to live thus still tormented
—John Dowland,
     "Can She Excuse My Wrongs"

Cordelia fretted as she helped Prudence and Maggie add the finishing touches to Sunday's dinner. Would the meal prove lavish enough for a duke? After last night's embarrassing encounter, she felt compelled to demonstrate her efficiency in running the vicarage. Every time she thought of Father falling to the floor, she burned with shame.

That's silly, she told herself as she stirred more cream into the soup. *Merely because Lord Waverley saw Father in his cups is no reason for me to scurry about and try to impress him.*

Her desire to impress him, however, stemmed from more than a simple need to erase that moment from his mind, and she knew it. For one thing, seeing His Grace again in church had affected her peculiarly. Who'd have guessed such a scornful man could be so . . . so remarkably appealing in formal attire? She'd expected to find him repulsive on second glance. But no, every time their eyes had met, something passed between them that was like every perfect fugue she'd ever heard.

He had this way of turning even a mocking stare into a caress. . . .

She shook her head, trying to blot the duke from her thoughts. No wonder respectable gentlewomen were always being ruined by noblemen. The peerage must have a special school to teach their men how to seduce women at a glance.

His glances wouldn't seduce her, however. She knew him for an arrogant sneerer, and at dinner she'd no doubt see those traits again. It was all well and good to admire a man from a distance, but it was his character up close that mattered. After last night's encounter and Father's stumbling delivery today, Lord Waverley would probably be even more contemptuous. She should be preparing herself for that instead of pondering His Grace's effect on her insides.

"No wine at Father's place," she told Prudence as the servant poured wine into her mother's prized crystal decanter. "The wine is only for His Grace."

"As you wish, miss." Prudence sniffed contemptuously as she always did when the subject of the vicar's "thirst" came up.

"Is His Grace going to dine with us often whilst he's in Belham?" plump Maggie asked as she wrestled a perfectly roasted leg of mutton onto a pewter platter.

Cordelia made a dismissive gesture. "Oh, I shouldn't think so. I don't believe he's staying in town long." She hoped not, at any rate.

"He's undoubtedly eager to return to London," Prudence muttered. "*Some* people only get their entertainment from the wild antics of the city. *Some* people think they're too good for honest country folk."

With a placid smile, Maggie ladled gravy over the roast. "He didn't seem uppish to me. Not at all. After the service, Old Jack started talking to him about sailing in India, and next thing I could see, His Grace and Jack were going at it full guns, chatting about banana trees and rajahs and such. You'd never've guessed His Grace weren't an old sailor himself."

Ah, so the duke only acted arrogantly with her, did he? "Somehow I can't see Lord Waverley shinnying up a rope in his velvet breeches and waistcoat," Cordelia put in as she concentrated on keeping the soup from lumping up.

"Oh, I can." Maggie pushed a damp lock of hair back with her wrist and strode to the carved-oak bread cupboard. "He's got a rough look about him, despite his nice clothes. I dare say I wouldn't want to meet up with him in a dark road some night."

Cordelia laughed. "Wouldn't you now? I should have thought you'd find him handsome."

"Handsome?" The discriminating Maggie rolled her eyes as she took some clapbread from the cupboard. "Heavens, no. Lord Waverley's too dark and hungry looking to be handsome. I mean, not compared to Peter. Now *he's* a man I'd call handsome."

Maggie's fiancé Peter was a strapping blond farm boy without a brain in his head. Privately, Cordelia thought *Peter* wasn't someone to meet on a dark road . . . or a light road, for that matter. He'd probably run a body down with his cart before he even realized someone was there.

"Not that His Grace would cast an eye *my* way," Maggie continued. "I ain't exactly the sort of girl a duke sets his eyes on."

Prudence snorted. "No, you're much too honest and modest for him, I'm sure." She actually seemed to mean it.

Cordelia and Maggie exchanged glances. Prudence normally railed at Maggie for being too free with her affections to Peter. Apparently contempt for the nobility overrode all such considerations today.

Suddenly, a knock came at the front door, alarming them. Cordelia glanced at the clock in disbelief. One P.M. She could have sworn she'd told him two, when the choirmaster and his wife were arriving.

"It's him, I know it's him," Maggie wailed, splattering gravy on herself. "The choirmaster would never be here early! We still got to finish the sauce for the custard and there's peas to boil and—"

"Don't worry your head about it." Cordelia wiped her hands on her apron. "If His Grace insists on arriving at the wrong time, he'll simply have to wait for his dinner like everyone else. No reason to rush it up for him." She gestured to the stove. "You and Prudence finish here, and I'll get the door." As she strode toward the dining room, she called back over her shoulder, "Where's Father?"

"Still upstairs," Prudence responded.

Passing through the dining room into the hall, Cordelia paused and stared up the stairs indecisively. Should she check on him before she opened the front door? What if he were at it again? Surely he hadn't had time to secrete more wine in his room since yesterday. She'd perish on the spot if Lord Waverley had to confiscate another flask.

A second knock came at the door, and she winced. Murmuring a quick prayer that Father would be presentable today of all days, she hurried to the door.

She opened it to find Lord Waverley with raised hand, apparently preparing to knock again.

He lowered his hand. "Miss Shalstone. Good to see you. I didn't make a mistake, did I? You did invite me to dinner."

"Yes, of course." *You simply can't tell time.*

He glanced down at her stained apron, then back to her flushed face, and his expression altered. "I'm early. I'd forgotten. . . . You told me two o'clock, didn't you?"

"It doesn't matter," she said in her most cordial voice, trying to tell from his courteous expression if he'd come early on purpose. She stood to one side. "Do come in. We're perfectly pleased to have you come any time."

He chuckled at her blatant lie before stepping through the door. "You needn't pretend with me. I know full well that this particular invitation was given under duress."

The color rose to her face as she relived the previous day's encounter. Ducking her head, she took his kersey surtout from him and hung it on a hook beside the door, then walked down the hall ahead of him. "You took Father and me by surprise last night, but I assure you my invitation was sincerely meant." *Or somewhat sincerely meant, anyway,* she thought.

"You took me by surprise as well," he murmured in that smooth baritone voice she'd admired before.

Last night, his voice hadn't been quite so smooth. She smiled bitterly. "I could tell. You seemed rather angry to discover that your brother's prized composer was a woman."

"In my surprise, I'm afraid I insulted you. I apologize."

She stopped short at the unexpected apology, then pivoted to face him. He was closer than she'd realized, and she suddenly found herself staring into the knot of a spotless white cravat.

Merciful heavens, he's tall, she thought as she craned her neck up so she could meet his gaze. Then again, she was quite short. Nearly every man towered over her.

His amber eyes stared down at her, dancing with amusement. "You do accept my apology, don't you? I didn't mean to be so incredulous about your abilities. I simply wasn't prepared for your revelation. But I was rude to doubt your word."

She hesitated, not quite sure whether to believe him. He'd said some very unflattering things yesterday. "Am I to understand that you no longer doubt I'm the composer of those chorales?"

One corner of his mouth quirked up in a crooked smile. "How could I doubt it? Your father made it quite clear you were telling the truth."

"My father says it and you believe it, but my word is insufficient to convince you." The flat statement needed no answer, for he wasn't the first to show her that few trusted the word of a woman. Even those in Belham who in a dire circumstance would trust her to see to their comfort nonetheless required her to hide behind her father's position whenever a major decision was required.

He regarded her thoughtfully. "Your father was, after all, the person with whom my brother corresponded. I don't think I was unreasonable in wanting to hear the truth from him."

"Oh, yes, the letters," she said in a small voice. The letters, one more deception on her head.

His eyes narrowed. "You also wrote the letters, I take it?"

Dropping her eyes from his, she stepped back to put more space between them. "My father knows little about music, Your Grace." She started to turn away, but he stopped her with his hand on her arm.

His fingers held her lightly, yet they immobilized her, pinning her in place like a rabbit caught in a snare. "But you know a great deal, don't you?"

"Perhaps you should ask Father, since you find my word on the subject unreliable."

He gave a faint, almost apologetic smile. "I needn't ask your father. I deduced as much from this morning's hymn."

Was that actually admiration in his voice? "The hymn?"

"The choir sang one of your hymns during the service, didn't they?"

Absurdly pleased that he'd realized it, she nodded.

"You're very talented." He released her arm, though his fingers brushed her hand as he did so, sending a strange quivering up her arm. He dropped his voice. "I made the mistake of assuming otherwise yesterday. I won't repeat that mistake."

The apparent sincerity of the compliment—not to mention the husky timbre of his voice—left her embarrassed ... and lightheaded. Discomfited by his gaze, she pivoted and walked briskly toward the parlor. He followed close behind.

Neither of them spoke. As they passed the kitchen, the clanging noises of pots and ladles made speech impossible anyway. Suddenly they heard a loud crash and

Maggie exclaiming, "That tears it! His Grace shan't eat *that* custard."

Cordelia opened the parlor door and beckoned Lord Waverley in. He entered, but not before they heard Prudence retort acidly, "That's what happens when you rush matters because some high and mighty nobleman takes a notion to arrive early."

Cordelia tried unsuccessfully to hide her grin as the duke faced her. But when she ventured a glance at him, he was also smiling.

"I've thrown your household into a dither with my early arrival, haven't I?" he said amiably.

"Not at all. Dinner was nearly ready anyway."

He watched as she nervously plumped the cushions on the settee. "Where's your father?"

"He's upstairs changing out of his robes. He should be down shortly." She wished he were here now to help her out of this uncomfortable encounter.

"Good. Then we have a few moments to speak alone."

Her gaze flew to his. So he *had* come early on purpose. "What about?" As if she didn't know.

"The trip to London, of course."

She dropped her eyes. "Now that you know the truth, I can't imagine why you'd still want Father to accompany you to London."

He sat down on the settee and stretched his arm out along the back. "Why not?"

"I told you," she said as she began straightening the stacks of music beside the harpsichord bench. "He didn't write the chorales. What purpose would it serve to have your brother meet him? Or Handel, for that matter? Father would only make a fool of himself and ruin all your brother's chances with Handel."

At his continued silence, she went on. "And you know that neither of them wishes to meet the real composer of the chorales."

"Miss Shalstone, stop that dithering, and come sit down."

At his impatient tone, her head shot up. For the first time since he'd arrived, she could sense the irritation he'd exhibited so fully yesterday. He might be trying to be cordial, she thought, but his eyes gave him away. They glowed with an energy barely tethered by his apparent desire to pacify her.

He dropped his arm from the back of the settee to pat the seat beside him. "Sit down," he repeated, putting more command in his tone. "I have a proposal for you."

She sighed. Best to get the whole thing over with, so His Grace could go on his merry way and stop bothering her. She sat on the harpsichord bench, well away from him. "What kind of proposal?"

Leaning forward, he compelled her to listen with the force of his stare. "My brother wants, no, needs, Handel to meet the vicar. And the vicar is here, the same one my brother believes has been writing all this music."

"The same one who's tone deaf and can't tell a musical staff from a walking staff."

He nodded grimly. "Nonetheless, your father is the vicar Richard thinks he wants. And although Handel doesn't know who writes the music he admires, he'll be far more amenable to accepting a vicar than a vicar's daughter. Well, I say we give them a vicar. We train your father in the language of composition, we have him memorize a few pat phrases about the chorales, and then we introduce him as the composer."

Sheer astonishment kept her in her seat. Surely he wasn't suggesting . . . He couldn't actually think . . . "You don't know what you're talking about," she whispered, thinking of her father trying to play any kind of role in his typically inebriated state.

Lord Waverley's face shone with all the fervency of an acolyte. "I know *exactly* what I'm talking about. All we need is for your father to play a charade for a short period. He merely has to pretend to be the composer of the chorales and present himself to my brother and

Handel. Then Handel will be pleased, and Richard's business will get the boost it needs." His tone softened. "Perhaps then Richard will find the will to live. It seems the best solution to our problem."

She jumped to her feet. "Not *our* problem, Lord Waverley." She punctuated her words with a finger stabbing the air at him. "*Your* problem. This has been *your* problem from the beginning."

He rose from his seat, too, his eyes blazing. "If my brother's business fails, it will be your problem, too, won't it? Who will publish your works when Richard goes bankrupt?" His lips thinned to a harsh line. "Tell me, Miss Shalstone, how much income do you derive from my brother?"

It appalled her that he could even think in those terms. Her face mirrored her outrage. "Not much, I assure you, not that it matt—"

"It's more than the money, though, isn't it?" he continued relentlessly. He approached her with fists clenched. "You live for that music, don't you? Even though it appears anonymously, you thrive on the knowledge that someone, somewhere hears the music *you* wrote, the notes that are no one else's but yours!"

Did he have to be so infernally perceptive? It was as if he read her thoughts, saw into the sadness of her soul. She lifted her chin, and cursed herself inwardly for not being able to stop it from quivering. "I can always write for the parishioners." She sounded defensive, even to her. "They hear my work, and that's all that matters."

His mocking smile cut her to the quick. "All that matters? It doesn't matter that the great Handel admires your work, that he no doubt speaks of it to other musicians, that my brother talks constantly of his brilliant discovery, that—"

"Stop it!" She lifted her hands helplessly, wishing she could push him from the room and find peace. "Of course it matters. Even if it didn't, I wouldn't want your brother's business to fail. I'm not callous, nor am

I unaware of how precious one's livelihood can be." She paused, fighting the tremor in her throat. "But I can't help you!"

"Ah, but you can. Handel's endorsement of my brother's business can make all the difference, and you know it. To get that endorsement, I need your father, and to get your father, I need you."

He took her trembling hands in his. "You can train your father to speak as a composer." She struggled to pull her hands away, but he clasped them tightly enough to keep her immobile. "Think of it as having a pupil to mold in your image. Have you no pupils?"

"Yes, but—"

"Think of your father as your pupil and impart your knowledge to him. That's all I ask of you."

This time when she jerked her hands from his he released them. "All? Have you no idea how difficult it is to compose music? It's not like riding a horse, where you merely need a good instructor to do it with minimal competence. No, writing music requires intuition, talent, knowledge, and instinct. I can teach Father the knowledge perhaps, but what about the other three-fourths? He can't carry a tune, and you want him to pretend to compose music?" She lifted an imploring face to him. "You truly are mad, Your Grace, or incredibly ignorant!"

His eyes glittered. "I'm incredibly desperate, Miss Shalstone. Richard is my only brother. He's young, only a few years older than you, but he's always been the one to keep the estates in order while I'm gone. More important, he's the mainstay of my sisters. But he's wasting away. . . ." His voice broke off, and her own breath caught in her throat.

Must he make her feel so reprehensible for refusing to help him? "You act as if this is all up to me. What about my father? What if Father refuses to be part of your charade?"

The intensity in his eyes arrested her. "He's been part of *your* charade, hasn't he? He's marched to your drum for quite some time. I'm sure you can convince him to participate."

She winced. He didn't understand. She didn't like having Father march to her drum. Unfortunately, he wouldn't march to any other. "That was a different matter, Your Grace. My charade was created for his benefit, to keep him from losing his living because he was too ... ill to adequately perform his duties."

"Too ill?" he clipped out. "Or too drunk?"

She closed her eyes, pain spreading over her like a disease. No one had ever been so straightforward about Father's problem before. She hadn't counted on it hurting quite so much.

Somehow she managed to answer him, the words little more than a whisper. "It hardly matters, does it? In either case, he can't perform his duties, which means he certainly can't participate in your charade."

When she opened her eyes once more, the duke was staring at her with abject pity. He held forth a hand to her, and she whirled away from him, less able to bear his sympathy than his condemnation.

But he wouldn't let her put distance between them. Quickly, he stepped behind her and clasped her shoulders. "I'm sorry," he murmured, so close she could feel his warm breath on her ear. "That was cruel of me."

"Please, leave ... me ... alone."

"Leave you alone?" His voice turned gentle. "To what purpose? Whether you see it or not, Miss Shalstone, I'm your savior. As matters stand, you balance on the brink of a precipice. If anyone should grow tired of having you for a vicar, all he need do is complain to the person who holds your father's living, and your father will lose it."

A shudder passed through her. She'd worried about that often, for although the old earl acquiesced in her charade because it was so difficult to find a vicar for Belham, he might not continue to do so if anyone made trouble about it. Even if he would, there were always the high churchmen in London, rumored to be scrutinizing clergymen's behavior more carefully these days. Belham's need for a vicar and remote location might not shield her father indefinitely.

"Then there's you to consider," Lord Waverley continued. "How much longer can you play this role while keeping up with the vicarage and your normal duties . . . not to mention composing? I know you want something better, but you'll not get it like this." His voice dropped to a seductive whisper as his fingers tightened on her shoulders. "You can't have a husband and family of your own as long as you have to be vicar, too, can you?"

Tears welled in her eyes, but she refused to let him see her cry. It was cruel of him, so cruel to voice aloud all her secret fears. Even his nearness, his husky baritone, taunted her by giving her a taste of what it would be like to have a husband, a young, virile man to love her.

Of course she wanted a husband, a house of her own . . . children. . . . But that wasn't to be. She forced nonchalance into her voice. "I merely want to be an independent woman."

"All right," he said, although he sounded skeptical. "But you're not one now."

"True. And your proposal won't change that, Your Grace," she choked out through the pain clogging her throat. "Even if I did as you asked and we were successful, I'd be back here in a few months, in the same situation."

"No, you wouldn't." His voice was filled with quiet confidence. "I would of course reward you for your help."

Slowly, she faced him, her eyes suspicious. "Reward me?"

"Yes." He regarded her pale face with earnest concern. "Once Richard's business is on its feet, I'll see to it that he publishes your work, under your name, not your father's—as much as you want, as often as you want for as long as you want." He grew more fervent the longer he talked. "And I'll use my influence to gain your work an ear, although neither Richard nor I can guarantee its success, as I'm sure you realize. But you'll have a chance to do what no other woman has done. You want to be an independent woman? Fine. This way, you'll no longer be tied to your father's position. You'll have your own income and be a musician in your own right."

Drawing a deep breath, she fought the sudden pounding in her heart. A musician in her own right? With a guarantee of publication? She could work on a major piece, instead of the chorales she'd been limited to because of time constraints. She could write oratorios or even an opera if she wished.

"If Richard's business fails anyway," he continued, "I'll settle a sum on you that would allow you to live independently. It's the least I can do."

He was offering her compensation beyond her wildest dreams, yet what he wanted in return was impossible. Any fool could see that. She could never transform Father into a musician. Such a trick would never fool Lord Kent, and certainly not Handel.

Your own income. The duke's words echoed in her ears like the tempting call of a siren.

"Your father would never want for anything, Miss Shalstone," the duke persisted. "If you wish, I could speak to the provider of his living. I could even offer him a living myself . . . or help you find a way to rid him of his . . . illness."

She blanched at his reminder of her father's current condition. There was no way to "rid him of his illness," she thought bitterly. That was the trouble.

That was also why she ought to accept the duke's offer. As he'd said, matters became more precarious daily. Lord Waverley was offering her a way out of her terrible trap.

What had she to lose? If she were unsuccessful, Lord Kent would be no worse off than before, and she and Father would return to their present state of affairs.

Granted, such a failure would be humiliating. It might also mean she could never publish with Lord Kent again, if he was even able to keep his publishing company going. But there'd be the income the duke promised. And if she should succeed. . . .

"I must speak to Father first before I give you an answer," she murmured.

He smiled, obviously sensing her weakening. "Of course."

"*If* I do it, I will need time."

"You may have it, but not here. I can't linger any longer. With the roads the way they are during this season, the trip to my estate will take us at least a week by coach, so you can use that time. Then if you need more, you can continue working with your father at my estate until he's ready."

The thought of Father tippling his way about a duke's estate jolted her. "We still haven't addressed the problem of Father's . . . illness." She swallowed hard. "As you can tell, I haven't been very successful with treating it."

Lord Waverley's expression hardened. "I believe I can take care of that myself."

A resentful laugh tumbled from her lips. "Can you, now?"

"Surely if he's isolated in a coach with us, we can control his access to 'medication,' don't you think?"

"You don't know my father—"

"This will work. I promise we can make it work."

Sighing, she met his imploring gaze. She must be mad to do this, but she couldn't resist the lifeline he offered. Nor could she ignore the urgency of his plea. "All right, Your Grace. You have a bargain."

Every muscle in his body seemed to relax, making him look suddenly young. He'd acted with such authority she'd had difficulty thinking of him as anything but an older man, despite the lack of gray in his hair.

"You've made the right choice, Miss Shalstone."

She'd made the only choice, she thought mournfully.

He looked as if he were about to say something else when Maggie stuck her head in the doorway, interrupting them. "Beggin' your pardon, miss, but your father's in the kitchen asking for you. Shall I send him in here?"

Cordelia's eyes met the duke's as Maggie waited.

He flashed Cordelia an encouraging smile. "I'll leave if you wish, so you can speak to him alone."

"That's unnecessary. He'll want to have you here to answer his questions." She turned to Maggie. "Is he ... is he—"

"He's well, miss," Maggie said reassuringly, knowing what her mistress spoke of.

Cordelia released a breath. At least Father wouldn't embarrass her today, she thought. "Send him in then, Maggie. The duke wishes to discuss something with him."

"Very good, miss," Maggie answered, then left.

Alone with the duke once more, Cordelia felt a stab of anxiety about the discussion to come. She glanced at Lord Waverley, unconsciously seeking reassurance.

He smiled. "Don't worry, Miss Shalstone. Everything will be all right. I'm sure you'll do your job more than adequately, and Richard will have his Handel oratorio." At her look of distress, a teasing note entered his voice. "As long as you don't have to write any sermons, you should perform splendidly. You write excellent music, but sermons aren't your forte."

As he'd no doubt intended, the thought of her father's mistakes that morning made her smile. "You certainly know how to warm a woman's heart with compliments," she quipped.

"I know what I like." A secretive expression crossed his face as his eyes lingered a moment on her face. "Yes, I do know what I like."

Something in the way he said it warned her he wasn't speaking of her talent as a musician. Something in the rough murmur started her wondering what a

week in a coach with a man like His Grace might
bring.

She was still wondering—and worrying—moments
later when her father entered the room.

Chapter Four

Favour is not won with words,
Nor the wish of a thought.
                              —John Dowland,
                              "Shall I Sue"

Oswald Shalstone wasn't stupid. He occasionally over-imbibed, but that didn't blind him to what went on around him. He could tell a meddling nobleman when he saw one—a meddling nobleman with a roving eye.

And that roving eye was fixed on his daughter.

True, the duke hadn't so much as touched Cordelia since Oswald had entered the parlor, but Cordelia's face flushed every time she looked at the man. Oswald found that suspicious. Very suspicious.

Nonetheless, he must be cordial. It was a vicar's duty to welcome all souls. Even a duke's.

Oswald gave a sketchy bow. "Good day, Your Grace. We're honored to have you join us at our humble home."

The duke nodded. "I'm honored to be here."

Neither of them mentioned the duke's previous visit, although Oswald vaguely remembered it. Abominably rude of His Grace to call when the house was all a muddle. Merely thinking of it roused Oswald's temper.

Ah, but far too much roused his temper these days. It was the blasted wine. He'd have to watch his consumption, he told himself, disregarding the little voice that said he'd broken that resolution countless times.

"Do sit down, Your Grace," Oswald said, sweeping

his hand to indicate the settee. He tried to hide his displeasure when both the duke and his daughter sat on it. It only mollified him slightly when they moved apart until they sat as far from each other as the seat would allow.

Cordelia settled her skirts modestly about her. "Father, His Grace is here on a mission of sorts. It concerns the music I send to London for publication. His brother is my publisher."

Oswald took a seat in his favorite chair and thoughtfully regarded his daughter as she fidgeted with her gown. Cordelia never cared a whit for her appearance. Something had upset her, and that worried him.

"I believe something was mentioned about Lord Kent last night," Oswald muttered.

When Lord Waverley and Cordelia exchanged glances, he bristled. Did they think him a complete idiot? He'd been in his cups last night, true, but he hadn't been deaf, for pity's sake, and he certainly knew who the duke's brother was.

Honorine's letters, which Cordelia always read aloud to him, had been full of news about the duke and his family. Honorine was an incorrigible gossip, but her sources in London were unimpeachable. She'd said quite a bit about the duke's sojourns in India. In fact, Oswald thought, what was the man doing here anyway?

"Actually, sir," Lord Waverley said, "I have a favor to ask of you and your daughter."

Nothing could rouse Oswald's suspicions like a nobleman asking a favor. Noblemen didn't ask favors of vicars, unless they wanted absolution for some crime. "A favor, Your Grace?"

With an almost condescending patience, the duke described the difficulties Lord Kent had experienced with his business. Then the duke elucidated an elaborate plan for deceiving Lord Kent and a composer named George Frideric Handel.

Apparently, Lord Waverley and Cordelia had concocted the preposterous scheme together, which only went to prove that thanks to the duke's smooth tongue, Oswald's normally intelligent daughter had completely lost her wits.

"Let me see if I understand you both," Oswald remarked caustically when the duke finished his recitation. "You want me to pretend to be a composer of church music in my daughter's place, thus deceiving not only your brother but a respected composer as well. All of this so your brother's business may prosper."

To Oswald's surprise, the duke contained his temper, although his eyes glowed like a devil's fiery orbs. "I think you've grasped the plan, sir."

Devilish eyes or no, Oswald wasn't intimidated. He turned to his daughter, who wore a much less fierce expression than the duke. "And you, gel? You approve of this scheme?"

She lowered her lashes to hide her eyes. "I can think of no other way to solve Lord Waverley's dilemma, Father."

"Ah, but why must *we* solve His Grace's dilemma?"

Cordelia colored. "Because Lord Kent has been very generous with us. He showed me a great kindness by publishing my work—"

Oswald snorted. "Nonsense. He showed good business sense, that's all. He's made money off your music, I'm sure."

"You misunderstand me, sir," Lord Waverley interjected, his jaw tight. "I'm not saying your daughter owes my brother anything. As you say, Richard has benefitted from her talent." He paused, a somber expression coming over his face. "I ask this as a favor, and only because I have no other recourse."

"No other recourse, eh?" Oswald pulled on his ear. These noblemen were all alike, coddled and spoiled. "Why don't you simply talk some sense into your fool brother? Remind him he has duties and a family to care for. Tell him to try harder and look to God for solace.

It sounds to me as if he needs a good dose of fortitude. Discipline, that's what he needs, discipline!"

Cordelia flashed her father an impenetrable look, then tossed her head as she always did when she was angry. For pity's sake, he couldn't imagine why she'd be angry. Surely she could see he was right.

"Father, old-fashioned discipline works for some, but certainly not all." Did he detect sarcasm in his mild-mannered daughter's voice? "You should know that more than anyone."

What was *that* supposed to mean? "Don't take that tone with me, gel—"

"Please, sir," the duke interrupted with a glance in Cordelia's direction. "I don't wish to cause problems between you and your daughter, but I do need your help. I know I'm asking a great deal, but I'll repay you for your efforts."

Oswald snorted. "That's always the way of it, isn't it, Your Grace? Throw a bit of silver at the clergy, and they'll snap to do your bidding."

Cordelia rose from her chair, her face flushed. "Father, you mustn't be rude."

Mustn't be rude? Oswald thought, suitably chastened. Yet he couldn't help this perverse desire to upbraid the duke. Now why was that?

Because the duke had seen him in his cups. Because the duke had heard him blunder during the sermon that morning. Because the duke kept looking at his daughter. And most of all, because Oswald need a swig of wine like a sinner needed absolution.

He shook his head. Nay, he didn't *need* the wine. He didn't. He could do without it any time.

"I'd think you'd want to help a man whose brother is desperate." Cordelia paced the floor and waved her hands in her usual expressive manner. "I'd think you'd help him solely because you're a man of the cloth and 'tis your duty."

He forced back the irritable words that sprang to his lips, and forced his tone to be smooth as honey. "Cordelia, pet, 'tis not that I begrudge His Grace my assistance, but surely you see this is impossible."

She hesitated, and he glimpsed the battle going on within her. Ah, so she wasn't as keen on this plan as she appeared.

Nonetheless, she drew a deep breath and faced him. "The scheme may be difficult to manage, 'tis true. Yet 'tis also impossible to continue as we have."

Her quiet rebuke stung. He'd led Cordelia a merry dance these last few years since Florinda had died, but he'd never guessed how deep her discontent went.

Nay, that wasn't true. He'd watched his daughter gradually slip away from him, and he'd been unable . . . unwilling to stop it.

He cracked his knuckles, striving to master his hurt. "How will aiding this"—he paused, glaring at the duke, who sat silently watching the battle between them play itself out—"this gentleman change matters?"

Seemingly unconscious of his question, Cordelia glided to the harpsichord with her usual quiet grace and stood beside it, stroking the keys with longing. She glanced at the duke before meeting her father's gaze. "His Grace has promised to make certain that my music will always be published, as much as I desire."

Oswald closed his eyes, unable to witness her eager expression. She need say no more, for her meaning was clear. If she could support herself with her music, then she needn't depend on her unreliable father.

He opened his eyes to find the duke staring at him, an unreadable expression on his face. Never had Oswald hated a man more. This blasted nobleman was offering Cordelia a way to abandon her father, and the man actually expected him to participate!

Then Oswald turned his gaze to his daughter. Cordelia was as fair-skinned as her mother had been dark, her features as strong as her mother's had been fragile. Yet despite her handsome face, she was unwed and fast approaching the age of spinsterhood. Even in his most

wretched wine-soaked hours, he'd been aware of her
sacrifices—the suitors she'd rejected, the time she
spent holding his parish together. Sometimes it even
shamed him to know how much of his duties she took
on herself, but then he always convinced himself she
was doing no more than was expected of a vicar's
daughter. His living merely required more time than
most.

Now this duke with all his finery and money and
power was offering her what he couldn't—freedom
from her father.

Or was he? In truth, it all depended on how Cordelia
regarded the duke's offer. She'd never abandon him,
would she?

Oswald fixed Cordelia with his most intimidating
stare. "Tell me, pet, what would you do if you had the
freedom to write your music and have it published?"

She toyed with a sheet of music on the harpsichord,
a dreamy smile stealing over her face. "I would find us
a cottage somewhere near London, a quiet place. We
could raise a chicken or two and buy a cow. I would
write music and you, Father, could study your books as
you used to before . . . before . . ."

Before Florinda died, he thought. No, Cordelia
would never abandon him. "What about my parish?
These people depend on us. What about them?"

A troubled frown wrinkled her brow. "If you
wanted, we could stay here. It wouldn't matter to me,
as long as I could write my music." She approached
him, then knelt and took his hands. Her face cleared,
glowing with a hope he hadn't seen there in a long
time. "But we wouldn't have to worry about whether
the living would be enough to keep us another year.
We wouldn't be at the mercies of the earl or the parishioners."

He wanted to ignore the appeal in her voice, but he
couldn't. He had no right. Besides, he'd be a fool to
refuse her this. It wasn't like the proposals of a suitor,
who'd marry his daughter and take her away. The duke

instead offered Cordelia a way to stay with her father, to care for him permanently.

One thing disturbed him, however. "What His Grace is asking us to do is wrong, pet, and you know it. It's a deceitful endeavor that can lead to no good."

The faintest of smiles touched her lips. " 'Tis no greater a deceit than the one we began when we told Lord Kent that you had written my compositions."

She had him there. Ironically, he'd insisted that she use his name to protect herself. Another father would have forbidden her to send the compositions off in the first place. But how could he have forbidden her? Letting her publish her chorales had been his way of atoning for all she'd suffered on his behalf. He'd thought to give her something of her own, even if it did bear the appellation "Anonymous." Now the whole petty deceit had come back to haunt him.

"Father, I don't know if this will work, but I feel guilty for having deceived Lord Kent," she whispered, her hands tightening on his. "This is a way to right that wrong. Lord Kent wouldn't have accepted Handel's support if I hadn't pretended to be a vicar. How could I bear it if Lord Kent lost his business, all the while thinking me, or rather you, an ingrate for not coming to his aid when he needed it?"

He didn't need to suggest that she tell Lord Kent the truth. Nay, he knew what reaction a man like Lord Kent would have upon learning he'd been taken in by a young woman. Nor had Oswald been so blind last night as not to notice how incredulous and condescending Lord Waverley himself had been over the matter. Oswald wouldn't allow Cordelia to endure that again from Lord Kent and Handel. Besides, the duke had emphasized that Lord Kent wouldn't profit from her revealing herself as the real composer.

What a pretty pickle she'd put him in. He turned to the duke for help before realizing he'd receive no quarter there. His Grace did smile, which reminded him of his other concern.

The duke's roving eye. Oswald stared at the unfortunately young and handsome owner of that eye. "Are we to travel with you, Your Grace?"

Lord Waverley nodded. "My coach should be here by this evening or tomorrow. I will of course pay any expenses along the way—meals and private rooms at the inns where we stop."

Oswald had to bite his tongue to keep from asking who'd be joining his daughter in her private room during the wee hours of the night. Instead he asked, "Will you allow us to take a servant?"

Cordelia looked startled. "A servant? But why?"

"As a chaperone for you. It isn't seemly for you to travel all that way with two men."

Lord Waverley chuckled. "Surely your daughter needs no chaperone with her father accompanying her."

"I wish to bring Prudence with us." Oswald's tone was firm. "If I am to participate in this preposterous scheme, I want a servant to accompany us."

The duke shrugged. "As you wish. You may bring one person or fifty as long as they don't slow us down."

Cordelia, however, looking none too happy. "Must we take Prudence, Father? Why not Maggie?"

"Maggie has aging parents to attend to, pet, or had you forgotten?" Besides, he had a far more important reason for bringing Prudence, one he could never reveal to his daughter.

"But Prudence—"

"Either Prudence accompanies us to serve as chaperone, or I won't go."

Pressing her lips together, Cordelia nodded, then rose to her feet.

Lord Waverley rose, too, his eyes fixed on Oswald. "May I assume you've agreed to help me? You'll pose as the composer?" The tenseness in his manner belied his nonchalant tone.

Oswald could feel Cordelia's eyes on him, questioning, probing. What choice had he? It was either help the duke and gain his daughter's good will or risk losing her ... if not now, then soon, when she tired of caring for the crotchety man who'd begrudged her a chance at independence. "Aye, I'll help you, though I don't believe it'll do you much good. Who'll believe me to be a musician when I've a tin ear?"

"But you'll try, Father, won't you?" Cordelia laid her hand on his arm and gazed at him with an innocent yearning that never failed to prick his guilt. "You'll try to make it convincing ... for Lord Kent's sake."

"I'll do my best to be a presentable composer, pet." Oswald patted her hand, then cast a quelling glance at Lord Waverley, before returning his attention to his daughter. "But not for Lord Kent's or even Lord Waverley's sake. For your sake. Only yours."

Chapter Five

I have entreated, and I have complained,
I have dispraised, and praise I likewise gave.
                              —Francis Davidson,
                                "I Have Entreated"

"The hollow circles are half notes, not quarter notes. I've told you that twenty times over!"

Cordelia's loud words echoed in the cramped confines of the well-appointed Waverley coach. Lord Waverley raised his eyebrows, but Prudence continued to snore peacefully.

Cordelia knew she sounded churlish, but her father's own churlishness had released a perverse demon in her. She'd expected his peevish complaints—after all, he'd been allowed no liquor since they'd left Belham that morning before dawn.

Still, it wasn't simply his temper that roused her anger. Merciful heavens, she'd never dealt with such a poor memory in all her life. Not one of her pupils had ever given her such trouble. She glared at her father, who sat beside Lord Waverley. Her finger tapped the sheet once more. "How is it you can memorize a hundred scriptures, Father, yet fail at remembering four simple notes?"

"Because it isn't four simple notes, is it?" he exploded, settling back onto the plush seat of the coach with a groan. "Half notes, quarter notes, rests, staves, clefs—marry, how do you musicians contort all that into a decent song? Greek is easier to learn than that tangle, and Greek gave me a wretched time!"

When Cordelia turned to Lord Waverley in helpless despair, she found him grinning. How could he laugh at her, the beast! He'd put her in this predicament in the first place!

Just then the coach hit a particularly deep rut, jolting them all half out of their seats. Instinctively catching hold of the nearest velvet curtain, she lost her grip on the sheet of music in her hand, and it flew into the duke's lap. He snatched it up before it could slither to the floor.

Once the coach settled into a more even rhythm—if the steady series of bumps and jerks over dismally bad roads could be called a rhythm—Lord Waverley perused the music with his smile intact. "Perhaps you should choose music more suited to your father's lack of . . . er . . . experience," he said as he did his best to keep the sheet still long enough to study it.

She rolled her eyes. "That's the piece I start my youngest pupils with, Your Grace. 'Tis a simple hymn, scarcely more than a melody."

" 'Tis a pile of chicken scratch!" her father protested. He cracked the knuckles of his right hand. "Besides, 'tis difficult to read it when we're traveling such wretched roads. My stomach fairly churns at the effort." He lifted a hopeful gaze to Cordelia, grimacing as if the "sickness" had gripped him again. "I could do so much better with this studying if I had my medication to settle my stomach."

Groaning, Cordelia shook her head, then glanced at the duke as if to say, "I told you so."

His Grace's smile vanished. "I'm terribly sorry we left your medication behind, Reverend Shalstone. As I told you before, I had no idea what your valise contained, or I certainly wouldn't have left it sitting on the doorstep."

He sounded so convincingly bland, Cordelia nearly laughed. She'd persuaded him yesterday that confronting Father about his liquor would only make him refuse to take the trip. Their only hope was to keep all liquor away from Father for another reason.

To that end, she and the duke had concocted a tale about Lord Waverley's dislike of strong drink, which he'd demonstrated immediately at Sunday dinner. For the length of the trip, His Grace was a temperance convert, determined to avoid liquor himself and have all those with him avoid it as well. Prudence had grumbled when told in private of the restriction—despite her disapproval of the vicar's drinking, she enjoyed her one glass of wine in the evening—but she'd agreed to abide by it.

Cordelia's father now looked even more disgruntled than before. "Perhaps we could stop and purchase more medication—"

"I told you, we must make good time," the duke cut in. This time he didn't bother to mask his harsh tone. "Besides, liquor isn't healthful, and I'd prefer you abstain in my presence."

Cordelia flashed her father a warning glance as Lord Waverley fought to keep his stiff-necked persona intact and his temper under control. Was Father so sunk in the quicksand of his drinking that he'd actually flout the duke's wishes?

Catching sight of her appalled expression, her father jutted out his chin in a stiff gesture of defiance. "Well, then, that's that, isn't it?" His tone grew more gruff. "Let's get on with it, gel. Explain about the half notes again, and I'll try to grasp it this time."

As Cordelia bent her head to the task of tutoring her father, she could feel Lord Waverley's eyes on her. It had been that way half the morning. Father had studied the music while Lord Waverley studied her.

The duke's perusal had been careful and intent, as if he weighed her measure. It irked her to have him watch her so fixedly with those eyes the color of antique bronze, like an Eastern idol keeping guard over his treasure.

Why couldn't he do like Prudence and snore the

morning away? She didn't expect him to stare out the window—with snowdrifts covering the barren wasteland, there was little to see but a vast expanse of stonewhite fields and dingy gray sky—but couldn't he find somewhere else to place his gaze?

Not sure she could bear another hour of his impertinent staring, she muttered, "This is probably most tedious for you, Lord Waverley." She thought of his horse tied to the back of the coach. "Perhaps you'd rather ride your stallion than languish of boredom in here."

He chuckled, making her wonder if he'd guessed the source of her discomfort. "Am I such an irritating companion, Miss Shalstone, that you'd banish me to the cold?"

She colored. "N-no, I didn't mean to imply . . . that is—"

"I'm sure Cordelia was only assuming," her father cut in, "that you'd prefer the freedom and softer ride of a horse to this bone-shattering coach." Her father winked at Cordelia, and she bit her lip to keep from smiling.

But her father's words had no apparent effect on the duke. "My ride to Belham was uncomfortable, although I endured it out of necessity. Unfortunately, my years in India have made me less than eager to brave the extremes of England's weather when I have a cozy coach at hand." He added in a smooth voice, "And such charming company."

When she glanced at him and witnessed the amusement in his eyes, she grew emboldened enough to challenge him. "I thought parts of India were quite cold."

He smiled, baring even white teeth. "Are you so familiar with India then?"

"I've read about it."

"Indeed. You must have read the best sources, for you're correct. Certain mountainous regions of India have quite cold weather. But I spent my time in the balmier regions."

Her father snorted. "Balmier regions, eh? I've heard

that hot weather can addle a person's brain, make him concoct all sorts of crazy schemes." He held up the sheet music and shot Cordelia a look of sheer disgust.

She twisted her hands in her lap nervously. How could Father be so appallingly rude? And to a duke, no less? She'd never dare say such a thing in front of His Grace.

Apparently unperturbed by the thinly veiled barb, however, Lord Waverley shifted in his seat, one of his leather boots grazing Cordelia's ankle. "Crazy schemes? No crazier than the scheme you and your daughter concocted for your parishioners."

Cordelia's father drew himself up. "I'll have you know, Your Grace—"

"That's enough, Father," Cordelia bit out. How on earth would she endure two weeks of Father growling at the duke, who played the bear-baiter to perfection? "Ignore His Grace for one moment, will you, and look at this music. We've gotten woefully away from the subject."

She cast the duke a pleading glance. He raised one eyebrow and tipped his head as if to acknowledge her plea and its implied reproof. Acknowledge, but not accept. She doubted he'd ever accept anyone's reproof.

She returned her attention to her father. "Now point out the half notes to me. There are five. Which ones are they?"

With a grumble, her father did as she bade. After a moment, they settled into a comfortable method of studying, despite her father's grousing. Although the duke continued his scrutiny of her, she forced herself to ignore him, to concentrate on her father's stumbling attempts to memorize the elements of music composition.

They had rumbled down the road peaceably for a while, her father actually beginning to absorb some of the material, when suddenly the coach lurched alarmingly, hurling them to one side. Amid the coachman's shouts and horses whinnying, the coach shuddered to a stop.

"Bloody hell," the duke exclaimed, and being nearest the door, now facing nearly skyward, he opened it and climbed out. Prudence stirred, complaining loudly about being awakened as Cordelia's father picked himself up off the floor.

Within a few moments, the duke stuck his head back in the coach. "The off-leader shied at a fox and pulled us into a ditch. Now we're mired down. The horses' harnesses are tangled and it's an ungodly mess out here, so you'll all have to get out while we free everything.

"With any luck, it'll take only a short time," the duke added as he gave Prudence his hand and helped her clamber onto the muddy road. "Once Hopkins gets the horses untangled, he and I will try to push the coach out."

Her father urged Cordelia to the coach door as she hastily donned her muff and settled her capuchin about her shoulders. The duke clasped her waist and swung her down as easily as if she'd been a child, careful to keep her free of the mud.

As soon as she had her footing, he gave her father a hand, and once the two of them were secure, stripped off his kersey surtout. Then he started on the brass buttons of his damask coat.

With a glance at the coachman, who'd nearly finished with the horses' harnesses, her father removed his own surtout. "I'll help you push."

After clambering up the side of the ditch, Cordelia turned to watch the men. As the duke peeled his coat from his shoulders, Cordelia stared, never having seen him without a coat. She'd certainly missed an interesting sight, she thought wickedly as he thrust his coat into the coach. His figured silk waistcoat hugged his trim waist and broad chest with the perfection only achieved by an expensive tailor.

Yet he looked quite different in his flowing white

shirtsleeves, not at all like a man who could afford an expensive tailor. In fact, when he unbuttoned his sleeves and rolled them up to his elbows, exposing sleekly muscled forearms, he looked almost ordinary.

No, not ordinary. Never ordinary. No one with such a fine build could look ordinary.

"Turn your gaze aside," Prudence hissed in her ear. " 'Tisn't fit for a maiden to see a man in such undress."

Cordelia wanted to laugh. Prudence was well aware of how many workmen Cordelia had seen attired thus. Apparently, Prudence believed that Cordelia should only be forbidden to witness men in their shirtsleeves when they had titles.

But pointing out the inconsistency to Prudence would be a waste of breath. Instead, Cordelia turned her back on the men. "As long as we shall be here a while, I think I'll go in the woods to take care of ... ah ... a necessary matter."

Prudence merely nodded. Cordelia scowled as she picked her way over some rocks toward the pines clustered along the road. She noticed that Prudence remained behind, hypocritically gaping at the men after she'd chastised Cordelia for doing so. Cordelia shrugged as she spotted a break in the woods where she might enter and find seclusion to do her business. Prudence would always be setting up rules for others that she didn't follow herself.

Yes, but I don't have to follow them either, Cordelia told herself, *no matter what Father says and Prudence thinks. Fie upon it, I've got more sense than the two of them put together.* She wrinkled her nose. *If I want to look at a man in his shirtsleeves, then I will.*

To make her point, she paused short of the woods to briefly watch the toiling men. Her throat went dry when she caught sight of the earl straining every muscle against the back of the muddy carriage. For all his figured silk waistcoat and his expensive leather breeches, he had no mark of the effete dandy about him, which probably had a great deal to do with his years abroad. He didn't even seem to care that his clothes were being soiled.

Faintly she heard him shout, "One, two, three, heave!" and she stood transfixed by the sight of his magnificent parts working in harmony together. She had a fine view of him from her vantage point, particularly of his behind, which tensed and flexed beneath the glove-tight breeches with every push.

Prudence looked back toward her, and Cordelia jerked around, her face flaming as she headed once more for the shelter of the trees. Merciful heavens, she'd been reduced to staring at a man's breeches for enjoyment! She scolded herself even as her pulse continued its silly racing. It wasn't seemly for her to take such pleasure in it, to want to stand gawking at him all day like the maids bringing the workmen their lunches.

Oh, but why did he have to be young? And so . . . so pleasant a sight for the eyes?

Try as she might to dismiss it, the image of the duke's corded body lingered in her mind, making her wonder what he'd look like without his clothes.

Giving herself another scolding for that unmaidenly thought, she hurried into the woods. This wasn't the time to dally, staring at the duke. The men would soon free the wheels so she'd best make haste.

It took her a few minutes to find a space wide enough to accommodate her skirts and petticoats, and with her skirts catching on every branch she passed, she had to stop often to disentangle them. When at last she did find a secluded spot, she doffed her muff and capuchin, hanging them both on a branch, and quickly went about the business of relieving herself.

Thank heavens she'd refused to wear a hoop for this trip. She'd never have managed to sit in the coach without looking like a kitten peeping out of a basket, and relieving herself would have required elaborate maneuvering.

She'd just finished and had dropped her petticoats

when a sound behind her made her whirl around. In the opening to the private space stood Lord Waverley.

A blush stained her cheeks as she jerked her skirt down over her petticoats. Surely he hadn't seen her attending to her needs? She'd die if he'd caught her with her petticoats up about her thighs.

If he had, he gave no sign, either by word or look. "You should be careful where you stray, Miss Shalstone." His voice was sharp with concern, and the anger glowing in his eyes took her quite by surprise.

"I'm fine. I had to . . . have a few moments alone."

He hesitated and seemed to rein in his worry. Yet when he spoke again, his tone was only a fraction milder. " 'Tis not the place for a woman to wander alone. Next time take Prudence with you."

His air of command irritated her, unaccustomed as she was to being ordered about by a man. Father had certainly never attempted to do so. "Are you afraid I'll be eaten by wolves?" she asked tartly as she picked up her capuchin and muff off the nearby branch.

"Human wolves, maybe." When she darted a surprised glance at him, he continued, "These roads are rife with highwaymen who'd delight to pluck a berry like you from the bushes."

None too happy to be referred to as a berry, she lifted her skirts and attempted to pass him. "I doubt they'd find much merit in that. I haven't a penny on my person."

He stayed her with his hand on her elbow. " 'Tis not money they'd be after, I assure you."

His husky words sent shivers through her, for she knew exactly what he implied. Nonetheless, he was being overly cautious, she told herself peevishly. Why must he always hover at her back like some jailer, even in the midst of a wilderness? He wouldn't leave her to tutor Father alone, nor did he trust her out of his sight to relieve herself. Merciful heavens, would he never give her any privacy?

Defiance building in her breast, she lifted her eyes to

his, then blanched at his expression. He looked far more like a human wolf than any highwayman, his eyes glowering and the muscles of his face taut over finely etched bones.

What had Maggie said? That he had too much of a hungry look about him? She hadn't lied, that was certain.

His eyes lingered over her face, as if memorizing it. Then they dropped to her lips, and she found herself wondering if he wanted to kiss her. It was a heady but disturbing thought, for if he did, she had no idea how she'd react.

Her breath quickened, as did his. A strange confusion of the senses made her drop her gaze and say as steadily as she could manage, "I knew all of you were but a call away, Your Grace. I'm not some green chit without a brain in her head. You can trust me not to do anything foolish."

"You don't know the dangers of these woods, Cordelia," he said in a rough-edged murmur, startling her with the use of her first name. "Anything could happen to you here."

Suddenly uncomfortable with his closeness, she wrenched free of his hand. " 'Tis no wonder your sisters prefer to be left to Lord Kent's care, if you suffocate them with hovering the way you do me!"

Horrified by her rude outburst, she clapped her hand to her mouth. But when she ventured a glance at him, the serious, ravenous expression had left his face and he was grinning.

He lifted her capuchin from her arm and moved behind her to settle it around her shoulders. "Am I that much of a bother, Miss Shalstone?" Gone was the intimate tone with which he'd said "Cordelia," and in its place was his usual maddening amusement.

She tied the strings of her capuchin, concentrating on the knot to keep from noticing how his hands rested ever so briefly on her shoulders before pulling the hood up over her head.

" 'Tis difficult to work when Your Grace is constantly watching me," she muttered. "You don't even trust me to teach Father properly without your overseeing the lessons, and I'll admit that galls me."

He sighed. "What do you wish me to do instead? Is that why you suggested I ride outside the coach?"

"Aye." She drew on her muff. "I realize it's cold, but . . . but if you'd give Father and me a few hours alone, I know we could accomplish more. Whenever the two of you are together, you argue, which is a monumental waste of time. Our purpose would be better served if you'd simply leave me to it." She faced him, a look of challenge on her face.

A half-smile played about his fine lips. "I had no idea I was such a trial. I only watch you work because I find it interesting."

Her anger melted away, and she softened her tone. "That's all well and good, but surely you tire of the cramped coach." When he continued to stare at her with laughing eyes, she muttered, "Besides, if the cold bothers you, surely your coachman has a flask he'd share with you. I'm told all the coachmen carry gin to—"

Gin. Merciful heavens, her father!

"Oh, dear, the coachman—" she said at the same time he muttered, "Bloody hell, I didn't warn Hopkins—"

Without hesitating, he grabbed her hand and pulled her behind him as he crashed through the undergrowth back toward the coach. Branches tore at her skirts again, but this time she paid them scant heed.

In moments, they'd broken through the forest onto the road, and a quick surveillance revealed the coachman and her father resting on a rock a short distance away. To her horror, the coachman lifted a flask, drank deeply, then passed it to her father, laughing as he did so.

"A pox on him!" the duke muttered, dropping her hand as they strode toward the companionable pair.

"Your father will be the death of me before this trip is over!"

Me, too, she thought despairingly as she saw the impossible man raise the flask and gulp a goodly portion of spirits.

He didn't even have the good sense to look guilty when he spotted them. "Ho, there, Your Grace," he called out, lifting his flask to toast the duke. "Here I'd been wishing for a spot of something to settle my stomach, and your man Hopkins had the perfect thing right in his coat."

"Yes, well, Hopkins knows I don't approve of strong drink," the duke said in a haughty tone, playing the temperance believer to the hilt as he snatched the flask from her father.

"Milord?" poor Hopkins asked, his expression confused, then pained as he watched the duke open the flask and pour the liquor out.

As her father stared with thwarted longing at the hole the gin left in the snow, the duke made a quick gesture to the coachman that Hopkins apparently understood, for his face cleared.

"Come, sir," Lord Waverley told her father. " 'Tis time to continue on our way. I've decided to ride my horse after all. You and Miss Shalstone shall have a few hours of peace to work."

Cordelia's father brightened as he stood, rather unsteadily, and wiped the gin from his mouth. "Well, then, let's be on about it."

The duke followed them to the coach, but when he went to hand her into it, her father scowled and took her hand, helping her in himself. With a shrug, the duke closed the door and turned toward the front of the coach.

As her father settled back onto the seat and she sat down beside him, she glanced out in time to catch the duke muttering a few words to Hopkins, then passing him a gold coin. The coachman nodded and said a few words in reply, jerking his head toward the coach with a chuckle.

Satisfied that the duke had taken care of the problem with the coachman's gin, she leaned back against the seat, only to come face to face with Prudence's malevolent glare. Prudence now sat opposite her, and her sour expression could've curdled the sweetest milk.

"You and His Grace were gone off together quite some time," Prudence accused. She surveyed Cordelia as if searching for signs of a sinful liaison.

Her father's head snapped up beside her.

"Oh, aye," Prudence continued to Cordelia's father. "Your daughter here ran off in the woods—only the good Lord knows why—and the duke himself went in after her. Gone ten minutes they were, back there in the woods alone."

"That's enough, Prudence," Cordelia snapped. "You know quite well why I went into the forest."

"Oh? What *were* you doing rambling about in the woods?" her father demanded.

Cordelia fought for patience, her hands tensing on her lap. "Why would a woman on a long trip go off into the woods by herself?" She frowned at him. "Think, Father. Why would *anyone* go into the woods alone when there are no chamber pots at hand?"

Under her critical stare, he blushed and mumbled, "Oh, yes, of course."

Before Prudence could start in with even more outrageous accusations, Cordelia added, "I was on my way out of the woods when His Grace found me and paused to lecture me on the follies of wandering off alone." She gave Prudence a pointed gaze. "He suggested I take *you* with me next time, Prudence."

"Yes, yes." Her father's anger shifted to Cordelia's accuser. "Surprised you didn't go with Cordelia anyway, you know. Not much of a chaperone, I'd say, if you're letting the gel gad about by herself in the woods."

The resentment gleaming in Prudence's eyes took

Cordelia aback. She knew the woman's thorny disposition, but her glare at Cordelia's father went beyond that. Bitterness, even hatred were balled up in that look, sending a shiver skittering along Cordelia's spine.

"Next time I shall," Prudence remarked, drawing herself up into the ramrod straight posture she favored. "Next time you can be sure I shall."

Wonderful, Cordelia thought as the coach rumbled along. *Now I'll have two "protectors" hovering about.*

She bent to pick up her satchel with its sheets of music. This trip would be longer than she'd thought. Much longer indeed.

The duke was thinking much the same thing as he rode behind the coach, wishing he hadn't poured out Hopkin's gin. The poor coachman had said he'd get more when they stopped, but Sebastian needed it now. Icy fingers of wind crept under his surtout through the slightest gap in the cloth, freezing everything they touched.

Unfortunately, he wasn't dressed with sufficient warmth for North England winters. After all, he'd come from India with lighter-weight clothing, not expecting to be sent north almost as soon as he'd arrived. There'd been no time to have warmer clothes made, and none of his old clothes at the estate had fit him, for after a few years in India eating native curries and tropical fruit, he'd grown thinner. Except for the surtout, he had no heavy clothing.

In truth, during his years in India he hadn't much missed eating great slabs of tasteless beef at every meal, but without all the heavy feasts to put fat on him, his body had trimmed to a whipcord leanness that left him even more susceptible to cold. He hadn't lied when he'd told Cordelia the weather was his reason for not wanting to ride. He shuddered, jerking his cocked hat lower about his ears, and for once regretted not wearing a wig.

A grim smile touched his lips. No, he'd rather freeze for a few months than shave his head and wear a scratchy piece of rug on it. Besides, if everything went as planned, he'd be returning to India before long.

He paused, examining that thought more closely. India. He missed it enormously, although he'd often been lonely in the vast foreign country. He probably didn't need to spend many more years there. Every day saw the adding of another English merchant to his roster of buyers. He gained capital with each new agreement signed, and the training of managers to take his place once he returned to England was going well.

Nonetheless, he'd left matters on a shaky footing to come back and attend to Richard's dying business. Besides, there'd been another reason for his return—to take Judith as his wife. She'd passed the age of her coming out, and her father was expecting a wedding. When the letter had come about Richard, he'd thought this would be the ideal time. He needed a wife to produce an heir, and he needed to repay his debt to Sir Quimley.

Yet now he found himself balking at the thought of the arranged marriage. He'd never balked before. He'd accepted it as one of the many labors he'd been forced to undertake for the sake of his family. Even Judith, who'd seemed hesitant to move to India at first, had eventually accepted that they must live there for a time. It wasn't her hesitation causing him to balk.

He scowled. No, it was Cordelia Shalstone. This time when a shiver passed over him, it wasn't from the cold. In fact, it warmed him through and through thinking of how he'd come upon her in the forest. She'd jerked her petticoats down too fast for him to catch more than a glimpse of smooth, white thighs and trim ankles. He'd nearly snapped her head off, but he'd really wanted to snap off a part of his own body . . . the part that was entirely too unruly where she was concerned.

Then when she'd looked at him in the dim light with

eyes bright and challenging and her bow-shaped lips parting as if begging to be kissed, he'd nearly lost all control.

Bloody hell, the chit made him feel like a virgin boy in a whorehouse, hot and bothered and most assuredly hungry. It was insane, his attraction to her.

And not only to her body. Something in the way she challenged him ... something in her competent handling of most situations drew him. He'd never met so forthright a young woman, one who didn't fawn over him and play coy. Unlike The Biddable Judith, who acquiesced to anyone she cared for, Cordelia was entirely her own person.

He shook his head, trying to shake off the keen, bitter ravening she roused in him. Years of being bombarded by sensual delights in India had made him forget how to behave in a more rigid England. In India, he'd had a mistress for those times when his body craved fulfillment; he'd had lush colors and sweet fruits and the rich, full air of the tropics. Now that he'd returned, his soul was starved for the light and air and beauty lacking in English winters.

Miss Shalstone had come along, and his body had responded with expectation. That's all it was. He wanted her as a thirsting man wanted water. It was perfectly understandable.

So why hadn't Judith made him feel this way since his return?

He scowled. Perhaps his attraction to Cordelia represented the last struggles of a bachelor being dragged to the altar. If he'd been engaged to Cordelia, Judith would have had the same effect on him.

That thought was so ludicrous, he nearly laughed aloud.

Well, it hardly mattered why Cordelia attracted him, he told himself. He still must guard against acting on the attraction. She wasn't the kind of woman to engage in a casual dalliance, and in any case, he didn't want such from her. Like an expensive wine, she deserved to be savored slowly and thoroughly. But he had no right to savor her at all, for no matter what his desire dictated, his engagement to Judith must be his first concern.

Yes, he must put the intriguing Miss Shalstone completely out of his mind, treat her as he'd treat one of his sisters—with forbearance and kindness and remote good humor. He must behave responsibly, remembering his fiancée and showing Cordelia only the concern necessary to accomplish their mission.

Yet as they crested a hill and the coach lurched down between endless stands of pine, a sudden image of Cordelia in the woods made him groan. Sometimes it was hard, he thought, to be so very responsible. Aye, sometimes it was hard indeed.

Chapter Six

Bold Assaults are fit for men
That on strange beauties venture.
—Thomas Campion,
"Woo Her and Win Her"

Night had long since fallen, and the riders in the coach were quiet, except for the soft snoring of Cordelia's father. Cordelia had been staring out the window at the stars for some time, but now she turned to survey her silent companions. In the dim light, she could barely make out her father's slumbering head, now fallen unceremoniously on the duke's shoulder.

She stifled a laugh as the duke flashed her a wry smile. First, his poor Grace had been forced to endure the freezing cold, and now a vicar using his body for a pillow. No doubt it was enough to make the man regret the mission he'd embarked upon.

"We'll stop in a few minutes at an inn I know," the duke said. The rumble of his voice made her father shift restlessly, throwing one arm across the duke's lap. Then the vicar snuggled up against Lord Waverley and smiled in his sleep.

"It's a good thing." She chuckled. "Much longer in this coach, and Father may claim you for a bed."

"I'll admit I would trade seatmates with you if I could."

At Cordelia's side, Prudence also slept, but true to her character, managed to remain rigidly erect.

Cordelia regarded her father thoughtfully. "Mother

used to say Father slept like a flooded river, always overflowing his banks."

"And no doubt stealing the blankets, too," the duke quipped.

She gave a tired smile, scarcely able to believe she was discussing Father's sleeping habits with a lord of the realm. Then again, Lord Waverley resembled no lord she'd met or imagined. Although a certain natural arrogance imbued him with a nobleman's demeanor, he kept it carefully in check. What's more, he always made her feel as if he regarded her as his equal. She knew that wasn't true—the class difference between them undoubtedly filled his thoughts as much as hers—but at least he didn't show it.

Not that they'd had much to do with each other in their long journey. He'd ridden his horse most of the afternoon, and when at last he'd entered the coach, she'd spoken to him little, thanks to her aching throat. Explaining music to her father and singing snatches of tunes to illustrate her points had taken its toll on her poor vocal cords. When her father had fallen asleep, she'd seized on the reprieve with a vengeance, retreating into her thoughts.

Nonetheless, she'd been more aware of the duke's presence opposite her than she'd have thought possible. His luminous amber eyes had watched her in silence, making her skin prickle with awareness. When she'd snatched a glance or two at him, he'd worn a thoughtful expression, the space between his thick brows wrinkling as he stared at her.

She'd tried to thrust him from her mind, but had failed.

Now the object of her obsessive thoughts smiled as he pushed her father's arm gently off his lap. "How long has your mother been deceased?"

"Three years. She caught a terrible ague from a parishioner and died shortly afterward."

"I'm so sorry." The sympathy in his voice sounded genuine.

An image of her mother filled her head. "She's in Heaven now. That's all that matters." She smiled. "No doubt she's busy petitioning God on my behalf. And Father's, of course. She always said she'd put in a good word for us."

"Your parents seem to have had an amiable marriage."

He sounded almost wistful. It made her ponder the way her parents had been together, which she'd always taken for granted. "Amiable? Interesting way to put it." She paused, remembering her father settling a shawl about her mother's shoulders without being asked and her mother's grateful smile in response. "Yes, they had a more than amiable marriage. They were quite in love."

" 'In love.' " Lord Waverley looked intrigued. "I didn't think such a sentiment survived in marriages anymore."

"Among your class, marriage for position is common, but those of us with little position to speak of look for something more satisfying in a lifetime union."

Silence reigned for a moment as he studied her, his eyes dark, curious. "Didn't your father's . . . ah .. predilection for wine disturb that satisfaction?"

Cordelia glanced at her father, but as always, when he slept, he was dead to the world. "Father didn't indulge in spirits then as he has lately. In truth, Mother never served much wine. She preferred 'invigorating' drinks like tea and lemonade." A sigh left her lips. "After Mother died, he grieved himself until he was sick. The remedies Belham's apothecary suggested were possets and tonics heavily laced with brandy, and he drank freely of them. Then he just"—she swallowed, her throat raw—"never seemed to get better. He grieved and drank, grieved and drank. Now he seems to know no other way."

"Ah. That's why he kept asking for his 'medication.' "

A tight smile was her only answer.

"So your father has grieved himself into drunkenness." Amber eyes pierced her defenses. "But what about your grief?"

"What do you mean?"

"Hasn't it occurred to your father that you grieve, too? That you need him to help you through your own grief? That he can't take care of you when he's in his cups?"

She crossed her arms over her chest. "He knows that. He does what he can to help me, although I know it looks as if he's very ... very ..."

"Selfish?" he finished for her.

Apparently Lord Waverley's arrogance had slipped its tether, she thought, angry that he could assume so much about a man he scarcely knew. "He's not selfish. Look at the way he allowed me to send my music to be published."

The duke snorted. "That wasn't unselfish. Quite the contrary. It enabled him to shirk his duties all the more while you acquired an extra income on his behalf."

Her eyes narrowed. Until now, she'd actually warmed to the duke. Merciful heavens, how foolish. He had nothing but ice water running through his veins. "He didn't do it for that reason."

Jaw tightening, he stared at her. "Didn't he?"

"Nay." His questions were eroding her thin shield of control. "He wanted to give me the chance to demonstrate my abilities."

"Which is why he insisted you write under his name and not your own."

She shook her head, his barbs striking a deeply buried, vulnerable part of her soul. "You're wrong." She couldn't keep the hurt from her voice. "Father is proud of me and my music. He only insisted on my using his name to protect me."

The duke opened his mouth to retort, then snapped it shut. She waited for him to strike again, to dig deeper into her pain, but his expression softened. "I hope so. For your sake, I truly hope so."

The rest of the trip passed in silence, but the closeness of the coach and the duke's steady gaze stifled Cordelia. Why did he continue to probe at her hidden fears, like a child scratching at a scab?

He acted as if Father were a monster. Father wasn't a monster. He merely grieved for his wife. But he cared for his daughter, too. He never spoke to her unkindly or raised his voice.

The trouble was, he scarcely spoke to her at all these days.

By the time they reached the beamed entryway of the inn, Cordelia was weary in both body and soul. She desired only to escape her companions, especially the duke. But they hadn't yet eaten supper and her empty stomach overrode her wish to be alone.

It took them a few moments to rouse Prudence and her father, but once the servant and the vicar saw the inn yard and knew that comfort was at hand, they were both all too eager to disembark. As Lord Waverley helped Cordelia down, she gazed up at the three-storied red-brick inn.

Hostlers scurried about tending to the horses as the innkeeper himself greeted them, drawn by the prospect of serving the wealthy visitors traveling in an expensive equipage with a ducal crest. The innkeeper's grin broadened as the duke introduced himself and his companions.

In no time at all, Lord Waverley had arranged for him and her father to share a room, ostensibly to save money, but in actuality so the duke could keep an eye on her father. Of course, she and Prudence were to share a room as well. Cordelia groaned at the prospect of sleeping with Prudence, wishing she could have her own room, but even if rooms were available for such extravagance, her father would never allow it.

Soon they were passing through the wide doors into a more luxurious inn than she'd ever seen. Prudence's mouth gaped as she stared at the gilt appointments, the broad staircase, and the well-lit hall flanked by parlors and private apartments for dining. Cordelia, however, was too weary and too hungry to think of anything but a soft bed and a plate of food.

And much too disturbed by the duke's presence.

"You'll be wantin' dinner, I suppose, Y'r Grace?" the innkeeper's wife, Mrs. Blifil, asked as she ushered them all into a private supper room. Without waiting for his answer, she babbled on in a cheery voice, "We can give ye a fine side of beef, a roast goose, and the tastiest leg of mutton this side of London, not to mention a wine that my husband's been savin'—"

"No wine." Lord Waverley shot Cordelia a glance, and she gave a faint nod in response.

Wiping her greasy hands in the deep folds of her apron, Mrs. Blifil grimaced. "I assure you our wine is first-rate, Your Grace."

Her father cleared his throat behind them. "Surely Your Grace wouldn't mind if the rest of us had a bit of wine with supper. After such a long day, my throat's a wee bit dry."

Lord Waverley fixed her father with a stern gaze. "I'm sure it is, but tea should suffice for us all."

"Not even ale?" her father protested.

With a stiff smile, the duke shook his head. He turned to Mrs. Blifil. "We don't indulge in strong drink, but thank you all the same."

Mrs. Blifil looked suspiciously at Lord Waverley. She probably seldom saw a duke abstain from liquor. She probably seldom saw a duke at all.

Nonetheless, she curtsied. "As you wish, Y'r Grace."

With a smile, the duke ordered an expensive repast for them that would have only been reserved for special guests at the vicarage. That went a long way toward soothing Mrs. Blifil's feelings. Now grinning broadly enough to split her face in two, the woman bustled off into the kitchen.

Her father dropped into a chair, a dejected expression on his face as he grumbled to himself. " 'No strong drink,' he says. 'We don't indulge,' he says. A madman, that's what he is. Completely mad."

As the duke and Cordelia exchanged glances, Prudence took up a position by the fire. "You'd think we could have stopped sooner. I know His Grace is in a rush, but did we have to travel into the night? I swear I'll be sore in my bones tomorrow. And I'm surprised we weren't accosted by highwaymen. . . ."

Prudence continued muttering her litany of complaints to no one in particular, but Cordelia ignored her. Removing her capuchin, Cordelia sat on a settee far from both Prudence and her father, then closed her eyes and rubbed her forehead. It ached unmercifully from hours of focusing on sheets of music. Notes still danced in her head. What she wouldn't give for time to tutor Father without contending with a moving seat.

Feeling someone sit down beside her, she opened one eye to find the duke watching her with concern.

"Are you all right?"

She sighed, closing her eye again. "I'll be fine after supper and a good night's sleep. You needn't worry about me."

"If I don't, who will?"

Coming after the long, hard journey, her empty stomach, and their previous conversation, his statement brought a sudden sting of tears. She hated that he'd seen all the vulnerabilities she'd tried so hard to hide.

She stiffened and opened her eyes, staring off at her father, who still grumbled to himself. She spoke in an undertone. "No matter what you think, Father truly does look out for me. He's more responsible than he seems. He's merely tired at the moment, as are we all."

"Really? Shall we test his responsible character?" Without waiting for an answer, the duke called out, "Reverend Shalstone, I believe your daughter feels ill. What do you think we should do to help her?"

"I'm fine," Cordelia protested. "I'm merely exhausted from our long journey." What blessed game was the duke playing now? He wore a peculiarly intent expression, a taut patience that worried her.

"Feeling poorly, dear?" her father asked. A smile of calculation muted the concern in his voice. "You see, Lord Waverley, we *must* have wine at supper now. Cordelia needs a touch of it for her stomach. All that riding in a coach and reading music is ailing her."

Her heart sank. Lord Waverley certainly knew how to make a point, she thought grimly. Gritting her teeth and refusing to look at Lord Waverley, she said, "Father, I'm sure wine would only ail me more. I'll be much better off with water."

Her father leaned forward to fix her with an earnest stare. "Water! Don't be absurd. The Bible says, 'Drink no longer water, but use a little wine for thy stomach's sake and thine often infirmities.' That's I Timothy 5:23, you know, and it's sound advice."

Prudence ceased her muttering, turning an expectant face to Cordelia. Cordelia could feel the duke watching her, too, no doubt gloating over how right he was. Men! Being proved right seemed their only joy. Didn't he care that every time he exposed Father, she died a bit inside?

Well, she was tired of it, tired of making excuses for Father's bad habits. She drew herself up until she was every inch the imperious temperance convert. "The Bible also says, 'Be not drunk with wine, but be filled with the Holy Spirit.' Ephesians 5:18, you know, and that's even sounder advice."

Taking her tart words as a challenge, her father quickly retorted, "Proverbs says, 'Give strong drink unto him that is ready to perish and wine unto those that be of heavy hearts.' I'd say I qualify on both those counts."

Oh, the man could tempt an angel to murder! She shot to her feet and planted her hands on her hips. "As I recall, we were talking about *me,* about what *I* need, not what you need." Anger, biting and hot, crashed through her, destroying all consideration for her father's feelings. "In any case, Proverbs also says, wine 'biteth like a serpent' and 'Wine is a mocker.' "

It was mocking her now, mocking her for ever thinking that Father's mind centered on anything but liquor. The reality galled her more than she could bear, and the duke's having instigated her lesson only made it worse.

"A mocker, eh?" Her father appeared completely oblivious to her distress. "Only if you drink too much. That's the trouble with all the scriptures you're choosing. They're the ones about immoderate drinkers."

When she glared at him in disbelief, he crossed his arms over his chest defensively and added, "I like the scripture that says, 'Wine is as good as life to a man, if it be drunk moderately: what is life then to a man that is without wine? For it was made to make men glad.' That's a true scripture if ever I read one."

"That's from the Apocrypha. You're cheating," she bit out.

"You're the one who's cheating. You keep quoting all those scriptures about drunkards. I am not a drunkard."

It was nothing short of miraculous that a thunderbolt didn't instantly destroy him for such a lie. Then again, Father's sad, dejected smile had always protected him from petty punishments, apparently even those administered by the deity Himself.

Suddenly, a perverse desire came over her to make him see himself as everyone else saw him, to remind him of what he lost each time he drank. "I have one more scripture for you, Father, from the very same I Timothy you quote so gleefully. Perhaps you remember it—'A bishop then must be blameless, the husband of one wife, vigilant'—she paused to emphasize the next word—"*sober,* of good behavior, given to hospitality, apt to teach.' "

When her father reddened, she knew he remembered the next line, and she spoke it very slowly, almost in a whisper. "And 'not given to wine.' You may not be a

bishop, Father, but you *are* a vicar after all, and sometimes tediously 'given to wine.' Well, you may use
scripture to condone your vices, but I won't."

"Bravo," she heard the duke say behind her, but she
ignored him, just as she ignored Prudence's shocked
exclamation.

Her father's jaw went slack with surprise, and his
expression shifted to the hurt one that always twisted
her heart.

Today, however, she'd have none of it. She sighed.
"I find my stomach is indeed unwell. I believe I'll skip
supper. Good evening, all." She allowed herself only
the briefest glance at the duke. "I'll have Mrs. Blifil
show me to my room."

Then snatching up her capuchin, she fled into the
hall, hoping she could escape without showing how her
entire body trembled with an unreasoning rage.

Unfortunately, she wasn't even allowed a gracious
exit. As she strode down the hallway, she heard the
door open behind her. Thinking it might be her father,
or even worse, Prudence, she ducked through the door
of the room nearest her.

To her relief, the room was a private supper room
much like theirs, and it was empty, though a fire had
been lit in the grate. Still, the flames couldn't repel the
chill in her heart. Drawing her capuchin about her
shoulders, she neared the fire. As she warmed her
shaking hands at it, she heard footsteps approach the
room and prayed they'd pass by.

They didn't. The door opened. Without a word,
someone entered and closed the door.

"Cordelia."

Only one person spoke her name with such husky
intensity, and he was the last person she wanted to see
at the moment. She kept her back to him. "Go away,
Your Grace. Please."

"Have you noticed that you resort to formality with
me whenever you're peeved?"

"I am *not* peeved, Your Grace." She paused, a grim

smile touching her lips. "All right, I'm peeved. In any case, I don't wish to discuss it. I want to be left alone."

"You must have supper." His gruff voice held far too much concern under the circumstances. "You'll truly be unwell tomorrow if you eat nothing tonight."

Couldn't he see that food scarcely mattered to her right now? "Don't worry. Unwell or not, I'll be ready to resume your farcical scheme in the morning, so please leave me be."

"You're angry with me, aren't you?"

Her hollow laugh sounded foreign to her ears. The duke's entrance into their lives had unearthed a world of bitterness in her. Had it been there all along? Had she simply pretended to be content?

That thought disturbed her more than she dared face, so instead she whirled on Lord Waverley. "Angry? Why should I be angry? Because you play games with people and care not a whit for the consequences?"

" 'Twas not at all a game to me."

She sniffed. "Don't try to convince me that your petty attempt to unmask Father's worst traits wasn't simply one more amusement. You find us all vastly diverting, don't you? The red-nosed vicar and his peculiar daughter. You delight in winding us up and watching us spar like mechanical boxing toys!"

The light from the fire lit half his face, enough to show her the frown spreading over his wide brow. "The sparring began long before I came along. All I've done is bring it out in the open. Don't you think it's time you spoke out against your father's obsession?"

She managed a brittle smile. "You think I haven't? Merciful heavens, did you think I'd ignored it for the last three years? I haven't. I know what Father is, and he knows I disapprove. I've thrown out his liquor, I've berated him . . . once I even locked him in his room until he sobered up, hoping that with a clear mind he could see what he was doing to himself. But he hasn't. He always finds someone to give him a drink when he goes on and on about Mother."

"Yet you make excuses for him. You say he cares about you, takes care of you, when anyone can see he's beyond caring. I wanted you to acknowledge that, so you'd stop letting him take advantage of you."

"I see." Rage boiled in her at his audacity. She attempted to still the furious beating of her heart. "Let me set your mind to rest. You've proven your case sufficiently, and I now stand corrected. Father obviously cares for his liquor more than life itself, and certainly more than for me." She dropped her eyes from his, her voice falling to a whisper. "Thank you for setting me straight. Now, if you're quite through destroying my illusions, I'd like to retire, Your Grace."

Drawing her capuchin more closely about her, she attempted to pass him.

He blocked her path. "You're being formal again. I shan't let you leave until you hear me out."

"It's rather too late to apologize."

"I don't intend to."

At the firmness of that statement, her gaze shot to his.

The firelight flickered over his face, making him look like some unholy avenger, but his tone was quiet as he answered her. "I merely demonstrated what was obvious, although I wish I hadn't hurt your feelings in the process. Nonetheless, don't kill the messenger simply because you don't like the message."

"Why was your 'demonstration' so infernally important? What could you possibly gain by it?"

"A little more help from you in keeping your father sober. You coddle him far too much."

Shock held her motionless a moment. His amber stare challenged her, and his implacable expression held not a hint of repentance. Her stomach tightened. How dare he!

"So Father's weakness for liquor is my fault. Is that what you're saying?"

He shrugged. "The weakness isn't your fault, but you do create the conditions that allow him to continue. You protect him from facing the consequences of his actions."

His unfair accusation rankled. "Letting him face the consequences would have left both of us homeless. But I don't suppose that would have occurred to you. Men of your position needn't deal with petty matters like putting food on the table and keeping a roof over your heads."

Harsh anger glinted in his eyes. "I've done my share of cleaning up after an irresponsible father, Miss Shalstone, so don't preach to me about earning a living."

"Miss Shalstone, is it?" Planting her hands on her hips, she mimicked his earlier tone, "My, my, have you noticed how formal you become when you're peeved? Could it be Your Grace is as testy as we common folk when your actions are questioned? Or are you the only one allowed to point out people's flaws?"

"That's enough, Cordelia." A muscle twitched in his jaw. "We're both tired, and this argument profits us little."

Her breath quickened as she strove to rein in her volatile emotions. Merciful heavens, until this contemptuous duke had entered her life, she'd never lost her temper. He had this knack of rousing her worst feelings while he controlled his own anger.

She mustn't let him turn her into some raging virago. He was right. Fighting him profited little, for who could argue with a man who thought he knew everything?

The only avenue was retreat. "As you say, we're both tired." She threw her head back and met his gaze, unable to resist a parting sally. "I'm tired of you and I'm bone weary of Father. Since you're obviously able to deal with him better than I, why don't you do so this evening? Take full charge of him with my blessing. *I'm* going to bed."

Again she attempted to leave the room. Again he prevented her, this time by clasping her shoulder.

"I'll happily shoulder that burden for the night, but please don't leave angry." When she glanced at him in disbelief, he added, "This trip will be unbearable if you and I are on bad terms."

He sounded almost conciliatory, but she knew he simply didn't wish to deal with Prudence and her father without her help.

She shook her head in a helpless gesture. "I'm afraid you and I are always destined to be angry with each other."

"Don't say that." His resonant murmur seemed to change the tenor of their discussion, especially when he punctuated it by sliding his hand down to clasp hers.

"There are many times, Cordelia," he added in a low, thrumming voice, "when I feel anything but angry with you. More times than you can imagine."

Suddenly she felt like a wanderer in a strange, treacherous bog with hidden traps. For heaven's sake, was he flirting with her? Men had flirted with her before, but not in such a private setting. How was she to deal with it . . . with him? Especially when his thumb now traced every crease in her sensitive palm with light, telling strokes.

She kept her face carefully averted. "Your Grace, I—"

"Please. No more 'Your Grace' or even Lord Waverley. Call me Sebastian. I hate that you regard me as some officious nobleman constantly spouting criticism."

The energy latent in his words put her on her guard. And called forth an answering shiver in her.

"I wish you'd think of me as a friend," he added. "After all, I have only your welfare at heart."

Was he trying to mollify her with this sudden attention or did he truly wish to make peace? The last thing she needed was this handsome duke treating her kindly, particularly when he could make her knees quiver simply by caressing her hand. "I'm sorry, but you and I have little on which to base a friendship."

"Do you truly think so?"

At the thread of gentleness in his tone, she lifted her face and what she saw made her mouth go dry. An enigmatic smile softened the tight lips and his eyes had lost their edge of critical fire. Another kind of fire lit them now, one that licked at her as well.

She was achingly aware of his fingers toying with hers, then enfolding them in a tight, intimate grasp. His other hand moved to her waist, and he drew her to him until she stood close, far too close.

Wide-eyed, she watched as he lowered his face to within a few inches of hers. "I think you and I have far too much on which to base a friendship." His breath was the barest whisper across her cheek. "More than any two people should have."

She murmured a protest, but it only seemed to tempt him closer as his gaze fastened on her parted lips. He hesitated, then sealed his mouth to hers.

She could pull away—his hands held her waist in the lightest of restraints. She could step back, and he'd release her. She knew it. Yet she stood like a statue in the circle of his arms, her eyelids sliding shut and her lips trembling against the slight pressure of his mouth.

It was all the response he required. With a gentleness as insidious as it was cautious, he slid his lips along hers, rubbing them apart and then skimming his tongue along the ridge of her teeth.

Her gasp of shock allowed him to slip his tongue into her mouth. It was the most intriguing thing a man had ever done to her. She stood stock still, her shock overcome by her curiosity.

When his tongue began a sensuous movement of withdrawal and advance that invaded her mouth with deepening strokes, she went limp. He melted and dissolved her, like an alchemist working gold, and the fires he used for it flamed higher and brighter with each caress. In moments she found herself sliding her arms about his neck, seeking to stretch her body as tightly against him as her clothing would allow.

He groaned, a guttural sound that roused unfamiliar longings within her. Then he molded himself to her, thigh to thigh and belly to belly.

Merciful heavens, she thought only half-consciously as his mouth became more and more demanding, slanting over hers in absolute possession as he swept the most sensitive parts of her mouth with his tongue. Her head spun and her heart pounded. It was assuredly the most enjoyable kiss she'd ever had.

"Bloody hell," he drew back to murmur, almost fiercely. "No wonder your father wanted a chaperone for you."

His words stunned her, then shot embarrassment through her. He must think her the worst wanton imaginable! Too late she regretted her easy capitulation to his kisses. Ducking her head, she tried to jerk away. "Please, Your Grace—" she murmured.

But he merely tightened his hold and began kissing along the pulse that beat madly in her neck. "Not 'Your Grace.' Sebastian. I want to hear my name on your lips, sweet Cordelia."

"We shouldn't . . . I . . ." It was hard for her to think with his hand splayed in the small of her back and his teeth nibbling at her earlobes. "Please . . . don't . . ."

"Sebastian," he rasped insistently against her ear. "Say 'Please don't stop, Sebastian. Hold me closer, Sebastian. I want more, Sebastian.' "

"I shan't say anything of the sort—" she gasped before he cut her words off with another long, needy kiss.

She tried to twist her head away, but his hands moved to cradle her head, holding it still for his merciless plundering. Then his fingers slid beneath her cap, dislodging it as they burrowed into the bun of her hair. Her cap dropped from her head, the pins came loose, and her hair tumbled down, but she did nothing, for his mouth was warm, hard, and utterly commanding as it pillaged hers until she abandoned all resistance.

Suddenly she heard noises in the hall and what sounded like her father's voice. It took a moment for the sounds to pierce her sensual haze, but as the voices grew louder, she froze in horror.

Thrusting her hands against the duke's chest, she wrenched her mouth from his. "Please, Your Grace, let me go at once!"

"Sebastian," he murmured, refusing to release her. His smoldering golden eyes raked her. "Let me hear you say my name."

"Let me go ... Sebastian," she obliged him, afraid that he wouldn't otherwise.

At the sound of his name, which she'd spoken more breathily than she'd intended, his hands tightened on her neck rather than loosening. She heard her father calling out to Mrs. Blifil, asking if she'd seen his daughter.

"You must let me go to my room," she urged, frantic with fear that her father would find them together.

The duke gave a shuddering breath and shook his head as if to throw off the effects of some terrible potion. Briefly, he looked almost dazed. Then he stared at her, his eyes clouding with self-reproach.

"Bloody hell," he murmured, releasing her suddenly. He raked his fingers through his hair, his jaw tautening. "Bloody, bloody hell. That shouldn't have happened."

The abrupt change from ardent lover to proper gentleman sent a shaft of disappointment deep into the pit of her stomach even though she agreed with him. "It certainly shouldn't have."

He closed his eyes and released a ragged breath. "I have a fiancée."

The phrase came so completely out of the blue that she didn't at first absorb it. Then awareness slammed into her. A leaden weight pressed on her chest, choking off all air. She'd known nothing permanent could come of any attention he paid her, for they weren't of the same class. Nonetheless, his admission stunned her.

It took considerable effort, but somehow she gained control over her whirling emotions. Somehow she managed a light tone, a bright smile. "Then probably you should have refrained from kissing me."

He opened his eyes and stared at her with a glittering gaze. "Most certainly. But I just—"

"It's all right. I understand," she cut him off, unwilling to hear what reason he'd had for touching her so, for arousing such feelings in her.

His lips thinned. " 'Tis bad enough you make excuses for your father, Cordelia. You shan't make them for me." He squared his shoulders and became the very image of a gentleman once more. "I had no business kissing you, but I assure you I won't disturb you so thoughtlessly again."

His words left her hollow, but she had no time to ponder that, for her father's voice echoed in the hall, calling her name. "I must go, Sebastian . . . I mean . . . Your Grace."

With a wry smile, he nodded. "I still wish us to be friends. I hope this, ah, incident won't prevent that."

She gulped. His "incident" had turned her world upside down, but he must never guess that for a moment. With a nonchalant shrug, she made it seem as if men forgot themselves and kissed her senseless every day. "What incident? It's forgotten. Don't trouble yourself another moment about it. Now, if you'll excuse me . . ."

She couldn't help it. Like the coward she was, she fled. She gathered up her skirts and got out of there as fast as her shaking legs could carry her, before she made a fool of herself. Before she started asking questions about his fiancée, who was no doubt a woman of a class and wealth more suited to him than Cordelia's could ever be.

Once clear of the room, she forced back the insane impulse to cry, to give vent to all the hurts of the day.

Obviously she'd been more enamored of the duke than she'd realized. But she wouldn't allow herself to cry simply because the man had kissed her.

She absolutely would *not*. She'd told him it was forgotten, and forgotten it must be.

Nonetheless, as she wandered through back hallways, avoiding her father while she searched for Mrs. Blifil, she wondered how one forgot such a kiss.

She feared 'twould be as impossible as keeping her father sober.

Chapter Seven

Now that the sun hath veil'd his light,
And bid the world good night,
To the soft bed my body I dispose,
But where, where shall my soul repose?
                                    —William Fuller,
                                        "An Evening Hymn"

Sebastian remained in the private supper room long after Cordelia disappeared. The image lingered: of her standing speechless with her hair scattered over her shoulders like threads of silk tossed in the wind, of her lips bruised a deep red from his kisses. Despite her light words, he'd caught the quick flash of betrayal in her eyes the moment after he'd told her he had a fiancée.

Guilt burned him, a savage brand on his conscience. He'd had no business kissing her like a man half-starved. Had he gone insane? Cordelia wasn't the kind of woman to take a kiss lightly. She'd make too much of it.

He groaned. Make too much of it? She couldn't make more of it than he had, even if he dared not admit it to her. Her luscious body and soft smile roused every predatory instinct in him, even while he felt an insane urge to protect her.

She had such a giving manner, wanting to care for everyone even when they didn't deserve it. She was talented, witty. . . . A quick smile touched his lips as he thought of the scriptures she'd thrown at her father so adroitly. Then his smile faded. He'd wounded her by pitting her against her father.

He slammed one fist into the other. He didn't regret

baiting her father—she needed to see how unfairly the vicar treated her, how much he took advantage of her.

No more than you took advantage just now, his conscience whispered, and he flinched. But bloody hell, it had thrown him off guard when she'd offered her sweetness up to him like grapes on a platter. He had wanted only a taste. Instead, he'd gotten a mouthful. And then he'd needed an entire delicious meal.

Sweet mother of God, if she hadn't heard her father in the outer hall, he'd have carried her to the nearest settee and taken her right there. When she pressed her body to his and spoke his name in that lilting, shy voice, he lost all reason. He became quite simply an animal, intent on only one thing—seduction.

That thought wrenched him. He whirled to the door and nearly slipped on her cap lying crumpled on the tile. Quickly he snatched it up. No one must find it here, for who knew what they'd conjecture about its presence.

Crushing the cap in his hand, he swallowed. He wanted Cordelia Shalstone. He wanted her badly. But he couldn't have her, not when he was pledged to Judith.

A scowl darkened his face. Dear Biddable Judith. When Sebastian's father had sunk into deepest depravity, Sebastian had appealed to Judith's father, Sir Quimley, for help. The old baron had generously agreed to cancel enormous debts owed him by Sebastian's father as long as Sebastian took the helm of the family finances and agreed to marry Judith. That had been the baron's main condition. Sebastian had agreed.

Now he must uphold that agreement. It wasn't a matter of money anymore. In time, Sebastian could afford to repay Sir Quimley, but he could never forget how the baron had stepped in when all seemed lost. Thanks to the baron's influence—and Sebastian's determination to wrest control from his father—Sebastian had been able to buy shares in the East India Company with the last of the family monies, shares that he'd parlayed into a sizeable income.

Without Baron Quimley, his sisters would have been forced to marry whatever scoundrels would have offered for them, Richard would have lost his publishing business, and Sebastian himself would have had to search for an heiress to replace the lost family assets.

Agreeing to marry Judith had seemed the least of several evils, and Sebastian had been glad to offer something of value to the old baron for all his trouble. At the time Sebastian had wanted nothing more anyway than a pleasant wife, a comfortable estate, and the assurance of future well-being for his siblings.

Yet he'd dragged his feet at marrying Judith. Sebastian shook his head. He must have known even then that he would eventually want a different wife. His native friends in India would say he'd sensed that Cordelia would come into his life, that he'd known what his karma would be.

His scowl deepened. His friends would be wrong. Happenstance, not karma, had led him to Cordelia. But pure strength of will must keep him from her, for if he stayed around her much longer, he'd have to kiss her again. Kiss her . . . and more.

With that thought, a growl tore from him and he stalked from the room, only to run smack into the vicar.

The man staggered back a step. "There you are, Your Grace! Have you seen Cordelia? When I talked to Mrs. Blifil a while ago, she said she'd not had a word with the gel. Yet I distinctly heard Cordelia say she was going to search out Mrs. Blifil to find out where her room was."

"I'm sure Cordelia has found her room by now," Sebastian clipped out.

The vicar's eyes trailed over him as if looking for signs of suspicious behavior. Unfortunately, he found one. "Is that my daughter's cap you have clutched in your hand?"

Sebastian suppressed a groan. He'd forgotten all about Cordelia's cap.

"Your Grace hasn't been making improper advances to my gel, now have you?" the vicar asked, his eyes alight with suspicion.

Because that was indeed what Sebastian had been doing, he went on the offensive, forcing as much haughtiness into his voice as he could muster. "I'll have you know, Reverend Shalstone, that I am engaged to be married to a noblewoman of wealth, beauty, and reputation. I therefore have no need to make advances to your daughter."

He hated dragging Judith into it, but perhaps it was just as well. If enough people knew of his fiancée, it might encourage him to remember her the next time he found himself alone with the delightful Miss Shalstone.

The vicar looked unconvinced. "A fiancée wouldn't keep a man of your class from dallying with the affections of a young gel. A nobleman can have ignoble intentions toward a woman he wouldn't marry, and my gel isn't used to such. I won't have you treating her like a light-o'-love for the taking."

Sebastian looked down his nose at the vicar, whose blustering words angered him all the more for being half-true. "I assure you I'm not the sort of man to seduce a respectable young woman."

"But you've got her cap—"

When he wanted to, Sebastian could act the pompous duke to the hilt. He handed the cap to her father, his face a mask of stiff self-righteousness. "I found it on the floor of the sitting room and thought it best that I retrieve it before someone made the same kind of unwarranted assumptions you make now about your daughter. No doubt she dropped it in her aimless wanderings." At least he was telling the truth, even if he was leaving a great deal out.

He sucked in his breath and continued before the vicar could retort, "You may not have noticed, but your daughter is a bit reckless. This afternoon she went into the woods alone and tonight she did much the same. When she has her head full of music, she's oblivious to her surroundings. You should speak to her about her tendency to wander. I'm sure it will cause us trouble later."

Just as he'd intended, the vicar bristled, but changed the focus of his concern. "A bit reckless, you say? Not at all, I'll have you know. She's a good gel, practical and perfectly capable of taking care of herself."

Sebastian fought the urge to point out that only moments before the vicar had assumed exactly the opposite about Cordelia. "Practical, yes, but rather innocent as you've said yourself. She needs a good hand guiding her."

"She has one!" the vicar exclaimed, his outrage evident in his reddening face. "I take care of my daughter!"

"Do you?" *If you took care of your daughter, she wouldn't have been melting in my arms scant moments ago.* "Have you seen to it that she eats? Have you made certain she's comfortable in her room?" *Have you halted your drinking?*

At least Sebastian could see to that. The vicar mumbled something about being unable to help her if he couldn't find the "blasted gel."

"Come then," Sebastian said, taking the man roughly by the arm. "We'll see to your daughter's comfort. Then we'll have our own repast." A wineless repast, he vowed.

The vicar nodded, although he shot the duke a speculative glance. "Aye. If you wish to retire after that, Your Grace, you mustn't wait up for me. I don't sleep much at night, and I promise not to wake you when I come in."

Sebastian suppressed a smile. The man thought to get him out of the way so he could get his liquor, did he? "Ah, but I usually retire late myself. And I'd certainly welcome your company until I do. It might be quite late, however. I never do like going to bed in these inns."

At the vicar's dark scowl, he allowed himself a self-satisfied smile. He could handle the old vicar's drinking if he kept his wits about him. Besides, perhaps it would take his mind off the vicar's intriguing daughter.

Perhaps.

Hours after her conversation with the duke, long after Mrs. Blifil had brought a tray to her room, Cordelia lay awake in the dark. When Prudence entered the room with a lit candle, Cordelia pretended to be asleep. The last thing she needed was a lengthy lecture from the servant about her disappearance. All Cordelia wanted was the heavy forgetfulness of sleep.

Unfortunately, sleep eluded her, particularly with Prudence wandering about the room. Cordelia hoped Prudence would extinguish the candle quickly so she could open her eyes and stare into the darkness once more. She forced her breathing to remain even and low as Prudence rummaged in her bag.

To her surprise, however, the woman didn't come to bed. Instead, she took the candle and left the room.

Cordelia sat up, staring at the closed door thoughtfully. Where on earth could Prudence be going this time of night? Then again, perhaps it wasn't as late as it seemed. Perhaps Prudence wanted to stay up longer to work on her embroidery by the fire.

With a shrug, Cordelia lay back against the pillow. Prudence ought to come to bed, for the woman had been half-asleep the entire day. Come to think of it, Prudence often seemed drowsy these days.

Ah, well, she thought, some people were like that. They liked the night hours and wanted to sleep half the day away.

Dismissing Prudence and her sleep habits, Cordelia fluffed up her pillow and tried to settle herself more comfortably on the thin horsehair mattress. She prayed there were no vermin. Unfortunately, even the best inns had infested beds.

Merciful heavens, could she at least be spared that this evening? She lay very still, imagining all sorts of nasty little beasts feeding on her. After a while, the odor of camphor, an ingredient in a concoction for ridding beds of lice, permeated her senses, giving her some reassurance. Perhaps Mrs. Blifil knew how to keep a bed free of vermin after all.

Trying to thrust her fear of bugs to the back of her mind, she rearranged the covers around her body. She attempted first one position, then another. She tried running through the notes to a very dull hymn in her head, her standard cure for insomnia, but it was no use. She couldn't sleep.

Unfortunately, it wasn't the possibility of bugs, nor the chill of the room, nor even the lumpy mattress that kept her awake. She'd dealt with those before.

It was the duke. "Sebastian," she murmured aloud. The word rolled off her tongue, giving her heart a queer flutter.

Unconsciously, she pressed her fingertips to her mouth. Nothing had prepared her for the devastating effect of Sebastian's kiss. She'd had a few awkward pecks from raw young men in Belham, kisses chaste as the blushing morn, but such kisses had roused nothing more than impatience in her and had made her uncomfortable. The men giving them had seemed hesitant, almost shy, and for some reason, she'd felt embarrassed for them.

No one could ever call the duke's kisses chaste or shy. Her toes curled as the delicious memory stirred a hot cauldron in her belly. Ah, how unexpectedly pleasant kisses could be. If she'd ever guessed what an experienced man's kisses could feel like, she'd have tried harder to attract older suitors, if only to know such delight.

Cordelia! You ought to be ashamed of yourself! she scolded. What had come over her in the last few days?

She'd been having scandalous thoughts more and more often, ever since the duke's arrival. Was it her age? Did all spinster women have wicked, lascivious thoughts as they grew older?

Or was it simply the duke who made her behave like a shameless hussy? She thought of that first startling moment when he'd plunged his tongue in and out of her mouth so intimately, when she'd pressed herself against him like a tavern wench. But who'd have thought his bizarre action would make her simmer and bubble like a kettle of hot soup?

She hated herself for it, but she'd give her eyeteeth to have it happen again. She sighed. That wasn't likely. After all, the wretched man had a fiancée, and he'd made it clear he intended to be faithful to her.

Of course he'd be faithful, she told herself, shocked that she'd even consider his being otherwise for her. After all, it wasn't as if the fiancée were the only thing standing between them. A river as wide and deep as the River Jordan itself separated them. Lords of the realm didn't have liaisons with vicar's daughters.

Well, perhaps illicit liaisons, she amended, but she could never engage in such a shameful union. Besides, the duke was too much of a gentleman to propose such a shocking thing.

What exactly was an illicit liaison anyway? she asked herself, then groaned. Merciful heavens, but the man had put thoughts in her head she'd never had before.

Illicit liaisons, indeed! She was a vicar's daughter, for heaven's sake! She shouldn't even have let the man kiss her!

She sniffed indignantly. She must put the man completely out of her mind. Twisting the sheet restlessly into a knot, she shifted to lie on her side and squeezed her eyes shut, determined to do just that.

Suddenly the door opened again, and she peered through half-closed lids, trying to see who'd entered. It was Prudence, of course, but the older woman was muttering to herself as she shot the bolt to. Cordelia strained to hear what she was saying, but could make out only a few phrases—"blasted duke," "wretched" something, and "a long, cold day in hell before . . ."

As Prudence trailed off into half-whispers, Cordelia's brow wrinkled. Prudence was cursing, for heaven's sake. It was quite unlike her. What had gotten her so upset?

Abruptly, Prudence turned and fixed Cordelia with her stare. Cordelia shut her eyes tightly, but not before glimpsing Prudence's resentful expression.

Cordelia could almost feel the woman's eyes boring into her, and she fought to keep her breathing steady. Never had she felt such dislike emanating from one person . . . and directed at her. What had she done to make Prudence hate her so?

She seemed to lie there forever, afraid to open her eyes or even move. She didn't know exactly when Prudence stopped staring, but just as she thought she'd have to open her eyes or explode from curiosity, Prudence slid between the sheets.

Cordelia held her breath, waiting for the sound of Prudence's even snoring. Suddenly the servant muttered, "Prissy little miss," then settled herself as far away from Cordelia on the mattress as possible.

A thin sigh escaped Cordelia's lips. She knew who the "prissy little miss" was. Was there some way she could soften Prudence toward her? Nay, for even when she'd made friendly overtures in the past, the servant had rebuffed them. And on the trip, Prudence had become even more bitter toward Cordelia. If only Cordelia could find out why the woman hated her so.

She shook her head. No doubt the woman was feeling the strain of their long hard trip like everyone else. She'd probably feel better in the morning.

Nonetheless, it was a long time before Cordelia could relax enough to sleep.

Chapter Eight

Care that consumes the heart with inward pain,
Pain that presents sad care in outward view,
Both tyrant-like enforce me to complain;
But still in vain; for none my plaints will rue.
                    —John Dowland,
                    "All Ye, Whom Love or Fortune"

A timid knock, followed by a soft voice murmuring, "Your Grace, 'tis dawn," brought Sebastian bolt upright out of sleep.

"I'm awake," he grumbled at the door, hearing Mrs. Blifil's footsteps recede as he swung his legs over the side of the rickety bed and buried his head in his hands.

It hadn't been an easy night. He'd tossed and turned trying to forget Cordelia's unsettling response to him. And the vicar's presence in the bed had only worsened matters. Sebastian had been right about the man's probable sleeping habits. More than right, as a matter of fact. Reverend Shalstone hadn't only stolen the blankets and taken up more than his share of the bed, but he'd also coughed and wheezed himself to sleep, then snored loud enough to rival a horse's thundering hooves. The man's bizarre assortment of night noises had kept Sebastian awake until the wee hours of the morning.

Now his head pounded, his eyes burned, and his bones creaked like rusty hinges. He rubbed his whiskered face, wondering how long it would take Mrs. Blifil to bring hot water. Perhaps he'd feel better after a good shave and a quick sponging off.

He wished he'd brought his valet. Granted, he was

without a valet often enough in India, but in India, no one expected him to observe the niceties of his rank as closely as in England. If he appeared at breakfast unshaven, he'd undoubtedly shock everyone.

Well, perhaps not the vicar, he thought as he glanced at the man who'd tortured him through the night. The vicar seemed decidedly unconcerned about anything but liquor and sleep. Now he slept like the proverbial baby, having ignored Mrs. Blifil's knock. His snores had lapsed into a rolling growl, but judging from the pleased smile on his face, the growl wasn't an expression of discomfort.

Sebastian groaned. Too bad he couldn't simply repay the vicar in kind. Suddenly a grin split his face. Clad in his drawers, which he'd worn to bed for modesty's sake, he rose and walked around the bed to the vicar's side. Then he bent down and cupped his hand, preparing to give the man the wakeup "halloo" of his life. But before he'd uttered a word he smelled it, a familiar sour odor that could only be one thing.

Brandy.

Sebastian scowled as he knelt beside the vicar and sniffed. The man reeked of brandy. Incredulous, he scanned the vicar's body. Then he spotted a flask cradled in the vicar's elbow.

With a roar of rage, he whisked the flask from the man and tossed it across the room. The vicar merely snuffled and snorted, then shifted his body and grabbed his pillow, clasping it to his chest.

Sebastian closed his eyes in sheer frustration. How had the man obtained an entire flask of brandy?

With his head aching even more now, Sebastian reconstructed the previous evening. He remembered its being abominably dull. He'd attempted to entertain the vicar when all the man spoke of was drink. They'd gone to bed at the same time. Then Sebastian had locked the door from the inside and tucked the key under his pillow, inventing some elaborate tale about thieves stealing keys from the inside locks of doors.

The vicar had even accepted the explanation with equanimity.

That thought sent Sebastian scurrying to check the pillow, but the key still lay where he'd left it. So how had the old fool gotten brandy?

Worse yet, how would Sebastian get him up? The devious wretch was obviously sleeping off a drunk. No wonder he'd coughed and wheezed in his sleep, then snored to the heavens. No wonder he'd stolen the blankets. He'd silently been drinking in bed, huddled deep under those stolen blankets to mask the scent of spirits.

Blast the bloody man to hell! Sebastian cursed, pacing the room.

It would take an hour at least to rouse him, then hours more to get him feeling up to snuff. They'd lose precious time on the road. What's more, Cordelia would be unable to tutor the man as long as he was suffering the after-effects of a full night of drink.

At the thought of Cordelia, Sebastian stopped short. She was going to kill him. He'd promised to take charge of her father. But he hadn't guessed he'd have to be a magician to do it!

Furious, he strode to the bed and shook the vicar. "Get up!" he shouted, loud enough to wake the dead.

The man merely groaned and muttered, "Shush, Florinda. Later."

Desperate now, he pushed the man out of bed, but the vicar merely curled into a ball on the cold hard floor and grumbled himself back to sleep.

Sebastian tried dragging him into a sitting position, but gave up when the vicar simply slumped back onto the floor. Resisting the urge to kick him, Sebastian shook his head. This was hopeless. Hopeless!

His stomach sank. He'd have to get Cordelia. She probably knew how to deal with her father the morning after much better than he did.

Still he lingered another moment, his pride pricked by his inability to cope with the vicar. The night before he'd been so self-righteous with Cordelia, telling her she coddled her father too much. Well, he hadn't coddled the vicar and look at all the good it had done him.

He went to the window and stared out, grimacing when he saw light flakes of snow falling on the road outside. They had to leave soon, before the snow fell too deep and they found themselves losing yet another day. There was nothing else for it. He'd have to swallow his pride and get Cordelia.

Dressing quickly, he cursed the fates that had saddled him with Reverend Shalstone. Why had his brother chosen a vicar with a penchant for spirits, who wasn't even the musician behind those precious chorales? Why couldn't the "anonymous composer" have turned out to be some stodgy music teacher or awkward young pupil? Sebastian could have handled either of those.

But he wasn't handling this drunken vicar well at all, and he certainly didn't know how to handle the man's daughter.

The man's beautiful, intriguing, and incredibly sensual daughter.

"Bloody hell!" he growled as he jerked on his coat, his loins throbbing at the thought.

He had to get them all to London and soon, because the longer he stayed in close proximity to Cordelia Shalstone, the more he wanted to bed her.

Angry at himself for his lack of control where the vicar's daughter was concerned, he strode from the room and down the hall to Cordelia's room.

He knocked impatiently, wondering if Cordelia and Prudence also lay abed, but in seconds the door opened a crack and Prudence's sour face appeared.

"Yes, Your Grace?"

"I must speak to Cor—, to Miss Shalstone. Is she dressed?"

"It isn't proper for you to—"

"What is it?" he heard Cordelia call from behind Prudence.

Prudence shut the door and he heard the low murmur of voices. Then the door opened to admit him, though Prudence scowled as she let him pass.

Cordelia sat fully dressed on a chair by a deal dressing table. She looked the picture of respectability, except her hair was down and she was combing the shining mass with long sensuous strokes that sent fire shooting to his already aching loins.

As he watched, she twisted the glossy fall of hair into a bun and pinned it at the nape of her neck, fluffing out a few short-cropped curls about her face. "What is it, Your Grace?" she asked, peering at him through the half-silvered mirror. She flushed as her gaze met his, and instantly he thought of their kisses.

He struggled against the urge to step forward and touch those gleaming curls. The effort to control himself made his words come out harsher than he'd meant. "I need help with your bloody father."

Her back went rigid. She dropped the comb on the table and turned to stare at him, not a trace of amusement in her eyes. "My 'bloody' father?"

"I can't get him up—" he began.

Instantly her expression shifted to fright as she sprang to her feet. "Oh, no! He's not ill, is he? Perhaps last night when he spoke of feeling unwell, he truly meant—"

"He's not ill," Sebastian hastened to reassure her. His lips thinned. "He's—" He sucked in his breath. "He's inebriated."

A strange expression passed over her face, of disbelief mingled with bitterness. She planted her hands on her hips. "What do you mean?"

She wouldn't make this easy for him, would she? "I mean, he's intoxicated, sotted . . . whatever word you wish to use. He's drunk. Or rather, he was drunk at some point last night. Now he's sleeping it off."

"I thought you were . . ." She trailed off, leaving the words unsaid, but the implied accusation was quite apparent.

"I stayed with him all evening. Never once did he

touch a drop of liquor. Yet somehow he acquired a flask of brandy while sleeping in *my* room with a door locked from the inside and the key stowed under *my* pillow!"

He heard a quick gasp from Prudence. He stared at the servant, noticing that she dropped her eyes under his intent gaze. Why was *she* surprised? Surely she knew her master's habits by now.

"So you see," he continued in a decidedly sharp tone, "I need your help."

Cordelia paled, and she shot Prudence a suspicious glance. "Of course. Father sleeps like the dead after a night of . . . of imbibing."

"I had noticed that." When she turned her back to him and rummaged among her bags, he snapped, "We've no time to waste with this, Cordelia. It's snowing, and I had planned to be on the road in an hour."

"Don't growl at me, Your Grace." Her hands closed on a curious-looking bottle. "I had nothing to do with it, if you'll recall."

Reining in his temper with difficulty, he watched as she stuck the bottle in her apron pocket, then snatched up a shawl that lay on the bed and settled it about her shoulders.

"Please accept my apologies," he bit out. "When I took on the task of caring for your father, I didn't realize flasks of brandy fell into his lap while he slept."

The glance she gave him then contained such woeful sadness that all his anger faded. She managed a faint smile. "I know. Believe me, I know."

Then she whisked from the room. He shot Prudence a glance, but the woman was busily packing up articles of clothing, apparently uninterested in the vicar's problem, so he followed Cordelia without a word to Prudence.

When he entered his room, he found Cordelia standing over her father with a pitcher of water. She started to tilt it over his head, and Sebastian darted forward in alarm. "What in bloody hell do you think you're—"

"Trust me. It's the most effective way to awaken Father when he's been at it all night. Generally, I let him sleep it off, but if he has to be up for something important, I resort to more drastic measures."

"Drastic!" Sebastian thought of the times when he himself had blissfully slept off the effects of a long night of carousing. "That's positively horrifying! That water's cold as a witch's tit!"

But she was already pouring the water out of the pitcher onto the vicar's shaved head in a thin, steady stream. The vicar shot up like a child's jack-in-the-box, sputtering and blinking his eyes as he waved off the evil that had disturbed his rest.

"Devil take thee!" he muttered, glaring at his daughter as he wiped water off his pale face with his sleeve. Then his gaze fixed on Sebastian. "Would you let her kill me then? Can't a man sleep without being attacked?"

Sebastian couldn't help it. He suddenly found himself enjoying the vicar's discomfort. "You know your daughter, sir, better than I. She gets these unusual notions in her head—"

"Come now, Father," Cordelia remarked, flashing Sebastian an unreadable glance. "We must be on the road. Snow is falling, and we don't wish to find ourselves snowbound only one day into our journey."

Reverend Shalstone grumbled as he rubbed his head. No doubt he had the devil of a headache, Sebastian thought with reprehensible glee. Who'd ever have guessed that Sebastian Kent, who'd had his share of mornings after, would be so vindictive toward a fellow drinker?

Then again, he'd never been a drunk. Sebastian watched as Cordelia tried to coax the man to drink from the bottle she'd brought into the room.

"What's that?" Sebastian asked as she got a little of the foul-looking liquid between her father's lips.

The vicar snapped, "Lucifer's concoction. My daughter whips it out when she wishes to torment me." That much speech apparently taxed his head, for he moaned and closed his eyes.

Cordelia ignored his distress. "Drink it all, Father. Every drop, or I swear I'll ask His Grace to hold you down so I can pour it down your throat."

The image her words brought to mind was enough to make Sebastian shiver. The thought of holding a cranky old vicar still so his daughter could force some dubious cure down his throat didn't appeal to him at all.

"You see?" the vicar told Sebastian, his nose wrinkling at the smell of the stuff in the bottle. "She's a witch, she is."

Cordelia's expression softened. "You know it settles your stomach." She thrust it into his hands. "Now drink!"

Apparently, even in his wretched state, the vicar could hear the note of command in her voice, for bracing himself, he tipped the bottle up and drank from it. He paled, and sweat broke out on his forehead. Then he jumped up, quite fast for an older man, and ran for the chamber pot to empty his stomach.

To Sebastian's surprise, Cordelia smiled at the retching noises. "Excellent."

When the vicar finished and stumbled back toward the bed, she handed him the bottle again. This time he swigged it tamely. A series of loud burps followed. Then he began to get some color in his face.

As soon as she saw he was feeling better, she corked the bottle and then bustled around the room, gathering her father's belongings and stuffing them in his bag. "Do you think you could eat something now?" she asked matter-of-factly.

Eat something? Sebastian thought. No man waking up the morning after downing a flask of brandy felt like eating.

Yet the vicar nodded. "A bit of toast perhaps."

His eyes narrowing, Sebastian remained silent, wondering about Cordelia's mysterious concoction. He watched the vicar and his daughter together, noting how the old man got himself painfully about as his daughter saw to his needs.

How many times had they followed this pattern before? How many times had Cordelia cared for her father after a night's drinking?

Part of him admired her for it. But another part wondered how long the vicar would have continued to take advantage of his daughter if she'd refused to help him after one of his nights. Then again, if she'd refused to help the vicar this morning, they'd all have been in a pickle. For one thing, how would they have endured the vicar's foul temper?

Guilt made him wince. If it weren't for Sebastian's inability to keep her father from drinking last night, she wouldn't have been forced to "cure" him this morning. Indeed, Sebastian had chastened her for not stopping her father's drinking, but he'd been equally unsuccessful. He began to understand why she found his statements about her father so presumptuous.

"I'd appreciate it if Your Grace would call a servant to help my father dress," her calm voice interrupted his unpleasant thoughts. "Normally, Father waits until he can manage alone, but today—"

"It's all right, Cordelia. I'll help him myself."

She smiled faintly, and Sebastian noted how sad she looked. For a while yesterday, she'd lost that careworn expression. It disturbed him to think he'd been partly responsible for bringing it back.

She started to leave the room, then turned to him, her hands twisting together. "If you don't mind, before you attend to Father, I . . . I need to speak with you about something. Privately."

Her father's head snapped up at that, but she went on, a glint of defiance in her eyes. "If you would step into the hall a moment, Your Grace—"

"Of course," Sebastian quickly said.

As soon as he'd followed her into the hall, aware of the vicar's angry gaze boring into his back, he closed the door behind them. "I thought after last night, you were going to call me Sebastian."

She glanced away from him. "I-I'd forgotten."

He wished *he'd* forgotten. In fact, he shouldn't have brought it up at all, he thought when she colored.

"About last night—" she began, and he flinched. She went on without seeming to notice. "You said Father never left your company."

He relaxed, then nodded.

Taking a deep breath, she gestured to her door down the hall. "Prudence was with you the whole evening, too, wasn't she?"

With a frown, he nodded again, wondering where this was leading. "She left for a moment to return to her room—*your* room—and retrieve her tambour. Then she returned to the parlor and worked on her embroidery until your father and I went to bed."

Cordelia looked perplexed. "Do you remember if she went near Father?"

He chuckled. "I don't think you need worry about your father and Prudence. The woman is too much of a termagant to attract anyone."

She shook her head impatiently. "I don't mean like that. I mean, did she come close to him at all, as if to show him her work or speak to him in a whisper or something like that?"

He thought back to the previous evening. "Why yes, I believe she did hand him her tambour once. She asked if he thought the colors were too bright. I thought it odd that she'd ask a man such a thing, particularly her employer, but—" He broke off as he followed her train of thought. "You don't think *she* gave him the brandy, do you?"

With a helpless wave of her hand, she stared off past him. "I don't know. I *have* been wondering how he manages to sneak his wine into the house under my very nose. Last night, Prudence slipped into our room, gathered something from her bag, then left. It was only the tambour, I'm sure but . . ."

"But what?"

With a flush, she bent her head. "This morning while she was downstairs calling for hot water, I searched her bags." Her eyes met his. "I found a flask of brandy among her clothes."

"One she no doubt intends to slip to your father tonight," he said grimly.

"I think so. I don't know. I didn't take any chances."

He looked at her quizzically.

With a wry smile, she said, "I poured out the brandy and replaced it with water."

"That will only solve the problem temporarily."

Her expression saddened. "I know. I'll have to confront her. But before I stir up trouble, I must make certain she's guilty. After all, she may have brought the flask along for herself."

He tried to imagine sanctimonious old Prudence tippling brandy, but failed. "You don't believe that, do you?"

She shrugged. "Tonight I can find out for sure, if and when she passes the flask to him. I'll have to trap her in the act, or she'll bluster her way out of my accusations. Will you help?"

A mischievous smile crossed his face. So he was to get his revenge on the vicar after all. "Believe me, I'll do whatever I can."

It was cold, bitterly cold, both outside and inside the coach, when they left the inn less than an hour later. To Cordelia's irritation, everyone was testy, but most especially her father, who grumbled at every loud sound and threatened to toss Cordelia's music out the window if they didn't give him some peace. Somehow she managed to calm him. She even tutored him for a time, but only when he'd lapsed into a restless sleep at her side close to noon had she been able to relax.

From the moment she'd been forced to get him up,

she'd struggled against the impulse to rail at him. Admonishing him did no good. She'd learned that long ago. He was stubborn and did precisely as he wished, no matter what she said.

Still, this time he'd gone too far. How dare he drink himself silly while sleeping next to a duke? It was embarrassing in the extreme, and no doubt frustrating for His Grace.

Of course, it served Sebastian right to have Father abuse drink beneath his very nose, she thought spitefully. She was still angry at the duke for all his overbearing statements the night before.

She shot him a glance, but he was staring out the window at the barren landscape, his body alert as if he watched for bandits. He probably did, she thought. The man seemed to revel in the role of watchdog. The only time he'd lost control was when he'd kissed her.

Warm thoughts flooded her, and she gritted her teeth, determined not to indulge them. Instead, she thought of all his insulting words the night before. *You coddle him far too much. You create the conditions that allow him to continue. You don't leave him to face the consequences of his actions.*

Hearing her father snore, she felt anger steal over her again, blessedly driving out memories of the duke's kiss. How dare Sebastian blame her for Father's condition? Sebastian had spent three days in their company, yet somehow he thought he knew everything about them. It was absolutely infuriating!

Despite her outrage, however, she found herself thinking about Sebastian's words. What did he mean, she created the conditions that allowed Father to continue? She certainly didn't give Father the wine. If anything, she'd always sought to make the house as free of liquor as possible. They hadn't had wine at the table in ages. In fact, they'd almost never had wine at the table, not even when Mother was alive. Ale, yes, but even that hadn't been available at every meal as it was in other houses.

For the first time, Cordelia wondered if Mother's preference for "stimulating beverages" like coffee and lemonade had been because Mother had known of Father's tendency to overindulge. The thought stunned her. She'd always assumed his drinking stemmed from his grief over Mother's death. Yet suppose it didn't? Suppose he'd always had been that way, but Mother had purposely curbed his tendencies?

Her father mumbled in his seat and shifted to lean against the side of the coach. Sebastian scowled at him, then at her. When their gazes locked, however, Sebastian's scowl faded into a hesitant half-smile that made her feel guilty for all her accusing thoughts. It wasn't as if the duke deliberately sought to irritate her with his statements. In truth, Sebastian was generally thoughtful to her, except when he kissed her like a man possessed.

Even then, he apologized afterward.

Merciful heavens, he was impossible to understand. One minute he showed concern for her health and in the next he told her how every problem with Father was *her* fault. *She* coddled Father and *she* didn't leave Father to face the consequences of his actions.

Face the consequences of his actions. What did that mean? Should she stand by and watch while Father lost his post, while he drank himself into oblivion? Where would they both be then? She had no choice—she had to keep him sober, even if it meant carrying his duties when he failed.

If she ever simply let go. . . . That was impossible. Too much was at risk.

But she could do a few things, she thought as she glanced at Prudence. She could get to the bottom of Prudence's involvement. Prudence had to be involved, she told herself, for the woman acted nervous as a cat today, all jittery and jumpy. Her eyebrows twitched every time she shot a venomous glance at Cordelia, and she fidgeted with her skirts constantly, pleating and repleating the black fustian. 'Twas enough to make Cordelia a raving lunatic.

At least the snow had stopped, Cordelia thought as the coach lumbered along. Sebastian had said if they could get as far as York tonight, the roads improved from there.

York. That was where Honorine lived. Cordelia hadn't seen her mother's old friend in years, not since the funeral, in fact. She wondered if she should mention Honorine to the duke. A visit with Honorine would be wonderful, but the woman mightn't even be home, and it would be rude in any case to descend on her with so many people and no notice.

On the other hand, Cordelia thought with a smile, Honorine would simply perish if she missed a chance to meet the Duke of Waverley.

"If you don't mind my asking, what is that smile about?"

Startled by the duke's comment, she regarded him thoughtfully. "It's nothing. Merely that you talked of stopping in York. You see, I have a friend there—"

"Honorine," muttered a low voice at her side.

Cordelia twisted to look at her father. "I thought you were sleeping."

His eyes were closed and his head was propped against the side of the coach, but he smiled.

She playfully swatted him with her reticule. "Why, you wretched pretender! You're trying to get out of your lessons, that's what you're doing!"

He opened one eye. "Not quite. When you mentioned that battle-ax Honorine, it woke me right up. Even asleep, my heart quaked at the sound of her name."

Cordelia rolled her eyes. "Battle-ax, indeed! She's not that bad, Father. She's only a bit forceful in her opinions."

Her father's snort of laughter made her swat him again.

Tugging her reticule away from her, her father

stuffed it behind his back, his eyes gleaming as he stared at Cordelia. "I know what you're thinking, gel. You're thinking we might stop and pay the widow Honorine a visit. Well, put that idea right out of your head. The last thing we need is Honorine's 'forceful' opinions."

"She's my friend."

"Aye." He shook his finger at her, only half in amusement. "But that friend has the will of a tigress, the mind of a judge, and the voice of a shrew. If she can't sway a man to her opinion by sheer force of will, she uses the devil's own logic on him. If that fails, she rails at him until he sees her point." A mournful sigh left his lips. "Eventually she wins. Honorine always wins, and I shan't put up with her nonsense when I've got all this other muddle on my mind."

"Father! She's not at all like that! She's generous and thoughtful—"

"And a tyrant to all who cross her," he finished for her.

"That's so ungrateful of you. Honorine has treated me with the kindness of a sister all these years, despite her superior wealth. Think of the countless times she's aided us with a donation when the church was in dire straits." Her voice dropped. "Nor did she hesitate to come to Mother's side at the end. If it hadn't been for Honorine—"

"Aye," he broke in, his voice softening. "Aye. Honorine does have a loyal streak in her."

"I relish the thought of meeting such an interesting woman," Sebastian broke in. To Cordelia's delight, he added, "I suppose we could manage a short visit."

Ignoring her father's groan, she said in breathless haste, "We needn't stay more than an hour or two. I know you wish to hasten back to your brother, but I'd be so grateful if we could at least spend a few moments with her."

"I could hardly refuse you when you make such an impassioned plea." His smile included her father, but the glint in his eyes was meant only for her, and she knew it.

"Thank you, Sebastian."

Then she cursed her slip of the tongue when Prudence looked at her with disdain, and her father glowered.

"Sebastian?" her father growled.

Lord Waverley shrugged. "I suggested to your daughter that we dispense with formalities since we were traveling in such close confines."

She shot her father a speculative glance, alarmed to see the rigid set of his chin. He replied in a stilted tone, "But Your Grace, 'tis inappropriate for us to be so familiar when we scarcely know you." He glared. "Perhaps if we knew your background, I'd feel more comfortable 'dispensing with formalities.' Why don't you tell us about yourself? You know . . . your parents, your work in India . . ." He paused to give Cordelia a sideways glance, and added in challenge, "Your fiancée."

Cordelia colored instantly. Father could have only one reason for making it clear to her that the duke was engaged. Did he know about the kiss? Merciful heavens, she hoped not.

Embarrassed to her toes to have Father warning her of the duke's ineligibility, she muttered, "It's impertinent to be so curious about personal matters, Father," and dug her fingers into his arm.

He ignored her not so subtle reproof. "We're letting the man carry us off to London with scarcely a day's notice. I don't see why we shouldn't expect him to be a bit forthcoming."

"You're perfectly within your rights." Sebastian's voice had a brittle edge. He crossed his arms over his chest and leaned back against the plush seat. "I'm perfectly willing to tell you about my life. Of course, you must do the same. I'd particularly be interested in hearing about your work as a vicar over the last three years."

Her father tugged his ear furiously, an expression of outrage growing on his face.

This is getting entirely out of hand, Cordelia thought. *Why can't Father and Sebastian get along together? This sparring simply can't continue.*

Her father leaned forward, preparing to give Sebastian a thorough set-down, so she dug her heel into his foot. "Father's work can't be nearly as fascinating as your travels in India, Your Grace," she said over her father's grunt. "It must have been quite interesting. You must tell us all about it."

The duke's eyes never left her father's face. "I think you father is more curious about the personal details of my life than my days in India."

Now it was the duke who received her disapproval. She glared at him until he turned his mutinous gaze to her.

Then she gave him her chilliest smile. "Whose curiosity will you satisfy then? That of a lady? Or that of an impertinent old man?"

"Cordelia!" her father protested. "Listen here, gel—"

"Which one, Your Grace?" Her gaze challenged the duke. "If you insist on satisfying Father's curiosity instead of mine, I shall feel quite wounded." She cast her father a quelling glance. "*Quite* insulted."

Her father knew better than to ignore that look. He grumbled and glowered at her, but he said nothing more. When she returned her gaze to Sebastian, the taut lines about his lips had softened, and he was almost smiling.

Raising one eyebrow, he said in an amused tone, "When you put it that way, Miss Shalstone, I can hardly refuse, can I?" He relaxed in his seat. "Tell me, what particulars about India would you like to know?"

She released a long breath, not realizing until then how nervous she'd been that the two men might come to blows, and all over the fact that she'd called His

Grace. "Sebastian." In the future, she must be more careful.

She cast about in her mind for some appropriate question, then said, "I'd most like to know why you went to India in the first place. It's not as if it's on the Grand Tour."

Sebastian smiled. "Indeed not. India is far too vibrant and outrageous to be considered an acceptable training ground for fledglings of Society."

"You mean, too pagan," Prudence cut in, surprising them all, for she'd been unusually silent all morning. "I hear 'tis a wicked, wicked place."

"Ah, but definitions of 'wicked' vary according to one's particular bias," Sebastian remarked dryly. "The Hindu, for example, consider us quite heathen for eating beef, and the Muslims rail against the 'wicked' forwardness of our women."

"The Muslims might have a point," her father mumbled at Cordelia's side as Prudence snorted and retreated back into her silence.

Cordelia shot him an arch glance, knowing quite well to whom he referred. "I pray you, Father, when did you acquire this eagerness to embrace Muslim ideas? Will you have Prudence and me covering our faces with veils?"

"I see you know something about Muslim customs," Sebastian put in.

"Oh, yes. Father made sure I had a thorough education. He's quite a lover of learning, you know. Thanks to him, I read widely from an early age. I've been tutored in mathematics, geography, the classics . . . oh, a number of subjects."

"And you see what it's brought me—an insolent daughter," her father grumbled, but she could hear the pride in his voice.

Sebastian regarded her father curiously. "Do you realize how unusual it is for a woman to be so thoroughly educated?"

She grinned, patting her father's hand. "Aye. 'Tis

quite unusual, or so Honorine and Mother used to tell me."

"Can't imagine why it should be," her father grumbled. "If women don't have things explained to them properly, how can men expect them to act with intelligence?"

"Most men don't." Sebastian leveled his thoughtful gaze on her father. "I think that's the trouble. Men treat women as half-wits, and women oblige them by acting that way."

"Aye, that's it exactly," her father agreed. "But it shouldn't be like that. Christ himself praised Martha for sitting at his feet and learning about truth when Mary tried to chastise her for not helping in the kitchen. I say a woman should be given the chance to fill her head with knowledge. Then if she chooses not to bother herself with it, that's her choice."

Cordelia could have hugged him at that moment. Truly her father could be a dear when he wasn't losing himself in drink.

"What about you, Your Grace?" She met his gaze with a daring smile. "You have three sisters, don't you? While you were in India, did you make certain they had an education? Or have they been taught only the usual pursuits—needlework, watercolor painting, etcetera?"

He grinned. "I assure you, my sisters have had tutors since they were old enough to chirp my name, and they're all quite as familiar with history, mathematics, and Latin as I am. Probably more so. I'm sure you'll enjoy meeting them and discussing learning. I suspect the four of you shall get along quite well."

The look he gave her then sent shivers to her toes, for it was the look a man gave a woman when no one else was there to see it. It was almost worse than his kiss, for it made infinite promises, ones she knew he couldn't keep. At least when he'd kissed her, she'd thought for a moment it meant something, but once he'd mentioned his fiancée. . . . A hard knot tightened in her belly.

As if he'd read her mind, her father asked tartly, "And your fiancée? Shall she and Cordelia get along well also?"

Cordelia suppressed a groan. Merciful heavens, could she and the duke not even be amiable without her father prickling?

Sebastian's smile faded. The solemn glint in his eyes dashed any hopes she'd had a moment before. "Undoubtedly, they will. Judith gets along well with everyone, so well that we call her The Biddable Judith. I'll admit she isn't much interested in books, but I'm sure she'll love Miss Shalstone's music."

Cordelia's stomach lurched, and she could think of nothing to say. She doubted she'd like this Judith, no matter what the woman thought of her music.

As if to stave off any more disconcerting discussions, Sebastian jerked out his pocket watch and glanced at it. "'Tis past two o'clock. Perhaps we should stop for dinner." He looked out the window. "We're nearing Ripon, which is as good a place to stop as any."

"A nice dinner would be good," her father agreed.

Sebastian and her father chatted another moment about what inns they had heard of in Ripon, but she couldn't concentrate. Their discussion had sunk her into unwarranted misery.

The duke hadn't shown her any other interest except that one spate of kisses, she chided, yet she was acting like a jealous wife, bristling every time he mentioned his fiancée. But she couldn't help it. Despite his arrogance and insistence on meddling, he was the most intriguing man she'd ever met. To her knowledge, no other man shared her father's peculiar views about women's education. Certainly, no other man had shown Sebastian's loyalty to family.

It would be so much easier to put him out of her mind if he were an old, gouty noble with a snuffbox.

Then she could treat him as the man who'd essentially employed her to train her father.

But she couldn't. Worse yet, she feared she never could.

Chapter Nine

Shall I strive with words to move,
When deeds receive not due regard?
Shall I speak, and neither please,
Nor be freely heard?
      —John Dowland,
        "Shall I Strive with Words to Move?"

Cordelia had thought she wouldn't have to deal with Prudence until that evening, but when her father excused himself from the table at dinner and Prudence did the same shortly after, she realized the time had come.

She looked at Sebastian, who was gazing after Prudence, his jaw taut.

"I guess I'd better follow them," she murmured.

"You think she's giving him the liquor now?"

"There's no telling, but it'll only take a moment to be sure."

"I'll go with you—"

"No." She stood. "No, they'll think it odd if we both claim to be searching for them."

He nodded curtly, and she felt him watching her as she left the room by the same door Prudence had taken. Finding herself in a long, empty hall, she hesitated.

A brief moment of doubt assailed her. Merciful heavens, Father was turning her into a silly fool, seeing conspiracies where there were none. They'd probably both needed to relieve themselves. It was perfectly understandable, considering—

A loud exclamation from around the corner at one

end of the hall put the lie to her thoughts. It was Father's voice.

Quickly she raced there, rounding the corner in time to see her father spit on the floor. Prudence stood beside him, a stony expression on her face as his eyes flashed murder.

"Water, blast you!" he shouted at the servant as Cordelia approached. " 'Tis water! Have you turned to temperance like His Grace?"

A cold, dark rage froze Cordelia's blood. She stepped forward, fighting to keep her fists at her side, for a ferocious urge to beat her father senseless assailed her.

"Nay, Father," she cut in before Prudence could answer. His gaze shot to her, and he reddened, thrusting the flask at Prudence, who refused to take it.

Cordelia snatched it from him. " 'Twas *I* put the water in it when I found the flask of brandy in Prudence's bags. For shame! Can't you even go one full day without needing your spirits?"

"Now, Cordelia—" he began.

"Don't!" Dimly she heard a door open and shut, but she ignored it, even when the duke rounded the corner to stand behind her. Her voice lowered to a cutting tone. "Don't try to apologize and tell me you merely wanted 'a bit to warm you.' You always say that before you drink yourself into oblivion."

Her eyes narrowed as she leveled an angry gaze on Prudence. "As for you, I can't believe you'd do this. You know what a problem liquor is for him. You know how it destroys him, yet you sneak around my back and—"

"My loyalty is to your father," Prudence spat out, having recovered from the shock of seeing Cordelia.

"I can't imagine why. 'Tis I who pays you while he's languishing in his cups!"

"Aye, and 'tis you who'd turn me out if it weren't for him!"

Prudence spoke the words with such vitriolic sincerity that it took Cordelia completely aback.

"What do you mean? I'll admit you and I have never gotten along very well, but I've never threatened to dismiss you."

"That's not what *he* said." Prudence shook one bony finger at Cordelia's father. "He said you wanted to dismiss me after your mother died. He said he persuaded you to keep me on. He always says he's the only one who wants me to stay."

Cordelia's mouth fell open. In disbelief, she shifted her gaze to her father. He stared at her in bleak silence, which in itself confirmed the truth of Prudence's words.

And here she'd thought he would eventually overcome his problem and become his old self again. Despair deep as a chasm threatened to swallow up those foolish hopes.

Scarcely able to hold her voice even, she whispered, "Father, is this true? Did you tell Prudence I planned to dismiss her?"

He dropped his eyes to his hands and cracked his knuckles. "You always said you didn't like her."

His defensive tone destroyed the last remnants of hope clinging to the sides of her wounded heart. "Did you tell Prudence I was going to dismiss her?" she repeated, more stiffly.

Pulling on his ear furiously, he muttered, "Maybe after your mother died, I might have implied—"

"After her mother died?" Prudence interrupted, astonishment spreading over her face. "You told me not three days ago that if I didn't come on this trip, you'd let the miss turn me off as she wanted to do. Three days ago you told me that!"

When he merely shrugged, Prudence appealed to Cordelia, her mouth now a thin, drawn line. "I swear, miss, he told me you didn't want me to stay on. I'd never have crossed your wishes about the spirits if I hadn't thought . . . I truly believed him when he said—"

"How long have you been supplying him with wine?" Cordelia asked woodenly. The duke stood at her back, hearing every word of the sordid tale and saying nothing, but she didn't care anymore. She wanted the truth.

Prudence glanced at Cordelia's father, who scowled at everyone. When she returned her gaze to Cordelia, she looked desperate. "Ever since you asked him to stop taking the possets. He came to me for the keys to the cellar, because he wouldn't ask you. I told him if he sneaked wine from there without you knowing, you'd think Maggie or I'd been stealing it. That's when he told me that if it weren't for him—"

"It was a lie, Prudence." Cordelia could hardly choke out the words. "I knew you were too old to find another position. I'd never have dismissed you like that, and I never said otherwise to Father."

Prudence's aged face crumpled, her wan lips trembling as she seemed to struggle for words. "Oh, miss, I-I thought . . . I'm so sorry. So truly sorry."

Cordelia felt lacerated, raw inside. They'd both been deceiving her, sneaking around behind her back, speaking of her as if she were some horrid monster. She couldn't bear to look at either of them, but especially not her father. Her lying, duplicitous father. She faced the wall, tears blinding her.

"I'll understand if you want to dismiss me now," Prudence said wearily.

The words trickled into Cordelia's consciousness from far away, but she could hardly respond. It was all too much to grasp at once. She thought of how often she'd poured wine out of his flasks, and her sense of betrayal increased. How many times had she bemoaned her father's lack of control to Maggie and Prudence? How often had they caught her weeping over her inability to help him? And all this time . . .

A choked sob escaped her lips. She must get away from them both. She must!

"Miss, what's to become of me?" Prudence asked plaintively. "Please, I need to know."

Cordelia wrenched her thoughts back to the situation at hand. Escape must wait until she dealt with this.

Still averting her face from Prudence, she murmured, "I won't punish you for Father's deceptions."

"Now, pet, it wasn't like that—" her father began.

She continued as if he hadn't even spoken. "But you'll understand why I can't let you continue on the trip with us. You may return to Belham and resume your duties. We'll . . . we'll discuss your situation at length upon my return."

"Thank you, miss," Prudence said in a rush. She clasped Cordelia's hand. Still Cordelia couldn't look at her.

Prudence dropped her hand. "'Tis most gracious of you," she said in a subdued tone. "I'll take the next post chaise back."

"You will not!" Cordelia's father protested. "Cordelia, you've no reason to send her back if she promises to follow your blasted rules about the wine. . . ."

Her mutinous glance made him trail off. He was probably right. There probably was no danger of letting Prudence continue with them, but right now Cordelia couldn't bear to have the woman in their midst. She simply couldn't bear it. "Prudence is going to return," she announced firmly.

"But you need a chaperone!" her father protested. His voice harshened. "If she returns to Belham, then we go with her. That'll put an end to the scheme concocted by you and that . . . that lord." He spoke the word "lord" with contempt as he jerked his head toward where the duke stood silent.

"Go ahead, Father, return to Belham if you wish," Cordelia said in a faraway voice. "But I won't go with you."

Stunned into silence, her father stepped back a pace.

She gathered her courage. "I'm going to London. With or without you, I'm going to meet Lord Kent . . . and Handel. With or without you, I'll help His Grace's brother. It'll be stickier without you, but I don't care."

"There's a post chaise leaving for Belham in a few hours," Sebastian offered wryly behind her.

Her father snorted. "You'd like that, wouldn't you, Your Grace? You'd like it if I simply took myself out of the picture. Then you could assault my daughter's virtue at your leisure!"

"Father!" Cordelia cried out in shock, mortified to the depths of her soul.

He went on heedlessly, resentment shining in his reddened face. "Did you plan this, Lord Waverley? Did you happen to notice Prudence gave me the flask last night and tell Cordelia about it, so she'd turn on me?"

When Cordelia started to vent her fury, the duke laid a stiff hand on her arm. "Have you no consideration for your daughter?" His voice shook with outrage. "You've spent the last three years shaming her before her neighbors and lying about her to her servants, and now you think to gloss it over by accusing me and insulting her? What kind of father are you?"

Her father's jaw sagged. He blinked, then shook his head. "It wasn't like that."

"What was it like then?" Cordelia blurted out, wondering if she'd ever get over the hurt. "What have I done that you should make my own servants hate me?"

His eyes looked like those of a cornered beast. "You took my freedom from me, that's what. It was my right to drink what I wished, but you forced me to sneak around. You kept the cellar locked, the wine rationed. . . ." He slumped, his face suddenly looking lined and weary. "Is it any wonder I twisted the truth to get what I wanted? I wanted a bit of wine for myself. What crime is that?"

In the past, his attempts to gain her sympathy had worked, but not this time. She thought of all the nights he'd drunk himself into a stupor, and she'd had to sober him up the next morning. She thought of the days she'd spent poring over the household accounts and wondering how they'd live if Father lost his post.

A profound sorrow swept her, numbing her with cold regret. Her father wasn't the man she'd thought. He was a selfish, inconsiderate drunk whose thirst for wine blurred his vision so totally he didn't even know his own daughter. Somehow he had come to see her as jailor. And she'd come to see him as the same thing.

No more, she thought. No more.

"I see I've made a grave mistake, Father," she whispered. She felt Prudence's startled gaze on her and knew the duke would wonder at her words, but she didn't care. "I was wrong to keep you from drinking. You wish to drink wine?" Her voice grew harder. "Fine. Drink what you wish. Drink yourself into oblivion."

She tossed the flask on the floor between them, her voice growing more hysterical by the moment. "Swill your wine and brandy. Wallow in it. Bathe in it. Enjoy yourself." She lifted her skirts. "But I'll not write another sermon for you while you're sleeping it off. I'll not clean up your vomit, and I'll never, ever excuse your behavior to the others in Belham." She fixed him with a wild stare. "You may invite them all to the vicarage for an eternal celebration to Bacchus." She pivoted on her heel, and added very quietly, "I won't be there."

Then she stalked off.

"Where are you going, gel?" her father shouted behind her.

Without a word, she headed for the nearest door that would get her out of the inn and away from her father.

"Wait!" he shouted.

The duke said, "I don't think she wants to see you at the moment, sir. Why don't you help Prudence prepare for the post chaise to Belham, and I'll take care of Cordelia?"

"Come back here, gel!" she heard her father shout as

she reached the door. She jerked it open, passed through, and slammed it behind her. Oblivious to the stares of the other travelers in the common room, she strode toward their empty table, snatched up her capuchin and threw it about her shoulders as she marched straight for the door that led to the street.

Seconds later she was out in the bracing cold, welcoming its bite as her rage carried her along the frozen, busy streets of the small market town.

"Fool! Idiot!" she muttered to herself. How could she have been so blind for so long? She'd saved them both from poverty, expecting him to be grateful. Her image of him had been all distorted, as if seen through a rippling pond. She'd thought he was struggling to deal with his grief, and thus temporarily incapable of caring for himself. But that hadn't been it at all, had it?

She jerked the capuchin close about her, fumbling with the ties as she stamped through the snow. No, the truth was he'd been resenting her interference, oblivious to everything she did for him. And she hadn't even seen it! What kind of ninny would work so hard for nothing?

Caught up in her private misery, she didn't hear the footsteps behind her until the duke fell into step at her side. He didn't try to stop her. He didn't even touch her, just walked next to her, his hands thrust into his pockets as he stared expressionlessly ahead.

They crunched through the new-fallen snow in silence for a while, oblivious to the bustle of the villagers around them. He didn't seem to mind that she didn't speak, and in truth she was so angry she couldn't put her fury into words.

As the wind chilled her body, however, it also chilled her anger. Her steps slowed to a steady, even pace. Soon they reached the outskirts of the town and village cottages became fewer and farther between. Coming to a crossroads, she took the more deserted road, and before long they were walking alone down a rutted country path that dwindled to a stop beside a frozen stream.

She halted beneath the stripped boughs of an ancient oak, staring off across the ice as she tucked her hands beneath her arms to keep them warm. The quiet stillness of their surroundings freed her to speak. "You were right," she said in a whisper, not looking at him.

"About what?"

The rumbling tenderness in his voice gave her an odd comfort. "You know. About Father. About me. About everything." She sucked in a breath of harsh, cold air. "I've fed him a cure every morning and helped him through the aftermath of his drunks. . . . I've written his sermons and made his visits, all the time excusing his lapses, telling myself that one day he'd no longer crave the drink. But that day will never come, will it?"

For the first time since she'd left the inn, she turned her face to his, expecting to see at least a hint of smugness. Instead she found him pensive, even angry as his eyes met hers.

"No, it never does seem to come. The more you cater to his whims, the more he'll demand. 'Tis better to cut him loose before he destroys you, too. If he destroys himself, so be it."

She hadn't wanted to hear her fears laid bare, but there they were, no less true because they'd previously been unspoken.

It was some time before she could bring herself to speak again. "I've made him this way, haven't I, by trying to keep his problems secret?"

"No!" Staring at her through eyes alight with anger, he shook his head. "Absolutely not. Your father chose to slide into the oblivion of liquor. You tried one way to break him of it. Someone else might have tried another. But none of them will work if he chooses not to relinquish his obsession."

"You said I should have made him face the consequences of—"

"Forget what I said." His face softened as he lifted his gloved hand to stroke a stray hair back from her forehead. "I didn't take into account the affection you bear for him. I thought him a selfish man who wanted only drink. I couldn't imagine why you defended him." He smiled faintly. "But today in the coach, I glimpsed the man who must have raised you, and I realized if I'd had a father like that, I'd have laid down my life to keep him from harm. It's hard for a child to be strong when strength requires hurting her parent."

Her lower lip trembled. "I-I don't know what to do anymore. Restricting his access isn't working." Tears clouded her vision. "Yet despite my words, I can't bear to see him drink himself senseless."

"You may not have a choice," he said, staring past her at the opaque ice covering the stream. "Sometimes you simply have to stand apart, to protect yourself from someone who would hurt you . . . even if you love them."

The faraway sorrow of his voice gave her pause. She searched his face, disturbed to see the bleak bitterness there. "You speak like a man who has stood apart himself," she murmured, wondering if it were Richard who'd caused this sadness. Or was it someone else?

His gaze snapped back to hers. He hesitated, as if weighing something in his mind. When he spoke, the words were clipped. "Surely you know the rumors about my own father, how he drove the family to ruin."

Unwilling to acknowledge that she'd heard everything from Honorine, she remained silent.

He averted his gaze once more. "They're all true. And my mother's love, her death, my own pleadings . . . none of them made a whit of difference to him. In the end, I went to India because I couldn't stand to watch him dig his own grave."

She reached for his hand, and he closed his fist around hers, squeezing tight.

A brisk wind ruffled his hair, softening the rough edges of his face. "I should never have presumed to

tell you how to handle your father." He met her gaze
once more, his lips almost smiling. "I suppose I'd
hoped to succeed with your father where I failed with
my own."

"I wish you could."

He enfolded her other hand in his, rubbing her cold,
bare knuckles with his leather-covered fingers. "Unlike
my father, yours is not entirely lost, you know. He
loves you. Somewhere within his wine-driven body is
a spark of humanity. It's faint, but it's there, waiting
for someone to fan it into life. And that someone probably won't be you, since he sees you as his nemesis."

"Who else is there?"

"Who knows? Perhaps he won't even need someone
else. Perhaps if you relinquish responsibility for him,
he'll find the strength in himself. He may surprise
you."

She swallowed. "After today, any change would surprise me. For so long I've thought he simply needed
time to adjust to Mother's death. But it's been three
years . . . and I'm afraid today I lost all hope he'll ever
be what he once was."

The tears she'd been holding back flooded her eyes,
spilling onto her frigid cheeks. She shuddered under
the weight of them, then turned away, not wanting him
to see her fall apart.

"There now, Cordelia," he murmured, and before
she could protest, he'd gathered her in his embrace.

It was all the encouragement she needed to release
her deadening sorrow. She pressed her face into his
open surtout and cried all over his beautiful waistcoat,
the sobs shaking up out of her in wild, gasping jerks.
He didn't seem to care, either that she was ruining his
clothing or that she clung to him like a frightened kitten, for he wrapped her in arms as welcoming as home,
stroking one hand along her spine as he whispered
soothing words into her hair.

"It's all . . . so . . . so very . . . useless," she choked
out between sobs. She fought for control over her tem-

pestuous emotions, taking in great lungfuls of bracing winter air. "I can't make him like ... he was. And I can't live with him as he is."

"Then you'll have to live without him," he whispered against her bent head.

She gave a hiccuping laugh. "Yes. Live without him. As if that's even a possibility." Sniffling, she rubbed her eyes and managed a more controlled tone. "As if I could abandon Father and set off for London to seek my fortune."

When he remained silent, she lifted her head to look at him. For once the confident duke looked perplexed, even disturbed.

"I realize that's not what you meant," she hastened to add. "We both know no respectable woman would hie herself off to London alone and attempt to establish herself as a composer of church music." She tried to sound light, but a note of resentment crept into her tone. "I mean, if it were that easy, London would be flooded with audacious women engaging in men's work—law, medicine, politics. It would destroy society as we know it."

"Undoubtedly," he said dryly, but she couldn't tell from his face what he thought of her words.

She drew in a shaky breath. "No, the only way I can succeed as a composer is if we first deceive your brother. And that's what you ... we ... need Father for. So living without him isn't possible, is it?"

Fruitlessly, she waited for his answer, her eyes fixed on his face. She wanted the impossible—for him to refute her assertion, announce that he'd changed his mind and the charade was off. For him to tell her he was prepared to present her to Lord Kent as the composer, or even more tantalizing, offer to take her on to London alone.

He wouldn't. She knew it in her head. But her heart didn't want to believe it.

Stupid, silly heart, she thought. *Why do you do this to me?*

He drew his mouth into a grim line. "You're right. Living without him isn't possible." He looked suddenly uncomfortable. "I spoke without thinking."

A leaden weight settled in her chest. "So unusual for you, Your Grace." She tried to wriggle free of his grasp.

Her capuchin billowed out behind her as his fingers slipped beneath and curled into her muslin sleeves, drawing her close. "You know if I could free you from your father, I would." His eyes, glittering gold with some hidden emotion, swept over her face.

She pressed her hands against his chest. "Would you?"

"Of course." He seemed astonished that she could doubt it.

"Why?" The word sprang out without her even meaning to say it. Yet she didn't, couldn't, take it back.

He regarded her with a bemused expression, his breath seeping out in little frosty clouds. "Why?"

"Yes. Why would you wish to free me of Father?"

His throat worked convulsively above his cravat, showing his agitation. "Perhaps because watching him hurt you reminds me too much of watching my own father torment my sisters. I can hardly endure it."

It wasn't exactly the answer she'd expected, but it made sense. She dropped her gaze to her fingers, which nervously traced the intricate embroidery of his waistcoat. "I see. I remind you of your sisters." She thought of his constant protectiveness, his incessant hovering. " 'Tis true that you often treat me like a sister."

At his self-mocking laugh, she raised her head. He scowled at her with a dark concentration that made her breath catch in her throat. "Like a sister," he echoed sarcastically. Lifting his hand to her throat, he stroked one glove finger over the place where the pulse beat. "A very close sister."

Then he dropped his hand abruptly and shut his eyes

as if blotting her from his vision would change everything.

She didn't want him to ignore her. After her father's
deception, she craved reassurance and perversely
wanted it to come from Sebastian. So she did something she'd never done with any other man.

She kissed him.

It was the barest wisp of a kiss, a mere brush of her
lips against his, but that was all it took. His eyes flew
open, and before she could draw breath, his mouth
crushed hers, his fingers digging into her arms to hold
her against him.

There was no mildness in this kiss, no coaxing, no
hesitation. There was only hunger, stark and sure and
demanding. Remembering the intimacy of their first
kiss, she parted her lips. With a low groan, he followed
her lead, plundering her mouth with bold assurance as
she slid her arms up to cling to his neck.

His hands clutched her waist, urging her flush
against his body as he drank his fill. He moaned. Or
maybe she did. She could hardly tell when she couldn't
even draw breath to sigh between the litany of kisses.
Her senses were too engaged in savoring his near-
assault.

An icy wind soughed around them and through the
tree over their heads, but it failed to chill his ardor. She
too completely forgot about the cold, for he was doing
intriguing things to her mouth that made her burn and
blaze amidst the winter snow.

At last his lips left hers to trail across her cheek to
her ear. "You should have let me treat you like a sister," he whispered before nipping her earlobe, causing
pleasure to skitter along her nerves. "You would have
been safer."

"I've lived a safe life too long." She sucked in a
quick breath when he kissed a path down her throat
and nudged aside her scarf to plant kisses along the
ridge of her collarbone. "What has it gotten me?"

Without a word, he tugged her modest scarf loose

from her gown, then pulled it from around her neck to drop it in the snow. As he trailed his tongue down into the valley between her breasts, she buried her fingers in his thick, shining hair.

"You're so sweet," he murmured, resting his head against her chest. He kissed the swell of one breast rising above her bodice. "So very sweet. Your father should keep you locked up."

Stiffening, she pulled his head back, stunned to see the stormy gleam in his eyes as he straightened. It frightened her with its ungoverned, wicked intensity.

"You . . . you keep saying that," she whispered. "You think I'm a terrible wanton, don't you, who should be chained away from men?"

A tight smile twisted his lips. "Not at all. But you're wild and dear, and I find you impossible to resist." He cupped her cheek in his hand, rubbing his thumb along her bottom lip. She tasted the leather of his gloves on her mouth. When she ran the tip of her tongue along the same path his thumb had taken, he released a jerky breath and kissed her quickly, a hard, bruising kiss that made her lips quiver afterward.

"We men are a dangerous lot, Cordelia. I shouldn't even be allowed to kiss your hand, yet I burn to kiss it. And more."

His hand slid down her throat, then slipped beneath her low neckline to caress the rounded shoulder. She stood stock-still, unable to think, and certainly not to move.

"Oh, yes, much more," he added as his eyes darkened and he slid her gown off her shoulder.

She couldn't imagine why she was standing there like a silly goose and letting him do such shocking things. Maybe because his caress made her heart thump faster and her hands tremble with the urge to touch him in the same way. Or maybe because she feared a tiny bit that hungry look in his eyes.

Or maybe because she'd simply gone quite mad.

Whatever the reason, she released only a small

whimper when his deft fingers skirted the sensitive skin of her underarm and trailed under the neckline of her shift and gown until they found her soft breast.

Her eyes widened when he pushed her bodice down, then thumbed her nipple into a hard pebble, his leather gloves surprisingly warm against her skin. Intrigued but horrified, she opened her mouth to protest, but it was too late, for without warning he sealed his lips to hers. As he covered her breast with his gloved hand, he dragged her body once more flush against his, imprisoning her with his arm about her waist.

Time paused to let them taste each other, to let her revel in a fleshly joy she'd only imagined before. He caressed her breast until it felt tight and ripe as a summer peach, his gloved fingers raising an ache, then soothing it with feathery strokes.

When he'd somehow made her want more than supple leather against her skin, he lowered his mouth to suck at her nipple. She'd never imagined a man doing such a thing to her, and she arched back, both appalled and thrilled by the touch of whiskered cheeks and the hot tongue swirling over her skin.

This was wicked beyond belief, she thought in a sudden panic and grabbed at his hair, meaning to pull his head back. Instead, her fingers caught in the ribbon of his queue, jerking it loose to free his hair, which scattered over her hands.

When he then sucked even harder on her breast, she sighed his name and clutched his head close, suddenly longing to have him touch her other breast, too. Her sense of modesty recoiled from the very idea, but she'd grown suddenly rather tired of listening to modesty. Modesty was clearly something old men had created to keep women from experiencing this incredible pleasure—men like her father.

At that thought, defiance heated her blood, prompting her to ignore caution and modesty. Threading her fingers through Sebastian's hair, she clasped him tight. And he rewarded her by making wild, wanton melodies hum through her blood, rousing it from slumber as a war song rouses a soldier.

His mouth left her breast to murmur, "This is mad," but he continued his sensuous caresses, merely shifting to trail hot kisses up her chest and throat to her mouth.

"And I said we men were a dangerous lot," he growled against her lips.

She could already see the regret entering his features, but she couldn't bear to hear his censure. So she kissed him full on the mouth.

He groaned, his golden eyes aglow with desire. "Bloody hell, not half as dangerous as a damned sweet virgin."

Suddenly she knew she'd gone too far, for he jerked her hard against him, his face set and his eyes determined as he thrust his knee between her legs. But any protest she might have made died when his mouth crashed down on hers, rough, blatant, and insistent upon gaining its pleasure. Half-consciously she parted her thighs as he pushed her against the tree trunk and hiked up her skirt.

That's when the tree dumped its load of snow on their heads.

They came apart in a flurry of wet flakes, the cold, melting stuff dampening their hair and blinding them both. She flung snow from her eyes and wiped it from her cheeks, then realized as it froze her breast that it had fallen inside her lowered gown.

It was that more than anything that brought her to her senses. Her face burning as she realized how indecently she'd behaved, she turned her back to Sebastian. Quickly, she scooped the snow from inside her bodice, so embarrassed she could hardly bear to face Sebastian, who cursed as he swiped snow from his shoulders.

She shivered, pulling up the cold, damp gown to cover her shoulder and breast, then jerking her skirts back down to cover her legs. She looked for her scarf with an almost frantic haste. When she saw it lying in the snow a few feet away, she snatched it up and tucked it where it belonged, as if somehow that would negate the last few minutes of lapsed modesty.

Sebastian's cursing had stopped, and she felt rather than saw him come up behind her. When he touched her shoulder, she flinched, though she didn't jerk away. Without a word, he pushed her capuchin, which still hung down her back like an abandoned purse, back up around her shoulders until it fell about her, shielding her from the cold. Then he turned her to face him.

His eyelashes were still dusted with snow, as was his glorious chestnut hair. But the savage look in his eyes threatened to burn off all of winter's snow, it was so very hot.

"What just happened was my fault, so don't blame yourself for it," he said, but his harsh tone belied his words. He paused as if fighting for control, then continued in a voice that was almost threatening. "Nonetheless, I give you fair warning, Cordelia. I'm a man, not a saint, and you bring out my basest desires. If I ever find you alone again, I can't answer for what will happen."

Dropping his eyes to her lips, his jaw went rigid. He jerked his gaze back to her face. "If you wish to keep your virtue intact, stay far away from me."

His words stung. It wasn't her fault, he said, but his entire manner blamed her. He told her to keep away from him, as if she seduced him with her very presence. Of course, she *had* behaved abominably, allowing him liberties and letting him nearly undress her. If she'd been more of a lady. . . .

Still, did he have to make it so painfully obvious that she couldn't behave properly when he kissed her?

Her confused emotions and wounded pride made it impossible for her to answer him reasonably as she fought the flush spreading over her skin. "Don't worry, Your Grace. 'Tis not my practice to tempt unwilling gentlemen. I promise you'll be quite safe from this strumpet's dangerous company in future."

"Bloody hell, that's not what I meant—" he bit out, but she had already drawn her capuchin close and whirled away from him, stumbling up the path they'd taken.

"Cordelia!" he shouted behind her.

"Leave me alone!" she choked out as she lifted her skirts.

Blessedly, when she fell into a run up the road to the village, he didn't stop her.

Chapter Ten

Our divided kingdoms now in friendly kindred meet,
And old debate to love and kindness turns, our power
with double force uniting.
Truly reconciled, grief appears at last more sweet
Both to ourselves and faithful friends, our undermin-
ing foes affrighting.
—Thomas Lupo,
"Shows and Nightly Revels"

Scowling, Oswald watched from the window of the inn's parlor as his daughter hurried up the road. The duke followed a few feet behind her, and at the sight of the handsome nobleman, Oswald clenched his fist.

If it hadn't been for that pompous, self-serving lord, Oswald thought, he and Cordelia would be safe at home now, secure in their vicarage. The blasted man had carried them both off, and when he'd separated them from the familiar, he'd somehow changed Cordelia.

Never before had Cordelia spoken to him as cruelly as she had these past two days. Why, she'd even reprimanded him with scripture! As if the girl knew a word of it that he hadn't taught her.

And what about this morning? he thought. She'd practically ordered him to send Prudence off; then she'd stormed out with that impudent lord.

Impudent, lecherous lord, he amended when he saw the duke following her movements with his eyes. In growing alarm, Oswald caught sight of Cordelia's flushed face and the snow in her hair. It wasn't snowing now, hadn't been since they'd arrived. Had she been rolling about in the snow? What had she been doing all this time with the duke anyway?

Oswald smeared away the condensation on the window to get a closer look, stiffening when he saw the duke catch up to her, clasp her arm and exchange words with her before she wrenched loose and continued stalking toward the inn.

The duke's dark scowl didn't reassure Oswald, especially when he realized the man's hair was unbound. It certainly hadn't been when the two of them had left. Horrified, he looked for signs of dishevelment in both his daughter and Lord Waverley and imagined he found them.

A low grumble escaped his lips. So help him, if that smooth-tongued noble had laid a hand on his daughter . . . there'd be the devil to pay. He'd see to that, even if it did mean taking on a highborn gentleman.

Cordelia passed into the inn yard, and Oswald flinched from the expression of angry betrayal on her face. Marry, she was certainly furious at someone.

It was the duke, he told himself. Of course it was. She'd argued with the man, and the blasted rogue had upset her. It had to be that. What else would have her looking so hurt?

Surely not his own foolish words a while ago. Could she still be mad at him for those?

He scowled. Aye, she could be. After all, he'd really gone and ruined things this time. He hadn't meant to say all those wretched absurdities about her locking up the wine and making him unhappy in his own house, but she'd pushed him to it with all her dithering about the brandy flask.

For pity's sake, did she think he didn't know he'd gotten too attached to his liquor of late? But it wasn't as if he were a drunk . . . he'd not have been able to preach such rousing sermons if he were some old sot tippling in the ditch.

He *had* been a trifle dependent on her recently, but he intended to improve . . . truly, he did. He'd have pulled himself up out of his slump eventually if that meddling Lord Waverley hadn't come along and ruined all his attempts.

Cordelia entered the inn, and Oswald left the window, wondering what he should do now. If she meant what she said about going on to London alone. . . .

Faith, that was completely unacceptable. Surely she wouldn't do that. Cordelia was too good a girl to ruin her reputation by running off with the duke to London. Wasn't she?

He cracked his knuckles with a vengeance. Well, even if she thought of doing such a mad thing, he couldn't let her. He *wouldn't* let her. He'd lock her up in the inn before he'd allow her to cast her pearls before swine like that.

The trouble was, the girl had a mind of her own. How was he to keep her from the evil clutches of Lord Waverley without making her even angrier?

The door to the room opened. He whirled to find Cordelia glaring at him like an angel of vengeance and Lord Waverley right behind her.

"Have you sent Prudence off, Father?" she demanded. "The innkeeper told me the post chaise left here a few moments ago."

Gone was the sweet, amiable daughter Oswald had always known, and in her place was a person he scarce recognized, full of fire and defiance. It made him want to blister her hide. Perhaps if he'd taken a rod to her a few times when she was younger, he'd not be in this pickle now.

Then again, she'd always been easy to manage as a child. What had happened?

"Aye." He paused. "Prudence didn't give me much choice. She refused to stay in the face of your anger."

"Wise woman," Lord Waverley muttered.

Cordelia flashed the duke a warning glance. "This is a private matter between my father and me, Your Grace. Please leave."

"Nay," Oswald broke in. "I want him to hear what I've got to say."

Slowly Cordelia pivoted to face him. Her chin shook as it had when she was but a wee girl in petticoats and he'd admonished her with a lecture. She hadn't taken well to the slightest criticism as a girl. She'd always gotten her feelings hurt if he so much as looked at her wrong.

He had a funny feeling he'd gone far beyond that this time.

"What do you have to say, Father?" she asked.

Wincing at the curt tone of her voice, he nonetheless stood his ground. "Do you still intend to go on to London?"

She hesitated a long moment. Lord Waverley's brow darkened, and the nobleman looked as if he would speak. But he wisely held his tongue.

"Yes," she said, to the duke's apparent relief and Oswald's chagrin. "As I said earlier, I don't want to go without you, but I will if I have to."

His temper flared. "Without a chaperone? Will you travel with the duke openly, not caring for your reputation?"

"No, she will not," the duke interjected.

Cordelia's hands balled into fists.

Lord Waverley stepped forward to stand beside her, but it was Oswald whom he addressed. "I'll not hold your daughter to her promise at the expense of her reputation. If you don't go with us, she won't be going either."

Cordelia refused to look at the duke. "I'm going to London, Father, with or without you and with or without His Grace's permission. I have funds of my own, more than enough to secure passage."

"Over my dead body!" the duke exploded.

"You won't alter my purpose." She whirled to face Lord Waverley as she planted her hands on her hips. "Your brother will, I'm sure, welcome any help he can get, and I owe him my help after the way I've deceived him."

Oswald bit back the impulse to ask what she thought she owed her father. At the moment, she might be inclined to say, "Nothing at all."

"I won't be responsible for destroying your future," Lord Waverley gritted out. He looked ready to throttle Cordelia, and Oswald fleetingly thought it might be a good thing.

"Don't worry. I won't hold you responsible for anything." She turned back to Oswald. "Nor you either, Father. I'm old enough to do what I want."

He could tell from the set of her jaw that what she wanted was to go to London. It was left to him to dissuade her, since it appeared she was going to ignore the duke's objections.

"Aye, you are," he admitted. "But I'm going wherever you go, gel, you can be sure of that, so let's not talk anymore of you galloping off to London on your own." He paused, pretending to consider the situation, then sighed. "Of course, now that Prudence is gone, there's still the problem of a chaperone. It won't look right your traveling with two men."

She waved her hand dismissively. "Don't be absurd, Father. You're a more than sufficient chaperone, and you know it." When he started to protest, she held up her hand. "But since you're obsessed with giving me a female companion, I've taken the liberty of choosing one. Honorine.

Oswald's jaw dropped. A pox on the girl for thinking of Honorine! He'd hoped that by insisting on a chaperone, he'd hold them up a day or two, long enough to get Cordelia to change her mind. He should have known Cordelia would outwit him when it meant getting her way. It had been the same thing with those troublesome chorales.

But Honorine, for pity's sake!

At his groan, Cordelia added, "We've only half a day's journey to York, so we might as well ask her.

Unless it takes her away from some pressing duty, I'm sure she'd be happy to oblige us."

No doubt, he thought. Honorine delighted in making his life miserable. It wasn't enough the woman had a sharp tongue and opinions enough to fuel it for an eternity. The blasted female was handsome, too. When Florinda had been alive, he'd managed to avoid Honorine most of the time. But with Florinda dead. . . .

He groaned, wondering if Cordelia had any idea what had happened between him and Honorine before he'd married Florinda. This wouldn't do, not at all!

"We couldn't ask Honorine to give up weeks of her time for us, pet," he protested. "She's got a life of her own."

Cordelia sniffed, lifting her head with a haughty assurance that actually reminded him of Honorine. "Her last letter said she was bored. I'm sure she'll jump at the chance to go to London. Besides, she's one of the few people who knows about my music and my deception. She'll be more than eager to help me out of a fix."

"Then by all means, let's not delay in continuing to York and enlisting her aid," Lord Waverley interjected.

Oswald shot the duke a furious glance, and received a blazing smile for his efforts. Blast the man! Any fool could see he was pleased at the thought of irritating Oswald. Someday Oswald would find a way to repay that arrogant noble for all the suffering he'd visited on the Shalstone family.

"Now Cordelia . . ." Oswald began in a wheedling tone, then paused. He knew he couldn't say a thing to dissuade her. She was insanely set on this. He could back out of his request for a chaperone, but since Cordelia hadn't yet realized that the only reason he'd insisted on one in the first place was to have Prudence along to slip him liquor, he'd best not stir up that hornet's nest.

And if he balked once more at going to London, the

impudent chit would simply set off on her own. She had him trapped.

"Mrs. Beardsley sounds as if she'd make a perfectly delightful companion," the duke added.

Seething inside but absolutely incapable of doing anything about it, Oswald recognized the futility of his objections and gave up the fight. Aye, a perfectly delightful companion Honorine would be, he thought. That was part of the problem.

"One more thing, Father," Cordelia said, interrupting his baleful thoughts.

The sadness had entered her face again. For a while, her anger had eclipsed it, but now she looked as she had a short while before, when she'd discovered his deception. It made him want to cry.

"Yes?"

"You were right. I should never have tried to keep you from your liquor."

When he gazed at her suspiciously, she added stiffly, "I only did it because I love you and hate to see you destroy yourself with drink. Nonetheless, I was wrong to attempt to change your life when you yourself don't wish to change it."

"I wouldn't quite say that—" he began.

"In any case," she continued firmly, her eyes dropping from his, "I do need your help." She drew in a deep breath. "To effectively accomplish our scheme, I must have you sober. You can't study music when you're drunk or sleeping off a drunk."

He bristled. For pity's sake, the girl talked as if he were a blasted sot!

Her tone softened. "I'm asking you to consider reducing your consumption of spirits until we finish our business in London. I've asked before, and you've told me there was no need, but even you must admit it would ease our labors if you could have a clear mind at all times." She stared at him, her lower lip trembling, and her eyes misting. "And it would mean a great deal to me."

Her soft plea struck at the very heart of him. She acted as if it would be a trial for him. Blast it all, if it meant so much to her, he would quit his liquor for a few days.

"Of course I'll not indulge if that's what you wish," he said soothingly. " 'Tis not as if I have to drink." He drew himself up proudly. "As you said, there was no reason to refrain in the past. But I suppose you're right in this case." He shrugged. "I can do without if it's necessary."

"I do think it's necessary, Father," she said in a small voice, and he realized she was fighting hard to hold back tears.

Something twisted inside him. His poor girl was hurting, and wretch that he was, he'd done it to her. A burdensome weight settled into his chest. Unable to bear her sad eyes a moment more, he drew her into his arms, something he'd done often before Florinda's death. With a shock, he realized he hadn't done it much since then. Well, he'd have to remedy that if he was to keep the girl from doing something foolish, like running to Lord Waverley every time she was upset.

She remained stiff in his embrace for a moment.

"It's all right, Cordelia, pet," he murmured, stroking her back. "I'll do whatever you wish if it'll keep you from harm."

A choked sob came from her. Then she buried her face in his neck and wrapped her arms about him, squeezing him tight. "Oh, Father," she whispered, in a voice that nearly broke his heart with its yearning, "how could you have lied to Prudence like that? How?"

A strange watering in his eyes clouded his own vision for a moment. "A man makes mistakes." He wasn't sure what else to say. His actions were truly inexcusable. He planted a kiss in her hair, tightening his arms around her. "I'll never do such a wretched thing again, I promise. It'll be all right. You'll see. Everything will be all right."

But when he looked up to see Lord Waverley staring at him with glittering eyes and a stark rigidity to his face, Oswald had his doubts.

He was beginning to think nothing would ever be all right in his life again.

Chapter Eleven

If I speak, my words want weight,
Am I mute, my heart doth break,
If I sigh, she fears deceit,
Sorrow then for me must speak.
—John Dowland,
"Rest Awhile, You Cruel Cares"

For once Sebastian welcomed the bite of cold wind against his face. He only wished he could drive his stallion into a gallop, so he could lose himself in the rush of icy air numbing him senseless. But no, he had to keep pace with his coach, which carried the most exasperating woman he'd ever met and her equally exasperating father.

He could ride in the coach with them, of course, and the time would pass more quickly. But that was out of the question after his last intimate encounter with Cordelia.

Soft, sweet Cordelia, who kissed more like a courtesan than a straightlaced vicar's daughter. His loins hardened against the unforgiving leather of the saddle, and a low curse escaped his lips.

This was all getting quite out of hand. If he'd had any inkling when he'd set out from London that he'd find a woman whose situation would so capture his sympathy, he might have left his brother's fate to chance. Cordelia had a dangerous way of making him want to forsake his every vow just to comfort and shield her from her rascal father.

He snorted, thinking of the vicar. Reverend Shalstone was infinitely more trouble than he was worth. It might indeed have been better to present Cordelia as the composer and dispense with her drunken father.

Then he groaned, thinking of the pretty scene Cordelia and the vicar had just played out in the inn. All the vicar's facile assurances made Sebastian want to put a fist to the bloody man's jaw. First the man tore her heart in two; then he thought to mend it by a hug and a few empty promises.

The man would never keep those promises. Some men would say anything when faced with a teary-eyed woman. But in the long hard hours of night when temptation danced through their fevered senses, those same men never did the right thing. Sebastian's father had been that kind of man, and the vicar would undoubtedly prove to be one as well, despite his good characteristics.

Snow began to fall again, soft, white, and treacherous. Sebastian cursed futilely into the wind. Now they were to have more snow on top of everything else. Was he simply plagued by ill luck, or was this God's vengeance upon him for being enamored of a woman other than his fiancée?

No doubt the latter. Sebastian swiped away the flakes settling on his eyelashes and cheeks, reminded of his earlier bout with snow. He grimaced, his knees digging automatically into his horse's sides. If it hadn't been for that tree dumping snow on them, how far would he have gone? Devil take it, he'd pawed her there in the open, where anyone could have come along and seen them. He must have been thoroughly mad.

He was gaining on the coach, but he spurred his stallion on anyway, needing the blessed relief of speed. Yet the wind blasting his body and the sting of snow against his face gave him no respite from his tormenting thoughts.

If only Cordelia hadn't been so ... so sweet, he thought against his will. "Sweet" seemed the right word for her, for even while she uttered low sighs and melded her body to his, her naiveté, her wide-eyed wonder at the pleasures of the flesh made something snap in him. There'd been no missish protests from Cordelia today ... except of course when he'd growled at her about staying away from him.

He winced, settling his three-cornered hat more tightly about his ears. Why was it whenever he got Cordelia alone, he reverted to pure animal instinct? What had happened to all his self-control? Bloody hell, it wasn't as if she paraded about in low-cut gowns or flirted with him.

She was simply ... herself. He sighed. Apparently that was enough to blot every thought of Judith right out of his head. He'd been criticizing the vicar for making promises the man would never keep, yet he himself was quite guilty.

His thoughts tormented him the entire ride to York. Occasionally the deepening snow captured his attention, but for the most part he brooded over Cordelia. And hated himself every minute for it.

By the time they reached York, he wondered how he would manage even one more day in her presence. He frowned as they entered the city. No question, winter cold or no, he'd have to spend his time in the saddle. Better to be half-frozen than to burn continually with the fires of hell under the vicar's suspicious eye.

The coach halted a moment at Cordelia's request so she could give Hopkins directions. Then they were off again, only stopping when they pulled up before an impressive Palladian town house of forbidding aspect.

To Sebastian's relief, the place glowed with lights. Someone at least was in residence. He hadn't realized how much he'd counted on finding this Mrs. Beardsley at home. Much as he'd laughed at the vicar's peculiar notions of propriety, he had to admit that the more people on this trip, the better his chances of staying away from Cordelia. On that, he and the vicar were surprisingly in agreement.

For once, luck was with them, for when they

knocked at the door, a footman met them who asserted that the lady of the house was indeed at home. Moments later, they were ushered into a vaulted entrance hall painted with elaborate *trompe l'oeil* and containing more expensive china gewgaws than Sebastian would have allowed in his entire London town house. The footman politely took their coats, then asked them to wait while he fetched his mistress, who was apparently holding an assembly in the salon. The lilt of lute music wafted through the house, quickly joined by the accompaniment of a harpsichord and bass viol.

This wasn't at all what he'd expected. Despite Cordelia's allusion to Mrs. Beardsley's wealth, Sebastian had imagined her friend to be a widow living in a cozy cottage like the vicarage, a woman who probably relished every opportunity for company. Now that he saw the extent of Mrs. Beardsley's wealth, he felt uncomfortable barging in on her without notice.

He glanced at Cordelia, who waited stiffly for their hostess to enter, her fingers worrying the braid that edged her gown. Unsurprisingly, her eyes avoided his, but he noticed she didn't shy away when he stepped up beside her.

"Are you sure your Mrs. Beardsley won't be appalled by our interruption?" he muttered.

"I'm not sure about anything." She had no time to say more, for a buxom woman burst through the doors nearest them, her face alight with smiles.

"Cordelia! Good heavens, how wonderful of you to appear!" The woman chuckled dryly. "Why, I can't remember the last time you attended one of my assemblies. And such a long way to come, too."

Cordelia laughed and threw herself into the open arms of the woman who could only be the famous Mrs. Beardsley, battle-ax of York. As the two of them hugged and exclaimed how long it had been, Sebastian keenly surveyed the middle-aged widow.

She was as unexpected as her house, for the vicar's words had brought to mind a matron of large proportions, with a haughty demeanor and a tongue sharp as a sword. This laughing, vibrant female with a handsome face, her hair powdered and her dress made of intricately embroidered silk, bore no resemblance to the "battle-ax" of Sebastian's imagination, except in her rather imposing stature.

He cast the vicar a speculative glance, to find the man grumbling under his breath. When the two women began chattering and crying for joy all at once, the vicar muttered, "Honorine, you old fool, we didn't come all this way to stand about watching you and my daughter slobber all over each other."

Mrs. Beardsley drew back from Cordelia, eyeing the vicar from head to toe, her eyes still watery. "Old fool yourself," she said. Something in the way she assessed the vicar with a saddening gaze, as if worried by his appearance, gave Sebastian pause. She continued in a decidedly shaky voice, "You never were much for 'slobbering,' were you?"

"I should say not," he retorted hotly.

She eyed him critically. "You could use someone slobbering over you. You look a sight too peaked. I'm sure Cordelia takes good care of you, but she's much too young to make you toe the line as you should."

The vicar's ears turned a bright red. "The gel's not foolish enough to think she knows what's best for me, unlike *some* people I know."

Mrs. Beardsley sniffed. "Pish, everyone knows what's best for you but yourself."

"Hush now, both of you!" Cordelia protested with a laugh. She tucked her arm into Mrs. Beardsley's, effectively deflecting the woman's attention from the grumpy vicar. "I have someone to introduce, Honorine." Cordelia's eyes brightened as she stared up into her friend's face, then at Sebastian.

When Mrs. Beardsley turned the full force of her piercing gaze on Sebastian, he had the feeling she'd prove a far more formidable protector of Cordelia's virtue than the vicar. Though he told himself that was for the best, he perversely didn't relish the thought of having her stand between them.

"May I present our traveling companion ... Sebastian Kent, the Duke of Waverley." A peculiar amusement glittered in Cordelia's eyes. "Lord Waverley, this is the dearest, oldest friend of both my mother and me ... Mrs. Honorine Beardsley."

Sebastian darted a curious glance at Cordelia, but her face revealed nothing of what had amused her. Then forcing his attention back to Mrs. Beardsley, he politely lifted her hand to kiss it ... and came face-to-face with her stunned expression.

"I'm honored," he murmured, wondering what in blazes was going on.

For a moment, she stared down at her hand blankly. Then she recovered herself. "Oh no, the honor is all mine, Your Grace. I'm afraid you took me quite by surprise. You're rather a long way from home, aren't you?"

He stared at her quizzically as he released her hand.

The vicar explained, with a faint edge to his voice, "Honorine is generally the most well-informed gossip in North England. She's no doubt surprised to find you here instead of in India." He turned to Mrs. Beardsley, whose face had turned a rosy color. "Isn't that where your last letter had said His Grace was? I can't remember."

"Father, behave!" Cordelia admonished, though her eyes twinkled. "You're telling all of Honorine's secrets."

Sebastian smiled at the beleaguered Mrs. Beardsley, although he wondered exactly what rumors the widow had heard about him and his family. He'd have to corner Cordelia later and see to it the woman hadn't been fed some gross untruths. "I think I'm flattered that you discuss me in your letters, madame, but I do hope you've portrayed my better side."

Mrs. Beardsley was now staring daggers at the vicar, but she managed a stiff smile for Sebastian. "I assure you, Lord Waverley, regardless of what Oswald might imply with his nasty words, I've never said a bad word about you or your family."

"Of course not," Cordelia interjected, a faint smile playing about her lips. "The only reason Honorine mentioned you at all was because I'd told her of my business with your brother. Father makes it sound quite awful, but it's really nothing."

Mrs. Beardsley sniffed. "Oswald always was rude and unmannerly. I can't imagine how he raised such a perfectly wonderful daughter."

"I'm sure Reverend Shalstone didn't mean to offend you," Sebastian said soothingly, resisting the smile that came to his lips when both Cordelia and the vicar looked at him in blank astonishment.

He'd ruffled the old man's feathers quite a bit over the last few days, and it was time he ingratiated himself with the man, before the vicar refused entirely to participate in his scheme. Right now it appeared that the vicar was outnumbered, and Sebastian figured he'd best even the odds if he were to get in the vicar's good graces. After all, the vicar's current liquorless state had already begun to make him peevish, and they had enough problems on their hands without his being a monster.

"Well, it doesn't matter anyway." Mrs. Beardsley waved her elegantly gloved hand. She'd now regained her composure enough to flash him a brilliant smile, the smile of a hostess completely in charge of her guests. "I'm delighted to have all of you here, and even Oswald's vile temper shan't dampen my joy."

She patted Cordelia's hand. "But I'm being awfully remiss, aren't I? Do come into the parlor and have some refreshment. After spending all day on the road, you must be weary."

"What about your assembly—" Cordelia said.

"Pish, who cares?" Mrs. Beardsley gestured for them to follow her into a nearby room. " 'Tisn't a large group, just the same people who come each week to hear the latest sonatas." She smiled proudly. "I am reputed to hire only the best musicians, so when *I* have an assembly, *everyone* attends."

"But I do regret bursting in on you like this," Cordelia protested as they entered a large parlor, as elaborately finished as the vaulted hall. "I suppose I didn't think about the possibility that you'd have company."

Mrs. Beardsley shook her head. "Don't worry another minute about it. I'm sure I shan't."

Stepping into the hall, she called for a servant and ordered drink brought for them and a light supper prepared. Sebastian and Cordelia both winced when Mrs. Beardsley asked for punch to be served along with coffee, but neither said a word. He couldn't resist glancing at the vicar, however, who maintained a carefully bland expression.

Having dealt with the amenities, Mrs. Beardsley urged them to sit down. She settled herself beside Cordelia on a lavishly upholstered sofa. "Now, you simply must tell me what on earth has brought you and Oswald to York." She nodded toward the duke with a winning smile. "And your auspicious companion, of course."

Cordelia grimaced. "Wonderful as our 'auspicious companion' is, I'm afraid he's proven quite troublesome. I can't think how to explain the situation he's gotten me into. You'll be appalled, I fear, and quite put out with me."

When the widow turned an alarmed gaze on Sebastian, he groaned. Cordelia obviously had no idea how the barbed words she'd meant to wound him could be misconstrued. He hastened to elaborate. "Cordelia is trying to say that she's landed herself in some trouble with her most recent endeavor—writing music under a false name."

As Mrs. Beardsley arched one brow, Cordelia went rigid. "His Grace has a way of making everything sound sordid."

When she cast him a brittle smile, he wondered if

she was referring to his statements about her father's drinking. No, more likely she was still angry over their disastrous encounter under the oak. He'd definitely have to get her alone later, if only to set her straight about whether he considered her a strumpet.

"Not everything," he shot back, eyes narrowing as they locked with hers. "But I'm afraid I often put things badly when I'm ... distracted. And Cordelia, it seems, is thin-skinned where I'm concerned."

Mrs. Beardsley's expression became speculative, but Cordelia jerked her gaze from his, her shoulders visibly shaking as she held her head erect. "In any case, His Grace came to visit us in Belham a few days ago with an interesting proposal."

"An insane proposal," her father muttered.

"Oh, tell me," Mrs. Beardsley exclaimed with all the anticipation of a notorious gossip. "This does sound exciting."

Cordelia licked her lips, then launched into a lengthy explanation of what Sebastian had proposed.

When she finished, Mrs. Beardsley's eyes were sparkling with good humor. "Really, Cordelia, I can't believe you agreed to do this impossible thing. Oswald is as tone-deaf as this sofa! How on earth do you expect to turn him into a musician in a week?"

"I tried to tell her that," the vicar interjected, "but she and His Grace have got this fool idea in their heads that it can be done and—"

"Why can't *you* meet Handel, Cordelia?" Mrs. Beardsley went on, scarcely acknowledging the vicar's comment. " 'Tis your music, and you should be the one to present it. It's all well and good to take Oswald along for company, but to give him such an important task"—she sniffed—"well, it simply makes no sense at all."

Cordelia crossed her arms and leaned back against the sofa, her eyes gleaming as she stared at Sebastian. "Oh, but you see, Honorine, His Grace is quite convinced that a woman composer would be of no use to his brother. After all, why would any genuine musician take the work of a woman seriously?"

"As I recall," Sebastian bit out as Mrs. Beardsley bristled, "you thought the same thing when I first proposed this."

With a haughty tilt of her chin, Cordelia glared at him. "Only because I let you convince me that Father could be tutored, which, after two days in a coach, I now seriously doubt."

"Let's not forget the little matter of the initial deception," Sebastian went on relentlessly. "You posed as your father. Remember, the root of my brother's business difficulties lies in his undeserved reputation for publishing suspect materials. Do you think Handel will be eager to champion him if he knows that once again my brother has attempted to pull the wool over the public's eyes?"

Cordelia sniffed. "Don't you think both Handel and your brother would be far more angered by having an impostor presented to them, especially a bad impostor? Besides, my works were published anonymously. Handel doesn't even know my father was involved."

"True. But my brother does, and unfortunately he'd never present you to Handel if he knew you were a woman."

"Ah, so your brother is a woman-hater," Mrs. Beardsley put in with an arch smile.

Sebastian sighed. "Not exactly, but he has very definite ideas about women musicians, I'm afraid. In the past he had some . . . ah . . . humiliating experiences that gave him a distinct bias. He's more liable to believe Miss Shalstone stole the chorales from a man than that she wrote them herself." A grim smile flitted over his face. "And he's had too much bad luck with stolen works to risk supporting her after that."

Cordelia's disappointment was immediately apparent, and he wondered how long she'd been toying with the idea of admitting the truth to his brother.

"In fact," Sebastian went on, determined to lay that

possibility to rest, " 'tis possible that if we present Miss Shalstone as the composer, my brother will refuse to publish more of her work. After all, she did deceive him, and untrustworthy composers have put him in a sticky position of late."

"Oh, dear." Mrs. Beardsley patted Cordelia's knee. "We wouldn't want that, would we? But I admit it's a shame your brother is such a stickler for truth. Almost no one is these days. It's rather a troublesome trait, don't you think?"

The vicar snorted loudly, but Sebastian decided he liked the widow Beardsley a great deal. "It can be. Obviously I'm not like my brother, or I wouldn't have proposed this elaborate deception in the first place."

Sebastian looked at Cordelia, who remained silent, staring into the fire with a dejected expression. If he'd known what direction her thoughts had taken lately, he'd have nipped them in the bud. Bloody hell, he wanted to cry her talent to the rooftops, but it was impossible.

At that moment a servant entered bearing a tray with a platter of fruit tarts and steaming bowls of spiced punch and coffee. To Sebastian's relief, the vicar passed up the punch for the coffee. He wondered if Cordelia had noticed.

"Well, I'm pleased you decided to visit me in the midst of your madcap trip to London," Mrs. Beardsley was saying. "This is a story well worth hearing, and much better heard in person than by letter."

"Actually, Honorine," the vicar broke in, "this isn't just a visit."

Mrs. Beardsley looked confused. "No?"

"No." Cordelia snapped out of her reverie. "Father, as you might imagine, has been testy about this whole endeavor. He doesn't approve of my traveling without a female companion."

No, Sebastian thought, her father merely hoped the lack of a companion would hinder their continuing.

But Mrs. Beardsley apparently noted nothing odd

about Cordelia's statement. Her eyes brightened. "Don't tell me. You want *me* to be your companion!"

"I know you have a number of pressing obligations," the vicar broke in. "We'll understand completely if you can't accompany us. I said the whole scheme was absurd from the very beginning—"

"Why, I wouldn't miss such an adventure for the world!" Mrs. Beardsley cut in eagerly. "What an opportunity!"

The vicar scowled and lapsed into a low grumbling, but Cordelia clasped her friend's hands. "So you'll go with us to His Grace's estate? And to London?"

"Of course, I will. Dear me, I wouldn't pass up a chance to stay at Waverley! My friends will be apoplectic with envy. Imagine what a crush there'll be at my assemblies upon my return—" Her eyes widened and her mouth formed an "O." "Oh, dear, I'd forgotten all about my assembly, and it does sound awfully quiet in there!"

In truth, Sebastian thought he'd heard the music end a few minutes before.

Laughing, Mrs. Beardsley jumped to her feet. "I've been having such a good time with all of you that I've quite neglected my guests! Ah, well, they'll forgive me when I give them the exciting news."

She hurried to the door, ticking things off on her fingers as she muttered half to herself. "I suppose I should pack the saffron gown . . . it's quite the color these days. And of course, my new silk mantua. . . ."

She paused in the doorway. "It's been ages since I was in London for the Season. I do hope we'll attend a subscription concert or two—" She gave a tinkling laugh. "Listen to me carry on while you three sit there exhausted. Just rest and take your time about supper. I'll get rid of my guests and rejoin you shortly."

Breathing in deeply, she flashed them a brilliant smile, then swept from the room, her skirts rustling.

"She hasn't changed a bit," Reverend Shalstone muttered as soon as Mrs. Beardsley was out of earshot.

"She's still a bubbling cauldron in petticoats. Mark my words ... we'll have no peace on the ride to London. She'll meddle in our private affairs. I hope you two are pleased with yourselves. You've harnessed us to a woman of waspish temper, and you'll regret it. You'll see."

"If I didn't know better, Reverend," Sebastian said dryly as he lifted a dish of punch and sipped it, "I'd think you were attracted to the woman."

While Cordelia hid a smile behind her hand and the vicar sputtered in outrage, Sebastian settled back to drink his punch, more than pleased with himself. Despite his determination to be on better terms with the vicar, he couldn't resist the barbed comment. Vicar-baiting was quite diverting.

In fact, it almost succeeded in keeping his mind off the vicar's daughter and her lovely body. And that was a definite boon.

Early the next morning, Cordelia sat in the breakfast room, sipping an herbal tea Honorine's cook had brewed for her the minute she'd noticed Cordelia up and wandering about the house.

This was only the second time Cordelia had been to Honorine's—the first had been when she'd spent a summer in York as the Beardsleys' guest—but she was pleased to discover that all the servants remembered her with apparent fondness.

She sighed, staring out the window across the table from her. It was a good thing she liked it here, for judging by the heavy blanket of snow that had fallen in the night, they wouldn't leave York today. In fact, they likely wouldn't leave for a number of days.

That should rile Sebastian, she thought with a bitter pleasure. At last there was something His Holy Grace couldn't control.

"I'd certainly hate to be the recipient of *that* look," a soft voice came behind her, and she turned to see Honorine draw back a chair and sit down.

Cordelia forced a smile to her face. "Don't worry. I reserve that look for self-important, overbearing men, and you're decidedly not one of those."

Honorine's eyes narrowed. "I'd think you were speaking of Oswald, if I hadn't watched you and His Grace spar last night. I take it you don't like the way the duke handles matters."

"You've summed up my opinion of him quite brilliantly."

"Then why did you agree to travel with him to London, hmmm? I had to wonder about that last night."

Cordelia stared into the bowl of tea. How much should she tell Honorine about life at the vicarage the last few years? Not much, she decided. Not with Honorine and her father already at daggers drawn. "His Grace has offered me independence. He'll see to it that my works are published forever . . . and that I'll be paid accordingly for them."

"I see." Honorine tapped her finger on the table. "Why would you want independence, I wonder? What about marriage? Children?"

Cordelia swallowed the acid retort burning her throat. "Oh, I haven't given up on all that. But I'm terribly choosy and haven't found a man to suit me. Besides, I'm growing into quite the spinster—"

"Nonsense. You have a duke enamored of you, after all, so you can't be too far gone."

Sudden alarm gripped Cordelia. Surely Honorine hadn't guessed at Cordelia's private encounters with the duke. "Why, whatever would make you say such a thing? His Grace isn't enamored of me. He has a fiancée."

"Oh?" Honorine shrugged, then clasped Cordelia's hand. "That's an obstacle, to be sure, but not an insurmountable one, especially when the man follows you with his eyes wherever you go."

Despite her fear of being found out, a delicious pleasure stole over her. Savagely she squelched it. Sebastian only "followed her with his eyes" because of her body, her treacherous body that melted under his hands. He obviously desired her, but that meant nothing. What man wouldn't desire a woman shameless enough to throw away all propriety when alone with him?

Improper women undoubtedly offered Sebastian their bodies often. Judging from his anger yesterday, he probably considered her that kind of woman and disapproved of her for it. Worse yet, she couldn't blame him.

It didn't bear thinking on, she told herself and changed the subject. "I'm glad you're coming with us. I'll have to spend most of my time tutoring Father, but you and I will probably have a few hours here and there to gossip. It'll be great fun, you'll see."

"No need to convince me." Honorine licked her finger, then slicked back a wayward strand of hair that had escaped her perfect coiffure. "But I don't think your father is happy about the idea."

"Of course he is," Cordelia lied, squeezing Honorine's hand. "He's simply being an old bear. You know how he is."

Honorine met her gaze with eyes of slate blue. "No, I don't. Not anymore." She drew in her breath, then sighed. "But I did once. In fact, that's what I came to talk to you about. Has your father ever told you that he and I knew each other before he met your mother?"

Cordelia stared at her curiously. "Why, no. He never mentioned it. Nor did Mother."

Glancing down at their two clasped hands, Honorine smiled faintly. "It's true. As a matter of fact, he proposed to me."

Odd bits of memory came back to her . . . of Mother talking about Honorine being an old family friend. Cordelia had always assumed Honorine had been Mother's particular friend. Certainly not Father's.

Honorine released Cordelia's hand with a little squeeze, then rose from the table. She wandered to the window, her back to Cordelia. "I thought you should know before you take me to London with you. Oswald and I have a tendency to snap at each other, and I want you to be forewarned. When your mother was alive, she stood between us. I don't think she ever knew why he and I always fought, but she kept us from killing each other."

Cordelia finally found her voice. "Why *did* you always fight? Because he proposed to you, but married Mother?"

"Not exactly." She sighed. "I refused his suit. Although I was but the daughter of a tailor, I had grandiose dreams about playing lady of the manor. Mr. Beardsley wasn't a lord, of course, but he'd already obtained wealth as a merchant and was certainly higher in station than me. He'd been courting me, and he had far better prospects than your father."

She pivoted to face Cordelia, a bright smile painted on her face. "Of course, I got everything I wished for—a rich husband . . . a place of respect among the gentry. . . ." She swept her hand around the breakfast room with its gilded stucco reliefs of gods and goddesses. "A glorious home." Her smile dimmed a fraction. "No children, unfortunately, but one can't have everything."

She dropped her eyes from Cordelia, her wistful tone becoming matter-of-fact. "I was absolutely right to refuse your father's suit, of course. We would never have rubbed along together very well, but he was quite angry about it, since I-I had actually gone so far as to tell him I loved him." She took a deep, shuddering breath. "Well, that's all quite in the past. I met your mother shortly afterward in Father's shop, liked her on sight, and introduced her to Oswald. I suppose it was my way of salving my conscience."

With a smile, she met Cordelia's gaze once more. "The rest you know. They fell in love at once. But Oswald and I haven't gotten along since. His pride was rather pricked, I think, over the whole matter."

"I can imagine it would have been," Cordelia said

dryly. Her father and Honorine. What a startling revelation. Cordelia sifted through childhood memories,
trying to pinpoint if she'd ever noticed undercurrents
between Honorine and her father, but she could think
of no time when she had.

Oddly enough, Honorine's confession didn't bother
her. That her father had been swayed by another
woman first didn't detract from her parents' love for
each other. Perhaps if it had been anyone else but
Honorine, she might have been disturbed, but
Honorine had been the nearest thing she'd had to an
aunt anyway. It seemed fitting that Honorine should
have once loved Father.

Still, knowing about their past altered many things
in her mind. It explained why Father had been so opposed to having Honorine come along, why he'd said
such vitriolic things.

She remembered Sebastian's comment to Father last
night, the one that had so angered Father. A slow smile
grew on her face. Honorine *was* a widow now, after all,
and Father a widower. . . .

"I know what you're thinking, and you'd best forget
it," Honorine warned, coming around the table. "Your
father isn't the least interested in me anymore, so don't
think you'll do any matchmaking on this trip. I only
told you so you'd understand why we don't get along."

Cordelia understood. She understood quite well. She
also noticed Honorine hadn't said a word about not being interested in Father anymore. Suppressing a smile,
Cordelia pasted on her most innocent expression.
"Matchmaking didn't even enter my head."

Honorine eyed her suspiciously. "Of course it did.
You're always wanting to please everyone, but squelch
any ideas you have about linking your father and me.
Whatever we felt for each other is quite in the past."

"I'm sure it is." By some miracle, Cordelia maintained a straight face.

Honorine cast her a warning glance and opened her
mouth to say more. That's when the duke entered the

room, looking polished and handsome, like a coveted shilling winking in summer sunlight.

Honorine's displeased expression faded, and she became once again the perfect hostess. "Good morning, Your Grace. I do hope you slept well."

"Quite well," he assured her with a smile. "After a night spent sleeping with the vicar, having a room to myself was a luxury beyond imagination." He winked at Cordelia, who turned her head to stare out the window.

At her rebuff, his voice grew more formal. "You have a lovely home, Mrs. Beardsley."

Honorine laughed. "You won't say that after you've spent a few days cooped up here."

"Cooped up?"

Honorine gestured to the window. "I see you haven't looked outside yet. I believe the trip to London will have to be postponed a short while. That is, unless you can produce a sleigh and some light-footed horses to whisk us over the extra two feet of snow that fell last night."

With a curse, he went to stand at the window and stared out, his shoulders tensing. "I believe you're right. It does look as if we're stuck for a while. I hope we'll not inconvenience you."

"Not at all." She winked at Cordelia. "There's nothing I like more than entertaining guests. In fact, now that nearly everyone is awake, I must see about breakfast."

"I'll help you," Cordelia hastened to say, rising from the table.

"No need." Honorine cast a sidelong glance at the duke, then flashed Cordelia a meaningful smile. "It won't take me but a moment to get Cook moving, so why don't you sit here and finish your tea?" Then before Cordelia could protest, Honorine hurried from the room.

Cordelia felt abandoned, and her sense of betrayal grew when Sebastian turned from the window to face her from across the table. He said nothing at first, just surveyed her with that devouring look that always made her feel like a hare run to ground.

Remembering his words yesterday, she met his gaze with her own mutinous one. "I'm alone, Your Grace, so you'd best leave, before I tempt you with my wanton manner."

A muscle twitched in his jaw. "The only one who considers you a wanton, Cordelia, is you."

"If you won't leave, then I guess I must—" she began, rising to her feet.

"Devil take you, why do you insist on misunderstanding me?" Bracing his hands on the table, he leaned forward. "I told you yesterday—'tis my own lack of control I worry about, not yours."

She hesitated, her hand gripping the top of the nearest bow-fronted chair. "But you were very angry at me yesterday."

"Not at you. At myself."

"You said I should be locked up. You said I bring out your basest desires, as if it were my fault." Swallowing hard, she continued in a lower voice, "And I know it *is* my fault for . . . for not slapping your face and . . . pushing you away . . . and . . ."

He uttered a low curse. "Look at me, Cordelia."

Stiffening her chin, she tilted her face up to his, struggling to retain the remnants of her pride and not be embarrassed by this peculiar conversation.

His eyes blazed. "Your only fault is in being young and inexperienced. And kind. I don't think it's in your nature to slap anyone's face. I wonder if you'd even shoot a wolf—you'd be too busy explaining to people that he only attacked you because he was hungry."

His implacable expression softened a fraction. "I, however, am not so young. And I'm most certainly experienced. I know better than to take advantage of a sweet young woman like you when I have nothing to offer but a few moments of stolen passion. My usual self-restraint, however, seems to fly right out the window whenever I find myself alone with you."

"Which only proves that it's my fault, since I'm apparently the one person who makes you lose your restraint." She turned to leave the room once more.

He threw back his head and groaned, then rounded the table, following her as she hurried to the door. "Nay. Is it the fault of the rider in the coach that the highwayman robs him? Do we send the rider to jail or the highwayman?"

His words stopped her short. She stood there confused. She'd been taught that it was a woman's responsibility to keep a man from taking liberties, that only a thorough trollop allowed more than the chastest kiss.

"But . . . but true ladies don't feel such . . . such . . ."

"Desires? Aye, angel, they do. They pretend they don't, but they do. Desire is natural for both men and women. 'Tis exactly why Richard guards my sisters. I know what my very proper sisters would be capable of if a man like myself came near them. And I assure you, I don't consider them strumpets."

When she glanced up at him with wide eyes, he continued in a rumbling voice, "If a man had laid a hand on one of my sisters yesterday as I did on you, I'd have cut it off. But I'd not have called her a strumpet for it, although I would have warned her to be cautious about being alone with him." His jaw tautened. "As I warned you."

"What if I don't want to be cautious?" she whispered, then clapped a hand over her mouth, horrified by what she'd just said, and the feelings it undoubtedly revealed.

His eyes glittered, sweeping down the length of her, then back to her face. "If ever you choose not to be cautious," he said in his low baritone, "I'm afraid you'd suck the civilized man right out of my body, and you'd find a very ungovernable creature in his place." He drew in a deep breath. "Then it wouldn't matter whose fault it was, angel. The result would be the same. I'd gobble you up with great relish. So take my advice. Don't ever, ever make such a foolish choice."

And before she could respond to that frightening speech, he swung on his heel and left.

Chapter Twelve

Music for a while
Shall all your cares beguile:
Wond'ring how your pains were eas'd,
And disdaining to be pleas'd.
                    —John Dryden, "Music for a While"

On the fourth day of their stay in York, Cordelia led everyone into Honorine's salon. Her father was already there, seated by the clavichord wearing his best wig and most expensive waistcoat. He looked uncomfortable sitting amid the grandeur of the salon's gilded scrolls and friezes of garlands, but he held himself erect with a dignity that made her proud.

As Honorine and the duke watched with obvious curiosity, Cordelia pointed to an armchair and a settee. "Both of you sit down."

"What's this all about?" Honorine strolled across the room in a rustle of satin skirts. "You're bursting to tell us some secret . . . I can tell. And Oswald is looking more sprightly than he has in days."

Cordelia ignored Honorine's question. "You're right. It's a secret. Now sit."

With a shrug, Honorine settled into the chair as Sebastian dutifully lowered himself onto the settee, amusement glinting in his eyes.

Cordelia flashed her father a reassuring smile. He did indeed look sprightly. Four days of sobriety had put healthy color into his cheeks and erased a few of the lines of dissipation about his mouth.

He'd been grouchier than usual, but she'd expected that, and he'd fought valiantly not to take it out on her.

Instead, Honorine had borne the brunt of his displeasure. Surprisingly, she'd endured it good-naturedly, laughing him out of his doldrums whenever possible.

What's more, Cordelia had been left in peace to tutor her father, for during the day both the duke and Honorine had judiciously avoided the salon where Cordelia held sway.

At night, she'd given her father a rest from music. Honorine had trounced her routinely at whist, and the duke and her father had carried on a congenial game of chess. An odd truce had existed between them all, as if they'd silently agreed to avoid unpleasant subjects and volatile emotions, as if the snow cocooned them in a world where harmony was possible.

Now that the snow had dropped to a manageable level, however, their peaceful stay at Honorine's was nearly over. It was time to test Father's knowledge.

"Well, get on with it, gel," her father snapped, although his eyes twinkled with a rare good humor.

Sebastian and Honorine looked to her expectantly.

She sucked in a deep breath, then smoothed down her skirts nervously. "All right, then." Adopting her father's ringing tones, she began. "Imagine we are in London at a fashionable assembly. You're both avid patrons of the arts and particularly interested in music. A new composer has come to town, and he's the guest of honor at the assembly, accompanied by his faithful daughter who plays the clavichord like an angel."

Honorine chuckled, and Cordelia held up one hand to signal that there was more.

"Honorine, of course, is the lady of the house, a stately countess with a burning desire to pick the famous composer's brain."

"Can't I be a duchess?" Honorine asked mischievously.

Cordelia's father snorted, but Cordelia nodded. "Certainly. If we're to have a duke, we must have a duchess."

Cordelia turned to Sebastian, barely suppressing her

smile. "His Grace is our reigning nobleman, lord of the manor."

"And patron of the arts," he reminded dryly.

"Enthusiastic patron of the arts," she corrected with a smile.

Honorine chimed in, "But not one of those sycophantic, fawning dandies you so often find at these things."

Cordelia clapped her hand to her chest in mock horror. "Certainly not. His Grace is allowed to be his usual arrogant self."

Sebastian stretched his arm out along the back of the settee, raising one eyebrow. "Thank you, I think."

Giving him a mock curtsy, Cordelia then gestured to her father. "The famous composer is a vicar, well-respected in North England, but generally reticent in speaking about his music. His work, however, is astoundingly wonderful—"

"Astoundingly," the duke broke in with a grin.

She shot him a arch glance. "And he's been asked to present a piece for his audience. Reluctantly he agrees to give them a prelude."

Sebastian looked nonplussed. "A prelude?"

A smug smile crossed Cordelia's face as she walked regally to the clavichord. Sebastian obviously had no idea how versatile a musician she was. "Now then. The vicar's daughter has been asked to play the prelude because the vicar has trouble with stiffening of the joints, so he doesn't play as well as he composes."

"Oh, dear, Oswald," Honorine quipped, "when did you start suffering from stiffening of the joints?"

"About the time you became a duchess," he retorted, cracking his knuckles in general defiance of everyone.

Amid the duke's and Honorine's laughter, Cordelia sat down at the clavichord, a determined set to her shoulders. She paused briefly in silence, her hands poised over the keys, her mind searching for a focus.

Then she sucked in her breath and without another word, played the first chord. This was her favorite prelude, the one she'd written in celebration when Lord Kent had first agreed to publish her chorales. She threw her whole self into it, her audience fading away as she coaxed lively sounds from Honorine's stately instrument.

The fugue unfolded with sweet delicacy for once, prancing forth on minuet steps that gave joy to her heart. She loved having a fugue fall into place with perfect precision, and today it was as if her fingers took wing.

By the time she reached the coda, her hands and the instrument seemed all one undulating creature of beauty. She almost hated to have it end.

As the last notes echoed into silence, she heard not a sound behind her. She twisted around to find Sebastian leaning forward in rapt attention and Honorine smiling. Cordelia's father wore a proud expression.

Despite their obvious approval, it was on the tip of her tongue to ask them what they thought. Then she remembered the purpose of the exercise.

With considerable effort, she forced herself back into the role circumstances had dictated for her. "That was Father's most exuberant piece, I think. Wouldn't you say so, Father?"

Her father went rigid when he heard his cue, like a soldier snapping to attention when his sergeant entered the barracks. "Aye." He paused. "I tried to make it so. That's why I avoided full cadences. Breaks up the flow, you know."

Although he sounded a bit like a child reciting scriptures, Cordelia hoped most people would attribute that to the nervousness of being forced to speak of his music when he'd supposedly been reticent before.

Honorine stared at Cordelia, then turned to Cordelia's father with a mischievous gleam in her eyes. "Reverend Shalstone, do tell us how you came to write the fugue's theme. It sounds like flutes trilling. I don't believe I've heard another quite so delightful."

Turning back to the keyboard, Cordelia slowly played the prelude's theme, counting out eight notes in her head. "That part, do you mean?" she asked from the clavichord.

"Yes, that part," Honorine answered.

Cordelia twisted around and gave her father the barest of nods.

He shrugged. "Flutes, eh? I suppose you're close, though I meant it to sound more like a lute improvisation. That's the purpose of the broken chords in the first five measures, especially that drawn-out A-minor chord."

Honorine's mouth gaped open as Cordelia beamed. She shot her father a approving glance, and he winked at her.

Suspicion glinted in Sebastian's eyes. "What about that . . . that rushed passage? The one where it sounded as if all the notes were tumbling after one another willy-nilly." She could see him floundering through his limited knowledge of music for a valid question. "Isn't it hard to keep all those little parts straight?" he finished weakly.

Honorine chuckled, but Cordelia merely fingered the notes she thought he was speaking of, carefully counting out ten. "You mean this passage?"

Her father shifted in his seat. "I suppose you're referring to the strettos I used to develop the main theme." He gave Sebastian an indulgent smile. "Well, of course it's difficult keeping all those notes straight in one's head, but for a musician, it comes as second nature."

Abandoning all pretense of adhering to her role, Honorine leapt from her seat in excitement, coming over to Cordelia's father and searching his hands. "No instructions or anything," she pronounced in amazement. She turned to Cordelia, her eyes wide. "I'm astonished. I'm truly astonished. Why, your father didn't know a stretto from a coda a few days ago!"

"He still doesn't." Cordelia couldn't keep from grinning. "Watch."

She played six notes of the fugue, then nodded at her father.

"This coda, with its simple harmonization of the principal idea, is one of my favorites," her father stated.

As Honorine gave a low murmur of surprise, shaking her head in amazement, Sebastian's eyes narrowed. "Is it some sort of code?"

"You're getting close," Cordelia said with a grin.

"But you couldn't possibly know which passage someone will ask about," Honorine protested as she stepped toward the clavichord and peered at it as if trying to find the answer in the keys of the instrument.

Cordelia and her father exchanged congratulatory smiles.

"I don't have to know," Cordelia explained. "You see, it was obvious to me that Father would never understand music. It doesn't come naturally to him. But he's wonderful at memorizing strings of words—scriptures, poems, passages from classical literature. And he *can* count, after all."

Her father took up the explanation. "So I memorized these set phrases of Cordelia's. When someone asks a question, she plays whatever passage they're asking about, but only a certain number of notes. Six notes means the question is about the coda. Ten notes is strettos."

"But those answers only fit this piece," Sebastian protested. "What if your audience doesn't wish to hear a prelude?"

"Father and I have worked up three pieces for your brother and Handel." Cordelia gave them all a self-satisfied smile. "I don't think either Lord Kent or Handel will require Father to talk about more than that. The prelude is our surprise piece, but we've also got two chorales we'll use."

Her father tilted his head with a haughty smile. "Six

notes in the first chorale means the answer should refer to the tonality change in the fourth measure," he recited, obviously pleased with his breadth of stolen knowledge.

Although Sebastian sat back against the settee with his brow furrowed, Honorine's face was flushed with excitement. She sat down beside Cordelia on the bench of the clavichord and patted Cordelia's hand. "This is brilliant, dear, simply brilliant! I'm quite thoroughly impressed."

"See here," Cordelia's father protested, "I've got something to do with this, too, you know. We couldn't pull it off without me."

"I'm not convinced you can pull it off at all," Sebastian interjected. "Reverend Shalstone could remember the wrong sequence—"

"Bosh!" the vicar cut in. "Anyone will tell you I have a memory like an elephant. Why, I can quote numerous psalms in their entirety and the whole of Ephesians."

Sebastian fixed him with a piercing stare. "What if the questions they ask are ones you haven't allowed for? What do you do then?"

Cordelia rose from the bench to pace the room. "I think we've made the twelve or so stock answers general enough that they'll suit nearly anything, but if we have a problem, I'll add my opinions when necessary. We merely have to make sure I don't do it too often or it'll look like I'm answering for Father."

Sebastian shook his head. "I don't know. What about general conversation? What if they question him and you're not allowed to play? I mean, your ploy worked in this limited instance, but—"

"But what, Your Grace? The only other choices are for Father to become a musician overnight, which we all know isn't going to happen, or for me to tell the truth, which you've said is impossible. Do you have a third choice to offer?"

With a sigh, Sebastian met her challenging gaze.

"Nay." He crossed his arms over his chest, his face still troubled. "I suppose I hadn't realized how truly untutored your father is in matters of music. I'd hoped you could make him actually understand how the music works."

She softened her expression. "Then you take me for a magician, Sebastian. You probably thought of your own tutoring. Perhaps *you* could understand a great deal about music in a few days if you worked at it, but that isn't true of most people. Not just anyone can be made to think like a composer."

A self-deprecating smile flitted across his face. "Once again, I've underestimated the complexity of your situation." Then he added, with a glance meant only for her, "And the enormity of your talent."

Honorine stood. "Well, I, for one, am quite sure it can be done." She paused, smoothing back a wayward lock of hair. "In fact, I'm so certain your ingenious trick will work, that I'm prepared to put it to a much harder test, which should settle the matter once and for all."

Everyone's eyes turned to her.

Now that she had their complete attention, she strolled around the room with languid grace, straightening a china figurine here and smoothing a tassel there. "As you must realize, the snow has melted enough to allow us to leave by day after tomorrow at the latest."

She stopped, sweeping her gaze around the room. "That gives me enough time to invite some friends for an intimate supper."

"A supper?" the vicar queried.

With a smile, she nodded. "Tomorrow night. I need only invite a few friends. The squire and his wife ... the rector, of course ... and the choirmaster." Her smile broadened. "I may even invite one or two of the harpsichordists from our local orchestra. That should provide the most accurate test of all. If you can convince them of your 'talent,' Oswald, then you convince anyone."

Sebastian's gaze settled on Cordelia, his eyes obviously searching her face for some evidence of reluctance. She threw her shoulders back proudly. "That sounds perfect."

She hoped she sounded more confident than she felt. As Sebastian had said, it had been easy pulling off their charade in the presence of friends. It might not be so easy to maintain it in front of an unknown audience. Yet Honorine was right. They needed a more convincing test of her plan before they risked fumbling all in front of Lord Kent and Handel.

"Do you think you're ready for such an endeavor?" Honorine asked Cordelia's father.

He shrugged. "Ready as I'll ever be, I suppose. The gel and I can practice a bit more tomorrow. If she thinks we can manage it, I'll not contest her opinion."

The doubt in his voice didn't reassure Cordelia, but the die was cast.

"Excellent!" Honorine proclaimed. "I'm sure it will be an evening to remember."

An evening to remember, Cordelia thought while Honorine began discussing what to serve for her "intimate supper."

Cordelia only hoped the evening was remembered with pleasure and not laughter in years to come. For despite her earlier enthusiasm about her plan, the duke's questions about its feasibility had raised questions of her own in her mind.

And she didn't know if she was ready to find out the answers.

Chapter Thirteen

When to her lute Corinna sings,
Her voice revives the leaden strings,
And both in highest notes appear,
As any challenged echo clear.
But when she doth of mourning speak,
Ev'n with her sighs the strings do break.
—Thomas Campion,
from *A Book of Airs* (no. 6)

Honorine noted the pale worry on Cordelia's face as they stood in Cordelia's room putting the finishing touches on her attire. Honorine had borrowed the attractive ensemble for Cordelia from her niece, but realized that Cordelia didn't even seem to notice the rich gold satin and embroidered stomacher with its tiny satin echelles. "Don't tell me you're nervous," Honorine commented. "I wouldn't have expected it of you."

Cordelia stared at Honorine's image in the ornate mirror. "Of course, I'm nervous. I'm terrified. 'Tis like His Grace said yesterday. Anything could go wrong."

"Ah, but it won't." Honorine turned her around so they faced each other. Her gaze swept critically over Cordelia, from her Dutch coiffure to her ivory silk slippers. With a frown, Honorine lifted the skirt of Cordelia's gown, which was tied back in front to expose the quilted petticoat, and settled it more smoothly over the fan hoop. Then she nodded her approval.

"Besides," Honorine added with a coy look, "who'll be able to think about music when faced with such a beautiful young woman? I assure you, our choirmaster will hardly be able to keep his questions straight."

A faint smile graced Cordelia's pretty face. "Come now, Honorine, you needn't flatter me to put me at ease. You're the one who's always saying the road to hell isn't paved with good intentions, but with false compliments. Yet here you are paving it for me."

Honorine stared blankly at Cordelia, realizing that the young woman actually believed every word she said. "But I'm not giving you false compliments. You truly look stunning in that dress."

Cordelia laughed. "It fits, at any rate, which is all I can ask for."

But Honorine noted that Cordelia took another look at herself in the mirror.

"It does more than fit," Honorine insisted, fluffing up the sleeves. "Rest assured, you fill it out with more . . . shall we say flair, than my niece ever did."

Honorine's eyes rested on the handkerchief draped around Cordelia's shoulders and modestly covering her chest, the ends trailing down over her stomacher. "Actually, if we wish to keep our guests completely off guard, we should take advantage of your nice figure." Untying the ribbon securing the handkerchief, she drew the strip of silk off and tossed it on the nearby bed.

"Honorine!" Cordelia protested, covering her exposed cleavage with her hands.

"There's not a woman in London who'd wear a handkerchief with her evening gown these days." Honorine smiled broadly, then twisted one of Cordelia's long sausage curls to trail over her creamy shoulder in front. "Besides, we need all the distractions we can get tonight."

Cordelia bent toward the bed, retrieving the handkerchief with a dramatic sigh. "That's not enough of a reason for me to dance in to supper looking like a strumpet."

Honorine chuckled. "*I'm* not wearing a handkerchief. Do *I* look like a strumpet?"

Cordelia winced. "You know I didn't mean . . . well,

you're a widow, after all. You're allowed to dress more—"

"Provocatively?" Honorine asked, one eyebrow raised.

"Maturely. In any case, a vicar's daughter should look the part." She held the handkerchief up to her chest with a mock expression of haughtiness. "I have my position to think of, you know."

"Oh, pish." Honorine snatched the handkerchief out of her hands. "You're young, and you have a lovely figure. You should flaunt it as much as possible."

Honorine held the handkerchief up to her own throat, thinking back to her courting days, when she'd been merely a tailor's daughter. She'd eschewed handkerchiefs as often as she could get away with it. Of course, she'd been considered somewhat outrageous even then, and time certainly hadn't dulled her love of excitement.

Her smile faded. But this life of parties and assemblies, late nights and lonely mornings, had long ago lost its thrill. As she grew older, she wondered if it couldn't be as exciting to make a life with the man one loved, no matter how remote his abode or how quiet his profession.

Ah, but those thoughts always led to Oswald, she told herself, firmly putting them from her mind.

Apparently aware of Honorine's pensive mood, Cordelia gently took the handkerchief back and stared at it in obvious indecision. "Father will have an apoplectic fit if I appear for supper without it."

"But His Grace will certainly sit up and take notice."

To Honorine's disgust, her words had the opposite effect from what she intended.

Cordelia's eyes went wide and she furiously threw the silk cloth around her neck, draping it carefully in front. "Aye, he'll notice, that's certain. And he'll think I'm the worst kind of flirt."

Honorine shrugged. "Then by all means, wear the

thing." She gave a dramatic pause. "Although I'm sure the squire's pretty wife and daughters won't be wearing handkerchiefs. Nor the choirmaster's fiancée." She took the ribbon from Cordelia and deftly began to tie it around the ends of the handkerchief. "Of course, His Grace would be much too polite to notice their . . . er . . . endowments."

Cordelia's eyes narrowed as she took the ends of the ribbon from Honorine. "Much too polite, you say?" Her gaze dropped to the handkerchief, and she paused a moment. Then with a low oath not at all fitting for a vicar's daughter, she whisked the handkerchief from around her neck and dropped it on the dressing table.

"Ah, dear girl," Honorine said amiably as she held out a fan for Cordelia's inspection. "Another week or two and I'd have every man in York eating out of your hand."

Cordelia rolled her eyes as she picked up the fan and flicked it open. "Then it's a good thing I'm not staying. Feeding men from my hands could get messy. Not to mention tedious."

Honorine smiled, gesturing toward the door. She bet she knew of at least one man Cordelia would want to feed from her hand—Lord Waverley himself. After all, for four days Honorine had watched Cordelia snatch glances at His Grace whenever she thought no one could see, and flush when he spoke to her in that low, husky undertone.

Nor was the duke any better, Honorine thought, following Cordelia with that wild, hungry gaze and pacing the halls like a caged beast whenever Cordelia and Oswald were closeted in the salon.

Then there were the evenings when the two of them spoke about trivialities with the kind of fervor only lovers could have in each other's presence. Oswald might be completely oblivious to what was going on, but Honorine had decided that Cordelia and Lord Waverley were furiously in love. Even if neither of them had admitted it yet.

What's more, they were perfect for each other, despite their difference in station. Of course, there was the small matter of that fiancée, but Honorine could get around that. Thank heavens she was going to London with them. With a little effort, perhaps she could—

"Are you sure I don't look too outrageous?" Cordelia whispered urgently, pausing at the top of the stairs.

"You look ravishing, dear, as should every girl your age. Don't worry, you have plenty of years ahead of you for dressing modestly." She quirked one eyebrow up. "I've no doubt that your future husband, whoever he may be, will prove to be quite a nuisance on the subject."

She noticed that Cordelia paled at the mention of a husband. She knew Cordelia had refused several suitors in order to stay at home and take care of Oswald, but Honorine thoroughly disapproved of that. It wasn't proper for a young girl to give up her life simply because her fool of a father had lost himself to grief.

Honorine's lips tightened. And apparently to drink as well, judging from a few odd things Cordelia had said. Honorine hadn't missed the strange undercurrents between Cordelia and Lord Waverley every time Oswald reached for something to drink or refused wine at dinner. Honorine also remembered vague hints from Florinda about how spirits "don't sit well with Oswald." How much had all of that to do with Cordelia's current spinsterhood?

She'd find out eventually, which was one more reason for her to go to London.

Resolutely, she pressed Cordelia's hand, turning her toward the stairs. "Come, now, dear, don't be a coward. It will all work out. You'll see. But if we linger any longer up here, they'll think we've perished." Then she began to descend the stairs, and after a slight hesitation, Cordelia followed.

A quarter of the way down, they caught sight of Lord Waverley and Oswald. The two men were chatting amiably. Honorine glanced quickly at Cordelia, whose face had lit up at the sight of His Grace in a sumptuous coat and waistcoat of gold brocade. Honorine congratulated herself on her forethought in discovering what the duke would be wearing so she could dress Cordelia accordingly. They would make a handsome pair tonight, no doubt of that, with their shining brown hair and their shimmering gold attire.

Honorine then turned her attention to Oswald's clothing, which wasn't half as awful as she'd expected after the silly man had refused her help in choosing something to wear. In fact, he wore a perfectly respectable suit of clothes, all sober black velvet except for his white shirt and cravat. No doubt the duke had intervened to make certain Oswald looked the part, for Oswald wasn't known for his fashionable clothing.

As they reached the halfway point of the stairs, Oswald looked up, but instead of gazing at his daughter and exploding into anger about her low-cut gown, which Honorine had half expected, it was Honorine he gaped at in slack-jawed surprise.

To her distress, she actually colored under his stare. Quickly she snapped open her fan, fluttering it in front of her face. It wouldn't do to let Oswald see her behaving like a schoolroom miss at her first evening ball. Still, it pleased her that he seemed only to have eyes for her as she and Cordelia descended.

Then she thought to glance at the duke, and what she saw made her hide a smile behind her fan. His Grace watched Cordelia's descent with glittering eyes that expressed almost volubly what he thought of her.

Never had Honorine seen such thinly disguised passion in a man's face. She wondered if Cordelia quite appreciated how rare it was to find a man who could look at you with such depth of feeling, such raw male power. Only one man had ever looked at Honorine that way.

Honorine's gaze instantly flew to Oswald, but Oswald had finally noticed his daughter. He drew himself up, opening his mouth to speak to Cordelia, but

Honorine pretended to miss a step on the stairs and practically fell into his arms.

"Here, now, be careful!" Oswald exclaimed, his attention temporarily diverted as he steadied her on her feet.

She glanced back at the duke and Cordelia in time to see Lord Waverley lift Cordelia's hand and press his lips to it in a kiss that stretched the bounds of propriety.

Oswald followed her gaze, his expression turning grim. "What have you done to Cordelia?" he hissed in Honorine's ear. "Not that she doesn't look beautiful, you understand, but 'tisn't right for her to be popping out of her gown like that. She's just a gel."

They watched together as Lord Waverley offered Cordelia his arm and she took it, a pleased smile curving her lips.

"Don't be absurd, Oswald. She's a woman. And it's high time for her to find a husband."

Oswald glared at her suspiciously. "What are you up to, Honorine? You're not trying to marry my daughter off, are you?"

Honorine couldn't hide the smug smile that rose to her lips. "I don't think I'd have to try very hard." She nodded at the duke and Cordelia, who were walking through the doors into the drawing room, looking like they belonged together.

Oswald stiffened. "Nay," he muttered angrily as he followed them, taking her arm none too gently and pulling her along with him. "Don't tell me you're thinking of catching His Grace for my Cordelia."

"Why not?"

"Why not? The man's a duke and he has a fiancée. That's why not."

"Pish. He wants Cordelia, *not* his fiancée. Any fool can see that."

Oswald's scowl was darker than usual. "Aye, he wants Cordelia, but that doesn't mean he wishes to marry her. If you care at all for my daughter, you'll not

encourage her in any foolish dreams about the duke.
Given half the chance, he'll take her virtue, then break
her heart. His kind always marries their own. They've
got no quarrel with deflowering sweet young gels like
Cordelia, but they always marry their own."

"Not all of them," Honorine said, a trifle peevishly.
Surely Oswald was being overly cautious.

"Oh, yes, I'd forgotten." His voice now held a hard
edge. "The wealthy Mr. Beardsley had no qualms
about marrying a tailor's daughter, did he?"

Honorine stopped in her tracks. It was the first time
Oswald had alluded to their previous relationship since
the day he'd stormed out after she'd refused his proposal. Her stomach knotted up as he fixed her with a
stern blue gaze.

She dropped her eyes from his. "I suppose he . . . he
thought I was worth it." Her voice trembled, and she
hated herself for it.

She could feel his eyes on her as she released his
arm, her heart pounding triple-time.

"No doubt you were," Oswald said softly. "The
question is, was he?"

It was a fair question. She had to admit that. And
Oswald of all people had a right to know the answer.
But she couldn't give it to him. She simply couldn't. It
would mean unleashing all sorts of emotions she'd
never wanted him to see or know about, and she wasn't
up to it.

Instead, she walked away.

But she feared, as he followed silently behind her,
that he'd not be satisfied until he got an answer. And
if she weren't careful, one day she'd have to give him
one.

Cordelia stared at her plate, at the plump capers resting atop a slice of roast hare. She was no more capable
of eating this dish than of eating the other nineteen.
She should have known Honorine's idea of an intimate
supper was to invite twenty-two friends to a feast that

had two courses of twenty dishes each, not including the dessert course. The first course alone had boasted a calf's head, stewed carp, pigeon pie, and the *coup-de-grâce*: a swan roasted with currant jelly sauce. Dessert hadn't even been served yet. She almost shuddered to think how elaborate that was bound to be.

But none of the dishes could outshine the centerpiece, Cordelia thought, looking glumly at the miniature artificial garden that stretched nearly a yard down the table. In the midst was a high round temple on pillars wreathed with artificial flowers. There were urns and a porcelain shepherd and shepherdess. . . .

Cordelia shook her head in amazement. If this were an intimate supper, what on earth did Honorine consider a large one? Any other time she might have delighted in Honorine's show of wealth, which was clearly meant to honor the duke, but tonight . . .

Tonight Cordelia feared she'd not last until it was over. Her stomach had long ago refused any nourishment and her knees were worn smooth from knocking together.

So far everything had gone well. Father had established himself from the outset in the role of modest vicar, a role guaranteed to fend off most questions. He'd explained that a man of the church shouldn't boast of worldly abilities.

In fact, he'd said, his music was intended for use only during worship. Normally he didn't approve of presenting it outside the proper context. However, for Honorine, he was willing to have his daughter play a piece or two, but only because Honorine had graciously come to their aid by housing them in York and agreeing to accompany them to London. The persona had worked nicely. Even Sebastian had seemed admiring of the adroit way Cordelia's father played the part.

Sebastian. Cordelia stole a glance at him, her fingers curling into the napkin in her lap. His hair gleamed like polished oak in the candlelight, and he looked perfectly at ease, obviously accustomed to roast swan and elaborate garden centerpieces. When he smiled, which was often, his spare, lean features relaxed, making him look roughly handsome. Over the past few days, she'd grown accustomed to having that sudden smile break over her like a welcoming summer shower. Until tonight, however, it had been reserved for her or Honorine.

Tonight, he had other women to dazzle with that smile. He sat between Honorine and one of Squire Hartford's daughters, a lively apple-cheeked blond girl of about seventeen prone to giggles and languishing glances. Admittedly, Sebastian had paid the girl no more than the polite attention expected of him, yet every time she gazed up at him, fluttering her fan in front of her face coyly, a thousand pins pricked Cordelia's heart.

Honorine had been right about one thing, Cordelia thought sourly. Although the girl's bodice was cut modestly, it was certainly low enough to hint at young, soft flesh, and the view was unobscured by a handkerchief. More was the pity.

Now you're being silly, she told herself. *If you're to be jealous of anyone, it ought to be Sebastian's fiancée.*

In truth, his fiancée, Judith, hadn't worried her nearly so much, since the woman remained faceless and Sebastian rarely mentioned her. The young, sweet-faced squire's daughter, however, was another matter entirely. . . .

The ludicrousness of her fears struck Cordelia with such sudden force, she nearly laughed aloud at herself. Merciful heavens, Sebastian was a duke, after all. He wasn't likely to be chasing after a squire's daughter.

Nor a vicar's daughter either, she reminded herself, her humor fleeing.

Just then, Sebastian caught her eye, and a lazy grin stretched over his face. She smiled in return, and he tipped his head toward her. For a second, it was as if they shared a secret no one else at the table was privy to.

Then the man sitting at Cordelia's right, a young, raw-boned harpsichordist, leaned over to whisper in her ear that he was looking forward to her playing later.

She mumbled some inanity about hoping he wasn't disappointed in her abilities, but all her attention was on Sebastian, whose eyes had darkened while the harpsichordist was whispering. His smile faded, and a muscle in his jaw jerked convulsively.

Suddenly she was reminded of all that had happened between them that day under the oak. His face wore the same stark desire it had worn then, the same instant possessiveness. Like a wanton caress, his gaze trailed downward over her mouth, her throat, the trembling tops of her breasts, before drifting back up to fasten on her face once more.

Did he notice that he was slowly stroking the rim of his wine glass with one finger as his eyes drank their fill of her? Did he realize that his lips parted slightly and that every time a breath escaped them, her lips trembled as if they felt the wisp of air slip warmly past?

Her stomach felt painfully taut, and not because of her tightly laced gown either. The longer he stared, the more he brought a blush to the surface of her skin until she wondered if she shone as pink as Honorine's poached salmon under the glittering candles.

They'd not had much of a chance to speak all evening. Their only moments alone had been when he'd escorted her from the stairs to the drawing room, and then he'd said only that "her beauty would put every woman to shame this evening." He hadn't said it glibly, yet she'd assumed it was the kind of polite comment a duke would make to any woman he escorted, and she'd taken it accordingly.

Now, however, she wasn't so sure. When the young harpsichordist again tried to capture her attention, Sebastian glared at the man with such venom, she had to fight back a smile. At least she wasn't the only one suffering the pangs of jealousy.

"How long have you been writing music?" the choirmaster asked Cordelia's father, breaking the spell between her and Sebastian, for they both instantly turned anxious eyes to her father.

But the vicar merely smiled congenially. "Oh, it's been years now . . . ever since I met my wife. Until then I'd been too caught up in my books and my . . . other interests to notice music."

To Cordelia's surprise, he glanced at Honorine before continuing. "But Florinda had a way of playing an air that made a fellow wish to learn more about it. She didn't seem to care that I didn't meet the qualifications for a musician, if you know what I mean. She was so happy to be with me that she didn't mind my being beneath her—in abilities, I mean."

Honorine dropped her fork and grew decidedly pale. "Yes, well, young people will be brash, won't they? I dare say a more mature woman would have thought twice about tutoring a man with no experience in music to speak of."

Sebastian looked questioningly at Cordelia, and she shrugged. Honorine and her father had taken the conversation where no one else could follow. Unfortunately, the choirmaster and the squire looked decidedly confused.

Cordelia shot Honorine a warning glance. " 'Tis a good thing Mother decided to teach Father despite his lack of knowledge. It enabled him to become what he is today."

Honorine looked as if she were going to retort, but then dessert was served, and she had to acknowledge her guests' compliments as two servants bore in an impressive pastry ship filled with an assortment of dried fruits and preserves.

Thankfully they were all allowed to finish the meal without any more barbed comments between Honorine and Cordelia's father, but Cordelia couldn't relax. The short contretemps had fueled her nervousness.

When Honorine announced it was time for their presentation, Cordelia rose from the table, her hands shaking so much she could scarcely hold her fan. She tried to make polite conversation with the harpsichordist, she tried to smile at everyone, but her doubts had surged back in full force.

What if Father miscounted? What if he forgot one of their set phrases?

She'd rounded the table and headed for the door when a hand touched her elbow ever so slightly, and she turned to look into Sebastian's face.

"It's easier to pull charades off when you look more confident, angel," he murmured in a low voice. "You should have learned that by now."

Undoubtedly, he was referring to her role in Belham, but that had been different. That had been a polite fiction everyone had conspired to maintain. This was true deception.

Hiding her face behind her fan, she whispered, "Our plan will never work. I was a fool to think it would."

"You can do it."

At the firm assurance in his voice, she looked at him skeptically. "Yesterday you weren't so sure."

"Yesterday I doubted your father's abilities. I've never doubted yours, however. And if your father can stay sober for five days, I suppose he can manage a parlor trick like this."

A dark scowl crossed his face. He nodded toward the door where the harpsichordist stood outside waiting for her. "Judging from the way your friend is glaring at me, you've already enchanted most of Honorine's guests, the male ones at any rate." His gaze dropped to her lips, and she could see him stiffen. "A parlor trick is all it will take to fool them."

She fluttered her fan more rapidly. "What about you, Your Grace?" she heard herself saying in a flirtatious manner uncharacteristic of her. "Have I enchanted you as well?"

Honorine's nonsensical remarks about her beauty had obviously gone to her head. She couldn't believe she was saying such outrageous things to a duke whose interests lay elsewhere. She steeled herself for the light retort sure to come, angry that she'd let her guard slip so far.

But he regarded her with a steady, unnervingly potent gaze. " 'Enchanted' is a flimsy word for what you've done to me, Cordelia." He jerked his head from her, as if aware of how revealing his words were. "In any case, it scarcely matters, does it? When we reach London, Judith will be waiting."

The wealth of meaning in the phrase "Judith will be waiting" struck Cordelia with the force of an unshielded blow. No matter what he felt for either his fiancée or Cordelia, his future was as certain as hers was uncertain.

Numbly she walked toward the door, her concern for the coming deception temporarily eclipsed by her despair. Her growing affection for Sebastian was worthless, and it was time she realized it, she told herself.

Yet as he followed her in silence, his face set in grim lines, Cordelia knew she was too far gone to relinquish her feelings so easily. For him, it was obviously a more simple matter, but that didn't change anything for her.

Thus when they all settled into the salon, she sat down eagerly at the clavichord, ready to take any step that would hasten the end of her association with Sebastian. She couldn't go on like this much longer—it was too wrenching on her heart.

And when Honorine introduced her with a few quick words about her abilities as a player, she attacked the instrument with a vengeance, pouring into the prelude all the savage emotions of her ruined hopes and futile dreams. She played like a woman gone mad. She let the soul of the music swell in her blood, the ache of its minor chords purge her as no physic ever could.

After a while, even Sebastian faded from her thoughts, and there was only the glorious enjoyment of a well-turned phrase and a simple repetition, the sweet slide into a new key, building and building until the coda ordered everything into a final harmony.

As the last notes of the coda faded in the room, she lifted her fingers from the keys. The stunned silence behind her told her that her frenzied performance hadn't been wasted on her audience. They, too, seemed to sense the anger, the despair, the heartache she'd been driven to express.

Swallowing, she pivoted on the bench. With an effort, she drew forth a smile and presented them with the nonchalant face of a performer who'd merely been showing her talents rather than indulging in an emotion-laden outpouring.

The sound of their enthusiastic applause brought her out of herself, reminding her that this was a charade in more ways than one. Warily she surveyed the group of people she and her father were about to deceive.

"You see?" Honorine exclaimed. "I told you she was magnificent."

She, Cordelia thought in alarm, but before she even had time to react to Honorine's slip, the choirmaster himself corrected Honorine.

"Oh, 'tis true that Miss Shalstone's playing is charming," he gushed, "but 'twas the piece itself that made it so. Such lovely harmonies, such intricate counterpoint!" He turned his gaze to the vicar. "I only wish we had a choir here so we could try out one of your chorales, Reverend Shalstone. If they're anything like this piece, they must be truly exquisite."

Nothing could have prepared Cordelia for the shock of hearing people publicly give her father the praise for her music, not Lord Kent's written praise nor the compliments of the Belham villagers. Lord Kent's letters had always been addressed to her father, but she'd substituted her name for everything she read. And in

Belham everyone *knew* it was her music and treated it accordingly.

This was entirely different.

Scanning the room, she caught the duke's gaze and found him watching her with a distinctly uneasy look on his face. He said nothing, of course. She hadn't really expected him to suddenly reverse his plans and proclaim her as the composer.

Yet when he jerked his gaze from hers, his expression impassive, it tore into her heart.

Even her father seemed to sense her pain, for he told the choirmaster, "Thank you, but you flatter me too much. The piece wouldn't have sounded nearly as good if Cordelia hadn't played it so well."

"Yes, yes." The choirmaster flashed her an impatient smile. "Excellent playing indeed." Then he leaned forward and fixed her father with a curious stare. "Tell me, Reverend Shalstone. How many voices were there? I thought I counted five, but surely there were not so many. And how many fugues?"

Cordelia remained silent. These were questions she'd known to anticipate, and Father had a stock answer for all of them.

"You were correct. This piece has five voices for its triple fugue." Her father talked for a moment about the intricacy of the piece in mostly general terms.

I couldn't have done better myself, she thought with pride.

The harpsichordist left his seat and came to stand by the clavichord. "I was particularly impressed, Miss Shalstone, with the way you managed the right hand on that one stretto toward the end." He reached across her to play a few notes on the clavichord.

Just what we need, she thought, *a harpsichordist with an excellent ear who can remember whole lines.*

She said hastily, "Aye, that stretto is difficult, but the contrast to the stately left hand makes it sound quicker than it is." She shifted on the bench, trying to make it harder for him to reach across and play. When he gazed down at her, a lecherous glint in his eyes, she suddenly realized he'd moved to her side not so he could play, but so he could have a more advantageous view of her bosom.

It took all her self-control not to leap up and leave the clavichord. But of course she couldn't.

When she returned her attention to the choirmaster, she realized he was saying something, and she'd missed part of it. Her father smiled in answer and glanced at her, then seeing her distress, said, "The coda, dear. Why don't you play the coda?"

Inwardly she groaned. Merciful heavens, what exactly was the question about the coda? She had to know in order to know how many notes to play.

Suddenly Sebastian's voice chimed in from the back of the room. "Yes, do play it. I too want to know if that was a skip of a minor ninth."

Forcing down her sigh of relief, she turned and played the coda slowly, counting out five notes.

"You can hear it now, can't you?" her father said knowingly to his audience. "That minor ninth was my outcry in the midst of an otherwise traditional fugue."

Everyone nodded with serious expressions. When Cordelia risked a glance at Sebastian, he was leaning against one of the pillars that flanked the bow window. Like a wolf poised to spring, he stood taut and silent as if waiting for some disaster to occur.

And disaster did occur, after she and her father had fielded three more questions successfully. It came in the form of the flirtatious harpsichordist, whom she knew she'd remember for all time with loathing.

Squire Hartford was asking her father a question when the harpsichordist bent down and said, in what he probably considered a seductive voice, "You make this old clavichord come to life with your playing."

"Thank you," she said hurriedly, trying to pay attention to what the squire was asking.

But the harpsichordist wasn't done with her. He laid his cold hand on her shoulder as he thrust his head closer until his lips were nearly against her ear. " 'Tis a pity you're going on to London tomorrow. I would so love to show you my own superior instrument."

Something in the way he said "instrument" made her flinch. With a shudder, she tried to scoot subtly away from him, but his hand held her prisoner.

Then her father's voice trickled into her consciousness. "Dear, play that last stretto again."

"No, don't trouble your daughter with having to play it once more," the squire said in his sonorous voice. "You know what I'm talking about—that last bit with all the notes."

The choirmaster chimed in. "Yes, the one that mirrors the first stretto? There's a theme that echoes throughout the final measures—"

She missed the rest of it when the harpsichordist murmured, "Perhaps when you return to York, I might call on you here. I don't think Mrs. Beardsley would mind, do you?"

Her father gave her a lame smile and said, "The theme is . . . er . . . one of my favorites. It's a lute improvisation. . . . I mean . . . 'tis supposed to *sound* like a lute improvisation."

At everyone's blank looks, she cut in. "No, Father, you're thinking of the other prelude. This one is more like horns."

"Horns, yes," he muttered.

The choirmaster shot her a quizzical look, then returned his attention to her father. "That's not what I asked, however. I counted at least five entrances of subject and answer in that stretto near the end." He turned to Cordelia. "Play that part again, Miss Shalstone."

Cordelia winced. He hadn't asked his question yet, and she didn't know how many notes to play. So she played more notes than were in her coded system.

Pleased with himself, the choirmaster nodded. "I did hear five entrances. How magnificent! So intricate and masterly."

She relaxed.

"Thank you," her father said, trying to look gracious as he cast her a confused look, obviously unsure why she'd given him no number of notes to use.

To Cordelia's chagrin, the choirmaster went on. "My question is, since you obviously intended to mirror the effect of the skip of the minor ninth there, why didn't you use the minor ninth skip once more? Why didn't you integrate it into the stretto?"

When her father looked completely blank, she said, "Well, you see, he wanted—"

"If you don't mind, Miss Shalstone, I wish to hear your father's opinion," the choirmaster said tartly.

His Grace pushed away from the pillar, watching her father anxiously.

"I didn't want to," her father said feebly.

"Yes, but why not? It would seem the perfect place to reinforce the 'outcry,' to repeat the theme, if indeed the theme was centered around that outcry, which perhaps it wasn't. Was it?"

Her father looked hopelessly lost as he began tugging madly on his ear. "Yes, of course it was . . . well . . . not exactly . . . Oh, blast it all!" He threw up his hands. "I don't know, do you hear me? If you want answers, ask my daughter!"

Then he jumped up and strode to the door, pushing away the restraining hand Honorine stretched out to him. He only stopped when he reached the door. Fixing the duke with an accusing expression, he muttered, "I hope you're pleased with the outcome of the experiment," then stormed from the room.

Cordelia's heart sank. She couldn't blame Father for being angry. At least he'd known when to give up the fight.

When every eye turned to her, she ventured a smile and said lamely, "He . . . he's not good with crowds, you see. He isn't used to talking about his music like this."

The choirmaster looked irate. "Nonsense! He's been

amiable and forthcoming all night. 'Twas a simple question, and all he would say is nonsense." He turned to Honorine with a pompous toss of his head. "What in blazes is going on here? The man keeps deferring to his daughter for simple answers, and doesn't seem to know a thing about his own compositions. Did he write the music or not?"

As Honorine looked at Cordelia helplessly and Cordelia struggled to find words, a familiar voice answered from the back of the room. "He did not."

The harpsichordist at her elbow gasped and the choirmaster twisted in his seat to look at Sebastian, who'd moved forward after making his bald statement.

"What is it then? Is it stolen?" the choirmaster asked.

Sebastian shot her a rueful glance, then shook his head. "Not exactly. Miss Shalstone wrote it."

Now all eyes turned to her, and she shifted uncomfortably on the bench. At least the harpsichordist moved away from her. Apparently, he wasn't at all interested in a woman who was more than simply a vicar's daughter for the plucking.

Squire Hartford looked down his bulbous nose at Cordelia. "What does His Grace mean, Honorine?"

"You've all been too sharp for us, I'm afraid," Honorine said lightly, coming to stand at the front of the room with a forced grin on her face, as if she expected them all to see it as a great joke. "I know it was terrible of me, but you know how I am. I love a good gamble. You see, I placed a bet with Lord Waverley that Cordelia couldn't pass her father off as a composer, and he took me up on it."

Cordelia swallowed, unable to look at any of the people in the room to see what they thought of Honorine's tale. Instead, Cordelia stared at the nearest *trompe l'oeil* of an open doorway leading into a garden and wished that the garden were a real one into which she could simply disappear.

"A bet?" the squire roared. "This has all been some dastardly trick you've played on your friends?"

Honorine shot him a sly glance. "Why, Squire Hartford! You know you'd have done the same thing if you'd heard His Grace boast of how provincial we are here in York and how easily we can be taken in by charlatans. I had to prove him wrong, don't you see?" She cast Sebastian an apologetic look. "Besides, I thought it might be a lark to show His Grace how easily my clever friends can detect imposters."

Cordelia stole a glance at the duke, thankful to see that he didn't seem angry. He watched Honorine, a faint smile tipping up the corners of his lips and his eyebrows raised.

Honorine fluttered her fan gaily before her. "Cordelia was more than happy to help me, for she took insult at his statements as well. We provincials must stick together, after all. Since she's been writing music for some time, it was an easy matter for her to prepare her father to present one of her pieces." She gave a dramatic sigh. "But you were all too astute to be taken in for more than a few moments."

"It wasn't a fair contest," Sebastian protested from the back of the room, throwing himself into the story with a vengeance. "Cordelia *wanted* to prove you right and me wrong."

"That's true, she did side with me in this." Honorine faced her guests. "But wouldn't all of you say she tried valiantly to fool you? I think she did her absolute best. It was just that you were all too smart for us."

Cordelia held her breath. Their answer would prove how they'd taken the whole thing.

After a moment's hesitation, the choirmaster shrugged. "Aye, she fooled me for a bit, I'll grant you, but only for a bit. I caught on that something was amiss when she kept trying to answer for him."

The squire nodded, settling his bulky frame more comfortably in his chair. " 'Twas a fair bet in my estimation." He twisted to glare at the duke, who regarded him with indifference. "Of course, Your Grace may disagree. After all, of what worth are the opinions of poor provincials like us?"

Cordelia had to bite her lip to keep from laughing, and apparently Sebastian wasn't in much better straits, for his voice sounded oddly strangled as he quipped, "What indeed?"

Instantly the others chimed in, protesting that they'd only been taken in for a few minutes, but hadn't wanted to insult Honorine's guest by making accusations. After a few minutes of rampant self-congratulation mixed with surreptitious glares at the duke, they were all smiling and before she knew it, they'd shifted to asking her questions about her composing.

"How did you come to write music?" asked one as another commented that it was unusual indeed for a woman to compose so well. She could tell they didn't quite believe that she'd written the music, but after she answered a few detailed technical questions about the piece, they seemed satisfied, and the talk turned to other matters.

Then cries came for her to play another piece. She looked about for Honorine, but Honorine had disappeared. At her questioning glance, Sebastian gave her a helpless shrug.

"Oh, do play another of your lovely pieces," the squire said, more amiable now that he was content he'd won the day. "After all, Honorine invited us to hear a virtuoso drown us in sound, and we've scarcely gotten our feet wet."

As he chuckled to himself over his metaphor, Cordelia glanced once more at Sebastian.

He smiled. "Yes, do play for us, Miss Shalstone. After all, I wouldn't have made the ... er ... bet in the first place if I hadn't thought you were talented. If you don't play for us, Honorine's guests will take to chastising me for my poor judgment in trusting to your abilities in the first place."

Amid general laughter, she blushed, warmed despite

herself by his compliment. Then she turned to the harpsichord and played her favorite variation.

Her mind wasn't on the music, however. Aside from worrying where her father and Honorine had gone off to, she couldn't help replaying the failed charade in her mind. It had been foolish of her not to anticipate that people didn't converse in straightforward patterns. Her plan would *never* work. There would always be interruptions, not to mention the occasional complicated question taking more than one pat phrase to answer.

Granted, if that blessed harpsichordist hadn't distracted her, she might have been able to field the more complex questions herself. Still, if she were truthful, she'd admit that the whole scheme had been doomed from the beginning.

So what was to become of them now?

Chapter Fourteen

But, O the fury of my restless fear!
The hidden anguish of my flesh desires!
The glories and the beauties that appear,
Between her brows, near Cupid's closed fires.
—John Dowland,
"Sleep, Wayward Thoughts"

Sebastian stood in the salon, which was filled with an unnatural quiet now that everyone had gone. Honorine was out front hastening her guests away after announcing that she and Cordelia needed their rest for tomorrow's journey.

That wasn't the reason for Honorine's haste, and he knew it. He glanced at Cordelia, wondering if she knew it, too. But Cordelia sat at the clavichord with a wan sadness lining her features. She held her fan clenched in her hand as she stared longingly at the *trompe l'oeil* of a garden.

"Are you all right?" he asked tenderly, knowing she wasn't, and not certain what to do about it.

She gave a helpless gesture with her hands. "I don't know."

They heard the entrance door shut.

A few minutes later Honorine entered the room. She now wore a heavy cloak and was pulling on thick gloves. "I'm sorry to leave you both so suddenly, but I must." Her gaze fell on Cordelia, soft and regretful. "Your father is gone."

That snapped Cordelia out of her passivity immediately. She rose from the bench in alarm. "Gone? What do you mean, gone?"

A false smile crossed Honorine's face as she avoided

Cordelia's gaze. " 'Tis nothing to worry about. Oswald apparently left the house as soon as he walked out of the salon. My footman told me Oswald took his coat, but left on foot, so I'm sure he hasn't gone far. I thought I'd go look for him."

Cordelia crossed the room quickly. "I'll go with you."

"No, you won't," Sebastian commanded, staying her with one hand. "Neither of you are going anywhere at this hour and in this weather. I'll go."

Honorine shook her head. "Thank you for offering, Your Grace, but you don't know where to go. I, on the other hand, know York well, and everyone in York knows me. It's a safe town. I shan't be in any danger, and I'll be able to find out where he is much quicker than either of you."

She turned toward the door.

Sebastian called out, "At least let me accompany you."

Honorine pivoted to face them once more, her features gentling. "Begging your pardon, Your Grace, but I'm afraid if Oswald saw you right now, he'd not listen to a word of reason. He blames you for much at the moment, and your presence will only anger him."

Sebastian scowled. "Your presence hasn't precisely pleased him the last few days either."

"That's true." Her blue eyes deepened to a rich cobalt. "Still, he'll not run from me. Nor will he attempt to throttle me as I fear he would you. He'll listen to me."

"But Honorine—" Cordelia protested.

"I won't let either of you come with me," Honorine interrupted gently. "You've had enough turmoil for one night, Cordelia, and the duke would only infuriate Oswald. Let me do this. Alone. I know I can find him, and I know I can talk some reason into him if he's . . . um . . . gotten into any trouble."

This time, she walked resolutely to the door.

Cordelia ran after her and grabbed her arm. "Wait."

When Honorine met her with a questioning expression, Cordelia's voice dropped to a low, mournful murmur. "You'd . . . best check the taverns."

Honorine nodded, her expression quietly sad. She lifted her hand and caressed Cordelia's cheek. "Don't worry, dear girl. It will be all right."

Then she left.

Cordelia stood stiffly in the doorway, watching as Honorine walked down the hall. The sounds of the massive front door opening and closing came to them both, but still she stood in silence.

Without speaking, Sebastian moved to her side and took her in his arms. She accepted his embrace, burying her face against his waistcoat and shuddering under the force of restraining her tears.

"It's all right to cry," he whispered as he stroked first her hair, then her back. "I wouldn't blame you."

"If only he'd stayed. . . ." she said shakily. "He'd have seen that everything worked out at the end. I know him. He's off somewhere thinking he failed me . . . thinking he ruined everything. . . . I-I can't bear him hurting so when he's done so well the last few days. . . ."

That's when she dissolved into tears, soft, mindless sobs that tore at his heart. With each shattering gasp, he clenched her tighter, closing his eyes and cursing himself for ever stepping into her life. If only he'd left her alone—

Then he caught himself. If he'd left her alone, she'd still be at the vicarage, cleaning up her father's vomit, despairing of the day when her father would stop drinking. No, that wouldn't have been good either. But wasn't there some way to halt her pain?

After a moment, she withdrew from him, her tears having subsided to sniffles. Wordlessly he handed his pocket handkerchief to her. She accepted it with a grateful nod and used it to dry her tears and wipe her nose.

A heavy sigh escaped her lips as she lifted her despondent face to his. "We have to talk about what happened tonight." Her voice sounded thin and small, like a wounded child's.

Anguish and sympathy for her tore at his heart. "Not now, we don't. You're distraught and tired and—"

"Now," she insisted. "I have some things to say to you while they're fresh in my mind."

"Cordelia—"

"Please?" Her sweet brown eyes begged him to hear her out.

How could he refuse when her plaintive expression turned him inside out? He groaned, but nodded.

She whispered a thank you and half turned to survey the room with its now empty chairs and the clavichord sitting silent at the other end. "None of them bought our 'parlor trick' for more than a few minutes. It didn't work, and I was mad to think it could."

"That's not true. It worked for a while. In fact, it far exceeded my expectations."

She managed a faint smile. "That only proves how low your expectations were in the first place."

"If that bloody harpsichordist hadn't distracted you—"

"Yes." Her eyes grew icy. "He certainly made himself troublesome, didn't he?"

Sebastian tensed. "When he put his hand on your shoulder, I wanted to break it off."

At the quiet menace in his voice, she looked at him, startled. Then her gaze dropped from his as she twisted his handkerchief in her hand. "I'll agree that he was . . . shall we say . . . a trifle forward."

"A trifle!"

"But I truly can't blame him for what happened. It could as easily have been the squire wanting to engage me in conversation or one of his daughters seeking instruction."

An uneasy feeling stole over him. Where was she going with this?

She met his gaze. "The point is . . . this charade

won't work. And I've already told you Father can't be taught to truly understand music. That leaves us with only one other possibility."

He shook his head. Now he knew exactly where her thoughts were leading. "You mean, tell the truth to my brother. Well, that's unworkable."

"Why? Why is it so impossible?"

"Because the minute Richard knows you're the composer, he'll refuse to present you to Handel, and that will end everything."

She shook her head. "I don't believe he'd do that." She paused a moment, a frown settling into her polished brow. "I know you're wrong. I *know* it." Then her face brightened, and she whirled on her heels. "And I can prove it, too. Come with me." She headed for the door.

"What?" he asked in utter confusion, but when she disappeared from the room, he shook his head and followed her.

With quick, light steps she darted up the stairs. He walked behind her, wondering what on earth she was up to now. When she lifted her skirts and marched down the second-story hall, he had to lengthen his stride to keep up with her. Then she stopped outside her bedchamber, took a candle from the sconce by the door, and entered her room.

He paused on the threshold as she began lighting the candles inside. This was the last place on earth he should be at the moment. Surely she realized that.

Apparently she didn't. "Come in," she insisted and returned to lighting the candles. When she finished, she rummaged through the contents of a bureau drawer, muttering, "Where did that silly maid put them?"

He stepped inside, careful to leave the door open. "Put what?"

"Aha!" she cried, then drew a packet of letters from the drawer and waved them at him.

His eyes narrowed as she undid the ribbon holding

them together. When she tossed the top one to him, he moved closer to the candle on the mantel and stared down at the handwriting on the envelope. It was Richard's.

"Read that," she commanded.

He glanced at her quizzically. She took up the second envelope and opened it, withdrawing a folded sheet of paper.

Quickly she scanned it, then read aloud, " 'This second piece is even more wondrous than your first. Such music coming from a country vicar is remarkable indeed.' "

She threw that letter down and snatched up the third, removing it from its envelope. Her eyes glittered at him as she read, " 'Your chorale would awe even the lowliest of God's creatures. It captured my soul from the first note.' " A glint of humor in her eyes, she muttered, "Your brother should be a poet."

Throwing that letter down, she picked up another, but after scanning it, her mouth drew tight. She tossed it on the bureau without a word.

He reached for it.

"Nay," she said, her gaze averted. "That one has nothing of importance."

With eyebrows raised, he took it up anyway and opened it. She watched him, her breath quickening.

He skimmed the familiar script before reading aloud, " 'Please forgive me, sir, but while I am of course honored that you would wish me to consider your daughter's music for publication, I regret that I must refuse. I have found that women aren't adept at the musical arts. No doubt her work is passable, but I venture to guess it doesn't compare to yours.' "

Sebastian raised his gaze to her and regarded her questioningly.

She blanched, hugging herself. "Lord Kent was merely refraining from involving himself with amateurs. I can't blame him. I—"

"It was more than that, Cordelia, and I suspect if I read through the rest of your letters, I'll find proof of it."

She glanced away from him. "Still, he obviously likes my music a great deal, even if he doesn't know I'm the one who wrote it. He'd *have* to put away his petty prejudices if I told him the truth."

Sebastian's harsh laugh made her flinch. He tossed the letter down on the bureau. "You're not the first woman who's approached him with music for publication, you know."

"I'm sure, but—"

"The first one offered him her body. She was a low sort, but not outwardly so. She made her living playing for the theater, but didn't tell him that, of course." His words were sharp, hard. He had to make her understand, even if it meant revealing his brother's most embarrassing secrets. "Richard was young and foolish. She pretended to be in love with him and let him make love to her. Then after he'd published a couple of her pieces and she'd realized there wasn't much money to be had in it, she told him to go to hell. She had no use for 'cripples,' she said."

Cordelia paled. "What an awful creature! How terrible for Lord Kent!"

He went on relentlessly. "The next woman was a sweet spinster teacher. He was careful with her. She had talent, and he nurtured it. Unfortunately, precisely because she was sweet and a spinster, she had no trouble convincing him to publish one of her more brilliant pieces." His voice grew bitter. "That was the piece that unbeknownst to him had been stolen from another composer, a man. That was the piece that ruined him."

The shock and sympathy in her eyes clutched at his heart. She'd never met Richard, yet she could feel for him. It was her ability to empathize that had enchanted Sebastian in the first place.

"Your brother has had a good deal of bad luck with women musicians, it appears." Desperation made her voice plaintive. "Nonetheless, he must realize that not all women are alike."

"If I could tell you how many women have scorned him because of his twisted legs, you wouldn't say that with such confidence." He drew in a deep breath. "Richard unfortunately always chooses those women most likely to spurn him, or worse yet, destroy him. Then he's wounded when they do. It has made him bitter. These days he tends to see women as deceitful, spiteful bitches who will do almost anything to get what they want."

She blanched. "What about your sisters?"

He forced himself to soften his tone. He *had* laid it on a bit thick, but for her own good. "Oh, Richard's all right with our sisters, but he claims they love him only because they're family. They tease him about his growling." He ventured a smile. "Secretly, I think he likes it, but he's unmercifully strict with them nonetheless. Besides, none of my sisters has shown the least bit of musical talent, so he has no one to refute his beliefs."

She remained silent a long time, staring into the fire that had been lit in the grate by a servant early in the evening. He watched the firelight play over her glossy hair and silky skin. How unfair that her beauty was the only asset society would acknowledge. If she'd had wealth, that would have counted, too, but her talent only helped her if she abandoned gentility and braved the rough ranks of artisans and musicians.

She'd not been raised for such, yet he sometimes feared that she'd enter that realm with only slight provocation. If it weren't for her father, of course, who needed her.

He wanted to go to her and hold her, to comfort her and whisper how sorry he was that life had dealt her such an unfair hand. Yet he dared not. Not as long as he stood in her bedchamber. Too much could happen.

At last she spoke. "What you're saying is that your brother's opinions mustn't be challenged, for if they are, he will abandon his only hope—the offer from Handel."

"Yes. I know my brother better than you do, Cordelia. If he won't take money from me, he'll not take help from you after you've deceived him. He won't risk trusting you."

"Then what solution do you suggest for this dilemma?"

She sounded calm and practical, but he didn't believe for a minute that she was, for her shoulders shook with the effort of keeping up the pretense.

"Tonight's charade might work," he told her, "in a setting where there are no distractions. After all, your presentation for my brother and even for Handel needn't take place with an audience. In a private setting, your scheme might be managed successfully ... if your father could be made a bit more knowledgeable. I think it's workable. In fact, tonight's trial only helped us determine the weak areas. Now we can go on to refine the scheme."

Her voice came to him as an agonized whisper. "So we perform our 'parlor trick' for your brother, we save his delicate feelings, and everything is as before. Is that it?"

For some reason, her words roused a deeply buried guilt. Angry that she could make him feel this way, he said harshly, "Nothing has changed, Cordelia, from when I first spoke to you."

When she turned, firelight glinted off the trail of fresh tears on her cheeks. "No, of course not. My feelings in this are as inconsequential as they were from the beginning."

Bloody hell, was there no way to avoid hurting her? He stepped close enough to touch her. Only by balling his hands into fists at his sides did he refrain from doing so. "Don't you see? 'Tis precisely your feelings I wish to protect. I don't want to see you flayed by my brother's harsh words. I don't want to see you lose your future income with him by exposing your deception."

She stared at him, then paled. "My future income. You mean, my father's future income, don't you? It was all a lie, wasn't it?"

"What the devil do you mean? What was a lie?"

"You said if I did this, you'd make sure Lord Kent published my work under my own name after it was all over. You said you'd make him champion me and that I'd be a musician in my own right. It was the bait you used to get me to come with you." Her voice broke. "But it was all a lie. Your brother will never champion me. He'll keep publishing my music under Father's name as before. He'll champion the reclusive vicar, but he'll never, ever champion me."

Closing his eyes, Sebastian released a low curse. He'd forgotten completely what he'd said at the vicarage in his fervent eagerness to convince her. He forced himself to face her wounded expression. "In truth, I don't know what Richard will do once the charade is done and Handel agrees to help us. When I told you I'd see to it he published your music . . . I was expressing my hope that he'd be so grateful he'd revise his opinion of women and show his gratitude appropriately."

She tilted her chin up, her lips quivering. "What were you planning to do if he didn't?"

"Pressure him to do the right thing." Seeing the pain flash over her face, his tone grew more desperate. "I didn't lie to you. I . . . I merely stretched the truth, but I thought I could make him honor my agreement. I still think I can, but only if we can keep Richard from balking before the visit to Handel."

Looking away from him, she said in a dull monotone, "Stretching the truth . . . lying . . . 'tis all the same."

"I'm not lying to you now, Cordelia. That should prove something. Now you know exactly what you're going to face when you reach London." He paused, half-choking on the words he was going to say, but after tonight he had to say them. "It's not too late for you to return to Belham, to have matters go on as before with you and your father."

She whirled away from him with a hollow laugh. "Except that you'd tell your brother everything, and he'd get angry. Then I'd most certainly lose my publisher."

"Sweet mother of God!" He grabbed her arms, twisting her around to face him. "You think I could do that to you? You truly think I care so little?"

Her solemn eyes met his. Tears glistened in them like crushed jewels on a fawn carpet. "If you cared at all, Sebastian, you'd know what it does to me every time Father is given the credit for my music."

He flinched, the heartbreak in her face nearly destroying his equilibrium. "I think I do know, angel."

A sigh shuddered forth from her. "How could you when you don't even know what it's like to create the music in the first place? To dredge up every loss that has made you weep, then distill it into notes and chords. To search for the most joyous psalm in your soul." Her voice dropped to a whisper. "To awaken in the darkest part of night, your mind exploding with so many unsung melodies there aren't hours enough to capture them nor notes enough to pin them down."

She bent her head. "If you knew what that was like, you'd know how I suffer when Father, who can't even appreciate the delicacy of the smallest trill, gets to claim that music as his."

After her wrenching speech, he couldn't help himself. He laid his hand on the smooth, pale flesh of her shoulder, needing to touch her, to comfort her somehow. "I don't need to know about composing to understand your suffering. It was written all over your face this evening."

He wished he could promise her that he'd see to it that her time came, but he doubted she'd believe him right now.

Her tone was acid. "But your brother's suffering is more important."

"Bloody hell, Cordelia, that's not true. You should know that by now. It's all connected, don't you see? As long as your only publisher is my brother, then what happens to my brother happens to you." He tipped her chin up with one finger. "No matter what you say, I care about you . . . very, very deeply. I don't know how I can convince you of that."

She met his gaze, her face surprisingly calm. Yet her eyes warred with that expression, for they were wild and dark, full of suppressed yearning and pain. The volatile, vulnerable look nearly ripped him apart.

"There is one way you could prove how much you care," she said, her voice quavering.

He hesitated, almost afraid to know what dangerous thoughts churned behind her seemingly calm facade. "What is that?"

Her eyes darkened as her voice dropped to a throaty murmur. "You could make love to me."

Chapter Fifteen

Speak then, and tell the passions of desire;
Which turns mine eyes to floods, my thoughts to fire.
—John Dowland,
"Unquiet Thoughts"

Why had she said such a shocking thing? Cordelia thought, as Sebastian blanched, then whirled from her and stalked to the mantel, bracing himself against it as he stared blindly into the fire.

She sighed. The truth was, she knew why she'd said it. Her future stretched before her like a bleak, dark monotony, filled with endless days tending her drunken father and writing music she could never claim as her own.

She'd had more joy in her week with Sebastian than in three years with her father. Now their time together was coming to an end, and in a few days, they'd be at his estate. Her father would meet Lord Kent and Handel, and it would all be over.

Afterward, what would be left for her? After what Sebastian had told her about his brother, she couldn't delude herself into thinking Sebastian would convince Lord Kent to publish her work in the future. Nor could she believe Sebastian would provide her with an income. The incomparable Judith, biddable though she might be, would never approve of that.

No, things would return to the way they were, and she'd be alone again in Belham. But she could store up memories for that time. She hushed the clamoring voice of conscience in her mind. This was her life, and she wouldn't live it out regretting that she'd let this opportunity pass by.

She came up behind him and lowered her voice. "If you care about me, Sebastian, show me." She slid her arms about his waist, laying her cold cheek against his warm back.

The muscles worked under her hands as Sebastian groaned. "I can't believe you're saying this."

"But I am. I want you to make love to me. I want you to show me you care." When she felt him stiffen, she added, "Please?"

Abruptly he twisted away from her, but his breathing quickened as he stared into her face with an almost desperate expression. " 'Tis precisely because I care that I won't make love to you. You deserve a man who will marry you, who will cherish you the way I have no right to do." Jerking his gaze from hers, he strode for the door. "I won't ruin your future simply because you're feeling hurt and betrayed at the moment."

She rushed to block him from leaving, clutching at his arms as she did so. "Don't you understand? There's not going to be a man to marry me!" Her voice shook with emotion. "Where do you think Father is right now, Sebastian? Where?"

Although his jaw tightened at the mention of her father, he remained silent.

Her fingers dug into his arms. "Your own father didn't resist the call of drink, did he? Father won't either, and you know it. He's out there in some tavern drinking himself sick. Oh, yes, he'll apologize tomorrow and say he'll do better, but nothing will change."

"You don't know that," he gritted out.

"I've been through this before, remember?" She slid her hands down his arms until she reached his hands. Gripping them tightly, she drew them to her waist and settled them there. He held her as if she were a fragile porcelain figurine, sure to break if he clasped her too tightly. And he still wouldn't look at her.

Near desperation, she twined her hands about his

neck and lifted her face to his. "How could you ruin a future that has no husband, no children, and no hope of independence in it? You know I'll not leave Father as long as he needs me." She shuddered. "Yet I must have something to see me through the years of being alone. If you care as much as you say you do, you'll give it to me."

When his eyes fell on her, they were fire in the ice of his expression. "Is that all you want of me? A bloody stallion to assuage your maidenly curiosity?"

His words shattered her. She'd not thought of how he might take her bold proposition, and she'd certainly not expected him to be offended.

But of course, he was. Shame choked her. "I-I didn't mean it like that. . . . I merely meant that . . . Well, you said before that you . . . you implied that you—"

"Desired you?" With infinite slowness, his gaze raked over her. "Aye, I'll not deny it. But I won't give you a night of passion just so you'll have something to remember in the lonely hours. I'm sure you can find any number of men who'll give you that. The harpsichordist, for example."

He'd misunderstood her completely. "I don't want another man. I never wanted any man . . . until you came. Until you touched me. Soon you'll leave, and I'll have nothing. I can't bear it, Sebastian!"

The planes of his face were stark and tight in the firelight. A wild look had entered his amber eyes.

"No one else has ever made me feel these yearnings," she told him, unable to hold back what lay in her heart, yet so very afraid to speak it. If he spurned her now, after she'd shown him her deepest feelings, she'd curl up and die. She bit her lip to hold back the tears. "I wouldn't have . . . made such an awful request if I hadn't thought you felt the same."

Something snapped in him then. With a groan, he dragged her body to his, crushing his mouth against hers with a violence she'd never sensed in him before. As his steely arm imprisoned her waist, he invaded her mouth, plundering it until she clung to him breathlessly.

Then he drew back, a ravaged expression on his face. "Feel the same? Bloody hell, it strikes the soul from my body every time I realize I can never have you."

Sucking in a ragged breath, she stroked his anguished face, scraping her palm against his whiskers. "You can have me for tonight, Sebastian."

His eyes mirrored the flames leaping and shifting behind her. "How can I make love to you and walk away? You know I can't make love to you and stay, for I've a vow to honor."

"I don't care. I need you." It was true. He'd become as necessary to her as bow strings to a violin. "I need you and I want you and—"

"Sweet mother of God," he bit out, then kissed her roughly, exploding fire in her brain. Next thing she knew, he'd kicked the door shut behind them and was branding her face with heated kisses.

"My beautiful, dangerous Cordelia," he murmured, burying his hands in her hair and shaking it loose. Gold hairpins tinkled on the marble floor as he destroyed her coiffure, but she didn't care.

All she cared about was him. She ached to touch him, to explore his body as he'd explored hers. With a feverish urgency, she tugged at his coat, and he shrugged out of it.

"Tomorrow we'll both regret this," he whispered as his fingers quickly unpinned her stomacher from her bodice.

"With us there's no tomorrow. There never has been, so why invent one now? There's only tonight, and that's enough for me."

Freeing her stomacher, he tossed it aside. "It will never be enough for me," he declared fiercely, pausing a moment in his hurried movements to stare at her flushed face. "Can it really be for you?"

No, never, she thought, but dared not say it aloud.

She mustn't think beyond tonight. She would have this night with him. It was better than a lifetime of regrets.

To avoid answering, she deliberately undid her gown at the waist and shoved it down over her petticoat and hoop. Then she pressed her lips to his, and he responded with a moan, taking her mouth with such abandon, she could scarcely breathe.

Her heart pounded beneath her tightly laced corset, and she wished to be free of the accursed garment. As if he could read her mind, he skimmed his hands over her back, finding the knot to her laces and undoing it, then loosening them. At last her corset fell away, leaving her in her shift and petticoat.

But the quilted petticoat dropped away next as his hands roamed her body, untying, unlacing, swift as a knife peeling the skin of an apple. In truth, she felt like a piece of fruit, filled to bursting with sweetness and aching to be tasted.

When her fan hoop collapsed to the floor, the enormity of her action hit her, for as long as the cagelike piece had kept her trapped, she'd felt protected from him. But now she stood in only her stockings and her shift, with its low bodice barely covering the tops of her breasts. She'd never stood so before a man.

After tonight, she told herself bitterly, *you shall never stand so again.*

That thought made her force back any hesitation, any shyness. Like a defiant urchin caught at pilfering, she lifted a determined face to his, refusing to be afraid of what she might glimpse in his eyes when he saw her in just her shift.

But his eyes held such wonder, her breath dried up in her throat. He trailed his gaze over her body, lingering over the swell of her breasts. "I had guessed you would be slender and nicely built." He fitted his hands to her small waist, running them down over her hips. "But you've the figure of an angel, Cordelia. 'Tis a pity to hide such a form beneath petticoats and hoops."

He knelt on one knee before her and lifted the hem

of her shift far enough to reach her garters. Untying
first one, then the other, he slid her stockings down
over her legs and removed them along with her slippers, pausing only to kiss the faint lines the garters had
left on her thighs.

While he knelt, she loosened the tie holding his
queue, running her fingers through his hair as she'd remembered doing when last they'd kissed. Touching his
hair seemed so intimate. In public, one could touch a
man's hand or his arm or even accidentally brush his
thigh and still not be considered improper. But to bury
one's hands in a man's hair . . .

He must have felt the intimacy of it too, for he
turned his face into her hand and kissed the palm before he rose. Emboldened by his response, she strove
for an even closer intimacy. She lifted shaky hands to
his waistcoat, slowly working loose the tiny buttons.

"You have the advantage of me, Your Grace," she
murmured lightly, trying to cover up her burgeoning
excitement at the thought of seeing his bared form.

He went very still, his eyes boring into her as she removed his waistcoat and cravat, then reached for the
ribbon ties at the collar of his shirt. But her hands now
trembled so much with the onrush of desire, she could
scarcely manage the knots.

Misunderstanding her distress, he closed his fist
around one of her hands. " 'Tis not too late to stop, angel." Lifting her hand to his mouth, he kissed each finger. He managed a pained smile. "I know you thought
this was what you wanted, but sometimes the
reality . . ."

He trailed off when her only answer was to urge his
hand to her breast, forcing him to rub his knuckles
lightly over the muslin-covered nipple. With a sound
that was half-growl, half-moan, he jerked her to him,
then lifted her in his arms and carried her to the cano-
pied bed, kissing her every step of the way.

He laid her down beneath the canopy, his eyes flaming as they swept over her body. "You would tempt the

Pope himself," he muttered almost angrily, undoing the buttons of his breeches with a frantic haste. An untamed fierceness had transformed his face, highlighting its wolfish features.

In seconds, he'd doffed his breeches, shirt, and hose, leaving only his form-fitting drawers, and had come to stand beside the bed, gazing down at her.

Rising to kneel at the edge of the bed, she stared in wonder at his well-muscled chest, sprinkled with crisp, dark hair that funneled down his stomach to a flat, firm belly.

With trembling fingers, she stroked the ridges of muscle and sinew that worked beneath the skin as he lifted his hands to her shoulders. Impatiently he brushed her hands aside so he could draw her shift down to her waist.

His breath quickened at the sight of her breasts with their peach-tinged nipples. Slowly he bent and kissed each one, then knelt beside her on the bed and began to caress them in earnest with his mouth, laving them with his tongue and sucking the nipples until she arched up against him. He caught her beneath her back and lifted her to him, fitting his knee between her legs as he trailed hot, sweet kisses over the curve of her neck and the hollow between her breasts.

Suddenly, his hand slipped between her legs to cup her in her most private part. She gasped, half in outrage, half in pleasure, but when he smoothed the thatch of hair with his palm, to her shame she found herself pressing against his rigid hand, rubbing herself against it as she closed her eye in abject enjoyment.

She couldn't help herself. He made her crave his touch in the most unspeakable places. By the time he dipped a finger into her dewy warmth, she was long past caring how "wanton" she might appear to him. Any woman who offered herself to a man would be thought "wanton." She'd accepted that.

But oh, how glorious it was to actually *be* wanton.

"Open your eyes," he whispered against her ear.

With only those words, he put the lie to her bold-
ness. Embarrassed, she shook her head wordlessly,
flinging her hair back from her face as her body shook
and her blood thundered in her ears.

"I want you to see what your pleasure does to me,"
he growled, nibbling at the corners of her lips. His
voice grew more demanding. "Open your eyes for me,
angel."

Slowly she did as he bid, swallowing hard at the
look of raw desire in his face.

"You wanted a night to remember." His eyes smol-
dered. "I want to see to it you remember all of it. I
want you to know what you've done."

With a subtle, sensuous motion, he plunged his finger deep inside her. She nearly shot off the bed in
shock, but he clutched her tightly and drove his finger
in again. As he thrust deeper and deeper, his eyes fixed
on her flushed face, she found she liked the intimate
caress. The more he did it, the more she yearned for
some unattainable goal only half met. When after a
moment, he rubbed his thumb over the petals of skin,
sending exquisite sensations shooting through her, she
cried out, thinking that perhaps the goal wasn't unattainable after all.

Soon she was shamelessly riding his hand, rocking
harder and harder, searching, reaching. Every time a
cry escaped her lips or a moan erupted from her throat,
his gaze darkened and he smiled, a deep, mysterious
smile.

She wanted to look away, but she couldn't, compelled by the erotic force of his gaze, by the taut, hard
passion in his flint-sharp features.

Soon the smile faded from his face. His breathing
quickened, and his eyes grew bleak. He must be ready
to explode with wanting her, she thought, yet he didn't
take her.

Something was wrong, she thought dimly, but
couldn't think what it was, for her mind lost its bear-
ings and now wandered in some tempestuous, thunder-

ing sea. Mindlessly, she dug her fingernails into his shoulders and arched back against the arm that clasped her.

With unexpected suddenness, waves of pleasure crashed over her, sucking her into a vortex of drowning sweetness. He was her only anchor, and she clung to him as unfamiliar sensations whirled through her body, wiping out all thoughts of anything but him and the incredible magic of his fingers.

It was only after she'd collapsed against his arm that he withdrew from her, laying her back on the damask coverlet. Slowly rational thought returned, and it came to her with a sudden jolt what he meant to do. He was trying to fulfill her wishes while still keeping her virginity intact. That was why he hadn't removed his drawers, why he'd brought her to such rapture and taken none of his own.

She knew there was more to lovemaking. Thankfully, her mother and Honorine, both eminently sensible women, had explained to her something about how women were bedded. She remembered enough of what they'd said to know that Sebastian hadn't made love to her. Not completely.

As he eased off the bed, she sat up and clutched him around the waist. "No, not yet," she whispered as she rose to her knees. "I want all of you, Sebastian."

He cursed. "You don't know what you want," he growled, his hands hard against her shoulders as he tried to push her away.

"Yes, I do." She dragged her hand down over the clenched muscles of his waist to his drawers. Swiftly she unbuttoned them. "I want you." She yanked the drawers down over his hips and let them slither to the floor, keeping her eyes on his tormented expression.

Their gazes locked for an endless moment. Finally, he said in a steely voice, "Virgins never know what they want." He glanced down at her upturned face, then lower at his own body, and gave a mocking laugh. "Bloody hell, you're such an innocent, you can't even bring yourself to look at the instrument supposed to do the dirty deed."

That much was true. The very thought of staring at his private parts frightened her inexplicably. All Honorine and her mother had said about a man's member was that it "grew excessively firm" when he was aroused, whatever that meant.

But if looking at him was what it took to make him see she truly meant her words, she'd do it. Timidly she dropped her gaze along the furred plane of his chest to the whorled hair at his navel and then lower to where the hair grew thick around . . .

Her eyes widened and a soft gasp escaped her lips.

"Touch me," he said hoarsely as he witnessed her response.

She did as he asked, running her fingers lightly along the silky skin, then enclosing his hard shaft. He sucked in his breath, his entire body going rigid as she explored him in timid fascination.

When her strokes grew bolder, he snapped.

"Sweet mother of God, Cordelia," he gasped out, then pressed her back onto the bed, following her down and covering her with his body. She had but a few moments to relish the brush of his naked skin against hers and the scent of brandy mingled with sweat that clung to him, before he'd spread her legs with his knees and was pressing his long, firm shaft between her thighs.

He paused, resting most of his weight on his arms as he fixed her with glittering amber eyes. "You want this," he said flatly, apparently unable to make it a question, though she supposed he meant it as one.

Her mouth went dry as she nodded.

"Then you've made your choice. Regret it later if you will, but you're mine now."

With those words, he inched into her until he met her virginal barrier. He hesitated, and she thrust her hips upward, feeling the tear as he was buried deep inside her. As she recoiled from the instant pain, he captured her mouth, muffling her cry. He paused a moment, kissing her senseless and allowing her to adjust to his invading maleness.

Cordelia didn't know if she liked this new sensation. Although it had a certain enticing appeal, it made her uncomfortable and sore. It had been much better when he used his finger, she thought.

Until he moved.

His eyes blazing with desire, he slid in and out in slow, sure strokes that drove out her soreness, replacing it with a thrumming awareness of his every movement—the plunge of his hips, the silken brush of his lips across her mouth, the caress of his chest against her sensitive nipples. Like the most talented of musicians, who knew how to use both firm and soft touches to wrest from his instrument awe-inspiring harmonies, Sebastian elicited from her body a tempestuous, wild music.

She wound her arms about his neck and gave herself up to the erotic power of his body's song, heedlessly raising her own hips to meet his in a delightful duet.

"That's it," he murmured hoarsely as his pace increased. "Show me what's in your heart tonight, my angel. Show me, and only me."

She did, revealing her feelings more fully and completely than when she was playing the clavichord. The rhythm between them became so instinctual, so right, that Cordelia knew she'd made no mistake in giving herself to him. In a counterpoint of kisses, caresses, and silken thrusts, they played each other's bodies, keeping time to the thundering of their hearts, the two of them surging and swelling in a quickening cadence until the room faded and there was only the night of their private enjoyment.

"Sebastian . . . my dear, dear Sebastian!" she exclaimed as she went taut as a violin string and hurtled once more into ecstasy. He gave one glorious, final thrust, burying himself so deeply within her, she thought she might never be freed of him.

He shuddered with the force of his release, and she

shuddered with him, her own release so intense she shook all over. Then slowly, achingly, they descended into normalcy.

He lay there atop her a few moments. She closed her eyes, savoring his weight on her. After a while, she became aware of other things—the settling of a log in the fireplace, the scent of rosewater emanating from the sheets, the ticking of a clock in some far-off room.

Opening her eyes, she glanced down to where her breast pillowed his head. His eyes were closed, but he wore an expression less of contentment than of regret. Fear intruded on her enjoyment then, and she ran trembling fingers over his stony cheek, longing to wipe away the remorse that had settled into his features.

Tenderly he covered her hand with his, then groaned and rolled off her to lie at her side on his back.

"Sebastian?" she whispered.

No sound came from him. Alarmed at the thought that he might have fallen asleep in her bed, she rose to one elbow and stared down at him.

But he was awake, his eyes gazing bleakly up at the bed canopy.

She laid her hand on his chest. "Are you angry at me?"

He stroked her fingers absently. "No. Only at myself."

"You shouldn't be angry with yourself." She started to touch his face, but the clatter of hooves in the street outside the house shifted her attention from him. She sat up and dragged the sheet to her breasts, holding her breath until the hooves passed by the house.

"You have to leave," she whispered, "before Honorine and Father return and find you here."

He met her worried gaze with a resigned one. "That hardly matters now, wouldn't you say? We'll be marrying as soon as I can obtain a special license, so it makes no difference if they find us together tonight."

"Marrying! What do you mean?" His words ought to make her happy, but something about the solemn way he said them struck her with dread.

He sat up and ran his fingers over the bloodstain on the sheets, his regret carved in the marble of his expression. "I don't make a practice of deflowering virgins and abandoning them, Cordelia. You were my first virgin, and I will, of course, do the right thing and marry you."

Her stomach sank. He spoke no words of love or even of mutual affection. This was a duty to him like all his others. That was all.

"You can't marry me," she said in a small voice.

"Why not?"

"For one thing, you're a duke and I'm a vicar's daughter."

His hard laugh chilled her. "I promise that wouldn't bother a soul. The first duke of Waverley was the bastard son of Charles II and an actress, and the second duke, my father, married a publican's daughter. Marrying you would be a step up for my family."

"But you're engaged to another."

He gritted his teeth. "Aye, I'm engaged to another. That will have to be dealt with."

"Sebastian, I didn't intend you to marry me when I asked you to make love to me. I certainly wouldn't want you to do so . . ." she half-choked on the words, "when you love someone else."

This time his laugh was genuinely bitter. "Love someone else? I'm not in love with Judith and never have been."

Her relief was palpable, and it was all she could do to keep it from showing. Still, if he didn't love Judith, why was he behaving as if Cordelia had just destroyed his life? "It was an arranged marriage then?"

"Yes, in a way." He stared at her a long moment, then explained about the Baron Quimley, who'd rescued the Kent family from certain financial ruin. Her dread grew the more he talked.

As if to block her from his vision, he closed his eyes. "It isn't the money he loaned me that matters. I could pay him back easily now. But he asked only one thing of me in return for his help—that I marry his daughter and make her a duchess—and I vowed to do so."

"Then-then you must keep your vow," she somehow managed to say.

His eyes shot open to flash her an angry glance, but his expression gentled when he saw her bloodless face. "If I keep my vow to Baron Quimley, angel, I must abandon you, and I can't do that."

"You're not abandoning me. I told you this was what I wanted—one beautiful night. You gave it to me, and I thought you understood. When I . . . when I made my request, I didn't mean for it to end with your marrying me. I knew it couldn't end that way." She forced as much sincerity into her words as she could manage. "I don't want you to marry me, Sebastian."

He raised one eyebrow. "What if you have a child?"

The question struck her with ominous force. The thought that he might give her a child hadn't once occurred to her in the midst of all their lovemaking.

With a shake of his head, he bit out, "You don't think of these things. I do. I've always fully understood what would be the consequences of making love to you. I knew it would mean being forsworn . . . and dishonoring myself before Baron Quimley." His mouth formed a grim line as he lifted his hand to brush her hair back from her face. "But tonight I didn't care. It seemed worth it all to have you. Therefore, angel, we *will* be married."

Tonight . . . It seemed worth it all . . . The words pierced her. While she'd been seducing him, it had "seemed" worth it, but now he was having second thoughts.

Heaven knew she wanted to marry him, but if she were to let him marry her at the cost of his honor and pride, there would be no happiness for them. She knew that as surely as she knew suddenly that she loved him.

She loved him. Her heart swelled with the knowledge of it. Merciful heavens, how she loved him. She loved his controlling manner and his gentleness and his self-restraint. But one of the things she loved most of all about him was his sense of honor and duty.

Honor and duty. She'd grown to hate those words, yet they meant even more to him than they'd meant to her. If she stripped him of his honor, he would be half a man, and he'd hate her for it all his days. His present anger was just the beginning of it.

Besides, he didn't love her, she thought, forcing herself to accept the truth. Perhaps he didn't love his fiancée either, but at least he had a real obligation to Judith. His only obligation to Cordelia came from a perverse desire to protect her reputation. He didn't love her, and if he married her out of duty, she'd be as unhappy as he.

Her only choice was to convince him that his duty did *not* lie in marrying her.

"You must stop speaking of marriage for us," she said flatly. "I won't marry you, and that's the end of it."

His eyes narrowed. She avoided his gaze, rising from the bed to find something to cover her. As she moved numbly about the room, searching for her wrapper, she could feel his eyes following her every move.

"You have no choice in this." His voice was tight. "If you refuse me, I'll simply tell your father what happened tonight. I assure you he'll make you marry me after that."

"You wouldn't!" she cried in horror, pivoting to face him. "I-I'll deny it . . . I'll tell him you simply want to destroy my honor . . . I'll—"

"I think you'd have trouble denying it when your virginal blood stains these sheets. Someone is bound to notice, don't you think?"

She clapped her hand over her mouth. How could he be so cruel? Had he no concern for her feelings, for how it would humiliate her to have him reveal this to her father? No, of course not. All he cared about was salving his unwarranted guilty conscience.

His expression softened. "There's no point in your being noble, Cordelia. All that talk about having one night to remember the rest of your life was absurd. If you didn't realize it, at least I did. Virgins don't do such things."

She increased her efforts to find her wrapper, almost insanely wanting to cover herself from his eyes. Stumbling across it at last, she jerked it around her and fought for the strength to do and say what she had to.

" 'Virgins don't do this,' and 'Virgins don't do that,' " she mimicked. Forcing a haughty demeanor to her face, she whirled on him. "For a man who's never had a virgin before tonight, you're awfully sure of what they can and can't do."

He rose from the bed, blissfully undisturbed by his own nakedness. She only wished she could be as undisturbed. Seeing him standing there in all his full male glory vividly brought back every intimate moment they'd shared.

Fixing her eyes on his rigid face, she forced them not to linger over his broad shoulders and sinewy arms and . . . "Besides," she snapped, "who said I was being noble? If I had wished to marry before now, I would have. 'Tis not on mere whim that I've refused all my previous suitors. Or did you think I had no suitors?"

He stepped toward her. "Your father's situation has prevented your marrying, but there's no need for it to do so now. I can more than adequately provide for him."

The sudden gentleness in his expression nearly undid her. It had been easy to resist his appeals when they were made in anger, but this considerate, kind Sebastian was the one she'd fallen in love with, and *he* was nearly impossible to resist.

But resist him she would. "That wasn't the only reason I never married. I told you from the beginning that I wanted to be an independent woman. Why should I relinquish my freedom to a man who'll expect me to cater to his every whim, when I have relative freedom in my father's house?"

She felt sure he could see through her patent lies,

but he watched her with a chilling silence that tore at her heart.

She drove another nail into the coffin of her hopes. " 'Tis true that I find you immensely attractive, Sebastian. And of course, you're a wonderful lover. But marry you? Why would I marry you and give up my chance at being a composer, at being independent?"

His face darkened. "I wouldn't keep you from writing your music, and you know it. I'd do all in my power to aid you."

"It wouldn't be the same thing," she said stoutly. "I can't prove myself if everyone is saying 'tis merely because of my husband that I've succeeded. I must do it on my own for it to mean anything."

He went very still, his hands balling into fists. "Is that truly what you want? To make your living alone among pompous choristers and raucous musicians?"

She tossed her hair back in faked nonchalance. "Of course. You know that having my music succeed means everything to me."

She forced herself to meet his gaze impassively as his expression grew frozen, his eyes icy shards in his anger.

"So all that rot about never being able to marry and wanting one night to remember was merely your sordid way of seducing me."

She couldn't speak words of agreement. That was expecting too much of her self-control. So she managed a shrug and hoped he would take it and her silence for consent.

To her horror, he came closer, stopping a few inches from her and lowering his voice to a bitter growl. "And I wasn't wrong when I said you only wanted a stallion to assuage your maidenly curiosity."

You were wrong! she wanted to cry out and had to bite the inside of her lip to keep silent.

He was near enough to touch her, but he didn't. She knew if she touched him, even lightly, he'd ignore all her words, pull her into his arms and renew his proposal. So she struggled against the insane urge to caress his cheek.

Instead she faced his accusing gaze with apparent unconcern, a part of her dying as the light of pleasure faded completely from his face. "I see. Well, I must give you credit, Cordelia. You were well worth bedding, virgin or no." He paused, his gaze raking her thinly clad body with blatant insolence. "In fact, I should have taken you seriously when you called yourself a wanton. You could give lessons to a courtesan."

Her stomach churned, and she feared she'd be sick. *Later,* she told herself desperately. *Later you can be as sick as you must.*

When he got no response from her, he slid by her and gathered his clothes, then strode for the door. She pivoted, watching incredulously as he opened it, his clothes held casually in a bundle in his hand.

"Sebastian! You can't go out there like that ... I mean ... what if someone sees you ... ?"

"What does it matter? You've already said you won't marry me, and I know you can wrap your father about your little finger with no trouble, so I doubt he'll squawk too much when you tell him I was merely an interesting erotic experiment."

She couldn't help the words that tumbled from her mouth. "Sebastian, please wait."

He hesitated in the doorway, his body stiff with rage.

"I-I didn't mean to hurt you," she said in a voice barely a whisper.

For a moment, fury so transformed him she feared he'd strike her, and she backed up a step. Then he said through gritted teeth, "If there's a child, let me know, and I'll provide for it. Otherwise, stay away from me. This time I mean it. Because the next time you play at seduction with me, you'll find out what it's like to tempt a beast. And I know you'd find it extremely unpleasant."

As soon as he slammed the door behind him, she dropped to her knees and burst into tears. She cried for him, for his wounded pride, and she cried for the loss of her hopes. But most of all, she cried for herself.

Chapter Sixteen

If the heart of a man is deprest with cares,
The mist is dispelled when a woman appears.
　　　　　　　—John Gay,
　　　　　　　　　The Beggar's Opera (air 21)

Honorine had nearly reached the end of her tether. Five taverns and no sign of Oswald. Worse yet, according to the last proprietor, Oswald had appeared earlier but had bought a bottle of wine and left.

She stood in the midst of a darkened street and gazed about her in frustration. Oswald could be anywhere. He might even have returned to her house.

No, that made no sense. Why would he buy a bottle of wine in a tavern and return to her house when he could easily take a bottle from her cellar? As she trudged up the street, she wondered what to do. 'Twas obvious he wasn't in a public place, but where could he have gone?

Then she noticed the faint glow of light coming from the windows on one corner of her parish church. The church. Could he have gone there? Hope leapt within her. It was probably the rector attending to some forgotten duty, yet she hastened her steps as she turned into the path leading to the church.

The heavy oak door stood ajar. Slowly she pushed it open, noting that the glow came from a brace of candles lit near the front pew. Peering in that direction, she frowned. No one seemed to be there. Nonetheless, she had nowhere else to try, so she walked up the aisle.

Five pews from the front, she suddenly caught sight

of a man's bent form in the front pew. Silently, she crept forward, her heart clicking almost as loudly as her boot heels on the marble.

When she stood even with the front pew, the man lifted his head. It was Oswald.

Her hands began to tremble as a rush of relief overwhelmed her. She hadn't known what to expect when she'd set out in search of him, but it hadn't been to find him meditating in a church.

Then she noticed the bottle of wine he held tightly clenched in his hand. She could see that the cork had been removed, but she couldn't tell how much of the wine he'd drunk, if any.

He surprised her when he spoke in a steady voice. "Come to fetch me, have you?" He hadn't even looked at her, although he'd obviously heard her footsteps.

She tried to make her tone even and calm, when all she wanted to do was berate him for alarming both her and Cordelia. "It was either fetch you myself or send the duke after you, and I doubted you'd want that."

At the sound of her voice, he visibly started, half turning to meet her gaze. "Honorine?"

Obviously he'd expected Cordelia. A scowl spread over his wide brow. "Why did Cordelia send you? Is the gel so angry with me she couldn't bear the sight of me?"

Honorine bristled. Sometimes men had no brains at all. "I could hardly allow her to wander about an unfamiliar city at night, could I? As for her being angry . . . she's worried sick, but I don't think she's angry." Honorine let her gaze rest meaningfully on the bottle. "At least not yet."

When he said nothing to that, merely sighing, she added, "May I sit? It appears we're going to be here a while."

Wordlessly, he slid over to make space for her on the pew. As she sat down beside him, she reached for the bottle of wine, and he let her take it from him. Another shudder of relief rocked her when she realized it was full. She set it gingerly beside the pew and waited for him to speak.

They sat there a long time in silence, long enough for her to notice the stained-glass window opposite them. It was her favorite, a depiction of the Biblical story of Ruth. Lately, she'd thought of Ruth a lot—the woman who married again when she'd thought her life as a wife was over. How bitterly ironic, Honorine thought, that she should now sit opposite that very window with Oswald.

Suddenly he spoke, jolting her from her unpleasant thoughts. "I ruined everything for her again tonight, didn't I?" He gazed forward at the altar, his forearms resting on his thighs.

"I wouldn't say that. After you stormed out, I convinced my guests that the whole thing was a bet between me and His Grace to see if they could detect an imposter. They decided in short order that it had been a great game, and then made Cordelia play her pieces until her fingers were sore. You see? You should have stayed for the grand finale."

He shook his head, a half-smile crossing his worn features. "That's so like you, Honorine. I'll wager the lot of them will wake up tomorrow still befuddled, trying to figure out exactly what happened."

"Probably. In any case, no one blames you, and certainly not Cordelia. The scheme was ill-conceived from the start, and if I'd had an ounce of brains about me, I'd have realized it."

"It's that blasted duke," Oswald snapped. "Him and his loyalty to family. He's dragging Cordelia through this torment just so he can save his idiot brother. I swear, any man as narrow thinking as Lord Kent deserves to lose his business."

"Perhaps. But Cordelia feels obligated to go through with it."

"Aye," he grumbled. "I should have put my foot down from the beginning. I should never have let her do this."

"Why did you?" Honorine had been dying to hear Oswald's side of things, but until now he'd always managed to avoid being alone with her.

Her question seemed to return him to the morose state she'd found him in. "I haven't done right by Cordelia these past three years, Honorine. The gel deserves much more than I've given her. She's had more than her share of troubles with me. After Florinda died, I . . . I began drinking heavily. It's been a bad time for her. So when she wanted this chance to meet Handel, I couldn't refuse her. In truth, it's only been on this trip that I've stopped drinking."

To her surprise, he suddenly told her everything— how life at the vicarage had been for the past three years, how he'd drunk too much and let Cordelia take over his responsibilities, and how Cordelia had confronted him at last and washed her hands of him.

Honorine listened in silence, murmuring a word of encouragement here and there. When he finished, she could read the remorse in his eyes. Clearly, he'd finally come to realize how much he'd hurt his daughter. Still, when she'd entered the church, he'd been clutching the bottle of wine as if his life depended on it.

She struggled for words, knowing that it was none of her business if he still chose to drink, yet needing to know. "Oswald?"

"Yes?"

She gestured to the bottle on the floor. "Why didn't you drink the wine after going to the trouble to buy it?"

An acid smile tipped up the edges of his full mouth. "It was a strange thing. I came here, because I thought no one would look for me here. I came so I could drink myself into sweet oblivion. I told myself that the Lord would understand, that he turned the water into wine, but deep inside I knew He wouldn't approve.

"Knowing that only made it worse, so I sat here holding the bottle, pitying myself for being a poor vicar and an even poorer father, hating myself for being unable to get a blasted thing right. I even opened the bottle. When I caught the first whiff, I suddenly saw Cordelia as she was that day at the inn." He paused, his eyes growing pensive. "You know what I remembered?"

"What?"

"Not the sadness in her eyes nor the accusation on her face. Nor even her humiliation when that fool Prudence lashed at her with her tongue." His jaw went tight. "I remembered that through that awful hour, all I could think of was how badly I wanted a drink, how angry I was that she'd dumped out my brandy. My mind worked at figuring out how to get more spirits without Cordelia finding out."

His expression was so bleak, she could hardly bear it. She wanted so badly to touch him, to comfort him, yet she didn't want to distract him from the confession he obviously needed to make.

After a moment, he continued. "It was only later . . . when I realized she fully intended to go to London without me that I understood how much I'd hurt her. Then it took a few days of sobriety before I understood how thoroughly the drink had entangled me.

"So I sat here with the wine, thinking over all that and staring at the altar. I thought about the promises I'd broken between me and Cordelia and me and God. I remembered how Florinda kept me from liquor because she knew what it did to me and how Cordelia had tried to follow in her steps. Suddenly, I was so . . . sick of myself, sick that I couldn't keep away from drink without a woman's hand."

He squeezed his eyes shut and buried his face in his hands. "Still, even while I thought these things, I wanted that wine. I wanted it so badly I could taste the sweet burn on my lips." His voice grew choked. "Truth be told, I want the blasted wine now."

She couldn't bear it anymore. She laid her hand on his shoulder, squeezing it tightly.

He didn't even seem to notice. "I poured some of it

in my hand, just a little, a few drops, and sniffed it like a thirsting animal."

He lifted his head, and she withdrew her hand.

"I sniffed my hand, savoring the smell, until the smell faded." A smile crossed his face, a genuine one. "Then it came to me. If I drank that wine, the pleasure of it would last as long as its smell on my hand. True, it would drown out my sorrows for a night, but they'd return in force on the morrow, except I'd have a blasted headache and I'd have shamed myself before Cordelia and God once more. Then I'd need a lot more wine the next night to forget my lapse, and even more the night after that." He sighed. "That's when I decided it wasn't worth it, after all."

Her heart swelled with pride and love for him. The only words she could manage, however, were "I'm glad."

He shrugged. "I don't know, Honorine, how long this . . . abstinence will last. I fear that bottle now as much as I craved it before. It's got a power over me that's stronger sometimes than even my love for Cordelia and my faith in God."

She fought the urge to hold him, forcing her voice to carry the weight of her sympathy. "Then you must increase the love and the faith until they're stronger. They can enable you to fight it. And if you should falter one night, simply pick yourself up and fight again."

She smiled. "You're not so different from other people, you know. People crave all sorts of things besides liquor—money, power, fame. Yet once they get what they crave, they find it wasn't what they wanted after all. Instead of seeing the truth, however, they seek more and more of that thing they don't want until they either destroy themselves or finally realize their true need lies elsewhere."

When he fixed her with questioning eyes, she shifted her gaze to the floor, suddenly aware she was no longer talking about him, but about herself.

He seemed to realize it as well. "You know,

Honorine, you never answered my question earlier this evening. About whether marrying Beardsley was worth it." His low, sonorous voice thrummed in her ears. "Are you answering it now?"

She sighed. "I suppose I am." She hesitated, then straightened her shoulders. Now that he'd bared his soul to her, she should give him the answer he craved. He deserved some satisfaction after the way she'd jilted him. "If it's any consolation, Oswald, you were right years ago when you warned me that a marriage built on the flimsy foundations I sought couldn't make me happy." She flashed him a self-mocking smile. "So was it worth it? I'm not sure it was."

When he remained silent, she plunged on. "Don't misunderstand me. Robert and I had a congenial marriage. He didn't beat me or treat me with disdain."

"I hadn't thought him the type to do that, or I'd never have let you marry him. If anything, he seemed the kind to let you have your way too much."

Her voice grew brittle. "I suppose you could put it that way. In truth, he didn't much care at all what I did. He wanted a beautiful wife to grace his table. That was all. The quiet demeanor he presented in courting me, which I'd imagined hid great depths of feeling, simply hid a very dull mind. Shortly after our marriage, we found our own pursuits. We only saw each other occasionally—when we entertained and when he felt the urge to—"

She broke off, unable to discuss that aspect of marriage with him. A shaky sigh escaped her lips. "I suppose we rubbed along tolerably well together . . . but there wasn't much feeling between us. After a while, I remembered that for all my family's difficulties with money, my mother had been quite happy with my lowly tailor father."

With a hint of defiance, she tilted her chin up and met his gaze, expecting to see smugness in it. But he regarded her with his steady scholar's eyes, his mouth a grim line.

"So you see," she continued, rather unsteadily, "I realized my mistake in the end. As it happens, you were far more blessed in your second choice than I was in my first." She swallowed her pride. "Hearing me say that should . . . satisfy your sense of justice for years to come."

He rubbed his chin, then shook his head. "I never wanted you to be unhappy, Honorine. You hurt me, yes, by refusing my suit, especially since I knew you loved me, even if you wouldn't admit it. But eventually I accepted it as God's path for me, and I certainly never wished you to suffer from your decision."

He shifted his gaze from hers. "When you used to visit Florinda, looking more and more brittle each time, I hurt for you. I watched you grow into what seemed like a shallow, unfeeling woman, and I mourned the loss of what you'd been, not knowing that the real woman still lay buried inside."

A smile graced his features. He reached for her hand, cradling it in his. "When I saw you here, I realized that your husband's death had freed you to be yourself again . . . that you hadn't changed at all."

Her breathing had nearly stopped. The way he stroked her hand gave her a hope she tried to squelch, but couldn't.

He was silent a moment, tracing the blue veins that lay beneath the surface of her translucent skin. "Honorine, I have something to say to you that you mustn't misinterpret." He drew in a deep breath. "I loved Florinda with all my heart. She was a good woman, more suited to me than I would have imagined. If she hadn't meant so much to me, I wouldn't have mourned her loss so bitterly, and in the process risked losing Cordelia's affection."

Without warning, he gripped her hand tightly, lifting his eyes to meet hers. They blazed with an emotion she'd never thought to see in them again, an emotion so strong it almost frightened her. "But I never stopped loving you either, or at least loving the woman I'd once known."

She gambled everything to murmur, "I've always loved you, Oswald."

A flush spread over his face, and for a moment, he looked as if he'd smile. Instead, he drew his bushy eyebrows together in a deep frown. "The thing is, there's a greater gap between us now than when we were young. You have power and wealth while I've been reduced to relying on my daughter for funds . . . although I plan to change that."

His hands squeezed the blood from hers. Did she dare hope he'd say what she wanted? She held her breath, fighting to keep silent. For once she mustn't rush or control the conversation. This was too important to botch.

He dragged in a heavy breath. "But even though I'm giving up the drink and planning to take back control of my parish and be a real vicar again, I'll never be wealthy. I have no desire to be and never have. You, on the other hand, have a fortune, a wonderful mansion, a thousand influential friends—"

"None of them have made me happy," she whispered. The time to speak had come, and she wouldn't let this chance pass her by again. "I would give every one of them up if, for example, you would . . . take me in your arms and kiss me . . . right now."

His lips parted as he stared at her disbelievingly. "Honorine, 'tis not as simple as all that. There's so much—"

"Please, Oswald?" Never in her life had she begged for anything, but she was begging now. Her female intuition told her that if she could simply get him to hold her . . . "Please kiss me? Once? For old times' sake?"

He groaned and glanced away, and for a moment, she feared she'd lost him. Then his gaze snapped back to hers, as fierce and intent as any young man's, and he muttered, "Blast it all, woman," before he pulled her into his arms.

The years melted away. Once more, they were in the garden of her father's house, standing behind the willow to avoid her mother's watchful gaze as they stole a kiss. Nothing had changed.

Yet everything had changed. Now they both had experience . . . quite a lot of experience she realized as he kissed her with a warmth and ease he'd lacked as a raw young man. She found she liked it. Very much.

After several long moments, he drew back to stare at her, wonder and latent desire in his eyes. "I have no right to ask you this, love, but—"

"Yes," she whispered, this time too impatient to wait for his cautious words. "Yes, Oswald. This time I'll most certainly marry you."

He laughed, and the sound rang joyously in the empty church. "You always were a bold one, Honorine. And I thank the good Lord that some things never change." Then he bent to kiss her once more as she echoed his words in her thoughts.

And in front of them the stained-glass picture of Ruth seemed to smile.

Alone in his room once more, Sebastian dressed in a furious frenzy, jerking on his warmest clothing in anticipation of having to go out after Mrs. Beardsley and Reverend Shalstone, who'd taken too long to return.

Entirely too long, he thought bitterly. If it hadn't been for Mrs. Beardsley's insistence on going out after the vicar alone, Sebastian wouldn't be standing here cursing himself for bedding a heartless woman.

How had Cordelia managed to stand before him after they'd engaged in the most passionate lovemaking of his life and flippantly announce she wouldn't marry him? Sweet mother of God, when he thought of how easily she'd seduced him. . . .

Stopping beside the fireplace, he stared at the flames. None of the whole bloody night made sense. When he'd gone to her room, she'd been so sweet, so anguished in her plea for him to make love to her. It was impossible to reconcile that adorable Cordelia with the one who'd stood there afterward claiming that she wanted her independence. The second Cordelia had been a coldhearted seductress desiring only to slake her thirst on the first man who'd agreed to satisfy her.

Still, that second Cordelia had been a virgin. He squeezed his eyes shut, seeing again the bloodstain on the sheets. No doubt about it, Cordelia had been a virgin, for he'd felt her hymen tear as surely as he'd seen the blood.

Oh, but what a virgin, he thought, unable to hold back other memories . . . of satiny skin, ripe sweet nipples, hair that tumbled over his hands like crushed velvet, and a body created expressly for love. Untaught and inexperienced, she'd brought him more pleasure in one short hour than he'd found in all his years in England and India.

He cursed aloud when he grew hard once more. If he hadn't made that bumbling proposal, he thought, he'd be making love to her again right now, more slowly and with infinitely more finesse.

That damned proposal. What a fool he'd been to ask her to marry him. He'd known she didn't want that—not independent, talented Cordelia. But his bloody sense of fair play had assaulted him with a vengeance the minute he'd come to his senses and realized he'd ruined her.

A sound in the hall put an abrupt end to his bitter thoughts. Stealthily, he went to his door and opened it a crack, gazing the length of the hall.

Cordelia was leaving her room. Now she wore one of her own plain, wrapped gowns, cinched at the waist with a belt and devoid of hoop and petticoats, and her glorious hair was stuffed beneath a mob cap. What's more, her hands were filled with sheets.

He went rigid at the sight. Of course, she'd have to get rid of the sheets, wouldn't she? She'd have to destroy the evidence of her scandalous behavior, especially after he'd threatened to show them to her father.

He watched as she came toward him along the dimly lit hall, heading for the top of the center staircase. She passed under a brace of candles, which for a second lit her face brightly. What he saw there stunned him— eyes puffy, cheeks pale, a reddened nose. In short, a face ravaged by tears.

He stood in silence as she rounded the staircase and began to descend, her steps heavy. Then he shut his door and leaned against it, his throat tight with pain.

Why would a woman who'd merely wanted an intro- duction to the pleasures of love be crying her eyes out now that it was over? He *had* said some cruel things to her, but nothing that wasn't true.

That is, nothing that wasn't true *if* she'd been telling the truth about why she didn't want to marry him. But what if she'd been lying? He thought a moment, his eyes narrowing. She'd only made her feverish protesta- tions after he'd revealed his indebtedness to Baron Quimley, after he'd also made it clear that he now felt duty bound to marry her.

He groaned, guilt washing over him in waves, and for the first time since he'd left her room, he replayed the entire conversation with as much honesty as he could bear. The picture it painted of him wasn't the best one. First he'd told her they would marry with no mention of how he felt about her. Then he'd threatened to show her sheets to her father, and in essence, to hu- miliate her. Never had he proclaimed that he *wanted* to marry her, despite all the trouble it would cause with the Quimleys.

Devil take it, he'd made a mess of proposing, hadn't he? It was just that she'd taken him so completely off guard. Their lovemaking, wonderful as it had been, *had* altered all his plans for the future, and in truth, he'd been furious at himself for succumbing to tempta- tion. He'd thought guiltily of Judith and his vow to Baron Quimley . . . and he'd secretly been glad that he now *had* to break the engagement. That had been what made him angriest of all, his private delight in thinking that he could finally marry Cordelia. It had increased his guilt tenfold and had made him wonder if he'd intended the seduction all along.

Then to compound everything, in his fury at himself, he'd acted as if marrying her would be some sort of necessary torture. A woman like Cordelia wouldn't want to marry a man who considered her a nuisance. A woman like Cordelia would do the noble thing. And a woman like Cordelia would certainly destroy the evidence of her indiscretion in order to protect both her and her lover from discovery.

A sudden awareness slammed into him. Half in panic, he pushed away from the door, then jerked it open. If Cordelia got rid of those sheets, he'd have no evidence at all that he'd bedded her. It would be his word against hers if it came to convincing her father to force her to marry him.

He'd already moved into the hall when what he was about to do hit him. He was attributing to her the intentions he wanted. Perhaps she genuinely *didn't* want to marry him. If he appeared out of nowhere demanding those sheets, and she really had meant everything she'd said, it would cause him more pain than he could stand.

Yet he couldn't believe she'd meant those words. The image of a cold, calculating Cordelia determined to find her pleasure without considering his feelings didn't mesh with the Cordelia who'd let her father take advantage of her because she couldn't bear to hurt him.

She simply wasn't a cruel woman.

But he still couldn't get those sheets from her, not until he was sure. There might be some truth to what she'd said about wanting her independence. She'd said that when he'd first approached her in Belham, too. If she were unwilling and he forced her to marry him, they'd both regret it.

As he stood in the hall, his head began to pound with a monstrous headache. The only way to settle this problem was to figure out the truth. He still had a few days to watch and wait for her to slip and reveal her true feelings.

Besides, that would also give him time to decide what to do about Judith. He couldn't marry her, that was certain, not now. Making love to Cordelia had shown him that. He couldn't deny Judith the chance to find a man who'd give her his whole heart, not a piece of it. Judith deserved better.

So what now? Well, if he couldn't go near Cordelia, at least he could do something to help her through this night. He could find her father.

With that resolution made, he descended the stairs. But as he began searching for his surtout, the front door opened, and Mrs. Beardsley and Reverend Shalstone entered.

"You see, Your Grace, I told you I'd find Oswald," Mrs. Beardsley said lightly when she spotted him.

Sebastian forced a smile to his face and surveyed the two of them. They both seemed different. For one thing, Mrs. Beardsley wore a glow he'd never noticed there before. She'd always been a cheery, bright woman, but now she fairly shone with happiness.

The vicar, too, seemed happy, his eyes alert and almost jovial, and his face less anxious than Sebastian had ever seen it. Then Sebastian noticed that Mrs. Beardsley's hand was tucked in the crook of Oswald's elbow, and the vicar was holding on to it as if afraid to release it.

In the midst of trying to figure out if Reverend Shalstone had been drinking, Sebastian didn't notice Cordelia coming up behind him until she'd flung herself at the vicar.

"Oh, Father!" she cried, burying her face in his shoulder. "I was so worried! What happened? Where did you go?"

"Now, gel, there was nothing to worry about. I went to the church is all. To think."

The vicar's words were steady, assured . . . not the words of a drunk. Yet he exchanged a meaningful glance with Mrs. Beardsley that made Sebastian wonder if there'd been more his story than he was saying.

Cordelia drew back to stare at him, her shoulders shaking. "The church? You went to the church?"

Mrs. Beardsley raised one eyebrow. "Can you believe that?" Her voice held the faintest tinge of sarcasm. "Your father . . . in a church. You'd think he was a vicar or something."

Cordelia blushed. "I didn't mean . . . it's just that—"

"I promised you I'd stop drinking," her father said gently. "I mean to keep that promise."

Mrs. Beardsley squared her shoulders. "Don't worry, I'll make sure he does." She squeezed the vicar's arm, and he looked at her. Some wordless communication passed between them, and then the vicar nodded.

Suddenly Sebastian knew precisely what was going on. It was with dread that he heard Mrs. Beardsley announce, "You see, your father and I are getting married."

It shouldn't have surprised him. Any fool could see they were suited for each other. But their announcement had new meaning in light of what had happened between him and Cordelia. Cordelia had asked him to make love to her because she thought she'd never have the chance to marry. Now Mrs. Beardsley and the reverend had freed her to marry whomever she wished, but she'd been ruined for marriage forever. By Sebastian.

He could only watch Cordelia with a horrifying sense of unreality, wondering if their announcement had struck her with the same painful irony. She did seem stunned at first, and then her face paled so much he feared she'd faint.

"M-married?" she whispered.

Her father scowled at her apparent distress. "Aye, married. Do you think it such an oddity that your father would marry at this age? Or do you object to Honorine? Because I tell you—"

"Hush, Oswald," Mrs. Beardsley interrupted, her eyes keenly surveying Cordelia. "We've given your daughter a shock. It's understandable that she'd be surprised."

Cordelia seemed to draw on some inner strength, for she plastered a smile on her face. "Yes, I'm merely . . . surprised. I mean, three days ago the two of you were at each other's throats and today . . ."

"I can't say as we won't be at each other's throats again," her father said congenially. "But we'll have a jolly good time making it up to each other afterward, won't we, love?"

Mrs. Beardsley's slow blush made Sebastian wonder exactly how long the two of them had been in the church together. Apparently, he and Cordelia hadn't been the only ones sharing stolen embraces tonight.

Cordelia's smile held genuine warmth now. She hugged Mrs. Beardsley. "I'm so glad, Honorine, truly I am. It'll be marvelous to have another woman in the house, and I know you'll make Father happy."

Mrs. Beardsley gave her a sparkling smile of her own. "Oh, but I hope you won't have to put up with the two of us too long. I mean to see you married too, dear girl. Now that your father is taken care of, it's high time you had your own husband and family. After this old fool and I marry, I'll have to see to *your* happiness."

Sebastian's eyes narrowed as he waited for Cordelia's response. She shot him a quick glance, then murmured. "I can't—I don't wish to marry, Honorine. I'd rather be an independent woman."

"Yes," her father said in an aside to Mrs. Beardsley, "she's always saying such nonsense, but I don't believe it for a minute. Cordelia's too sweet to be one of those brash, outspoken women who spend their time stirring things up."

Mrs. Beardsley gave him an arch glance. "Be careful, Oswald. You're marrying one of those women."

He chuckled. "Aye, and it shall be my pleasure to tame that wild tongue of yours, love."

"Oswald!" Mrs. Beardsley protested with another blush, before she launched into a frank and detailed account of all the aspects of his behavior that she expected to change.

Soon they were squabbling goodnaturedly like a couple who'd already been married for years. Cordelia looked relieved that they'd abandoned the subject of a husband for her, but Sebastian wondered how deep her desire to be independent ran. She refused to look at him at all, yet he knew his presence affected her, for her hands nervously worried the buckle of her slender belt. He stared at her boldly, willing her to look at him.

Suddenly, he felt Mrs. Beardsley's eyes on him. The conversation had petered out into an awkward silence, and he snapped his gaze from Cordelia to find Mrs. Beardsley and the vicar staring at him.

"Oswald," Mrs. Beardsley said brightly, her eyes never leaving Sebastian's face, "our engagement calls for a celebration, don't you think? Why don't you and Cordelia go into the drawing room, and I'll press His Grace into helping me search for my best champagne." She paused, casting Reverend Shalstone a loving glance, "And tea for you, of course."

Cordelia's eyes widened, but she didn't protest when her father drew her off into the drawing room with a firm hand.

Sebastian braced himself. Something in Mrs. Beardsley's demeanor told him to expect trouble.

In fact, they'd only gone a short way toward the kitchen when she asked crisply, "What happened while we were gone, Your Grace?"

Only with great effort did he affect a nonchalant air. "Why do you think anything happened?"

"Because Cordelia looks like her entire world was turned upside-down."

He scowled. Devil take the woman for being so observant. "What do you expect? She just heard that her father is remarrying."

She stopped him as they entered the kitchen. The hand she placed on his arm was as imperious as any chaperone's. He turned to stare at her with a frosty smile.

"You know quite well I'm not talking about that," she snapped. "So I'll ask you again. What happened while we were gone, Your Grace?" She spoke in a slow, deliberate tone as if she considered him a man of damaged faculties.

Bloody hell, but the woman had her nerve! "Why don't you ask Cordelia?"

Her lips tightened. "I don't think she'd tell me, but I'd erroneously assumed that you might." She paused, her eyes scrutinizing him. "I would hate to discover, Lord Waverley, that my high regard for you has been misplaced. I thought Cordelia would be safe if I left her alone with you, for you seemed an honorable gentleman."

It took every ounce of his self-control to refrain from informing her that even an honorable gentleman had his limits, that when a seductive young beauty threw herself at him, he seldom thought about being honorable.

"So I ask you only once," she continued, "and then I swear I'll never speak of this again. While I was gone, did you do anything to . . . harm my future step-daughter?"

Not even by the flicker of an eyelid did he betray the inner turmoil her questions roused in him. This was his chance. If he told Mrs. Beardsley the entire story, Cordelia would be wed to him so fast she'd not have time to think.

But that wasn't how he wanted it. He wanted her to want this marriage. He wanted to be sure she embraced the idea on her own, and Mrs. Beardsley's interference would destroy any possibility of that.

It was the easiest lie he'd ever spoken. And the

hardest. "No," he said quietly. "You of all people should know your future stepdaughter would never allow me to harm her."

She didn't seem to know whether or not to believe him. For a moment, she looked as if she might say more, despite her promise not to.

At last, she gave a great sigh and led him toward the door of the wine cellar. "Good," she said, then added enigmatically, "because Cordelia deserves to have a proper marriage."

One day she would, he vowed with clenched teeth. He'd see to that.

Chapter Seventeen

See Life is but a dream, whose best contenting,
Begun with hope, pursued with doubt, enjoyed with
fear, ends in repenting.
                                        —John Ward,
                                          "Retire, My Troubled Soul"

The next morning passed in a nightmarish blur for Cordelia. Sebastian had convinced her father and Honorine to continue the scheme they'd tested at Honorine's, and Cordelia had given him her support because she had no choice. She owed it to Lord Kent to finish out the charade, even if she didn't think it would work.

But she could scarcely concentrate on tutoring her father. She'd already spent a restless night remembering every harsh word Sebastian had spoken and aching over each one. And now today she was forced to pretend as if nothing had happened.

Sebastian had certainly mastered the technique, she thought bitterly. She'd expected him to ride his horse and maintain a cold distance from her. Instead, he spent every hour in the coach with them, his air of nonchalance wounding her. How could he be so casual when his very presence burned her like salt on a deep cut? To make matters worse, occasionally she caught him watching her with undisguised interest as he had before.

Was this some sort of torture he'd invented to make her regret what she'd said? If so, it was working. Every time he handed her out of the coach with proprietary gentleness or inquired about her comfort, she suffered. Fie upon the man! Why must he torment her like this? Wasn't it enough that his looks seared her, his smiles destroyed her? Did he also have to treat her with false solicitude after he'd warned her to stay away from him and said cruel things to her?

It took all her energy to hide her chagrin behind a mask of indifference, to pretend she was as unconcerned about what had passed between them as he. Only through great force of will did she stick to her tutoring.

Fortunately, her work with her father was a little easier than it had been before. Although he hadn't changed his feelings about the duke's mission, he'd acquiesced to Honorine's wish to see the entire thing played out. In fact, Honorine threw herself into helping Cordelia tutor her father with an eagerness that perplexed Cordelia. The woman had something up her sleeve, that was certain. Never had Cordelia seen her friend so diligent to make something work.

The first night after they'd left York, Cordelia found out why her friend was so eager to continue the ruse and travel all the way to London. As she and Honorine prepared for bed, Honorine bombarded her with questions about what had happened while Cordelia and Sebastian had been alone together. Apparently, one of the servants had informed Honorine that Cordelia had been washing out sheets in back of the kitchen. Now Honorine was determined to ferret out the truth, even if it took the rest of the trip to do so.

Cordelia gave Honorine a feeble explanation, but refused to admit that anything at all had passed between her and Sebastian while Honorine and Oswald were gone.

Honorine sniffed after she heard the explanation. "I tell you, dear girl, if the man behaved inappropriately toward you—" She paused and flashed Cordelia a searching look. "Then he must be made to do the right thing. You must be honest with me on this matter. No one will blame you if ... if ... well, you know what I mean."

When she trailed off with a meaningful expression on her face, alarm skittered through Cordelia. Honorine obviously had guessed far too much. This wouldn't do at all.

Cordelia drew herself up with her best air of stiff civility. "His Grace has been nothing but the soul of courtesy to me. Besides, I would certainly never let him take liberties. What kind of woman do you take me for?"

"A young, pretty one with the same urges as anyone else. As I said, no one will hold you to blame. 'Tis Lord Waverley who is in the wrong—"

"He's done nothing," Cordelia choked out. She had to get Honorine to believe her, or she'd find herself forced into marriage anyway. "You wound me deeply by implying that I might have acted improperly while alone with His Grace. I can't believe that you'd think so little of me." Then she burst into tears, thankful that they came so easily to her these days.

With a sigh, Honorine gave a curt apology, but Cordelia could tell she was still suspicious. Although Honorine didn't pursue the matter further, Cordelia couldn't help but feel that the woman watched her with a keen eye.

But she couldn't be worried about that. She had other more important worries ... like whether she might be with child. At first, it alarmed her to think Sebastian's baby might be growing in her belly, but by their second day in the coach, the thought began to warm her, even comfort her. If she couldn't have Sebastian, she could at least have his child.

Of course, that would present enormous problems, she told herself. But by that night, she'd formed a plan for handling those problems. She could never tell either her father or Sebastian the truth, assuming it came to that. Her father would insist that Sebastian marry her and Sebastian would do "the right thing" in his bloodless, noble fashion. That didn't even bear thinking upon.

No, she'd stay in London, telling Father and Honorine that she wished to make her way alone in the music world. She'd have a few months before her pregnancy became evident, and in that time she'd amass as much money as she could by taking in pupils and composing for Lord Kent. Then she could hide herself away until the child was born, return home with it, and invent a story about finding a poor abandoned orphan to whom she'd become attached.

But then she'd have to lie about her own child, she thought despairingly. Still, wasn't it better to lie than to be locked forever into a marriage where the man she loved didn't love her and in fact resented her for making him forswear himself?

By the third day after they'd all left York, she'd half-resigned herself to being pregnant when she awoke early to discover that her monthly courses had come in the night.

To her horror, the realization brought on a fit of silent weeping. Fighting to make no sound so she wouldn't wake Honorine, she slipped from the bed, took care of her problem, and returned to lie beside Honorine.

She swiped scalding tears from her face as she stared blindly at the ceiling. No child. She wasn't even to be granted Sebastian's child. It was silly for her to feel like this. No unmarried woman wanted a bastard child, yet the more she thought about it, the more tears streamed down her cheeks.

It took her some time to get her emotions under control. She ought to be rejoicing, she told herself sternly. How many times had she heard of a maid impregnated after a single indiscretion? She was fortunate to have had a night with Sebastian without having to suffer for it.

Without having to suffer for it. As if she weren't already suffering. A pregnancy would have caused her less pain than this daily torment of being, yet not being, with Sebastian. Making love to him had altered everything. Before he'd come along, she'd resigned herself to a tedious, unfulfilled spinsterhood. If she'd thought occasionally about what she might miss in not marrying, she'd squelched such unproductive thoughts. Now that she and Sebastian had made love, however, her sense of loss was acute.

If Father had announced two or three months ago that he planned to marry Honorine, everything would be so different. She wouldn't be balking at Honorine's announced intention to find her a suitor, and she'd shyly be anticipating marrying and have her own family.

Now that all seemed unreachable. She could never marry, and not only because she was no longer a virgin. How could she marry any man when she loved only Sebastian? The very thought of having another man do to her the intimate things Sebastian had done filled her with loathing.

The wretch had unfortunately been right to try to dissuade her from giving herself to him. Her act had been rash and unthinking, prompted by her despair over her father and a sudden desire to have Sebastian for her own.

Still, she didn't regret it. A ghost of a smile touched her lips. At least she'd experienced true passion for a few glorious hours. How many people could say the same?

When the knock came at the door to awaken them, Cordelia started. Time to begin another dreadful day in Sebastian's presence, aching to touch him and knowing she couldn't. A day without even the slim comfort of knowing she bore his child.

At that thought, her eyes suddenly widened. She had to tell him. He'd said to let him know if there was a child. She clutched the blanket to her chest, her thoughts whirling. He hadn't said to let him know if there was *not* a child. Still, it would be unfair to keep him in the dark. Despite all the cruel things he'd said to her at Honorine's, he had every right to know. After all, she *had* wounded his pride by refusing his suit. The least she could do was assure him he wasn't a father.

Unfortunately, by the following afternoon she still hadn't found a way to get him off by himself. Honorine and her father watched them both like hawks, and every time she manufactured some excuse for speaking with him alone, Honorine insisted on joining her.

In truth, Cordelia didn't want to be alone with him, to relive the pain of their last encounter, to risk his hurting her again. Yet she knew she must. They were to reach his estate in the morning, and she couldn't wait until then. She might not see him at all once they got there. For all she knew, he'd be spending his days attending to business in London while she and her father put on their show for Lord Kent and Handel.

It had to be tonight. But how?

That night, she was still wondering how to get Sebastian alone. They'd all spent the evening dining with some friends of Honorine's in Huntingdon. Honorine had even convinced Cordelia and her father to try their "parlor trick" again, and this time it had succeeded. Now they were returning to the inn in Lord Waverley's coach.

"I told you it would work," her father said jovially.

Honorine slapped his arm with her fan. "How can you even say such a thing with a straight face, Oswald Shalstone, when you know quite well you've been opposed to this scheme from the beginning?"

He chuckled. "I've only been opposed to it, love, because I knew we could pull it off. I didn't wish to find myself suddenly assailed with invitations to assemblies near and far."

His good humor even infected Cordelia. It had been so long since he'd behaved as the father of her youth.

Seeing him happy and his mind clear was one of the few joys left to her.

Her eyes twinkled. "Perhaps we could make this into a traveling show. With Honorine providing the victims, Father could expound upon his talents and I could play the harpsichord for a score of bored provincials. We could eat and lodge free for months!"

They all laughed, even the duke.

"Jest if you will," her father said, "but we did a mighty fine job tonight. I wager even Lord Waverley will admit it."

"Oh, indeed." The duke's warm gaze rested briefly on Cordelia's face. "Richard will be impressed. Let's hope he also proves grateful enough to want to publish Cordelia's works for all eternity."

"Let's hope," Honorine echoed, with the faintest tartness in her tone. "If she wants to be independent, she'll need as much of your brother's money as he can give her."

"Honorine!" Cordelia protested, but the woman scarcely noticed the admonishment, for Cordelia's father was shamefully intent on stealing a kiss from her, and she was laughingly trying to fend him off.

Sebastian fixed his eyes on Cordelia's face. "Oh, I doubt she'll need Richard's money. Men in London swarm around women as pretty and talented as Cordelia. One of them will surely be willing to be her patron." His gaze dropped to her mouth. "I know I wouldn't be averse to it."

Cordelia felt suddenly incapable of speech. She blushed, then glanced at Honorine and her father in alarm to see if they'd noticed, but they were still too busy with their own conversation to have heard the duke's words.

Thank heavens, she thought. If they realized how he was looking at her now, like a wolf contemplating a particularly tasty sheep, they'd never let her get him alone.

Why was he looking at her like that? After his words

the night they'd made love, she'd never thought to see him look at her with desire again. It made no sense whatsoever.

She was still wondering about it when they reached the inn. Her father handed Honorine out, drawing her aside and whispering in her ear. Honorine glanced to where Sebastian was helping Cordelia out of the coach and whispered something back, but Cordelia's father merely shook his head and said something that made Honorine blush.

"The two of you go on in," Honorine murmured, "and we'll follow in a moment. Oswald wants to . . . show me something in the garden."

"Don't be too long," the duke said with laughter in his voice. "We wouldn't want the two of you to catch cold."

When Honorine colored again, both Sebastian and Cordelia's father chuckled, but Cordelia barely managed a smile. Her chance to get Sebastian alone had come. It might only be a few moments, but it was better than nothing. Still, now that it was here, she found herself reluctant to speak to him of such intimate things.

Yet speak to him she must. So as soon as they gained the entrance, Cordelia whispered under her breath, "I need to talk to you in private, Sebastian."

She thought his lips tightened, but he said nothing, merely nodding as he took her arm and led her through the winding hall until he found an empty room. As soon as they entered, he shut the door behind them and stood, quietly waiting for her to speak.

Now that the moment was upon her, she didn't know quite how to tell him. She'd thought all day about delicate ways to inform him he wasn't a father, but as he studied her with raised eyebrows, not saying a word, she blurted out the first thing that came to her mind.

"My monthly courses came yesterday."

For a moment, he seemed not to understand and she worried she'd have to explain in more detail. Then a strange expression came over his face, almost sad. "Then you're not with child."

She shook her head, dropping her eyes from his. There, she'd told him. Her obligation was finished.

"You don't seem happy about it," he added softly.

Somehow she managed a smile. "Of course I'm happy about it. It would have . . . complicated matters dreadfully."

"Yes."

An uncomfortable silence stretched between them. There was no point in her talking with him further, she thought, and turned toward the door. "I—I thought you should know," she stammered, placing her hand on the knob.

"Wait!" He came up beside her.

Wordlessly, she twisted to face him, a questioning expression on her face.

His gaze was unreadable. "We haven't had a chance to talk alone since your father and Honorine announced their engagement. I wondered what you plan to do after they marry."

She swallowed. His nearness oppressed her, but she couldn't bring herself to move away. "I-I hadn't much thought about it."

"You could marry now, you know." His probing gaze unsettled her. "Your father and Honorine won't expect you to stay with them if you don't want."

"As I told you before, I have no wish to marry."

A muscle jerked in his jaw. "So you intend to intrude on the newlyweds?"

His tone told her he didn't approve. Automatically, she crossed her arms over her chest. "That wouldn't be unusual," she said stiffly. Then she sighed. "But I probably won't. I'll establish my own household and leave them in peace to find their way together."

"I see. You'll be an independent woman and set yourself up as a composer. Perhaps even in London."

Furiously, she nodded. She had to get out of here and away from his peculiar questions.

He was having none of that. To her alarm, he grasped her arm and drew her away from the door. He gestured to one of the spindled Windsor chairs. "Sit down, Cordelia. I wish to discuss something with you."

Full of dread, but not wanting to provoke him any more than was necessary, she sat gingerly on the end of the chair.

He scrutinized her so carefully, she squirmed under his stare. Then his eyes narrowed. "Tell me, did you enjoy your experience with lovemaking the other night?"

His straightforward manner in asking the question shocked her almost as much as the question itself.

"Sebastian, please—"

"Did you?" His eyes wandered slowly, meaningfully over her trembling mouth, her bare throat, the swells of her breasts. Then they snapped back up to her face and his voice lowered. "I thought you did. I believe your exact words were, 'You're a wonderful lover.' Did you mean that, Cordelia?"

Dragging in a heavy breath, she murmured, "You know I did."

A faint smile touched his lips. Firelight played over his features, highlighting every sculpted plane of his face in minute detail. It was all she could do to meet his gaze, but she refused to be a coward. If he wanted to punish her more for her casual rejection of his suit the other night, she wouldn't stop him.

But this was the last time she'd let him torture her like this, she told herself.

He was the first to look away. "Well, then, it shouldn't surprise you to know that I enjoyed it, too."

His husky tone left her breathless. What did one say to that? she wondered. I'm glad? How wonderful? For lack of a better choice, she remained silent.

"In fact," he continued, "it has occurred to me that there's no reason on earth we can't repeat the experience."

This wasn't at all what she'd expected. She leapt

from her chair in a panic. "I told you, Sebastian, I won't marry you!"

"I'm not speaking of marriage," he said dryly as his gaze swung back to hers. There was a hard determination in it that sent shivers rippling over her skin.

He stepped toward her. "But if, as you say, you have no desire to marry, and you admit to enjoying our lovemaking, there seems no reason you couldn't be . . . my mistress. It would solve both our problems, wouldn't it? I could still marry Judith, and you could have your independence without having to sacrifice the new pleasures you've discovered."

Her blood roared in her ears. It was all she could do to stay on her feet after such a horrible suggestion. Solve both their problems? Perhaps it would solve his, but it would give her intolerable agony. She could never share him with Judith, nor could she live the life of a kept whore. It was unthinkable. How could he even suggest it?

She clenched her fists. "I couldn't be your mistress, and you shouldn't even ask it of me."

He moved closer, too close, his eyes glittering. "You made it quite clear the other night that your emotions weren't involved in our lovemaking. And you found pleasure in it. Why should you object to continuing such a delightful involvement when I've removed any of the restraints you fear?"

"What if I had children?" she blurted out, seeking for something, anything to halt the cruel flow of his words.

He shrugged. "I'd provide for them. 'Tis not that uncommon, Cordelia, for dukes to keep mistresses and sire bastards."

"I-I couldn't live like that, Sebastian. It-it's truly awful of you to think I could. I could never endure it."

He took another step forward, and she backed away from him.

His eyes probed hers as if seeking to delve into the secrets of her mind. "I don't understand why not.

Surely 'tisn't the impropriety of it that disturbs you. The other night, you were quite heedless of propriety. Most women of independence are. They take lovers when they wish. Why can't you do the same if you intend never to marry? What difference would it make? It's not as if you have to guard your virtue any longer."

Oh, that was too cruel. "I-I have to go now." She whirled toward the door, but he caught her arm.

"Unless, of course," he said in a seductive whisper, "you truly didn't find pleasure in what we did. Unless you've merely been saying you liked it to avoid wounding my manly pride."

She squeezed her eyes shut. Merciful heavens, what a trap lay before her! If she said she wanted to be independent, he'd point out she should be his mistress. If she said she wanted to marry after all, he'd ask why she couldn't marry *him*. And if she claimed she'd enjoyed their lovemaking, he'd want to make love to her, and that would surely drive her over the edge of sanity.

Only one alternative remained. "You're right. I-I didn't enjoy it. It was . . . interesting, o-of course, but that's all. I wouldn't choose to do it again." Lies, all lies. So many lies. How long could she go on lying?

"Really?" His throaty murmur made her shiver. Turning her to face him, he tipped up her chin with one finger. "I don't believe you."

When he stroked her lower lip with his thumb, her eyes shot open in terror. "You *must* believe me! It's true! Please, Sebastian, I want to be left to live out my life in peace . . . alone."

Now his index finger traced the line of her jaw. An involuntary shudder shook her. She felt unbearably hot, even though she was nowhere near the fire. She had to get away from him, but when she backed away, he captured her around the waist with one arm.

"Let . . . me . . . go," she begged. "Please?"

"I've just now had an intriguing thought," he murmured, his palm cupping her cheek, then sliding ever so slowly down the curve of her neck and behind into her hair. "I think you should prove how . . . unappealing . . . you find my caresses."

She groaned and then his lips were on hers. She tried to remain aloof, to pretend the entire thing disgusted her. She kept her teeth tightly clenched and her arms at her sides. But when she finally succeeded in dragging her mouth from his, he assaulted her cheeks with kisses, then spilled more kisses over her neck and throat.

To keep from clasping him the way she wanted, she dug her fingernails into her palms and kept her body rigid. Yet he held her so close she felt the iron-hard muscles of his thighs and his arousal rising between them. The hard heat brought a myriad of erotic desires slamming into her at once.

He gripped her chin as he kissed her on the mouth again, his thumb caressing the corner of her lips. When his other hand slipped from her waist to cover her breast, she gasped and he drove his tongue into her mouth.

That's when she lost all control. Throwing her arms about his neck, she kissed him back furiously. This was Sebastian, she thought in mindless delirium. He wanted her, and she wanted him. Nothing else mattered. Nothing.

The kiss continued forever. His mouth was by turns gentle and demanding, giving and taking as he taught her that kissing could be as close to heaven as lovemaking itself. His stubbled chin scraped her smooth skin, but she didn't care. He smelled of brandy and tasted of fruit, a heady combination that made her dizzy with pleasure.

When he tore loose her modesty piece and slid his hand inside her wrapped gown, she trembled all over, wishing there weren't so many layers of clothing between them. Baring her breast, he covered it with his hand. His fingers plucked at her nipple, and she moaned, pressing herself against him.

"Ah, angel," he whispered against her lips. "You *are* mine."

"Yes," she murmured unthinkingly, planting kisses on his rough cheek, his bold chin, the place where the pulse beat in his throat.

"This isn't the time or place for us. But you'll come to me in London."

He wasn't asking, but commanding, and his words shook her partly out of her sensual haze.

"You said to stay away from you." She couldn't keep the hurt from her voice.

"I was a fool." He bent his head to suck her breast.

"I-I can't be your mistress," she protested halfheartedly.

He lifted his head, though his hand continued to fondle her. His imploring expression cut to her heart. "Come to me in London. That's all I ask."

In London where his fiancée awaited him, Cordelia thought.

"I—"

The door flying open behind them cut off her words. Her face flamed as she pushed him away, fumbling to straighten her gown and not daring to look and see who'd interrupted them.

The stiff expression on Sebastian's face was enough to tell her. She pivoted to find Honorine standing in the entrance, her face livid with fury.

"Cordelia, I'll meet you upstairs," the woman announced in a voice that brooked no argument.

"Please, I know it looks awful, but—"

"Upstairs. Now. Before your father comes."

Those words were all it took to send Cordelia fleeing. With a backward glance at Sebastian, she ran from the room.

Sebastian watched her leave, his heart soaring. He didn't care that Mrs. Beardsley had caught them or even that his interlude with Cordelia had been interrupted. There'd be time for that later.

But he thought he'd gotten the answer to the question he'd been pondering ever since York. He couldn't be sure, of course, but he was surer than he'd been three days ago.

Mrs. Beardsley shut the door behind her. "Thank heavens Oswald is still in the garden, or I'd be keeping him from murdering you right now."

Sebastian fought for control over his loins. Wryly, he realized why Oswald had stayed behind. . . . Sebastian only wished *he'd* had more time to compose himself.

"It's time you and I had a frank discussion, Lord Waverley," she continued, her eyes flashing.

"Before you launch into the lecture you're itching to give me, I think you should know I intend to marry Cordelia."

He paused to let the full import of his words sink in, a smile tugging at his lips as an astonished expression spread over Mrs. Beardsley's face.

She held a hand to her throat. "M-marry?"

"Yes. Surely it doesn't come as a surprise to you that we have feelings for each other?"

"No, but . . . but she . . . she hasn't said a word to me about marrying."

"She doesn't know, or at least she doesn't believe I will. And you mustn't tell her otherwise, not until I've taken care of matters with my fiancée."

Her eyes narrowed. "If this is some trick to give you time to seduce her—"

"Nay." He bit back the retort he wanted to make— that he could seduce her—and had—without resorting to tricks. "But until I'm free to do so properly, I won't ask her again to marry me."

"Again?"

Of course Mrs. Beardsley had shrewdly pounced on his unintentional slip. He groaned, then decided perhaps it would be best after all to tell her everything . . . or almost everything. He could use an ally like Mrs. Beardsley.

Sebastian drew in a deep breath. "You asked me

what happened that night in York. Well, the truth of it is I asked Cordelia to marry me." His body went rigid, remembering that night. "She refused me."

Mrs. Beardsley looked stunned. Pressing one hand to her temple, she moved toward the fireplace. "I don't believe it." She shook her head and stared into the flames. "Has the girl gone quite mad?"

He searched for some explanation that wouldn't reveal what had happened between them. "I'm afraid I proposed rather clumsily. She thought I was doing it out of pity for her situation with her father. If you'll recall, he'd left without explanation, and she thought he'd gone off to drink."

Mrs. Beardsley pivoted to face him, her eyes darkening at the mention of Reverend Shalstone's problem with drink. "Oswald was merely thinking through some matters."

"Yes, we learned that later. At the time, however, even you thought he might be drowning his disappointments in brandy, didn't you?" He gave her no opportunity to answer. "Besides, it didn't matter what he was actually doing. Cordelia feared that he was falling into drunkenness once more. She felt despairing of her future, and I . . . took the opportunity to offer to marry her."

Mrs. Beardsley looked skeptical. Her eyes narrowed. "I know more about that night than you realize, Your Grace. For example, while Cordelia will say nothing else, she did admit to accidentally soiling her sheets that night, an action which prompted her to wash them out herself. You wouldn't know anything about that, would you?"

Obviously, Mrs. Beardsley had attributed a great deal to the soiling of the sheets. With a tight smile, he said stiffly, "If you have an accusation to make, Mrs. Beardsley, make it. Otherwise, I suggest you don't speculate on matters that are none of your business." Some things he refused to discuss even with an ally.

Her eyes locked with his. She'd probably guessed

the truth, but he didn't care. He wouldn't have changed a moment of his night with Cordelia . . . except perhaps for its botched ending.

After a moment, she gave him a deferential nod. "Go on. What exactly did she say when she refused you?"

"I had already foolishly told her about my situation with my fiancée, that I had vowed to marry Judith in repayment for her father's financial help. So when I suggested to Cordelia that I could marry her instead, she became rather stubborn about the whole thing. She told me she didn't wish to marry, that she wished never to marry. She wanted to be independent, she said."

"And you believed her."

"I did at the time. Now I'm not so certain. I don't know if she was trying to avoid causing trouble for me . . . or if she really has no desire to marry me. Mayhap she truly wants independence."

"Pish. Even men don't want independence, or they wouldn't take on wives and children."

"In any case, the only thing of which I'm absolutely certain is her strong feelings for me. Our . . . er . . . discussion this evening confirmed that."

Honorine gave him a frosty look. "I still say if you tell her you intend to break your engagement and marry her—"

"That's what I told her the first time." He shook his head. "I'm not going to do that again until I'm free to offer for her." Giving in to the urge to lay all his cards on the table, he said, "You have to understand, Mrs. Beardsley. Cordelia is bound to me by only one thing—desire, both mine and hers. It's up to me to convince her there's more between us, but I can't do it with you always fighting me."

"So you want me to stop chaperoning her?" she snapped. "Is that it? Allow you to have your way with her whenever and wherever?"

He shook his head. "I think that would be asking a bit much of you. I merely request that you don't speak against me or alarm Cordelia unduly. If you so much as hint that you'll force me to marry her because of what she and I . . . have done together, you'll drive her out of my grasp. I'm sure of it."

She stared at him, thin-lipped and pale.

"Please," he begged, swallowing his pride. "Give me a few days to deal with this in my own way."

Closing her eyes, she released an exasperated and very unladylike oath. She seemed to think for a moment, tapping her finger against her chin.

At last she opened her eyes and fixed him with a stern gaze. "All right, Lord Waverley. You may have your few days. But if Cordelia isn't engaged to you by the time we leave your estate to return to York and Belham, I'll tell Oswald everything I know and suspect, and he'll make sure you wed her."

He gave her a solemn smile. "I assure you, if Cordelia isn't engaged to me by the time you leave, *I'll* tell her father everything. Because one way or another, I'm going to have Cordelia."

And as Mrs. Beardsley stared at him in openmouthed surprise, he opened the door, bowed, and left the room.

Chapter Eighteen

If she at last reward thy love,
And all thy harms repair,
Thy happiness will sweeter prove,
Rais'd up from deep despair.
—John Dowland,
"Awake, Sweet Love"

Richard Kent sat in the parlor of Waverley staring sightlessly at the note before him. He reread it, then crumpled it and threw it into the fire with an angry jerk of one hand.

Damn Sebastian! They were all descending on the household today! Why did it have to be today?

Richard had expected his brother to take at least a month traveling to Belham and back. Last week, that had seemed like forever. Last week, he'd cursed himself for not going with Sebastian, for being too proud to approach the vicar after he'd been rebuffed more than once. Last week, he'd eagerly anticipated his brother's return, when this thing with Handel and his business could be settled.

In one short week, everything had changed. Not quite everything, he reminded himself. If anything, now it was even more essential that he redeem his reputation, that he regain the business he'd nearly lost.

Because without his business, he hadn't a prayer of a chance with Judith.

Judith. His heart stilled as an image of her filled his mind. He'd always admired her, always found her friendly and pretty and enticingly naive, from the time they were children. Because she lived on the estate adjoining theirs, she'd played with all of them at one time or another. Yet somehow he'd been so caught up in watching over his sisters and dealing with his business to notice how she'd blossomed into a woman.

And oh, what a woman. Barely twenty, her buxom figure and sweet disposition would make a dead man rise from the grave, and he was no exception.

Still, it was hard to believe that until a month ago, he hadn't thought of Judith that way. Not for him. Until a month ago, the Biddable Judith had merely been his brother's fiancée. His brother's engaging, beautiful fiancée, but his brother's nonetheless.

Then Sebastian had left for Belham after telling Judith they would set a date for the wedding upon his return. Suddenly, the engagement that everyone had taken for granted had become a serious matter. Richard's sisters had begun talking about the wedding, and Judith had been constantly underfoot, familiarizing herself with the workings of the house over which she'd soon be mistress.

Suddenly, she'd been around whenever Richard looked up. He'd begun to look forward to her presence at their dinner table, to miss her if she didn't join them in the evening, to take note of what she wore and how often she smiled.

But the worst had come a few days ago when she'd come upon him early in the morning, poring over his accounts for the hundredth time, his eyes bloodshot and his hands shaky from lack of sleep. She'd scolded him. She'd taken his accounts from him, sat down in a chair to peruse them, and urged him to sleep.

Surprisingly enough, he had. When she'd awakened him from a damnably real dream of her by placing a gentle hand on his shoulder, he'd jolted awake to see her smiling face above his. On impulse he'd kissed her.

To his utter surprise, she hadn't drawn back in shock or slapped him or berated him. And when he'd pulled her head back for a better kiss, she'd let him take that one too, afterward swaying breathlessly against his chair.

Then she'd left without a word. Since then, he'd found moments here and there to spend with her and had noticed that she regarded him with shy, sweet smiles whenever he was in the room.

He sighed now, pounding his fist on the arm of his chair. Judith, for God's sake! Why Biddable Judith, who could never be biddable for him? He'd sworn off women for a long time now. He'd successfully squelched any feelings of desire or affection for the women who crossed his path.

But Judith had slipped under his guard, probably because he'd grown up with her and never thought of her as a woman. In truth, she wasn't like other women. For one thing she had no interest in music at all, so he knew her interest in him wasn't another ploy by an amateur musician to gain his attention.

For another, she didn't avert her head in shock when he entered a room, leaning heavily on his crutches. She didn't make snide comments about "that poor, crippled Lord Kent." He'd heard fashionable ladies say such things when they thought he couldn't hear, in whispers that might as well have been shouts for all their subtlety. He'd spend a lifetime building up a protective shell, relying on his sisters for female companionship and ignoring the rest of them.

Until Judith. Damn her! She was the one woman with whom he felt safe, the one woman he could trust.

The one woman he had no right to care for. She belonged to Sebastian. And Sebastian was arriving to claim her in a few short hours.

A quiet knock at the door startled him out of his thoughts.

"Come in!" he barked.

When the woman who'd plagued his thoughts all morning entered, he glared at her, hating her for looking cheery and beautiful, and hating himself for noticing.

"My, but aren't you in a wretched mood today," she

said with her usual mild smile as she neared his chair. "I thought you told Belinda you wanted to see me."

He'd sent his sister after Judith as soon as he'd gotten the note from Sebastian, but now he found he wasn't quite ready to give her the news.

"Why don't you sit down?" he said, forcing some pleasantness into his voice.

She shrugged and sat in the chair next to him before the fire, her hands placed primly in her lap and her posture erect as she waited for him to speak. This was the Judith he'd grown up with, yet she seemed as foreign to him now as an exotic hothouse flower.

"I suppose—" he began, then stopped when he noticed that his voice sounded strangled, even to himself. He modulated his tone. "I suppose you're eagerly awaiting Sebastian's return."

"Of course."

At her placid reply, his gaze swung sharply to her. She met it with an even smile that told him nothing.

"I suppose you can't wait to become a duchess," he added peevishly. Studying her with narrowed eyes, he watched for some indication of how she really felt.

Although she colored and shifted her eyes from his, she gave a haughty tilt to her head. "A duchess. Oh, yes, that should be grand."

Had that been sarcasm in her voice? It wasn't at all like Judith to be sarcastic, yet he could have sworn he hadn't imagined it. Was he merely reading into her answers what he wished to hear?

This shilly-shallying wasn't getting him anywhere. He grew bolder. "Are you in love with my brother, Judith?"

Her soft blue eyes widened in surprise. Nonetheless, she answered him. "Of course not. You know that. Nor is he in love with me. This is a bargain between our two families, arranged by Father. Most marriages among our class are arranged, you know."

She spoke as if he were a fool to ask, but something in her expression, a flinching, made him go on.

"Don't you wish to marry for love then?"

"What I wish scarcely matters, does it?"

Now he knew it was there, pain and a hint of something else—resignation. Yet still she wouldn't speak her mind.

He slammed his hand against the arm of his chair. "If you wish to marry for love, why not stand up to your father? Tell him you don't want to marry Sebastian."

She stood abruptly, her composure shaken. With her back to him, she said in a faraway voice, "Stand up to Father? I knew you were a cynic, Richard Kent, but I didn't think you'd advise a young woman to go against her father's wishes." Her shoulders were shaking now, and her voice had risen to an emotion-laden pitch. "Why, it's my duty to marry as Father sees fit. He knows what's best for me, even if I don't."

Her innocent answer filled him with such hopelessness, he almost groaned aloud. What a fool he'd been to think she might abandon Sebastian for him! Even if she had some small affection for him, and he had little enough evidence that she did, she wouldn't ignore years of training to flout her father's wishes. She hadn't been nicknamed the Biddable Judith for nothing.

Then again, perhaps he was merely fooling himself. Perhaps she didn't care for him at all, and he'd been utterly mistaken in thinking she did. He was a second son, after all, with only the possible future of his business to commend him, and even that depended on the whims of an unknown vicar and Handel.

Few women found him attractive, thanks to his deformity. Why should Judith care at all for him, when she had whole-and-hearty Sebastian to care for?

He shook his head, staring morosely into the fire. "You're a good daughter." He couldn't keep the bite out of his tone. "I'm sure you'll make Sebastian a good wife."

She faced him, an arch expression on her face. "I'm

so glad to have your approval. Is that all you wished to
see me about, to find out how I feel about your
brother?"

Her words reminded him about the note. He scowled.
"Sebastian has sent a boy ahead to let us know he'll be
here in a few hours' time. I thought you should know."

Later he couldn't say why he'd turned to watch her
reaction, but he was glad he did.

Her face went white for the briefest moment, disappointment shadowing it before she recovered herself.
"I see."

It wasn't the expression of joy a fiancée should wear
when told her future husband was arriving. And it delighted him.

He abandoned all pretense. He had to take this chance.
He had to. "You don't have to marry Sebastian if you
don't wish to."

She gave him a forced smile. "Sebastian will make
a good husband, I'm sure." When he frowned, she continued, "Besides, you know how he is. He promised
Father to make me a duchess, and he'll stand to that
promise no matter what." There was no mistaking the
bitterness in her voice now.

"Do you wish to be a duchess?" He had to hear her
say the words before he would believe them. "Tell me
the truth, darling. Please."

At his use of the word "darling," she became quite
agitated. "I wish to please Father. Don't you understand that? I'm his only child, and he has placed much
of his hopes on my becoming a duchess and joining the
Waverley estate to his."

Richard leaned forward in his chair, fixing her with
a stern gaze. "Yes, but do you wish to be a duchess? I
must know, Judith."

Paling, she turned to the door. He thought for certain
she would walk out without giving him an answer, but
suddenly she stopped and ran back to his chair.

Quickly, she bent and kissed his cheek. "Leave it be,
Richard," she murmured. Her mouth was trembling,

and she looked ready to cry. A yearning expression on her face, she cupped his cheek with delicate tenderness before she dropped her hand. "Just leave it be."

Then she ran from the room.

He sat there stunned. Then a slow smile crossed his face. At least he had his answer.

Well then, he thought, damn her father and damn Sebastian and damn them all. He'd have his success with Handel and then he'd have his success with Judith. Because regardless of what Judith said, he would not leave it be.

As the coach rumbled toward London, Cordelia noticed that the number of carts, coaches, and post chaises on the road tripled. Midmorning, Sebastian told them that his estate lay to the northeast of the city, a few miles from its outskirts. After giving them that terse piece of information, Sebastian lapsed into an almost somber silence as he watched out the window.

Cordelia didn't know what to make of his brooding. Undoubtedly it had something to do with his discussion with Honorine last night. Cordelia wanted badly to know what they'd said to each other, but Honorine hadn't told her a thing.

After being closeted with Sebastian for an eternity, Honorine had returned to the room she shared with Cordelia. All she'd said was "I suppose you're old enough to know what you're doing, though I hadn't thought you'd turn fool on me all of a sudden."

Was that all? Cordelia had thought. She'd expected a more stinging lecture from Honorine. In fact, she'd already prepared a speech about being twenty-three and perfectly capable of fending for herself, so Honorine's dismissive comment had taken the wind right out of her sails. It had also left her wondering what had passed between Honorine and Sebastian.

Nor could she stop wondering about it now. She glanced at Honorine and then Sebastian. Both of them were unusually quiet, a fact that even her father commented upon.

Nervously rolling up the piece of music in her hand, Cordelia gritted her teeth and tapped the roll against her knee with impatience. The two of them were enough to drive her mad with wondering.

Especially Sebastian . . . him with his practical talk of lovemaking and horrible propositions!

Not that she could blame him for expecting her to agree to be his mistress. After all, she'd been thoroughly shameless yesterday. But why on earth had the man insisted on venting his anger on her in such disturbing ways, kissing her and provoking her into kissing him back?

She tapped the roll even harder. At least she hadn't promised to go to him in London.

"You're going to beat that sheet of music into a tattered mess before we even reach Waverley," Sebastian said mildly.

She glared at him. For the first time that day, he smiled, a dark, sensuous smile that reminded her of how he'd touched her at the inn, how he'd caressed her senseless. As if he read her thoughts, his eyes trailed slowly over her body, then back to her face, and his smile widened.

Heat blazed in her nether regions, making her shift uncomfortably in her seat. How truly wicked of him to flaunt her weaknesses before her.

She snapped her gaze from him, her hands squeezing the roll of music until it crumpled. If only it were his neck, she thought. The blessed wretch was so sure of her, so sure she'd come to him in London, despite all the miserable things he'd said about her wantonness. Any liaison between them was futile, yet he was too dense, and too arrogant, to see it.

Well, she'd show him she had some pride. The beast would find that out if he tried to corner her in his house.

Then her trembling hands belied her thoughts. As if

she could resist him for even a moment if he cornered her anywhere. The man could shatter her rock-hard determination to dust with one blessed kiss. Oh, heavens, if he touched her again as he'd touched her yesterday, she'd agree to be his mistress without a thought.

She forced herself not to think on that. Perhaps he wouldn't touch her after all. Once he was reunited with his fiancée, he might forget all about her.

Unfortunately, that thought gave her no comfort either.

Suddenly Sebastian sat up straight, a grin splitting his face as he leaned out the window. They had topped a slight rise, and the road stretched below them, passing between a number of large manors and far-reaching estates.

"Look there!" He pointed in the distance to a mansion of pale cream brick and freestone. "That's Waverley." No one could mistake the pride of ownership in his voice.

She strained forward to get a better view of the house. A hipped roof topped a huge house with projecting wings at either end. Judging from the number of windows, the place held at least fifty rooms. The main house was flanked by two pavilions, one probably containing the kitchens and the other the stables. Of course, Sebastian probably had more than one coach and a full complement of blooded horses.

As they grew closer, she noted that the house needed work—the roof of one wing looked battered from some recent storm and the other wing's gables were in disrepair—but efforts were clearly being made to set it to rights, for a few men could be seen working the stone to replace the crumbling gables.

All in all, it was an impressive group of buildings. She sighed wearily as the house loomed larger and larger. Its very expansiveness depressed her. How different her world was from Sebastian's. Despite his disparaging remarks about his lineage, he'd grown up in a splendor beyond anything she'd ever seen in Belham. Even Belham's earl hadn't such a magnificent home.

Think of it, she told herself, Sebastian regularly dined with earls and marquises, perhaps even princes. He no doubt had a valet to help him dress and a steward to do his accounts. This was his life.

No wonder he'd been so bitter when he'd proposed. No wonder he'd only thought later in terms of her being his mistress. This wasn't the place for a vicar's daughter. He knew it, and she should have known.

"There's the garden," he said, pointing it out as they drew closer. "And there's the chapel. We have a fine chapel, vicar. I know you'll like it."

Suddenly he glanced at her, his amber eyes still alive with the pleasure of seeing his home once more. "What do you think, Cordelia? Is it beautiful or am I simply blinded by sentimentality into thinking it so?"

Tears stung her eyes, and she glanced away to keep him from seeing them. "It's quite beautiful," she whispered and meant it. "The most beautiful house I've ever seen."

Sebastian turned to Honorine. "What do you say, Mrs. Beardsley?" He had a sudden gleam in his eye. "Will it do?"

As Cordelia wondered what he meant by that, Honorine cast him an enigmatic look before a smile tugged at her lips. Her gaze fell briefly on Cordelia. Then she nodded. "It will do, I think."

Sebastian laughed, all his somber manner seeming to disappear. He was like a boy as they reached the bottom of the rise and drove up the drive to the mansion. He pointed out his favorite spots, showing them the stream where he'd first learned to swim and the tree he'd tumbled out of as a child, breaking his arm.

When they passed a crumbling cottage, he told them with fervor that one day all of Waverley would be restored to its former glory. He'd been working at it for some years, but he expected it shouldn't take too many more.

His enthusiasm infected Honorine, who began to question him about the extent of his estate, and even Cordelia's father, who wanted to know more about the chapel. But it merely discouraged Cordelia. She tried to tell herself that staying in such a mansion would be a grand adventure, that she'd never get another such chance, for even Honorine's opulent house bore no resemblance to this luxury.

Unfortunately, it seemed just another terrible trick Fate had played on her. This was the last straw, to have Sebastian's wealth thrown in her face, reminding her what a little wren she must seem to him.

Her stomach sank even further a few moments later when they pulled up before the grand entrance to find all of Sebastian's family awaiting him on the stairs, looking splendid and elegant in clothing she could never have afforded.

It was easy to pick out Lord Kent, standing with his hands on his crutches. But the four women beside him gave her a start. Three of them were Sebastian's sisters. So the fourth must be Judith. Lady Judith, Cordelia silently amended.

Cordelia could probably have figured out which one was Lady Judith by watching Sebastian's face, but she didn't want to see how he reacted when he caught sight of his fiancée. Instead she tried to determine it on her own.

It proved easy to figure out, for as soon as the coach halted and they alighted, the three sisters gathered around Sebastian, fussing over him and gabbling excitedly like an unruly flock of geese. They seemed to range in age from about thirteen to about eighteen, and all were relatively pretty.

One woman stood aside, however, a placid smile on her finely formed features. Cordelia stifled a groan. This must be Lady Judith. Although Sebastian had told her his fiancée was only twenty, Lady Judith had an older woman's composure. No wonder Sebastian was marrying her. She was the quintessential London beauty, all perfect blond ringlets, creamy skin, and pale blue eyes.

Sebastian bowed to the woman, confirming Cordelia's fears. "I hope these three minxes haven't driven you mad in my absence."

"It's good to see you, Sebastian," Lady Judith said, then approached him with an easy grace Cordelia envied. Sebastian took Lady Judith's hands and bent to kiss her upturned cheek.

It was the slightest of kisses, a mere social formality, yet it stabbed Cordelia right through the heart. Merciful heavens, how would she ever endure the next few days?

"You should be more worried about how *I* put up with our sisters," Richard interrupted dryly.

Sebastian turned to his brother, who stood back from the others, balancing on his crutches. "You mustn't have done too badly." He regarded his brother with approving eyes. "You're looking much better than when I left you."

Lord Kent laughed. "With all the cosseting and pampering the girls showed me ... and Judith, of course, when she was here ... I couldn't help but improve."

Cordelia regarded Lord Kent with curiosity for the first time since they'd driven up. Any fool could tell he was Sebastian's brother. They were both lean and tall, and both men eschewed wigs, preferring to tie their chestnut hair back in queues. Like his brother, Lord Kent was attractive, although his handsomeness was of a more conventional kind, unlike Sebastian's rough good looks. What's more, Lord Kent had brown eyes. And at the moment, his face was quite pale.

Yet not as pale as she'd expected. In fact, for an ill man driving himself into the grave, he didn't look bad off. She could see the "twisted limbs" Sebastian had referred to, but they didn't seem to affect his mobility much, since he was standing out on the stairs with everyone. Except for his paleness and the problem with his legs, he didn't look ill at all.

Had Sebastian lied to her about the severity of his brother's condition? No, she thought as she glanced at Sebastian, realizing that he too seemed surprised to find Lord Kent looking relatively healthy.

Lord Kent jerked his head toward where Honorine and Cordelia and her father stood. "Are you going to introduce us, or are you simply going to stand there gawking at me as if I'd grown horns?"

Sebastian's perplexed expression faded, and he smiled. He introduced his sisters—Belinda, Margaret, and Katherine—before formally introducing Lord Kent and Lady Judith.

Then taking her father's arm, Sebastian led him forward. "This," he said, "is the Reverend Shalstone you've spoken of so many times." He nodded to Honorine. "This is Mrs. Beardsley, the vicar's fiancée."

He paused. Then with a stubborn set to his chin he added, "The young woman here is Reverend Shalstone's daughter, Cordelia."

The change that came over Lord Kent's face at Sebastian's introduction of her was immediately apparent. She could see his displeasure in the way he wrinkled his brow.

"A nice family group," he said, the barest acidity in his tone. "I'm afraid we weren't expecting anyone but the vicar, so we haven't made the proper arrangements."

"But of course, we'll do so now," said Belinda, the oldest sister. "I'll see to it at once." She ran up the stairs, stopped, then ran back down and impulsively kissed Sebastian. "We're all so glad you're home, Sebastian. And this time you mustn't run off too quickly." Then she left.

Cordelia could feel Lord Kent's eyes on her. She met his gaze, disturbed by the dislike she saw there. Then she remembered what Sebastian had told her about his brother's suspicions of women, and remembered, too, that Lord Kent had refused to look at her music when her father supposedly had offered it to him.

Suddenly Lord Kent smiled, a warm smile that reminded her of Sebastian and made her wonder if she'd been mistaken about his seeming dislike.

He gestured behind him to the entrance. "All of you, please come in."

"Yes," Sebastian seconded. "It's too cold to stand out here chatting."

Lord Kent allowed them all to pass him and enter the manor. As he fell in behind them, moving with surprising agility for a man on crutches, he muttered, "We're delighted to have the three of you. I shall have to tell Cook to set two extra places, of course, for we weren't expecting—"

"You've already said that," Sebastian broke in, an edge to his voice. "Since you're obviously wondering why Mrs. Beardsley and Miss Shalstone are here, I'll tell you. Aside from the fact that it's perfectly understandable that Miss Shalstone should wish to travel with her father, we also needed her. Reverend Shalstone has a deplorable problem with stiffening of the joints that keeps him from being able to play the harpsichord as he once could, so Miss Shalstone is his hands. We didn't know if Handel would wish some of the music played for him, but we brought her along in case he did. Mrs. Beardsley is her chaperone."

"I'm glad all of you came," said a gentle voice at Cordelia's elbow.

To Cordelia's surprise, it was Lady Judith who'd spoken. Smiling softly at Cordelia, Lady Judith went on. "It will be wonderful having someone about who can play well. You see, Miss Shalstone, I can't play an instrument to save my life."

"And my sisters aren't much better," Sebastian put in. "Except for Richard, we're completely unmusical. It drives poor Richard insane half the time, particularly since he has perfect pitch. Belinda's singing offends his ears, he calls Margaret 'stumble fingers' for she never hits the right notes on the spinet, and Katherine . . ." He lifted his eyes heavenward. "Even *I* can't abide hearing Katherine torture the keys."

"Sebastian, you devilish rogue!" Katherine protested, half in outrage, half in laughter. She was the prettiest of the three sisters, and the one who looked most like her brothers. At the moment, her eyes twinkled as brightly as Sebastian's, and she wore an engaging grin like his.

"You see how quickly I wear out my welcome," Sebastian announced to general protests from both Margaret and Katherine as they all entered a great hall where servants descended upon them, gathering coats and cloaks and hats. "Soon you'll be accusing me of being as cynical as Richard."

"Not them. They think you walk on water," Lord Kent growled, but he, too, wore a smile on his face. " 'Tis only because they don't have you constantly carping at them. *I'm* the one who has to crack the whip, so *I'm* the one with the reputation for being a cynic."

"You know it's a reputation you richly deserve," Sebastian retorted.

"Aye," Katherine put in sarcastically. "But carping is a mild term for a man who raps his sister's knuckles whenever she uses the wrong fingerings on the spinet."

In rapt amazement, Cordelia watched the four siblings sparring. Their words seemed harsh to her, but it was clear they jested. The entire family seemed used to such rampant teasing. But that was probably typical for large families, she told herself.

"Well, Lord Kent won't be rapping my daughter's knuckles, I can tell you that," her father said, flashing her a smile as the footman took his greatcoat. "Tell them, Lord Waverley. She plays like an angel, doesn't she?"

"Indeed," Sebastian replied. "You must hear her, Richard. I doubt even angels can play as sweetly."

Cordelia didn't look at Sebastian, nor he at her, but

she felt intensely aware of him. Despite everything, his compliment made her feel more welcome in his home than anything his brother or sisters could have said.

Oblivious to the undercurrents swirling around them, Margaret, the youngest, who was short and plump and looked the least like her brothers, chimed in, "We'll have to have a concert . . . but not until after dinner." She linked her arms with Sebastian. "Judith's staying, of course, and we've got the grandest dinner prepared. As soon as Richard got your note, we told Cook to make all your favorite dishes. There's pigeon pie and sweetmeats and . . ."

The rest of it was lost in the confusion of voices rising around them—Kathering asking Honorine about their journey, Richard barking orders to the footmen, Judith inquiring about the vicar's health.

Momentarily left to herself, Cordelia surveyed the grand entrance hall. There were frescoes painted all around, interspersed with Ionic pilasters, and the floor was marble. The huge central staircase had an intricate wrought-iron balustrade and walls painted with pastoral scenes, stretching up as far as she could see.

She sighed. The Kents might seem like a typical family, but they were far from it. They had wealth, power, and connections that they undoubtedly took for granted. Even if they'd once fallen on hard times, they were already recouping their losses, thanks to Sebastian, and they had probably never lost their ties to a society she didn't understand and wasn't part of.

Their kind were the patrons for her kind. Always had been, always would be. She must make herself remember that.

That dismal thought was made more dismal by the sight of the amiable Lady Judith beckoning them all into the dining room. The woman wasn't officially part of the Kent family yet, but it scarcely mattered. She was part of their society. She would always be comfortable with them, always fit in.

Cordelia couldn't even hate her, for the woman was

as nice as anyone, even if she was a paragon and strikingly beautiful. In fact, she'd make the perfect duchess for Sebastian.

She groaned. Ah, well. At least Lady Judith wouldn't have to worry that Sebastian might keep a mistress on the side. Because after seeing all this, there was no way Cordelia would agree to be his mistress.

After all, it was one thing to have a man be patron to one's music. But it was quite another thing entirely to let him be patron to one's heart.

Chapter Nineteen

Die not, fond man, before thy day.
Love's cold December
Will surrender
To succeeding jocund May.
     —John Ward,
      "Die Not, Fond Man"

From his seat at the head of the table, Sebastian watched Richard intently. Something was different about his brother. Nor was it merely the improvement in his physical condition. This wasn't the despondent Richard he'd left behind a few weeks ago. This Richard had an air of steely determination about him. Little trace remained of the chilling despair or bitter resignation Richard had worn like an invisible cloak last month.

Perhaps Richard simply anticipated the successful continuation of his business, Sebastian thought as he noted how animated Richard's expressions were, how expansive his smile.

Yet somehow Sebastian didn't think that was it. For one thing, the feverish urgency behind his request that Sebastian fetch the vicar seemed to have faded. Before they'd arrived, Sebastian had expected to have Richard whisk them off immediately into the music room for a discussion. Instead Richard seemed content to bide his time through dinner.

Not that Richard ignored the vicar. Quite the opposite—he addressed a number of comments to him, but the comments were social and had nothing to do with music. Of course, Richard couldn't speak much to the man, for Belinda had unthinkingly placed Reverend

Shalstone at the end of the table farthest from Richard, making it difficult for them to talk except in generalities. Sebastian made a mental note to thank Belinda later.

Then he scowled and rethought that idea. He shouldn't be so hasty to thank his sister. After all, Belinda had also placed Cordelia at Richard's right hand.

He glanced at his sister, noting how she kept her eye on Richard, a smile on her face. Devil take the girl for her matchmaking ways. Obviously she'd decided Cordelia would be perfect for Richard, since Cordelia had an interest in music. The girls were forever trying to find a woman for Richard. Normally Sebastian would have approved, but not today.

It hardly mattered that Richard paid no attention to Cordelia, and she even less to him. Other men would have discounted Richard as a rival because of his twisted limbs. Sebastian, however, was no such fool. Richard was otherwise quite attractive, and Cordelia had a soft heart. Crippled legs wouldn't bother her if she took a liking to him.

Bloody hell, he didn't approve of this at all. Although he told himself his jealousy was foolish— Cordelia loved him no matter what she said—it was maddening to sit at such distance and pretend to have no claim on her.

When Richard spoke to her at last and she responded, smiling, Sebastian's fingers curved about the handle of his fork instinctively, and he stabbed the slab of roast on his plate. He must take care of this matter of breaking his engagement soon, he thought, before Richard got any ideas about Cordelia.

Or she about him.

"The Shalstones seem a respectable sort," Judith said at his elbow, jerking him from his thoughts. "And Mrs. Beardsley is a delightful woman."

He forced a smile to his face as he bent his head to answer her. "Aye, it was most kind of them to come all this way."

He returned to his perusal of Cordelia only to find Richard regarding him with a murderous expression. That was odd, thought Sebastian. Perhaps Richard had seen through Belinda's matchmaking and was angry, but if so, why be angry at Sebastian, who'd certainly had nothing to do with it?

Judith touched Sebastian's arm as she said something more, and Sebastian noted with curiosity that Richard's scowl deepened.

He glanced at Judith's face. She gazed up at him with her usual placid expression, yet he imagined he saw more indifference there than before.

Was this wishful thinking on his part? Surely Richard and Judith weren't . . . Surely they couldn't be . . .

It was an intriguing idea. In fact, a thoroughly wonderful possibility. Yet how could he know for sure? A new affection between Richard and Judith would explain the differences he'd noted in Richard earlier, but that wasn't proof.

Forcing his tone to be casual, he said to Judith in a voice loud enough to carry, "So, dear, did you spend a lot of time here while I was gone?"

Had he imagined that flicker of guilt in her eyes, quickly masked?

"Of course." She dropped her gaze from his. "I thought I'd begin learning my responsibilities early."

"Judith's been ever so much help," Margaret piped up, reaching for her third piece of pigeon pie. "She's good in the kitchen and much more sensible in talking to the steward than Belinda or I could ever be."

"She's even been helping Richard with his accounts," Katherine added. "She's had much more success with making him sleep and eat right than the rest of us."

How very interesting, Sebastian thought, shifting his gaze first to Judith, who colored, and then to Richard. As his eyes met his brother's, Richard squared his jaw defiantly, as if daring him to say anything about Judith's visits. There was also something else in Richard's expression as his eyes fell on Judith—a hint of possessiveness.

Sebastian had to tamp down his instant impulse to believe what he thought he saw. Obviously he'd been too long away from home or he wouldn't be making such broad interpretations based on so few facts.

Still, he couldn't let go of the idea that Richard might desire Judith. Of course, it would do no good if Judith didn't share those feelings, but she did seem to have changed toward both brothers since he'd left.

If only he could be sure. . . .

Richard was thinking much the same thing as he watched Judith and Sebastian. He'd been waiting to see how they were together. He'd never noticed before, because it hadn't been important to him, but now it was of the utmost importance. If Judith wanted Sebastian and Sebastian wanted her, then Richard couldn't very well continue to pursue her. Unfortunately, he couldn't think of any reason why Sebastian *wouldn't* want Judith, for what man in his right mind wouldn't? Still, Richard could always hope.

To his secret delight, he noticed that Judith didn't blush when Sebastian paid her a polite compliment the way she colored lately when Richard did so. If anything, she seemed distant from all of them, like Venus rising from the sea, beautiful and dispassionate.

She truly was a Venus, he thought, but golden-haired and purer than even the goddess. He would give whatever health he still possessed to have her. Yet he had to be sure she wanted him. Perhaps he'd misread her kiss that morning, perhaps it had been born of pity for him.

He wouldn't take pity from Judith. He wouldn't take it from anyone, but especially not Judith.

"My father would never say so," a voice came beside him, disturbing him from his ruminations, "but he's very flattered by your words of praise for his chorales."

Reluctantly, Richard shifted his attention from Judith and Sebastian, leveling a quiet stare on the young woman beside him. Miss Shalstone was pretty, he admitted grudgingly. He hadn't failed to notice Belinda's blatant attempts at matchmaking. As always, he resented them, but thankfully the vicar's daughter didn't seem to have recognized his sister's machinations.

In fact, although he'd feared at first that her father had brought her along to push her music on him, Richard had revised that opinion when she'd been anything but pushy at dinner. Actually, the poor woman seemed tragically sad.

Forcing himself to remember what she'd said, he replied, "Your father's work is exquisite. I can't help but praise it."

A ghost of a smile touched her fine lips. "You've always been so kind in your letters."

He scowled. "My letters? You've read my letters to your father?"

When she colored and dropped her gaze from his, he winced. If she'd read his letters, she knew he'd refused to look at her music.

"I help Father with his correspondence," she explained, "but you needn't worry. Your letters were nice. I knew from them you'd be nice in person."

He raised one eyebrow in a gesture unconsciously like his brother's. "Nice? You're undoubtedly the only person to use that adjective in reference to me."

Her smile broadened. "I don't believe that. You took a chance on a new composer, and I think that's very nice."

Ah, now it comes, he thought, dismayed. *She'll suggest that I consider her own music, and I'll have to create an absurd reason for not doing so.*

But she surprised him again. "Have you been publishing music long, Lord Kent?"

He smiled and relaxed. "Five years."

"It's a young company then." She paused. "How did you manage to come by a music publishing concern? Or did you buy it on a lark?"

He chuckled. "I do nothing on a lark, Miss Shalstone. My father, however, did a number of things on a lark. One of them was to win a publishing business in a game of loo."

He'd apparently managed to surprise her, for her eyes widened. "A game of loo?"

He nodded. "Sebastian didn't tell you?"

"No. He said your father had 'acquired' the business."

"And he had, although in a more unconventional manner than most. I'm sure Sebastian has told you about Father's deplorable tendency to gamble excessively. This was one of the few times Father actually won."

Thinking of the day his father had announced he'd won a business at cards, Richard was reminded of what had become of the business. The presses were still and silent, and the beautiful sheets of music with Kent Publishing printed in lovely golden letters on the top sat in piles in a storehouse, since no one would buy them.

He glanced around the table, noting that nearly everyone had finished their dinner. Dessert was on the way, and Sebastian was bending his head to say something to Judith. Richard clenched his jaw and decided he'd waited long enough to resolve this matter of what was to happen to his publishing company. Without his company, he hadn't a prayer of convincing the baron to let him marry Judith instead of Sebastian.

Abruptly Richard rose from the table, turning his attention to the vicar. "There's dessert coming, but I'm too excited about the vicar's being here to wait. I hope you don't mind, Reverend Shalstone, but if you'd accompany me to my study, we can discuss what we'll say to Handel. Everyone else can eat dessert without us."

The entire table fell silent. Sebastian started, and Miss Shalstone and Mrs. Beardsley blanched inexplicably. The vicar himself looked stunned. What on earth had he said to shock them all so?

"Why . . . ah . . . certainly, my lord," the vicar muttered, glancing anxiously at his daughter.

"Oh, come, Richard," Sebastian put in. "Can't it wait until after dessert? Then we can all be in on the discussion. After traveling all the way to Belham to fetch the vicar, I'd like to at least hear what you plan to do."

Richard stared incredulously at his brother. "Don't be absurd. You're lost in discussions about music. There's no point in your being there. Stay and entertain the ladies. The vicar and I won't be long. We merely have to discuss some strategy."

The vicar motioned to Cordelia, and she rose.

With a frown, Richard noted that she was leaving the table, too. "No, no, Miss Shalstone. No need for you to bother yourself. A few words with your father is all I need."

"But he can't play music without me."

Richard's irritation grew. "He doesn't need to play a damned thing. I simply want to talk to him about a few of the pieces, the ones Handel likes best."

She paled even more as she dropped into her chair, a forced smile on her face. "Of course, my lord."

"I don't see what the bloody hell is wrong with Miss Shalstone entering the discussion," Sebastian said in clipped tones. "Let her go if she wishes."

Richard thought something decidedly odd was going on here. What was putting them all into a dither?

"No," he insisted. "The vicar and I will have our discussion alone. Then you're all free to bombard him with your own questions if you like, although the amount of knowledge the rest of you have concerning music could probably fit into a thimble." He paused. "Excepting Miss Shalstone, I'm sure."

Stepping away from the table, he gestured to the vicar. The man rose, his face reddening from ear to ear. He cracked his knuckles rather loudly, then stared down at his hands and stuffed them in his pockets. After flashing Richard a hesitant smile, he walked toward the door.

As Richard led him into the hall, he found himself wondering why a musician with stiffening of the joints would do something so foolish as to crack his knuckles. Then he dismissed the thought and headed down the hall with his prized composer.

So much for that, Cordelia thought in despair. In five minutes, Lord Kent had destroyed two weeks' work. Then she brightened. Perhaps Father could hold his own after all their hours together. Maybe he now had enough general knowledge to pass for a composer in his short interview with Lord Kent.

"Cordelia," came Sebastian's voice from the other end of the table. She looked at him.

His grim demeanor told her he didn't have quite as much hope as she did that her father could successfully pull off the deception without her. "May I have a word with you in the hall?"

She nodded, rising from her chair.

"None of that now," Katherine complained. "No secrets here. Tell us what the bloody hell is going on, Sebastian."

"Katherine!" Belinda admonished. "Where are you getting that awful language?"

"From Sebastian, of course." Katherine twisted in her chair to grin at her brother as he came around the table. "Oh, please tell us what you and Miss Shalstone are up to. It's obvious there's a grand conspiracy underway."

"It's none of your concern, brat," Sebastian told her, chucking her under the chin as he passed her chair. "Come on, Cordelia."

With a sinking heart, Cordelia followed him into the hall. As soon as the door closed behind them, he took her by the arm and led her away from it.

"I wouldn't put it past Katherine to listen at the

door," he explained. He fixed her with a troubled gaze. "Do you think your father can manage this?"

"I don't know. He seems to have learned a great deal since Honorine began helping me. I think he wanted to impress her. But the fact remains, his strength lies elsewhere." She managed a woeful smile. "I don't suppose your brother's fond of sonorous scripture recitations."

"Afraid not."

The door to the dining room burst open, and Lady Judith emerged, an anxious expression on her face. "Sebastian, I can understand your not wanting to say anything to the girls, but surely you can tell *me* what's going on. You aren't pulling some trick on Richard, are you?"

Cordelia wondered about Lady Judith's apparent distress, but Sebastian didn't seem to notice that Lady Judith appeared more concerned for his brother than for him. If anything, his smile widened. "It's not exactly a trick, but I don't know if I should explain. You see—"

That was all he managed to get out, for the door down the hall from them swung open, slamming against the wall, and Lord Kent himself stormed into the hall, his crutches clicking along the marble floor.

"Sebastian!" he roared, coming toward them with amazing speed. He jerked to a halt when he reached them, and he focused all his attention on his brother. "I want to know what's going on, and you'd better tell me the truth or I swear I'll beat you over the head with one of these crutches until you do."

His face wore a mixture of pain and anger that shot a bolt of guilt to Cordelia's heart. She bit her lip to keep from telling Lord Kent the truth. It was up to Sebastian to decide what to say now that everything had fallen apart.

"What's wrong?" Lady Judith blurted out.

Lord Kent turned his glittering gaze to her. "What's wrong? For one thing, this supposed vicar has only the most cursory knowledge of music. The man couldn't remember which chorale had the two diatonic countersubjects or which one changed tonality in the coda. When I asked him about his preferred composers, he confused Froberger with Corelli."

His flushed face grew redder the more he shouted. He leveled a bitter gaze on Sebastian, who seemed frozen in place. "For another thing, there's nothing wrong with his hands that less knuckle cracking wouldn't cure. He's a damned impostor, and Sebastain knows it. What happened? You couldn't find the real vicar? You thought if you passed some fake off on your stupid brother he'd straighten up and behave himself? Well, that vicar couldn't fool a music student, much less me or Handel! You've damn well gone too far this time with your controlling ways, dear brother!"

He said the word "brother" with such sarcasm, Cordelia flinched, her heart aching for Sebastian. Sebastian himself seemed incapable of speech, though abject betrayal suffused his face. Behind Lord Kent, her father had stepped into the hall, giving her a look of helpless regret and making her wish she could comfort him. But first she had to set this muddle straight, since Sebastian seemed content to let his brother bludgeon him with words.

"It's all my fault, Lord Kent," she said softly.

"Oh?" His voice held such sarcasm she could feel his contempt. "How surprising to find that a woman is at fault."

"Shut up, Richard," Sebastian bit out as her father came toward them bristling. "You've had your say. Now you're going to listen to me—"

"No, this is my fight," Cordelia interrupted. Her hands were shaking, so she tucked them under her arms as she fixed Lord Kent with a defiant gaze. "*I* wrote the chorales that you've been publishing. I'm the one who wrote you the letters and who approached you about publishing the music in the first place. My father only signed his name to the letters."

Lord Kent glared at her for a long moment, his jaw rigid. Then his eyes narrowed. "I don't believe you."

Sebastian cursed. "That is precisely why I invented this bloody charade in the first place. I knew you'd never accept her as the composer. You're so . . . caught up in your past mistakes you're convinced a woman can't produce your precious music." He was breathing hard now, and Cordelia feared he might strike Lord Kent. "I tell you, Cordelia's music could rival that of the angels, but you're too stupid to believe that all your preconceptions might be wrong."

Richard sneered at his brother. "I see I'm not the only one who can be fooled by a pretty face into ignoring the obvious."

As Cordelia's mouth dropped open in shock, Sebastian lifted his arm, his hand already forming a fist.

Cordelia threw herself between him and Lord Kent. "No! Stop this, both of you!"

"This has nothing to do with you, Miss Shalstone," Lord Kent growled. "Get out of the way."

"This has everything to do with me, my lord," she hissed as Sebastian tried to thrust her aside. "I *am* the one who wrote the chorales whether you wish to believe it or not."

"I'll give you credit, Sebastian," Lord Kent bit out without looking at her. "The wench is persistent with her story."

At Sebastian's outraged roar behind her, she thrust her finger into Lord Kent's face, forcing him to look at her. "So you think I didn't write them? Then explain how I know this. The first chorale I sent you is the one with the two diatonic countersubjects. The last one changed tonality in the coda, although you've also published two others that did. And I prefer Corelli's concertos to Froberger's suites because I enjoy hearing each instrument have its say."

As his face registered surprise, she lowered her voice. "Furthermore, you are not the gentleman I took you for. You're certainly not the Lord Kent of those letters, for he was kind and openminded where you are not."

Lord Kent's expression altered subtly, but she merely paused for breath before rushing on. "I left my responsibilities and the only home I've ever known to travel two weeks in the dead of winter because your 'controlling' brother begged me to help you. I swallowed my pride and let my father get the credit for my music because your brother asked me to. Meanwhile I attempted to teach Father everything I know, despite the fact that he's tone-deaf. I did all that just to have you tell me I'm lying."

She planted her hands on her hips, working up into a royal rage. "Well, my lord—though I'm sure I use that term loosely—for the first time in a long time, I am not lying about who wrote those chorales. But since you seem determined to believe I am, you won't have to worry about publishing them anymore. I'm dismissing you. I won't write for a bloody man who holds me in contempt."

Merciful heavens, she thought with a shock, Lord Kent had so infuriated her she was even adopting Sebastian's deplorably bad language. If she stayed a moment longer, she'd be cursing like a laborer.

She sucked in a deep breath. "That's all I have to say." Glancing up, she caught her father's bemused expression. "Come, Father. We must tell Honorine we're leaving at once."

"Now, Cordelia, don't be hasty—" Sebastian began, but she ignored him, whirling toward the dining room.

Unfortunately, Lady Judith blocked her path. The woman wore an alarmed expression as she held out her hands to Cordelia. "Please, Miss Shalstone, wait."

With stiff, barely maintained composure, Cordelia shook her head. "I have to leave."

"You mustn't let Richard's foolish words drive you away. He has a temper, I'll grant you, but he's not the ungracious fool he pretends to be."

"I'm sorry—" Cordelia began as tears filled her eyes. Merciful heavens, she mustn't break down right here, not in front of this woman of all women.

"He needs you," Lady Judith added softly, placing a

hand on Cordelia's arm. "He won't admit it, but he needs your music for his business."

"I-I can't—"

"Judith is right." Lord Kent's voice behind her sounded shaken. He paused as if gathering his thoughts. "You . . . you mustn't let my foolish words drive you away."

Although his tone seemed more gentle now, a far cry from his earlier one, Cordelia stood there uncertain, her shoulders trembling with the effort to keep from crying.

"Please, Miss Shalstone?" Lord Kent gave a shuddering breath. "Please. Will you accept my apology?"

Not sure she'd heard him right, she pivoted slowly to face him. A shock of his hair had come loose from his queue and had fallen onto his cheek, making him look somehow boyish and pitiable. All of Sebastian's words about Lord Kent came back to her, striking at her ridiculously soft heart. She wished she could tear it out at that moment.

"Why should I accept it?" she whispered, fighting her urge to forgive him.

He breathed deeply and clenched his fists about the handholds of his crutches. "Because Judith tells the truth when she says I need you."

It was a tribute to how desperate he was that he could say such a thing, Cordelia thought. His whole body seemed to strain with the effort of lowering his pride.

" 'Tis bad enough that I've lost Handel's support," he continued. "I can't lose yours, too."

She gave one last resistance, her words deliberately harsh. "I thought you didn't believe I wrote the music. I thought you believed women were incapable of composing."

He winced. "I'm sorry. I did speak in anger. But to be honest, I've been rethinking my opinions about women lately." He glanced beyond her to Lady Judith, then returned his gaze to her with a weak smile. "Besides, anyone who prefers Corelli to Froberger can't be an impostor."

Their gazes held for a long moment as they assessed each other. She didn't want to trust his sudden about-face, yet he seemed genuinely sorry. In truth, until this day, she'd admired his quick understanding of her music and his willingness to take a chance on an unknown vicar. It wouldn't be right of her to abandon him now, especially when he'd swallowed his pride to apologize.

"Come on then, gel," her father put in from behind Lord Kent. "Accept the man's apology and be done with it. I'm sorely tired of playing musician."

Scanning the expectant faces around her, she sighed. "All right. It seems I'm outnumbered." She lifted her face stiffly to his. "I accept your apology, Lord Kent."

"And you'll continue to give me your music to publish?"

She stared at him, then nodded. "But on one condition."

Lord Kent eyed her warily. "What's that?"

"I want to drop the 'Anonymous' and put my own name on the works."

He flinched and said in a shaky, disbelieving voice, "Your name?"

"Yes." She took a deep breath. She was tired of pretending to be someone else and having everyone take her for granted. This was her blessed music, and she wanted everyone to know it. "I have the right to use my own name. If you can't accommodate that, then once again, I must withdraw my music from publication."

It was his turn to glance at the expectant faces surrounding him. He looked fierce for a moment, like a cornered bull about to be butchered. Then he shook his head. Beetling his brow, he grumbled, "Oh, all right. It isn't as if it could make things any worse."

Relief flooded her as she heard Lady Judith exclaim softly behind her.

"Speaking of not making things worse," Sebastian

interrupted. "Why do you assume you've lost Handel's support now? I think you should introduce the composer of the chorales to Handel as planned. Perhaps he won't mind that Cordelia is a woman."

After Cordelia got over her shock, she felt her heart soar. When had this happened? Suddenly, Sebastian was on her side. She could kiss him for saying the words she dared not say herself.

Lord Kent moved toward a nearby chair and collapsed into it, his crutches clattering to the floor about him as he buried his head in his hands. " 'Tis true that Handel won't mind that she's a woman. But he'll damned well mind that she's not a vicar."

Confused, Cordelia stared at him. "I thought he didn't know who I was supposed to be. I thought that was the whole purpose of this—to introduced him to the 'Anonymous' composer of the chorales?"

Lord Kent lifted a ravaged face to hers. "It was. Unfortunately, I . . . I got overeager after Sebastian left. I broke my promise to keep your identity secret, and I told Handel the composer was Vicar Shalstone of Belham, who was at this very moment on his way to London."

"Bloody hell," Sebastian muttered.

"Now we'll be back to the same suspicions Handel had before," Lord Kent continued. "He expects a vicar—I bring him someone else. He'll wonder if I'm lying, if I'm trying to deceive him, if I can be trusted." He pounded a fist on his knee. "This whole damn thing came about, you know, because I trusted a woman who lied about the music she claimed to have written. If I introduce Miss Shalstone to Handel, he'll think I've gone and done it again."

"If you *don't* introduce her, then what?" Lady Judith asked gently. "You'll lose your business without him. How can it possibly hurt now to approach him?"

Lord Kent blanched and cast Lady Judith an imploring glance. "You don't understand—"

"I do, Richard, truly I do." Lady Judith stepped toward him. "I know it would be humiliating to be publicly chastised by Handel if he chose to be cruel. But aren't you strong enough to take that?" A pleading note entered her voice. "If you're wrong, however, and he *doesn't* turn you away, you've gained everything. Dear heaven, Richard, what have you to lose?"

In astonishment, Cordelia watched Lady Judith turn from a sweet Madonna into an impassioned Mary Magdalene. The woman seemed very concerned about what happened to Lord Kent.

"Judith's right." Sebastian moved to his brother's side, laying a hand on his shoulder. "You have nothing to lose. Why not try?"

Lord Kent lifted his eyes to stare at Judith, whose face implored him to relent. Some communication seemed to pass between them.

Suddenly he shifted his gaze to Cordelia. "Do you realize what meeting Handel would mean, Miss Shalstone? It would mean braving the lion's den, risking harsher criticism than even I gave you. I couldn't ask you to do such a thing."

She met his gaze steadily. "I've already braved a great many things in coming here, my lord. It hardly matters now what happens to me, as long as I finally get the chance to claim my music as my own."

With a grimace, he pushed himself out of the chair, balancing against the edge as he reached for his crutches. "I don't know," he murmured. "I don't know if I could endure it if Handel refused. Handel gossips as much as the average person. Just as his words of praise could save me, his words of disapproval spoken to a few influential friends could also ruin me forever."

He shook his head mournfully. "I must think on this. You must all give me time to think on this."

Cordelia fought down her disappointment. She'd known to expect Lord Kent's reluctance. Still, it was a blow one could never adequately prepare for.

"In the meantime," Judith interjected as she noted the disappointed faces around her, "the first London subscription concert for one of Handel's new oratorios, *The Messiah*, is tomorrow night. Perhaps it would help if Miss Shalstone could attend and at least familiarize herself with the composer's latest music so she can speak intelligently of it when she meets him."

Lord Kent's eyes bored into Judith. "*If* she meets him."

The woman smiled apologetically. "Of course. 'If' is what I meant to say."

"Going to the concert is a wonderful idea," Sebastian interjected. "I'm sure I can procure seats in a box."

When Lord Kent said nothing, Cordelia felt encouraged. If she and Lord Kent attended the concert, perhaps he might be persuaded to . . .

Then again, he might not be, she told herself, trying to prepare herself for disappointment. Yet the thought of meeting Handel in person struck too much hope in her heart for her to dampen it. Despite herself, a growing excitement rose in her.

At last, she thought. *At last I might have my chance.*

Chapter Twenty

I saw my Lady weep,
And sorrow proud to be advanced so:
In those fair eyes where all perfections keep,
Her face was full of woe.
                                    —John Dowland,
                                    "I Saw My Lady Weep"

The Theatre Royal in Covent Garden was packed for the first performance of Handel's new oratorio. In fact, the newspapers had published a request that "ladies come without hoops and gentlemen without swords," so there'd be more room in the theater, and most had honored that request.

Although London nobility had resented Handel for some time because of his Hanoverian loyalties, many of them had attended the oratorio anyway, unable to resist finding out if the piece was as magnificent as rumored by those who'd heard it in Dublin.

Thanks to his title and reputation, Sebastian had obtained four box seats even though the concert had been sold out for weeks. As he surveyed the theater from an excellent vantage point opposite the King's own box, he allowed himself to relax. After everything else that had gone wrong today, at least he'd managed this.

Amid the chatter and the sound of instruments being tuned, he glanced over at his brother, who sat beside him and behind Cordelia. Richard's eyes were fixed on Judith, who was seated in front of Sebastian.

Don't we both make a pretty pair, Sebastian thought bitterly. Richard pined for Judith, and Sebastian pined for Cordelia. It was absurd. Sebastian wanted to pound his fist against the flimsy walls of the box in frustration.

Obviously Richard desired Judith as much as Sebastian desired Cordelia, yet Sebastian couldn't take advantage of that as long as they were all bound by promises to Baron Quimley. Besides, Judith's feelings were still unclear to Sebastian. Perhaps he'd only imagined that she fancied Richard. Or perhaps she only cared for his brother a little. Sebastian didn't wish to force the issue with her until he'd spoken to the baron, especially since she never went against her father's wishes on anything. First he'd have to secure the baron's agreement. Then Judith would do as her father said.

Unfortunately, this morning when Sebastian had gone to the Quimley estate, he'd discovered that Judith's father had left town suddenly to attend to an emergency at his Suffolk estate, putting Judith in the care of his elderly sister.

Sebastian groaned as his gaze shifted to Cordelia. Her pale face reminded him of yet another complication. At dinner, the vicar had announced his desire to return to Belham on the morrow. Only Cordelia's pleas had made him agree to stay until Richard had made up his mind about the meeting with Handel. Unfortunately, Sebastian couldn't be certain how long Cordelia could hold the vicar at bay. The vicar clearly wanted to return to his parish so he could "marry and get on with my life." When he'd made that bold statement, Mrs. Beardsley had shot Sebastian a questioning look, to which he'd been unable to respond.

Bloody hell, what did the woman expect? He'd only had two days and not a minute alone with Cordelia. There was no telling when the baron would return, and Richard refused to make a decision. How in God's name was Sebastian to persuade Cordelia to marry him when he still couldn't offer her anything but the promise of a broken engagement? Devil take it, she still hadn't even admitted that she *wanted* to marry him.

With a hunger bordering on madness, he watched Cordelia as she stared wide-eyed at the theater around her. No one apparently noticed him, so he let his gaze wander where it would over her form. When he glimpsed the pearl pins in her simple coiffure, he smiled. He knew she'd resisted having her hair powdered. His sisters, Judith, and Mrs. Beardsley had all complained of it. Cordelia had told them that powdering her hair would be like "gilding a wren, totally inappropriate for a vicar's daughter," and at last they'd let her alone. But apparently they'd persuaded her that pearl pins would not be too much "gilding."

Belinda and her maid had also convinced Cordelia to wear an embroidered mantua, and she looked anything but a wren in the rich rose satin. She couldn't look like a wren if she tried. Her skin gleamed above the mantua's low décolletage, and her throat seemed impossibly slender with her hair swept away from it. In short, she looked stunning, and yet she hadn't the slightest realization of it. While Judith wore her beauty like a gift to be displayed, though not flaunted, Cordelia seemed completely unaware of hers.

Ah, what he'd give to lean forward and run his finger along that creamy curved shoulder, up the exposed neck to the soft curls at her nape. He'd slide his fingers in her glossy hair and shake it loose from its pins, then wrap the silky rope in his fist so he could pull her head back to press a kiss on her pale throat. She'd give a small, surprised gasp before lifting her warm mouth to his and—

"There's something I've been meaning to ask you and Miss Shalstone," Richard said next to him, and Sebastian's vision disintegrated, leaving him hard and ravenous and unfulfilled.

"What's that?" Sebastian asked, a bit too sharply.

Cordelia turned her head toward Richard with a quizzical expression.

"Why did the two of you assume the vicar's performance would fool me?"

As Cordelia's face reddened, Sebastian sighed. "You mustn't blame Miss Shalstone for that. She told me from the start the scheme was ludicrous."

Richard scowled. "So why didn't you listen to her?"

Sebastian hesitated, uncertain what to say to assuage his brother's obviously hurt feelings.

Cordelia glanced at Sebastian expectantly, and when he looked blank, managed a wan smile. "Lord Kent, surely you know your brother better than that. He thinks he can manipulate events to his advantage by the sheer force of his will. I think he truly believed if he browbeat me enough, I'd miraculously endow Father with enough musical talent to serve his purposes." She gave a brittle laugh. "Alas, Father is as tone-deaf as your brother is arrogant, and I had some trouble getting around that."

Richard flashed him an assessing look. "If I may speak from experience, Miss Shalstone, Sebastian doesn't take refusals lightly. It's nearly impossible to thwart him once he sets his mind to something."

"You seem to be having no trouble thwarting me in this matter of the Handel interview," Sebastian snapped.

His brother bristled. "Perhaps I recognize what you do not—that this matter is much too important to rush."

Sebastian bit back the harsh retort that sprang to his lips. It did no good to badger Richard. The man became mutinously stubborn when cornered. Still, Sebastian was weary of catering to his younger brother, of worrying about his delicate health. These days, Richard's health seemed far from delicate, which made Richard's grumbling and mulishness even more irritating. The waiting was killing Sebastian, who wasn't very good at it anyway, especially when it might mean losing Cordelia.

He glanced at her. Ever since their arrival, she'd been clutching in her arms the satchel containing the sheet music for her chorales. Ignoring Richard's disapproval, she'd come prepared for an interview, explaining that if it should occur naturally, she wanted to be ready.

Now he could tell from her dejected expression that Richard's words had dampened her hopes. When she placed the satchel gingerly at her feet, he sighed, aching to assure her that her preparation wouldn't be for naught, but knowing better than to try to shield her from the truth. Uttering silent curses at his brother, he forced himself to turn his attention from her to Judith, before he made himself conspicuous in his sympathy.

Judith sought to break the strained silence. "They say His Majesty plans to attend this evening," she said with a bright smile fixed on her face.

"It will take that to squelch the mumbling of the naysayers," Richard muttered.

Cordelia frowned. "Naysayers?"

Judith nodded sadly. "Aye. A few of the most pious members of fashionable circles are outraged that a sacred oratorio should be performed in a playhouse. Heaven only knows why Handel insisted on it. It's brought him a bale of trouble from them and from scandalized clergymen."

Richard nodded. "Several clerics tried to prevent the performance, claiming that the theater is a place of worldly amusement and that public entertainments during Lent are sacrilegious. Somehow Handel persisted in having it go on as planned." A dark gleam entered his eye. "What about you, Miss Shalstone? Since you're a vicar's daughter, I suppose you have strong feelings about such matters."

Sebastian noted the gentle smile that crossed her lips. "I suspect the only people who can't worship God in a playhouse are the same ones who attend the playhouse for more profane entertainment, so their opinion hardly counts, does it? Besides, why do they believe a mere theater can profane God's music? 'Tis more likely that God's music will ennoble the theater."

"An eminently sensible answer, Miss Shalstone," Judith responded with a shy smile.

Sebastian thought how right he'd been to tell Cordelia that she and Judith would get along well. Cordelia was outspoken where Judith wasn't, yet the two women were both tolerant when it counted.

True to Judith's prediction, a short while later the king himself did enter, settling his large bulk in an ornate chair as his hangers-on fluttered about him. It took only a few seconds for the rest of the crowd to respond to His Majesty's entrance with murmurs and pleased smiles.

When Richard pointed His Majesty out to Cordelia, however, Sebastian noted that she seemed unimpressed. In fact, Handel's entrance affected her far more. The instant the composer took the stage to polite applause and not so polite whispers, she straightened in her seat, her eyes darkening in her eagerness.

Then Handel lifted his arms and all fell silent. Cordelia leaned forward, an expectant expression on her face. As the piece titled "Sinfonia" began, Sebastian found himself watching her every move, curious about how she would take the music. After all, he told himself, she'd probably never heard a concert of such magnitude ... not in Belham, and possibly not even in York.

As cascading fugues, intricate polyphonies, and resonant chords surrounded them, wrapping them in shimmering sound, he noted how her eyes lit up and her head nodded to the music. When her lips parted and her face brightened in an expression of pleasure not unlike the one she'd worn when they'd made love, it almost made him jealous.

Yet he couldn't blame her for her delight. The music rippled forth like a glistening bolt of gold-shot silk exposed to light. Even his jaded ears reaped unexpected pleasure from the lilting violins, the sudden shock of trumpets, the thrumming, insistent organ. How much more enjoyment must Cordelia find in it, he thought, when all she'd previously heard were her tinny harpsichord and Belham's wheezing organ? It was as she'd said—the music ennobled the theater. If he closed his eyes, he could easily imagine he was in St. Paul's Cathedral, not the middle of Covent Garden.

When the first chorus came, Cordelia grew even more entranced. As the choir sang, "And the glory, the glory of the Lord shall be revealed," her face mirrored the glory. If the instrumental music had enticed her before, the choral music now transformed her into a wild, wanton creature. Her body swayed, her lips moved with the words of the familiar scripture, and her smile shone so bright, he marveled at the fervency of her joy.

Admittedly, a great gap stretched between these voices and the untaught ones of Belham's choir. Still, it must be more than that, for she looked as if she'd ascended into heaven. Her eyes blazed like fiery jewels in the thousand candles of the theater, and her breath quickened with each accelerated rhythm. If he could only touch her, glean from her ecstasy a small measure for himself, he too might glimpse heaven.

When an unusual rhythm elicited a gasp from her, Richard leaned forward, as if planning to comment, but Sebastian tapped his arm and shook his head. His instincts told him she'd not respond kindly to any interruption, and he wanted badly to see her have her full enjoyment.

In truth, this taste of Handel was his gift to her, and he relished the reflected glow of her pleasure, even though it excluded him. Her joy eased a heart sore with guilt over the way he'd shattered her future. Settling back in his seat, he basked in the light of her enthrallment.

After an hour of plaintive arias and stirring choruses had passed, the music stopped for an intermission. As soon as Handel left the stage, the theater hummed with chattering voices, but Sebastian noticed that Cordelia sat in complete silence for a full minute before stirring, as if out of a long sleep. To his enormous delight, it wasn't to Richard she turned first or even Judith, but to him.

"Isn't it magnificent?" she whispered in an awed voice. "Isn't it the most brilliant music you've ever heard?"

"The most brilliant," Sebastian echoed in a husky voice, thinking more of her smile than of the music. Then he felt Richard's thoughtful gaze on him. Less intensely, he added, "Not like anything you've heard before, I'd wager."

This time her smile included everyone. "Oh, no. I think even Father would appreciate the beauty of this music. And Honorine would love it. We must bring them next time. . . ." She trailed off, and her smile faded. "I-I suppose that must wait until another visit to London."

Not if I have anything to say about it, Sebastian thought fiercely, wishing he could speak the words aloud.

But Richard stepped in with his own comments about the performance, and soon he and Cordelia were thoroughly engrossed in an analysis of the technical aspects of the work. Watching them speak so intently together was more than he could bear.

"I'm going outside for a breath of fresh air," he grumbled to Judith as he stood.

She smiled, then rose. "If you don't mind, I'll go with you. I believe our companions won't be good for real conversation for some hours."

As they passed down the stuffy aisles behind the boxes, she snapped open her fan and fluttered it in front of her face, casting him a sidelong glance as she did so. "Miss Shalstone seems to be very nice."

Her words brought him up short. What had prompted her statement? Was she simply making conversation? He tried to sound casual. "Yes. And she's talented as well."

Judith digested that comment. "You know, despite their rocky beginning, she and Richard seem to get along well."

This time her face looked decidedly strained, and relief flooded him. Jealousy in Judith was a good sign, a good sign indeed when it involved Richard's reactions to Cordelia.

He tested his impressions. "Oh, I think so. I don't mind telling you, it wouldn't bother me to see Richard find an amiable woman he could settle down with." *Just not Cordelia,* he thought.

Her fan working furiously, she asked, "Do you think they would suit?"

He debated how to answer, then decided he'd tormented her enough. "It hardly matters, does it? She's returning to Belham quite soon, I believe." When Judith remained silent, he added, "But no, I don't think so. Miss Shalstone is too independent for Richard. He needs a woman to fuss over him, to agree with him, at least on the surface. Richard requires more attention than I think Miss Shalstone would give him."

Judith stopped in her tracks and looked at him, eyes narrowed. For a fleeting moment, he thought she might speak of her feelings. He thought she might even have guessed his. It was all he could do to refrain from speaking of it himself, but he couldn't until he'd talked to Baron Quimley.

Then Judith dropped her gaze, and the moment passed. Instead they spoke of his estate and what she'd done while he'd been gone. It was a congenial conversation between friends, yet it reminded him how much more he wanted from a woman now that he'd known Cordelia.

When he and Judith returned to the box, the orchestra was tuning up for the second portion of the oratorio and Richard was still talking to Cordelia.

Richard lifted his head and scowled as Sebastian and Judith took their seats. "You two might have told us you were running off."

"I'm surprised you even noticed we were gone," Judith retorted hotly.

Sebastian smiled. It was a bloody shame he didn't have more time. Another week and perhaps Sebastian wouldn't have to say anything to the baron after all. By then Judith's jealousy might so influence her that she'd beg him to break off their engagement.

The music began, banishing his thoughts, and once more he ignored the orchestra. It was Cordelia who held his attention, Cordelia who captured his gaze. As before, she seemed to melt into the music, to become part of it. With her fan she tapped the rhythms on her thigh, and her head bobbed in time as well. Certain sequences of notes made her eyes go wide. Others made her shut them in dreamy contemplation. He thought he would watch her forever.

At one point, she jerked her satchel onto her lap, opened it, and removed a sheet of music and a pencil. Her brow furrowed in concentration, she jotted marks in the margins of the sheet, stopping occasionally to listen, then jotting some more. After a while, she relaxed and put all of the implements back in the satchel, returning it to the floor.

They'd been listening for nearly three-quarters of an hour when an aria faded, and the orchestra broke into a joyous introduction that made even Sebastian sit up. The bassoons and bass viol ascended and descended in bold notes accented by the thrill of oboes and violins. A strange anticipation gripped him, and he leaned forward in his seat. Suddenly jubilant "Hallelujahs" burst from the choir in a solid wall of rapturous sound. His heart stilled as more staccato "Hallelujahs" rained down, starkly splendid.

He'd never heard anything like this before.

Instinctively, he glanced at Cordelia and what he saw there struck him as numb as the music. Tears streamed unheeded down her cheeks. As the purest joy suffused her face, she rose in a trance, drawn upward with the strains of voices and bassoons and trumpets. The words, "for the Lord God Omnipotent reigneth," were answered by "Hallelujahs" and thundering timpani, and Sebastian abruptly realized he and Cordelia weren't the only ones affected. Around the theater, people stirred in their seats, their faces rapt.

Suddenly everyone else in the surrounding boxes stood, and that action rippled through the lower levels. For one mad moment, he thought Cordelia's reaction had prompted the concert-goers to follow her example, as if the other listeners were as tied to her reactions as he.

Then he saw the reason for their rising, and he jerked to his feet himself. Across the way, George II had also struggled to a stand, his face nearly as full of awe as Cordelia's. Everyone else had merely followed the king's lead as the sumptuous fugue unfurled before the crowd like a victory flag.

"King of Kings," the choir sang, and then "Lord of Lords," rising higher and higher until the bell-like soprano voices sang "King of Kings" in an impossibly clear, sweet pitch.

Suddenly Sebastian glimpsed what Cordelia meant when she spoke of searching "for the most joyous psalm in your soul." For the first time in his life, music pierced deeper than the surface of his mind, clear through to the darkest parts of his heart. For the first time, he glimpsed the full extent of creation, the absolute glory. He'd never thought much about God, yet the music made him think he saw God for the briefest moment illuminated in all His power and omnipotence.

Wanting to share the shattering awareness with Cordelia, he stared at her, at her tearstained face and shining eyes, her body straining to unite with the sound. And in an instant he knew he'd do anything for her. He'd give her anything if he could simply share his life with her.

She'll have her interview with Handel, he vowed as the music drew them together like an enveloping cloak. *A pox on Richard and his caution. A pox on Judith and her fears. Tonight Cordelia will have Handel. Tonight I'll give her what she's rightfully earned, by God.*

Then he'd make her his own, regardless of the baron's absence and Judith and all the things holding him back. *Tonight,* he thought, watching her weep un-

ashamedly as the music crashed and roared around
them, saturating the theater with an almost pagan joy.

*Tonight Cordelia will be mine. Tonight. And then
forever.*

Drained yet exhilarated, Cordelia sank into her seat
as the stunning chorus ended. Another intermission began, but she scarcely noticed, her mind too full of
wondrous images and her pulse racing furiously. She
swallowed and flexed her fingers, forcing feeling back
into limbs numb with ecstasy. Never had she heard
such exquisite music. It had nearly been worth everything she'd suffered in the last few weeks just to hear
it.

Shifting in her seat, she sought Sebastian, wanting to
witness his reaction to the chorus she'd reveled in, but
he'd left the box. She stared blankly at his empty seat,
before Lord Kent captured her attention with comments on the chorus. Soon she was so wrapped up in
discussing the concert with Lord Kent that she didn't
notice how long Sebastian was gone until she looked
up as the intermission ended to find him back in his
seat, conversing with Lady Judith.

After the music began, a young boy entered the box
and handed Sebastian a note, and Cordelia wondered at
the smile that curved the edges of Sebastian's lips as
he read the note and dismissed the boy. Then he caught
her questioning gaze on him, and his smile widened.
For a moment, their gazes held. There was a different
look in his eyes than before, a savage yearning so keen
it roused an answering yearning in her. He seemed to
understand her enjoyment and even to share it. His
smile promised worlds. His smile offered her himself,
and she knew it instantly.

An endless moment passed, poignant, private, and
sweet. Then she snapped her attention away from him,
the young boy and the note forgotten in her confusion
over the emotions he stirred in her. It was so unfair of

him to do this to her. How could she ever ease the ache of not having him, of wanting him?

Turning for comfort to the beautiful music, she fought to blot out the pain. But she was constantly aware of his eyes on her, gauging her every response. Oddly enough, it sharpened her enjoyment, for she could feel the connection between them through the music, a connection she craved shamelessly.

The oratorio ended far too soon in a fugue of "Amen's" spun together with silken tones. Applause roared around them as Handel took his bows, and it was some time before another sound could be heard in the theater.

She applauded as wildly as the rest, her throat tight with emotion. She would always remember this night and the man who'd given it to her. If only she could repay Sebastian. . . . But how was she to do that without honoring his request that she come to him in London? That was out of the question, for he'd enslave her for certain if she did that.

Besides, she thought with a pang, he hadn't even tried to get a moment alone with her since yesterday. It was all too likely he'd forgotten about his request. He might feel something for her, but surrounded by his family and fiancée, he'd decided to put all that aside.

Yet his eyes when he looked at her . . .

She forced those thoughts from her mind as Handel left the stage and the audience began to chatter and push from their seats.

Lord Kent gave a loud sigh. "We might as well wait until the crowd thins a bit."

"We're not leaving the theater yet anyway," Sebastian announced in an imperious voice.

All eyes turned to him, especially Cordelia's.

"Why not?" Lady Judith asked.

Sebastian held Cordelia's gaze as he answered. "I'm introducing Miss Shalstone to Handel."

Cordelia's blood thrummed in her ears as she stared

blankly at him. Had Lord Kent changed his mind while she was engrossed in the music?

No, that couldn't be. Lord Kent's face looked stony as he rose shakily from his chair. "What the devil do you mean?"

As Lady Judith glanced from Lord Kent to Sebastian, Cordelia gripped her fan so tightly it snapped. Surely Sebastian didn't mean to override his brother's wishes.

Sebastian smiled at her, then faced his irate brother. "I meant what I said. Miss Shalstone has endured a great deal from you and me, and I think it's time we give her the chance she wants."

Lord Kent clutched the back of his chair with one hand as he ran the other through his hair. "I can't believe you're saying this. You can't decide to take this step without consulting me."

"Why not?"

"Because this is my business, my future you're talking about!" Lord Kent's voice rose menacingly. "Must everything occur on your timetable, at your discretion? Have you no damned concern for what *I* think should be done?"

Sebastian rose, his face rigid. "I've given you two bloody days, and you're still trying to decide what to do. In the meantime, Cordelia's father is ready to leave and your business languishes. I won't make her wait another day. This is her future, too. She has a right to have it settled."

Cordelia sucked in her breath, deeply touched yet surprised that he would champion her so before his fiancée. A part of her wanted what he urged, but another part understood Lord Kent's anger.

"What if I refuse?" the younger man bit out.

Sebastian's eyes glittered. "That's your choice. But I've already sent a message to Handel asking for an interview, and he has agreed to meet with us . . . tonight."

Lord Kent's hands squeezed the back of the chair until his knuckles whitened. "Tonight?"

"Yes." Sebastian's voice lowered. "You don't have to go. If you don't, I'll tell him you discovered the truth about Miss Shalstone and refused to back her. I'll explain that I am introducing her on my own initiative, and that you've washed your hands of involvement with her and her music."

"That's not a choice!" Lord Kent protested. "Then I lose her works too!"

Now that Sebastian had raised her hopes, Cordelia felt compelled to speak. "But Lord Kent, if you continue to publish my works under my name as you promised, Handel will learn the truth anyway. I think Lord Waverley is merely pointing out that you'll be making a choice by not making a choice."

Sebastian nodded. "It's not fair to Miss Shalstone for you to avoid taking a firm stand, so decide what you want to do about her music. Go with us and face the fire, or go home, but for God's sake, choose!"

Lord Kent gritted his teeth, his gaze darting first to Lady Judith, who stared at them both speechlessly, and then to his brother. His eyes narrowed to slits. "All right then. You've forced my hand. I'll go with you."

Cordelia's breath came out in a long sigh, and Sebastian visibly relaxed.

Lord Kent wasn't finished, however. "But I won't allow you to interfere in my affairs any longer, Sebastian. This is the last time you take matters into your own hands." His eyes grew cold, aloof. "As soon as possible, I'll be moving out of Waverley, and I shall stay in the town house until you've returned to India. After tonight, I wish nothing more to do with you."

Lord Kent's pronouncement stunned them all, especially Sebastian, who looked temporarily thunderstruck before his jaw tightened. "Whatever you wish, Richard."

"Don't say that!" Cordelia cried out. Her eyes wide, she clutched at Lord Kent's arm. "Please, Lord Kent, you can't mean to do this. I won't let you. I need not see Handel if it means causing a rift between you and your brother—"

"He knows it's the right thing to do," Sebastian snapped. He knows it, and that's why he's angry."

Richard glowered at him. "I'm tired of having you tell me the 'right thing to do'—"

"Stop this, both of you!" Lady Judith's voice shook with barely suppressed alarm. "You're both behaving like . . . like children!" the two men looked at her, obviously surprised to see her so outspoken.

She colored, but lifted her chin as she faced Lord Kent, "Sebastian is right, you know. It isn't fair to Miss Shalstone to keep her waiting like this. Why not end the matter now? Please, Richard? And let's have no more foolish talk of . . . of moving out of your own home."

Lord Kent's lips tightened. For a second, he looked as if he might strike something or someone. Then he glared stiffly down at the emptying theater. "I see that you're all against me." He cast Lady Judith a look of betrayal, but although her shoulders quivered, she stood her ground. As he stared at her, he softened. "All right then, since it's what you all want, we shall accost Handel tonight."

Then he grabbed his crutches and left the box. His face set, Sebastian reached for Cordelia before he caught himself and took Lady Judith's arm.

Cordelia followed them uneasily, fully aware that Lord Kent hadn't taken back what he'd said about moving. This wasn't how she'd wanted this to happen, yet she felt powerless to stop it. As Lord Kent had said, once Sebastian decided to do something, he did it.

Besides, she didn't want to stop it. Sebastian *was* right. It was time Lord Kent made a decision. She only hoped he'd made the right one.

Then other worries assailed her. What if Handel scorned her? What if he laughed at the possibility that she'd written the chorales? She wouldn't be able to bear that, not now that she'd heard his own wonderful music.

By the time they'd reached the backstage, her stomach muscles were tense from worry and her head ached. So much depended on this interview. She was about to enter the presence of greatness, and she mustn't make a fool of herself now that she'd been given this chance to prove her talent.

But what if he didn't believe her? What then?

She clasped her satchel under her arm. All she could do was tell the truth. If he didn't believe her, she'd be no worse off than before. She only hoped that was also true for Lord Kent.

They found the composer in the theater's tiring room, awaiting them. Most of the other musicians had gone, and although a few people lingered in the pit, most of the audience had left, too, so the theater was relatively quiet.

As they entered, Handel rose. He was in his stocking feet, Cordelia noticed, warming his hands before the fire. That little detail relaxed her a bit, for it reminded her of her father after a long service. He too had always removed his shoes the second he'd gotten the chance.

But her father had never looked quite so imposing in his stocking feet. Despite his short stature, Handel seemed even more impressive in person than he had from the box. His figured silk coat and waistcoat bespoke his status, and his flowing powdered bagwig towered above a full face dominated by large, heavy-lidded eyes and a stately nose. He was stout, yet that imbued him with power, as if the sheer size of him increased the size of his talent.

"Thank you for seeing us, sir," Sebastian said reverentially as he stepped forward and bowed. "I am Lord Waverley, and this is Lady Judith Quimley. You know my brother, of course."

"Yes. Lord Kent," Handel answered in a heavy German accent, then gave a dramatic bow before returning his attention to Sebastian. "It is a great honor to have Your Grace attend my oratorio. What did you think of it?"

Sebastian smiled. "It was excellent. Truly inspired."

"It was the most sublime piece of music I've very heard," Cordelia found herself saying. Then she stopped, aware suddenly that she hadn't yet been introduced.

Handel turned his gaze to her with an indulgent expression. Stepping forward, he took her hand and kissed it. "And who is this lovely creature? Other than a lady of exceptional taste?"

Cordelia's hand trembled in Handel's as she glanced at Sebastian, who looked at Lord Kent.

Drawing a deep breath, Lord Kent said, "This, sir, is Miss Cordelia Shalstone."

"So pleased to meet you, Miss Shalstone," Handel murmured before releasing her hand. Then he pursed his lips and frowned. "Shalstone? That name is familiar."

Lord Kent shifted on his crutches. "Her father is the vicar I told you about."

Handel's face brightened. "Ah, yes, the wonderful vicar. Such beauty, such talent in his music." He stopped, then turned to Lord Kent. "Where is he? Could he not come as well?"

Lord Kent didn't speak, but merely leveled a challenging gaze on her. Cordelia swallowed. He was leaving it to her to tell the truth. She supposed that was only fair, since she'd been the one to perpetrate the deception in the first place.

Cordelia drew in a deep breath. "My father didn't come, sir, because . . . because he didn't write the chorales that Lord Kent publishes anonymously." She swallowed. "I did."

Handel stared at her in dismay. "I don't understand." He pivoted to face Lord Kent. "What does she mean?"

A muscle jerked in Lord Kent's jaw. "When I told you that Vicar Shalstone wrote those chorales, I believed it to be so. His name was always signed to them. But when the Shalstones arrived in London yesterday, I was informed that the real composer is the vicar's daughter. And this is she."

Handel's gaze swung back to her *"Gott in Himmel,"* he muttered as he scrutinized her. His face reflected his disbelief, and when he spoke again, his tones were decidedly chilly. "If you will permit me to say so, madame, you are not what I expected."

Cordelia squirmed under his disapproving scowl. "I-I know, sir. It was wrong of me to use my father's name on my music, but Father urged it, for he feared I would be ... condemned if I wrote under my own name. Ladies who compose aren't generally taken seriously."

He pondered that a moment, his heavy eyebrows lifting in question. "You wanted very badly to compose?"

Wetting her dry lips, she nodded. "Very much. My mother taught me about music, but I always found it more interesting to create my own arrangements than to play someone else's."

Sebastian and Lord Kent were still as statues as they watched Handel, their faces taut. Even Lady Judith seemed anxious. Cordelia herself felt her pulse race as the great man leveled on her a considering stare. She felt almost naked before him, as if he could read her every thought and wish. It gave her an insane urge to flee before he could denounce her as a charlatan and cast her from the room.

His gaze fell to the satchel. "What have you there?"

She opened the satchel with trembling fingers. "My music, sir. It is everything I have done."

He nodded at the satchel. "Allow me to see one of your chorales, a new one."

Forcing some steadiness into her hands, she drew out her latest piece, which she was very proud of, and handed it to him.

He perused it in silence, mumbling under his breath

and here and there humming a few notes. When he looked up, he wore a frown on his face. "You double the third too much in your pieces," he growled. "It is much better to double the fifth."

It took her a moment to find her voice. "I ... I ... of course, you're right. I'm afraid I've gotten in the habit of doubling the third because our choir has weak tenor voices."

He waved his hand dismissively. "Yes, these singers can be troublesome. Even in my oratorio I had to alter the arias to fit my soloist's range. It is so much trouble, is it not?"

She nodded, scarcely able to belive he was speaking to her as if she were an equal.

"Why chorales?" he asked suddenly. "Why did you choose such paltry exercises? Is it the best you can do?"

She stiffened. The worst wasn't over yet. "I've written other things, a prelude or two, but as a vicar's daughter, it made sense to create music the choir could perform at services." She paused, her eyes challenging him. "My domestic duties kept me from having time to compose something as complex as an oratorio, although I'd love to work on a larger piece."

A grave expression crossed his face, drawing the heavy brows together. "Ah, yes, domestic duties. A woman composing has a different life from a man composing, does she not? It hampers your work to do these things. If you want to be serious about your music—"

"I *am* serious about my music," she cut in. "But I also have duties I can't neglect. If anything, having so little time makes me more careful as a musician. I can't afford to play with arrangements as you can, so I must choose the best one the first time I write." She dropped her eyes. "But you're right that my situation presents problems. I could never come close to producing something as magnificent as your *Messiah*." Her voice grew earnest. "I know you must have spent months on it and shed many tears for it."

Something flickered in his eyes and a ghost of a smile played over his lips. "Tears . . . and blood and all those other things we composers are rumored to shed when we create."

He had said *we*. Her heart raced madly, and she jerked her head up to his in shock, but he merely looked at her with a shuttered expression.

"You must tell me all about your chorales," he said gruffly, inclining his head to a settee and some chairs.

Cordelia glanced at Lord Kent, who nodded. Lady Judith's eyes were alight, and Sebastian gave her a reassuring grin as they took the chairs Handel offered. The room was cold, but Cordelia scarcely noticed, for her blood pumped so furiously in her that she felt almost feverish.

It took enormous effort to concentrate on the questions Handel asked. Sitting tensely on the edge of her chair, she buried her damp hands in her skirts for fear they'd betray her nervousness. This was clearly Handel's test of her, to assess her knowledge of music. But as her answers apparently pleased him and his questions became more genial, she relaxed. She even asked a few questions of her own about the "Sacred Oratorio."

After nearly half an hour, Handel suddenly said, "You are a talented beginner, Miss Shalstone, and I have enjoyed our conversation. I wish you good fortune with your music."

There was a note of finality to his words that worried Cordelia. She forced a smile. "Thank you, sir. It has meant a great deal to me to meet you."

He nodded, then rose abruptly. "Unfortunately, I am very tired, so I must be going. If you will all excuse me—"

Cordelia stood too, as did the others, bewildered by the abrupt end to the interview.

Lord Kent cleared his throat as Handel stood there,

obviously waiting for them to leave. "Pardon me, sir, but does this mean you'll agree to let me publish one of your oratorios?"

Running one finger under the collar of his shirt, Handel avoided Lord Kent's gaze. "You must realize you've placed me in a difficult position."

Cordelia sucked in her breath.

"How so?" Sebastian asked boldly.

Handel shrugged. "Nothing has changed from before, Your Grace. I can't support your brother's company after his disastrous mistake with the other young lady's stolen music. My own fortunes rise and fall with the whims of your English lords. I cannot risk the appearance of impropriety."

Lord Kent's face filled with outrage. "You said that if I brought you the vicar—"

"*Ja.*" Handel's voice rose, and his accent grew heavier. "But you have not brought me the vicar. While to me it is obvious that Miss Shalstone wrote the music you publish, to others it will not be so obvious."

"Others? What others?" Lord Kent protested. "The works have been published anonymously. What does anyone care if the writer turns out to be a woman, as long as you and I support her?"

With a sigh, Handel shook his head. "You told me of the vicar. I told others. I will look like a fool if I admit my mistake. It will also rouse old accusations about you. They will say, 'Ah, Lord Kent has found another paramour,' and, 'Whose work has he stolen this time?' "

When Cordelia stiffened, he added more gently, "I know what the truth is, but truth does not matter here in London with wagging tongues everywhere. I am in a precarious position these days. I cannot afford to tarnish my image now that my works finally receive praise again. For me it is too risky."

He flashed Cordelia a kindly smile. "Of course, I will not stand in the way. Continue to publish her music as you see fit. In time people will see its worth . . . if you continue to put the vicar's name to it."

Her heart sank. Despite his harsh manner, she'd been so sure when Handel had talked with her that he would take her side . . .

Sebastian stepped forward, his face livid. "Richard can't continue to publish her music if you don't help him now, sir. Do you truly wish to see it end for her? You said she's a talented beginner, yet you cut her off like this. How is she to proceed, to become 'serious' about her music, as you put it, when she has no publisher?"

Handel fixed her with an intent gaze. "Lord Kent is your only publisher?"

She nodded.

He grew pensive. "Then you must apply to *my* publisher, John Walsh. Perhaps he would deign to publish a piece or two, if I speak with him. You may use your own name, so no one need ever know of your involvement with Lord Kent's company. In such a case, I may be able to help you."

His casual offer struck her dumb. To publish with Handel's publisher! It was a dream beyond belief. Handel himself was offering her a chance greater than she'd ever hoped!

Then she felt Sebastian's eyes on her. Lord Kent wouldn't look at her, but Lady Judith seemed to be waiting with indrawn breath for her answer.

Suddenly she knew she could never betray them all that way. Without Lord Kent, she'd never have had any chance at all. And of course, there was Sebastian. How could she look him in the face if she abandoned his brother?

Regretful tears stung her eyes. "I'm sorry, sir. Your offer is very generous, but . . . but I can't abandon Lord Kent simply because he has fallen on hard times."

To her surprise, Sebastian shook his head. "Cordelia, at least consider—"

"No," she said before she could change her mind.

She'd already caused one rift between Sebastian and his brother. She couldn't cause another. "Thank you, Lord Waverley, for your concern, but I must do this. It wouldn't be right for me to accept Mr. Handel's offer, no matter how graciously he makes it."

Handel regarded her with a different light in his eyes. "You are loyal. *Das ist gut.* I only wish matters could be different." He faced Lord Kent. "Forgive me. I wish you every success with your venture."

Then returning his gaze to her, he gestured to her satchel. "At least leave one piece with me to show my friend. So he will know what he is missing, *ja*? Who knows? Maybe if Lord Kent decides to give up the publishing . . ."

When she hesitated, Sebastian took the satchel from her, opened it and withdrew a sheet of music, then thrust it at Handel.

"Not that one—" she began, for it was the sheet she'd used to make notes during the oratorio.

It was too late. Handel had seen the notes. He glanced at them, then peered more closely, his face darkening. He stabbed one finger at her scribblings. *"Was ist das?"*

"It-it's some notes I made about the oratorio . . . during the arioso, 'Their sound is gone out,' " She held her breath, praying he wouldn't think she'd been trying to steal his music.

He peered at her hastily drawn staff. "You change it into a chorus."

She nodded stiffly. "Excuse my impertinence, sir, but I thought it would make a delightful chorus."

Handel's hard stare made her want to run, yet after all that had happened, it also angered her. If she wanted to experiment privately with his music, it shouldn't concern him. He wouldn't have known about it at all if Sebastian hadn't given him the wrong piece of music. Handel had no right to look at her that way, especially when he'd refused to help Lord Kent.

She crossed her arms over her chest as she threw

caution to the winds. "You know how *we* composers are, sir. We are always toying with new arrangements, but I assure you, I wasn't attempting to steal your arioso." Jutting her chin out, she added arrogantly, "Feel free to use my version if you wish."

His eyes widened at her insolence, but she didn't stay to hear whatever scathing retort he might make. She'd had enough of being forced to prove her worth. Let him think what he wished. Like all men, he'd do what he wanted no matter what she said.

So gathering her tattered pride about her, she stalked from the room.

Chapter Twenty-one

Awake, sweet love, thou art return'd:
My heart, which long in absence mourn'd
Lives now in perfect joy.

—John Dowland,
"Awake, Sweet Love"

Everyone remained silent as the coach neared Waverley. No one had spoken a word since they'd left Handel. What, after all, was there to say? Cordelia thought.

She couldn't bear to look at any of their faces and see their disappointment. She'd done what she could, but still she felt guilty. Perhaps if she'd explained to Handel how much Lord Kent had done for her ... Or perhaps if she'd told him—

Oh, what was the use, she told herself. Handel only cared about his own future, not hers or Lord Kent's. And could she really blame him?

"Would you like the coach to take you home after we disembark?" Lord Kent asked Lady Judith.

That brought Lady Judith out of her silence. "No. We promised everyone at home that we'd have a late supper and tell them all about it. I shan't disappoint them."

Lord Kent snorted. "I don't feel like pretending to smile and be merry when we all know 'tis the end for my business."

Lady Judith ignored his grumbling as she turned to Cordelia. "What about you, Miss Shalstone? Will you have supper?"

She wished she could say no, but her father and

Honorine deserved to hear a full account of all that had happened. "I suppose so."

Sebastian remained quiet, although she felt his eyes on her. It suddenly occurred to her that now there was nothing to keep her in London. Father and Honorine would want her to return with them, and tomorrow would be as good a day to leave as any.

That thought weighed her down as they reached the manor. Nor did it lessen her sadness to find the whole company eagerly awaiting them, filled with excited questions. When she wouldn't meet Honorine's inquisitive gaze, her friend stiffened, apparently sensing that something was wrong. Placing an arm around Cordelia, Honorine didn't ask a single question, but merely squeezed tightly.

But as they all strolled toward the dining room, Sebastian headed for the stairs.

Lady Judith stopped and turned. "Sebastian, where are you going? Won't you join us? Even your grouchy brother is supping."

Sebastian shook his head. "Perhaps I'll be along later." He flashed Cordelia an enigmatic glance. "I have some matters to attend to in my study."

Lady Judith shrugged and followed the girls into the dining room, but Cordelia couldn't resist looking after Sebastian in disappointment. One night was all they had left, and he wouldn't even give her that. She forced back tears. No doubt he was disappointed in her inability to convince Handel. She sighed. There was nothing she could do about that.

Supper was an elaborate affair. Mercifully, Lady Judith carried the bulk of the conversation, somehow managing to explain what had happened without placing blame on anyone. Even that didn't soothe Cordelia's hurt. She wished Sebastian were there, then cursed herself for wishing it.

They'd just begun the second course when a servant boy entered the room and came quietly to Cordelia's side, handing her a note. She opened the note and stared at the words before her, at first not quite able to believe them.

Come to me was written in a bold male handwriting. She'd never seen Sebastian's handwriting, but she knew it was his nonetheless. *I'll await you in my study. We must speak.*

The boy had already left, no doubt to keep her from sending a refusal. She clenched the note in her hand. *Come to me.* The words spawned a turmoil within her. They were such small words to bear such great meaning.

She glanced around the table. Had the others noticed the servant boy giving her the note? No one seemed to have done so. Apparently, they'd all been too busy questioning Richard about the night's events. She could remain here, and no one would be the wiser.

Come to me.

The words burned into her thoughts. He'd written, *We must speak,* but was that all he intended? If he wished to make love to her, she couldn't allow it, for it would lay waste to all her resolve. If he asked her again tonight to be his mistress, she feared she'd accept, and that would be unforgivable.

Yet she wanted to see him alone one last time. Besides, if she didn't at least go and tell him he must pursue her no more, he would keep at it until she'd left. Worse still, he might accost her tonight in her bedchamber, and that would be disastrous. No, she must see him, if only to put an end to this.

Before she could think another moment about it, she rose from the table. "I-I'm sorry." All eyes turned to her. "I'm more tired than I realized. I think I shall retire early."

Now it's done, she thought as she hastened from the room, her heart hammering in her chest. She could still turn back, could indeed go to bed, but she knew she wouldn't. Her only fear was that someone else might wonder about the fact that both she and Sebastian were absent from supper.

To be certain no one followed her, she waited outside the dining room, fearful that Honorine at least might guess where she was going. But when no one came, she relaxed. Thank goodness no one had noticed anything odd about her departure.

Her mind more at ease, she climbed the stairs.

But someone had indeed noticed the circumstances of her departure. Judith. The minute the boy had entered and given Miss Shalstone his message, Judith had watched the woman, only half listening to Richard give his own gruff version of the evening's events.

Now Judith wondered if the note had anything to do with Miss Shalstone's sudden exit. Who could be sending the woman a message? Judith wondered, looking to Richard to see if he'd noticed too.

But the sight of his grim face as he spoke bitterly of the Handel interview drove all thoughts of Miss Shalstone's mysterious exit from her mind.

She sighed as she noted his worn expression. Oh, what were she and Richard to do now?

A month ago she'd been content to be Sebastian's fiancée. He was a fine man, after all, and they'd had an amiable friendship since childhood. She'd always thought that was the most she could expect from her marriage. Then Richard had kissed her, and everything had changed.

In truth, it had begun to change before that . . . when she first realized how ill he'd become. Richard had always simply been there, someone she could depend upon to advise her as he did his sisters. When it had become evident he might not survive the loss of his business, it had thrown her into an inexplicable panic. That had been the real reason for her increased presence at Waverley while Sebastian had been away.

Yesterday when she'd told Richard she couldn't go against her father's wishes and refuse to marry Sebastian, she hadn't considered how differently she might feel when she saw Sebastian again. Now she knew she couldn't marry Sebastian when all she wanted was

Richard. Unfortunately, tonight's events had put Richard beyond her reach, thanks to his stubborn pride. Richard would never marry her now, when he had no prospects and he knew his brother could offer her everything.

She sighed. In truth, even if Richard would offer for her, Father would never accept him. If only she could convince Father that a marriage to Sebastian would never work. But how could she when Sebastian was the most upright, honorable, wealthy suitor she'd ever had and a duke besides? Father wouldn't believe a word of her protests, nor would he countenance them. And marrying Richard without Father's approval was unthinkable.

She brightened. Maybe Sebastian could be convinced to cry off. It was true he'd changed toward her since his trip to Belham. He seemed far more interested these days in furthering Miss Shalstone's prospects as a composer than planning for his own upcoming marriage.

Suddenly she froze as all the events of the night passed through her mind ... Sebastian's comments about Miss Shalstone's unsuitability for Richard, his strange absorption in the woman, his fervent words in defense of her right to see Handel....

Miss Shalstone had left after receiving a note, Judith mused, and Sebastian was the only one not present at the supper. Her pulse quickened. Could it be? Was it possible that Sebastian and Miss Shalstone ...?

Excusing herself from the table, she left the room and searched out the servant boy who'd brought the message. It took only a few careful questions to determine that the message had indeed come from Sebastian in his study.

Her expression grew calculating. Obviously something improper was going on or Sebastian would have asked to speak with Miss Shalstone in front of everyone before they'd gone in to supper. And Miss Shalstone, after receiving the message, would have said exactly where she was going.

She clapped her hands together. This was too perfect! If Sebastian and Miss Shalstone were at present engaged in some tête-à-tête, all she had to do was happen upon them as if by accident and catch them in a compromising kiss or embrace. Then no one could fault her for calling off the engagement. No one, not even Father!

Then she frowned. Such a situation was bound to be embarrassing. She'd have to pretend to be angry, and endure a fight with Sebastian. She wasn't very good at that sort of thing.

Besides, breaking her engagement was only the first step in ensuring that Richard offered for her. With his business in its present state, he might still balk. . . .

Suddenly it occurred to her exactly what she must do. She glanced quickly toward the second floor, where Sebastian's study was situated, then nodded to herself.

Yes, that would work quite well, she thought as she strode the length of the hall. She'd have to give Sebastian and Miss Shalstone a little more time together, but then she could put her plan into place.

With a slow secret smile all her own, she returned to the dining room.

Sebastian furiously paced the floor of his study. What would he say to Cordelia when she came? Perhaps if he told her right out that he loved her, that he wanted to marry her, she'd relent.

It was true, after all. He did love her. He'd finally realized that. Until tonight, he'd admitted to liking her, to wanting her, but not to loving her. Until tonight, he'd believed love to be a silly emotion invented by bored women. Marriage was a business proposition, to be considered only in that light.

But from the moment Cordelia had entered his life, he'd been forced to question all his beliefs. Then tonight, when her face had glowed with rapture, he'd known she meant everything in the world to him. That was love, wasn't it?

If he told her all that, she'd marry him, wouldn't she?

Her words came back to him, "I want to be an independent woman," and he cursed under his breath. If he told her he loved her and wished to marry her, would she believe him? And if she did, would she admit she wanted the same, or would she continue to uphold her brave front? Would she insist she wanted only to be independent? His instincts told him that no matter what she professed, she didn't feel it in her heart. But how to make her admit it?

One thing was certain—he mustn't alarm her as he had before. First he must force her to admit she loved him, that she wanted him as much as he wanted her. Then he'd use her own words against her to prove she didn't truly want independence. Somehow he'd make her see they were meant to be man and wife.

But before any of that could happen, she had to come.

Bloody hell, what if she didn't? What if she ignored his summons? What if it had been a mistake to send for her this way?

He hadn't seen any other discreet choice. Going to her room tonight was out of the question, for her room adjoined one of his sister's. Asking her to come to his room wouldn't do, for that would drive her away quicker than anything.

With the Handel incident over, she'd probably leave tomorrow. He couldn't let that happen, of course. If forced to it, he'd publicly propose to her, before Judith and everyone.

But he wanted to avoid hurting Judith with such an abrupt announcement. Well, perhaps if Cordelia didn't come tonight, he could speak to Judith privately, convince her to break the engagement even though it meant her standing up to her father.

Suddenly, he heard the door to his study open. He whirled to find Cordelia in the doorway.

His pulse raced at the sight of her looking so frightened and so utterly, wrenchingly beautiful in the candlelight. "You came," he whispered.

Her hand went to her throat as she realized he'd shed his coat and waistcoat and now wore only his open-necked shirt and breeches. With a sudden start, she jerked her gaze back to his face. "Clearly I shouldn't have."

He hurried to the door, pulling her inside and shutting it behind her before she could flee. "You did, and that's all that matters."

She shook her head violently, her eyes wide as she backed away from him. "I came only to say that you must stop this."

Ignoring her words, he clasped her waist and drew her to him. Her lips tightened as she pressed her hands against his chest. "No, Sebastian. There can be nothing between us. You know that. Tomorrow I'll leave and—"

He kissed her before she could say another word. Ah, her mouth was silky sweet and every bit as delectable as he remembered. She was stiff at first, like an untried maiden, but after a few seconds she went limp beneath his hands. Only then did he allow himself the pleasure of stroking her body, of reacquainting himself with its contours . . . the gentle weight of her cloth-draped breasts, the slender waist, the pleasant fullness of her hips.

He hadn't intended to make love to her here. His bedchamber adjoined his study, and he'd wanted to carry her there, but now he feared if he stopped long enough to do so, she'd dash away. He drew back a moment, glancing around the room until his gaze fell on the huge bearskin rug before the fireplace.

"No," she whispered as she followed his eyes. "I didn't come here to . . . to . . ."

His gaze snapped back to hers, and he raised one eyebrow. "Yes, you did." With slow, deliberate movements, he removed the pearl pins from her hair and tossed them to the floor. "You may not admit it, but you came because you want me as much as I want you. And you couldn't leave without letting me love you again."

Her hair untwisted and fell about her shoulders, mantling them in glossy brown. "Th-that's not true. You said we needed to talk."

"We do." He smiled. "But first, we'll talk with our bodies, and you'll admit all the things you refuse to say with words."

Her eyes dropped from his. "Wh-what things?"

Capturing her chin with one hand, he tilted her head up until she was forced to look at him. "That you want me. That you relish every kiss, every caress between us." He rubbed his thumb along her delectable lips. "By the end of this night, angel, you'll admit that . . . and so much more."

Her breath quickened as alarm flickered in her gorgeous eyes.

He lowered his mouth to within an inch of hers. "I'll make you admit how much you care."

Then he covered her trembling lips again, coaxing them to part, plunging his tongue deep into the heated softness and reveling in her answering moan. Bloody hell, but she drove him mad. How he wanted her. But he must be careful. He must entice her to him with offers of pleasure she couldn't resist. He waited for the tension to ebb from her body again as her urges overwhelmed her.

Only when her arms stole around his neck did he release her chin, dragging his thumb along the line of her jaw and down her smooth neck. His lips followed the same sensuous path, nibbling and kissing as she arched back, baring her throat even more to his tasting.

He ran his tongue along the ridge of her upper jaw, then around her ear before he whispered, "You don't want to leave me tomorrow, do you, angel?"

"No-o-o," she said in a long drawn out murmur that fired his blood.

He kissed her temple, then her brow and her closed eyelids as his hands circled her back to find the ties of her laced bodice. He tugged them loose, but when he then untied the laces of her corset, she gasped and twisted against him in alarm, which only served to loosen her clothing further. As the offending garments slid away from her chest, he dropped kisses along the edge of her flushed cheek and down into the sweet hollow of her throat.

Then he pressed her against the closed door, letting her feel his arousal. Her eyes shot open. She looked wary, yet he could see the wanting in her face. Her lips parted, and he joined his to hers in a greedy kiss. When he drew back, her head had fallen against the door.

"I want to make love to you," he murmured, sliding one hand beneath her shift to cup her breast. "Please, angel, let me love you."

She closed her eyes, a frown creasing her brow as she wrenched her head to the side, laying her cheek against the walnut door. "You'll destroy me."

Her whisper held so much fearful urgency it confused him. Couldn't she see that her power over him was thricefold his over her? Couldn't she see he didn't seek to destroy her but to love her?

Slowly he kneaded her breast, watching as her face grew flushed. "Does this destroy you?"

She nodded even as her hands clutched his waist. "You want me to give up everything for you . . . my pride . . . my . . . my independence."

"Devil take your bloody independence! I love you. Tell me that means nothing to you."

Her eyes flew open, and she stared at him, startled. A sudden panic filled her face. "Don't say those words! I don't want you to say you love me if it only means . . ." She twisted her head away, her face taut. "I don't want you to say you love me."

"If it only means what?" He thumbed her nipple until she moaned. "Tell me, Cordelia, what you were going to say."

"Nothing. . . . I-I only want you to leave me alone."

It was on his lips to tell her he was breaking his engagement, that he would marry her, wanted to marry her. But he'd said the words once before, and she'd refused him. Bloody hell, first he'd make her admit she loved him. Then she couldn't refuse him again.

He cupped her face in his hands. "You refuse to be my wife . . . you refuse to be my mistress. . . . You say you want independence, then melt when I touch you. Apparently, the only thing you want from me is my body."

"I don't . . . want your body either," she whispered, but she refused to look at him.

She tried to drop her arms from around his waist, but he caught her hand and brought it to his cheek. "My poor liar. 'Tis a pity your body tells the truth so sweetly."

When he released her hand, her fingers stroked his skin as if of their own accord, and he turned his head to catch one finger in his mouth, sucking the tip until her cheeks grew rosy.

"Your blushes say you want me," he rasped. "Will you deny it?"

He trailed his lips to her wrist and tongued the place where the pulse beat madly. "Your blood races with wanting me. Will you deny it?"

Entwining her fingers with his, he lifted their joined hands to the top of one breast, sliding them against the thin muslin shift. Her breath came in staccato gasps as she watched him rub the nipple into a hard pebble. "Your body aches for me. Will you deny it?"

Before she could answer, he untied her shift and pushed down the low neck, then covered her breast with his mouth. As he sucked hungrily at the velvety soft skin with its hard little crown, her body melted against his like a cat's when stroked.

He raised his head then and stared at her flushed face. *"Will you deny it?"* he repeated earnestly.

With a low moan, she shook her head.

That wasn't enough. "Say it, Cordelia. At least say you want me."

"I want you."

The throaty murmur nearly undid him. He covered her face with kisses and she tore at his shirt, her inhibitions gone. He jerked his shirt over his head, then feverishly began working her gown and shift down her body.

When he'd gotten her arms half-free, he stopped. A smile spread over his face as he realized that the tight-fitting sleeves trapped her arms. He suddenly had a thoroughly devious idea.

She stared at him, her eyes now heavy-lidded and dark with desire. "Sebastian?"

Groaning, he lifted her in his arms and strode to the rug, laying her down on it, then standing over her as he unbuttoned his breeches. He hesitated a moment, scarcely able to believe he'd gotten her at least to admit she wanted him.

Cordelia herself couldn't believe she'd admitted it. Was it as he'd said, that she'd intended this from the moment she'd come to him? She squirmed under his lingering gaze, suddenly aware that she couldn't get out of her gown without help.

He removed the rest of his clothing leisurely, his eyes hotly raking her body. Her throat felt painfully raw with desire, especially as he slowly revealed the full extent of his arousal. Merciful heavens, but his body was splendid—sleek, long-limbed, and well-muscled. As she surveyed the body she craved, her tongue darted out to wet her lips.

He gave a half-smile, then knelt and ran one long finger over her mouth and chin, searing a path to her breast. She tried to wriggle out of her gown, but he lowered his body next to hers and continued to caress her breasts and the part of her belly he'd already bared.

"What are you doing?" she choked out.

"I'm going to make love to you."

"Yes, but . . . you must—" She blushed. Surely he knew she couldn't get free alone. "You must help me with my . . . my . . ."

"Not yet," he murmured, his eyes devilish.

She tried to wriggle free of the sleeves, but she couldn't.

"Not yet," he repeated more firmly. He covered her body with his, essentially trapping her arms at her sides.

A moment of real fear assailed her. Then his mouth slanted over hers, and she forgot everything. Merciful heavens, but the man could kiss. He stabbed his tongue deep, then withdrew it in enticing strokes that made her squirm against him.

When his hands slid her over-skirt and petticoat up her legs, the cold kernel of resistance in her belly exploded into hot, hard wanting. He ran his fingers over her hose, past her garter, then along the inside of her bare thigh, tickling the silky skin. Mindlessly, she twisted beneath him, struggling to free her arms so she could clasp him close.

But she was still trapped. When she tore her lips from his to murmur, "Please, Sebastian, let me touch you, too," he gazed into her feverish face with his wolfish eyes.

"Do you love me?"

She shut her eyes to blot out his face. It wasn't fair, she thought, her fingers digging into the fur rug. He said he loved her, but only so he could enslave her, and now he wanted her to give him the key to her imprisonment. He wanted her to admit everything, so he could have her at will, make her stay in London and be his mistress while he ruled his dominion with Judith at his side. She mustn't let him gain that advantage over her, for then she'd be lost. Utterly lost.

Then his finger stroked the secret place between her legs, and she gasped.

"Do you love me, angel?" he repeated, his voice hoarser now.

"I-I want you."

"Bloody hell, I know that."

The arrogance behind his words made her eyes fly open, but his face showed no hint of arrogance. The muscles were strained into a pained grimace, as if he struggled to control himself. She could even feel his heated shaft against her leg. Why wouldn't he take her and be done with it? Why was he holding back, tormenting her like this?

He stroked her again with such an achingly slow caress it made her throb all over. "Do you love me?" he growled.

In a flash she understood. He was using her desire as a weapon. His finger thrust deep into her, and she arched up against it despite herself.

Oh, he was such a beast. Well, his weapon could cut both ways, she thought. She, too, could make him relinquish control, and she must do so before he made her reveal her heart. She shifted her thigh to rest against his shaft, rubbing along it as she thrust her breasts against his chest.

He moaned, his amber eyes afire, but he shifted the lower half of his body away from her. "Not this time, temptress. This time *I* will do the seducing."

Then he lowered his head to her breast and cupped her nether regions, and she knew it was war. His warm fingers explored deeper and deeper in the slick inner passage, but whenever the sweet urgency in her loins built to a peak, he pulled back, then began the dark torture all over again. He stormed every entrance, fondling, kissing, making her ache and sigh as she bucked beneath him.

And though she knew he burned, too, for he uttered a guttural groan every time she cried out for more, he wouldn't relent. He dangled fulfillment within her reach, then denied it to her.

At last he withdrew his magical fingers completely

and lifted his head to fix her with a wild gaze. "Do you love me?" he growled as sweat beaded his forehead. "Admit you love me, Cordelia, and I swear I'll move heaven and earth for you, tonight and every night for the rest of our lives."

His words barely reached her in the midst of her sensual haze. She wanted to scream in frustration, to pound his chest, but she couldn't. If she could only calm her thundering heart, somehow ignore the fires he stoked with each new assault. . . .

"You're a devil, Sebastian—" she choked out.

His lips tightened in a grim crease. "Sweet mother of God, Cordelia, I love you and I know you love me. Admit it, damn it! I swear I'll not stop until you admit it!"

With those ominous words he removed his hand from between her legs. She gasped, both relieved and disappointed, thinking perversely that he'd given up. Then he shifted his body lower until his head was below her belly. Slowly, he pushed her petticoat and over-skirt up around her waist, exposing her completely to his view.

Her cheeks were aflame as he boldly surveyed what her bunched-up clothing blocked from her own eyes. She held her breath, wondering, fearing what he intended.

Then he lowered his head and kissed her in the most unusual place. Shocked, she flinched as he lifted his head and flashed her a challenging smile. His audacity outraged her, yet she sensed that he intended more.

And oh, he did. He dropped his head again, and after that, her thoughts disintegrated into nothing. For he did more than kiss her. His mouth did to her what his fingers had done before, only better.

His warm tongue stroked, and she writhed at the exquisite sensations darting through her like a million tiny pleasure shocks. As he grew bolder . . . and rougher . . . she twisted her head from side to side. After all his earlier torment, this was too much. . . . No, it was too little. She wriggled beneath him, thrusting against his mouth in a vain attempt to get more.

A cry tore from her throat, but that merely made him torture her with more delicacy. "Sebastian ... please ... oh, please—"

"That's it, angel," he muttered. "Beg as you've made me beg. Tell me what you want."

"I-I want you to ... to ..." She trailed off, not even knowing how to ask for it.

His hot mouth closed over her again and she bucked so hard, she nearly shook him off, but he knew exactly what he was doing. He settled into a rhythm that enticed her so powerfully, she lost all sense of place or time. It was a heartless heaven and a holy hell, and he ruled both. She didn't even notice anymore that her arms were trapped, for Sebastian's sensual music thrummed through her body, forcing her to dance to his pace.

When he had her near to exploding, he drew back again and raised himself over her, his rock-hard shaft nudging between her legs as he glared down at her, his face stark, hungry. She could tell he was as near the breaking point as she.

"Do you love me?" he ground out, sinking in an inch and then withdrawing. "Bloody hell, Cordelia, say it!"

Despite her despicable craving to feel him inside her again, she choked back the words. If she said them, she'd be enslaved forever. There'd be no dignity left to her.

"Please let me h-hold you," she whispered instead, a helpless whimper escaping her lips.

His eyes widened, and a bleak expression crossed his face. Then with a savage groan, he pulled back and tore down her gown, freeing her arms and baring the rest of her body.

As he tossed the gown to the side, he covered her body. "Sweet mother of God," he growled, "I can't take any more." Then he drove into her.

Free at last, her arms clutched his back and her fingernails dug into the expanse of skin-wrapped steel. Then she held on for dear life as he rode her with the same frenzy he'd roused in her. His sweet torture had heightened her desire to a fever pitch, and now she hungered so urgently for release that she met his stabbing thrusts with violent, arching thrusts of her own.

You want a bloody stallion, she remembered him saying. Yes, she thought. She'd wanted one and she'd gotten one, lunging and bucking with the savage energy of untamed force as he carried her on the wind toward a release that came closer . . . closer . . .

"Angel, angel . . ." he murmured, his breath coming hard and fast against her taut neck. "Be *my* angel . . ."

His strokes quickened, but he'd teased her too long, and now her release came in a fiery stroke of pure light that split all her pride in two.

"Sebastian . . . ah, Sebastian . . . I love you!" she cried out as his thrusts shattered her defenses and she shuddered, her body straining up to fuse with his.

Then he, too, gave a wrenching cry as with one mighty final lunge, he spilled his seed into her.

He fell on her, and she clasped him possessively against her slick, spent body. They both breathed hard, like horses after a race, except that he had won this race. Blast the man, he'd won.

But had he even heard her cry out the words he'd tortured her for? she wondered as her mind reasserted dominion over her wayward flesh. He buried his face in her shoulder, his breath there tickling her. Allowing herself to enjoy the moment, she stroked his back and tried to forget that she'd just given him the ultimate weapon against her.

"I love you, too," he whispered against her ear.

So he had heard, she thought despairingly as she stared up at the coffered ceiling. Then again, what did it matter? After what they'd just done, she could never leave him now. Mistress or wife, it was all one. She must have him. It was as she'd thought. He'd enslaved her.

She was so intent on her painful thoughts that she scarcely heard the door to the study open. But an explosive curse brought her completely out of her reverie.

She and Sebastian jerked apart and stared in startled amazement at the doorway. And there, his face white as death, stood Lord Kent.

"Bloody hell," Sebastian muttered.

For once she shared his sentiments completely.

Chapter Twenty-two

But when with moving accent thou
Shalt constant faith and service vow,
Thy Celia shall receive those charms,
With open ears, and with unfolded arms.
—Nicholas Lanier,
"Mark How the Blushful Morn"

Richard couldn't believe his eyes. When he'd heard strange cries coming from behind Sebastian's study door, he hadn't bothered to knock. All he'd thought of was how worried Judith had been that Sebastian might be distraught over his earlier threat to leave Waverley.

Richard had rushed in, never expecting to find his brother and a naked woman. And not just any woman, he realized as he glimpsed Miss Shalstone's startled face before Sebastian threw her discarded gown over her.

At that point, another man might have muttered an apology and withdrawn, but not Richard. He was already too angry at his brother for interfering in his business, and at Miss Shalstone for not being a vicar. This was the last straw.

He slammed the door behind him, deriving a perverse pleasure from his brother's shocked face and Miss Shalstone's growing embarrassment.

"For God's sake, man, get out!" Sebastian commanded as his shock altered to fury. He stood and jerked on his drawers. "Bloody hell, Richard, haven't you the decency to leave?"

"Decency? You speak to me of decency while you're rutting on the floor with your paramour? Never mind that your fiancée is sick with worry over you. Never mind that Judith's an innocent woman who never did you a day of harm. Damn you, Sebastian, isn't it enough that you have Judith? Must you also bed any wench with a sweet face and fine ass who happens to cross your path?"

A choked cry came from beneath the pile of clothing, and Miss Shalstone's "sweet face" emerged to cast a scathing glare his way.

But Sebastian's glare was ten times more lethal. "I could kill you just for having seen that 'fine ass'! Get out, before I forget you're my brother and do something I'll regret later!"

"I expect some explanation from you. After this, there's no damned way I'll let Judith marry you." Richard's outrage knew no bounds. "I'll die before I see you treat Judith with this lack of conscience."

Sebastian uttered a low curse, his gaze flitting to Cordelia. He motioned to the door a few feet from her, the one that led to his bedchamber. "In there, love," he murmured gently. "I'll be with you in a moment."

Careful to shield herself from Richard's eyes with her clothing, she fled in the direction Sebastian had indicated, her expression showing she was all too eager to escape.

As soon as the door shut behind her, Sebastian whirled on his brother in a rage. "I don't plan to marry Judith, and if you hadn't been so bloody inconsiderate as to barge in on me, you'd have found that out tomorrow. I'm marrying Cordelia."

Richard opened his mouth, then snapped it shut. Sebastian was marrying Miss Shalstone instead of Judith? "When did you decide this? Why hasn't Judith said anything to anyone?"

Sebastian sighed. "I haven't told her yet. I was waiting to speak to the baron first, but I didn't think she'd be too shattered."

At Sebastian's ironic tone, Richard's sense of horror grew. "As usual, you don't consult anyone before you set off on your own path. How could you treat her this way ... how could you ...?" He trailed off when he realized the full implication of Sebastian's words. For God's sake, this meant Judith was finally free! So why was he so upset?

"What are you doing here anyway?" Sebastian grumbled, his fingers stabbing through his disheveled hair as he glanced anxiously toward the door to his room. "And what's this about Judith being sick with worry over me?"

All of Richard's righteous indignation came flooding to the fore. "She's the one who sent me looking for you. She said she was worried you might be brooding over my words earlier. What a jest! I can see 'brooding' isn't exactly the word for what you've been doing!"

Sebastian seemed to ignore his sarcasm. Instead he went still, his eyes narrowing. "Judith sent you to look for me? Why didn't she come herself? Or for that matter, why didn't she come with you?"

The very thought of Judith witnessing this ... outrage made him feel sick. "Aren't you glad she didn't?"

When Sebastian's eyes grew calculating, Richard stared at his brother in amazement. And when his brother then smiled, he had to clench his fist to keep from walloping Sebastian with his crutch.

"Well, well," Sebastian remarked. "So the Biddable Judith has an aggressive streak in her after all. And a devious one as well."

"What on earth are you talking about?"

"I suppose she thought this was the only way to make you take the plunge. I wonder how she knew—"

"Would you mind explaining what the hell you're blathering about?"

Sebastian shrugged. "Judith has shown about as much concern for me since my return as a mare shows a bull. It didn't take me long to figure out she had another companion in mind." He shot Richard a searching glance. "And I suspect the stallion she wanted was close to home."

It took a moment for Richard to realize what his

brother hinted at. Richard drew a ragged breath and said tightly, "I don't know what you mean."

"Come now, I know you want Judith. I'm delighted, tickled pink, especially since Judith returns the feeling. She must, or she wouldn't have sent you in here—"

"She didn't know you were here with your . . . your . . ."

Sebastian chuckled. "Didn't she?"

Suddenly the last hour passed before Richard. He remembered Judith leaving the dining room shortly after Miss Shalstone had, then returning with a smile on her face. And later, when she'd urged him to find Sebastian, she'd been more insistent than he'd ever seen her. He'd wanted to wait until the morrow; she'd said no. It hadn't occurred to him to wonder why she insisted on waiting in the drawing room for his return instead of going with him. He'd been too furious at her apparent concern for Sebastian to note much of anything.

His heart began to pound. In a daze, he pivoted toward the door.

"Now don't scare her off," Sebastian said jovially from behind him. Then his voice deepened. "Speaking of scaring someone off, I hope you can take care of this alone, because I have to—"

But Richard was already out the door, moving as fast as his crutches would allow.

When he reached the drawing room, he paused for a moment to gather his scattered and impetuous thoughts. Could Judith possibly have intended him to find Sebastian and Miss Shalstone in the midst of . . . It didn't seem like her, yet everything Sebastian had said made sense.

He stared at the drawing room door, his lips tightening. One way or the other, he'd find out. And so help him, if this was Judith's peculiar way of getting him to propose . . .

He grinned. He'd do this right, so he could catch his wily little love, but by God, he'd teach her a lesson while he was doing it.

He opened the door. Judith whirled the moment he

entered, and he felt sure he saw the faintest hint of guilt on her face. Then she stared at him, as if to assess what he'd seen, but when he closed the door and leaned back against it nonchalantly, her face registered disappointment.

"Did you find Sebastian?" she asked.

"Oh, yes."

"Is-is he all right?"

"He's fine."

Confusion spread over her face, and he had to clamp down on the laugh of joy that bubbled up in his throat. Sebastian had been right. The woman did indeed have a devious streak in her, but not wide enough to fool him.

"You spoke with him?" she persisted.

"I could hardly do that," he said in an even tone. "Since he and Miss Shalstone were quite engrossed in a private conversation, I didn't think it appropriate to interrupt them."

This time her disappointment was acute and unmistakable. "A conversation," she said dully.

"Yes." His tone was acidic. "A very intriguing one, which they engaged in while naked. I'd say it was most unusual."

Her eyes widened in such shock that he fleetingly worried he'd made a vast mistake.

"N-naked?" she stammered. "I thought they'd be kiss—" She broke off, then colored as she saw the grin spreading over his face. She sought to cover her slip. "I-I mean, Sebastian and Miss Shalstone? How appalling! I never would have thought—"

"It's all right, Judith. You don't have to pretend."

"Pretend?"

He wiped the smile from his face, leveling an earnest gaze on her. "Tell me one thing, darling. Why didn't you go with me to speak with Sebastian if you were so concerned for him?"

She twisted her hands together, her face white as

chalk as she dropped her eyes from his. "Because . . . because I thought you'd . . ." She trailed off.

"Find them together, get angry, and make Sebastian give you up to me?"

Her head shot up, and she shook her head. "No, of course not! I-I didn't even know they were together!" Her expression grew bleak as she met his searching gaze.

Damn, he thought, now she'd retreat into her polite distance, and he'd never get the truth from her. Well, he knew all he needed to know now. It was time for more effective tactics. "Come here, Judith."

She swallowed. "You're angry with me."

"Not at all. Now come here," he commanded.

"Why?" The word was the merest whisper.

He released his crutches and they clattered to the floor as he let the door behind him take his full weight. "Because I can't hold you while I'm grabbing at my crutches, and I very badly want to be holding you when I propose."

At first, she stared at him blankly, as if disbelieving her ears. Then she gave a sweet little cry and flew to him. As her body met his, he closed his arms around her and sighed in absolute contentment.

"That's better," he murmured against her hair. Then he turned her face up to his for a long, drugging kiss, which she returned so thoroughly that any other doubts he might have had were immediately quelled.

He drew back and began stroking her hair. "You know you didn't have to resort to such drastic tactics to get my attention."

"I was so afraid," she whispered. "After Handel turned you down, I knew you'd never offer for me. And after Sebastian's return, when I had the chance to compare the two of you . . . well, I knew I could never marry him."

That confession brought another deep kiss. This time when he pulled away, she was blushing.

He cradled her head against his shoulder. "I wish you'd simply told me."

"I-I thought it would be better if I forced the issue."

He chuckled, and she glanced up, her eyes wide. "They weren't really naked, were they?"

"Oh, yes, love. Naked and in the midst of what looked to be a thoroughly intimate encounter." He suddenly realized he was speaking of the man she'd meant to marry. He stiffened. "You don't mind, do you?"

"That Sebastian was intimate with Miss Shalstone? Not at all. Although I do hope he intends to treat her fairly. It sounds most uncharacteristic of him to take advantage of a young woman that way."

"Apparently, Sebastian plans to marry her, but he was waiting to speak to your father before he said anything to you." His eyes darkened. "Damned impudent bastard. As usual, everything goes by his schedule."

"Was he very angry at you for . . . for . . ."

He smiled. "At first. But he was delighted to hear that you'd sent me."

She colored. "You didn't tell him that!"

"Oh, yes, darling. And from now on, you're going to let me in on the secret when you plan something so outrageous."

She shook her head. "I would never have thought Miss Shalstone would have let Sebastian . . ." She trailed off delicately.

"Why not? You're going to let *me* bed *you* tonight." He relished her shocked gaze.

"I shall not! We'll be married first, Richard Kent!"

With a sigh, he said, "Fine. I can see I'll have to wait a week or so longer. But that's all, because we're setting off for Gretna Green as soon as you gather your things."

Her eyes narrowed suspiciously. "Gretna Green?"

"Aye, love. Your father shan't like our arrangements at all, so I think we should remove him from them. And since eloping is out of the question for Sebastian and Miss Shalstone with her father so close by, that leaves us to make sure this comes off to everyone's advantage."

He held his breath, waiting for the protest he thought sure she'd make, but she seemed to consider his words carefully.

Then she flashed him a tentative smile. "Are you sure you can travel so far as Scotland? 'Tis a long journey."

"I can travel anywhere for you. Does this mean you'll go?"

"Whenever you want, however you want, and as soon as you want," she whispered, her eyes shining as she laid her head against his chest.

At last, he thought. He tipped her chin up to kiss her again, relishing the way she softened like wax under his fingers. At last the Biddable Judith was *his* Biddable Judith.

Cordelia had somehow managed to get her gown back on by the time Sebastian came through the door, still wearing nothing more than his drawers.

He halted in the doorway at the sight of her attempting to make herself presentable enough to flee to her bedchamber. "I'm afraid you're doing that all wrong, angel," he muttered, his jaw taut. "You should be removing the gown, not putting it on."

Keeping her face averted from his, she bent to draw on her stockings. It took all her strength to keep her voice from revealing how absolutely shattered she was. "You can't expect me to stay around waiting for your fiancée to denounce me as your 'paramour.' "

"Oh, I doubt Judith will have time to denounce anyone. She's too busy just now listening to my brother's marriage proposal."

That stopped Cordelia. Lifting her head, she fixed him with a questioning gaze. "What do you mean?"

"I'm free. My brother is marrying Judith."

She sucked in her breath, her mind racing through

the implications of that. "That's rather a surprise, isn't it?"

"Not to me. As soon as we arrived yesterday, I figured out that the two of them had grown ... er ... close in my absence. It only remained to make sure that Richard found the courage to ask her."

A horrible thought gripped her. "You didn't ... didn't plan ... that embarrassing—"

"I'd never have done that to you, and you know it," he said tersely. Then his expression softened, and he came closer. "I had planned to be more subtle with my own marriage proposal."

"Proposal?"

"Come now, Cordelia. We've played this scene before. You know I want to marry you."

His words sent her thoughts scattering in a thousand different directions. Oh, so now he again wanted to marry her, did he? Because he'd been caught with her? Because his stupid actions had made his fiancée refuse him?

She shut her eyes. Merciful heavens, she was being horribly unfair. She'd refused him when he wasn't free. What did she want from him, after all?

He rested his hands on his hips with their low-slung drawers that molded every inch of his iron-hewn body. His eyes shone like dark honey in the firelight.

He took another step forward, his expression vividly intent. "I'd meant to wait until I could work things out with the baron and explain everything to Judith before I spoke again to you of marriage. But the baron was gone and you were so determined to return to Belham that I had to work more quickly. Unfortunately, Richard interrupted before I could ... state my case."

She said nothing, stunned by the realization that he'd planned this night all along, that he'd intended to marry her for some time.

A smile spread over his face, utterly sensuous, making her breath catch in her throat. "What's wrong, angel? And don't give me your 'I want to be independent' speech again. I won't believe a word of it." He reached for her and worked the gown back over her head, tossing it aside as she continued to stand in amazement.

One quick motion and her shift was lying at her feet. "You said you loved me." His voice held all the tenderness in the world. "I heard you say the words, and I won't let you take them back, not when I love you so much that I ache with it."

He enfolded her in his arms, and she sighed, lifting her face up to his, a slow joy building beneath her breast that made her breath quicken and her heart thunder.

His eyes glittered as he stared down at her. "I'm free, and you have no more reasons to refuse me. You *won't* refuse me."

As if to demonstrate his power over her, he slid his hand between her legs and gave her impudent, intimate caresses that reminded her of his earlier delicious torments.

She attempted to look indignant, which was difficult under the circumstances. "You are the most conceited, controlling lout," she muttered, but her body turned to butter beneath his expert hands.

"And you love me anyway."

He kissed her hard, then walked her backward until her legs came up against his bed. Next thing she knew they were lying across it, and his body was covering hers.

"Say it, angel," he murmured against her lips. "Say you love me anyway."

As she stared up into his face, which even now held the merest hint of uncertainty, her heart swelled with joy. Could she really be hearing right? Was she at last to see her dreams realized, after all the disappointments of the past few weeks?

"Say it!" he growled.

Yes, apparently she was. "I love you anyway."

"And you'll marry me."

Marriage. To Sebastian. What heaven! Still, she felt a need to torment him a little, especially after the way he'd used her desire earlier to force her into revealing her feelings. "I want to be independent," she said, but her giggle immediately afterward took away from the effect.

"Independent, eh?" he grumbled as he parted her legs with his knee. "Don't tell me I'll have to resort to extreme tactics again to make you tell the truth."

She could already feel his arousal growing against her thigh. "As I recall, your insolent tactics were less than successful last time. You didn't force me to say anything. I said it because I wanted to."

He captured her arms and pinned them at her sides. His brilliant smile held promises of things to come, and she squirmed beneath him, already anticipating the pleasures he'd give her.

Then the smile faded, and he stared at her with eyes gone serious and dark. "Say you'll marry me, angel, and you may punish me for my insolence in whatever way you wish."

For a long moment, she stared into the face of the man she loved, the man she could never get enough of. Love for him filled her expression. "Now that's an offer even an independent woman can't refuse."

He gave a satisfied chuckle, then lowered his head to suck her breast as he released her hands. "Ah, I do so love forcing an independent woman to surrender."

She reached down between their bodies and closed her hand around his silky shaft. "By the time I'm finished with you, Your Grace, you may regret those words. I accept your offer to punish you for your insolent torments earlier."

He groaned blissfully as her hand began to caress him. "Punish away, angel. I suspect this will be only the first of many, many battles. And I look forward to every one of them."

So do I, she thought as he captured her lips in a thorough kiss. *So do I.*

Chapter Twenty-three

Hark! The echoing air a triumph sings,
And all around pleased cupids clap their wings.
— Henry Purcell,
"Hark! the Echoing Air"

Cordelia came awake slowly amid vague sensations of warmth and contentment. She kept her eyes closed, wanting to revel in the delicious feelings. Gradually she became aware of Sebastian's arm thrown over her naked belly and his even breathing on her cheek. Dear, wanton memories assailed her, of Sebastian making love to her in a variety of interesting ways.

And we're to be married, she thought in wonder.

She opened her eyes to gaze at him and instead bolted upright in bed. Oh, merciful heavens, she was in trouble now. Sunlight flooded every inch of the well-appointed bedchamber. Sebastian had persuaded her to stay the night with him by promising that he'd awaken her in enough time for her to sneak to her bedchamber before dawn. Dawn had obviously passed long ago.

"Go back to sleep, angel," Sebastian mumbled into his pillow.

Devil take the wretch, she thought.

She turned to glare at him and ended up staring at his peaceful expression, at the tousled hair and stubbled chin. A faint smile touched her lips.

Then she heard noises in the hall and the smile fled her lips. She jerked the pillow from under Sebastian's head, then hit him with it.

His eyes shot open, and he scowled. "I hope you're not going to awaken me like that every morning." Then he seemed to realize how bright the room was.

To her complete dismay, he threw his head back and laughed.

"It's not funny. You said you'd wake up." She slid quickly out of bed and glanced about for her clothes.

"I think we've missed dawn." Amusement lingered in his voice. "Ah, well, we might as well throw caution to the winds then. Come back to bed."

She didn't even grace that with an answer, but unearthed her crumpled shift from beneath his drawers at the foot of the tester bed and jerked it on over her head.

"What's a few more minutes?" he said. "Besides, Richard has probably told *someone* what he saw."

"If he'd told anyone that mattered, we'd not have slept late. I assure you, if he'd told Father, you'd be standing in a church at this very moment."

"I can think of worse things," he said congenially as he sat up and rubbed his chest. His eyes raked her insolently, and his voice lowered. "Come back to bed, angel. Lovemaking is even better in the light of day."

Her expression of disgust brought another laugh from him.

"Oh, just stay in bed!" she muttered. "I'm perfectly capable of getting back to my room without your help."

Shaking his head, he slid from the bed. "I can see you're going to force me to continue this in your bedchamber."

He grabbed her and kissed her soundly.

And she melted, as he'd no doubt known she would. "You have an insatiable appetite, Your Grace," she whispered against his mouth. Then she thought of one of his sisters looking for her after finding her bedchamber empty, and all her irritation returned.

She shoved him. Hard.

He fell on the bed and groaned. "I never had an insatiable appetite until I met you."

She threw his breeches at him. "Well, if you want anything more today, my hungry suitor, you'd best get me to my room with my reputation intact."

Between his stealing kisses and her mostly futile attempts to resist, it was another quarter hour before they were finally dressed enough to leave.

"Let's go out through my study door," he told her. "That way, if anyone discovers us, we can tell them we had things to discuss and happened to get an early start."

She rolled her eyes. "Yes, and we just happened to wear the same clothes we were wearing last night." Nonetheless, she followed him through the study.

They opened the door carefully and peeked out. There in a chair in the hall sat Honorine. Cordelia stifled a groan, and Sebastian started to shut the door, but it was too late. Honorine had seen them.

Honorine leapt from the chair and went straight for the study door, catching it and swinging it open.

"So," she snapped, "the lovebirds emerge at last!"

Her voice dripped with sarcasm and her face was the reddest Cordelia had ever seen it. Cordelia winced. This business of being caught with Sebastian by Honorine was certainly getting tiresome.

"Been waiting long?" Sebastian asked, not a whit of embarrassment on his face.

Cordelia wanted to strangle him. Merciful heavens, how many more people could discover them in compromising circumstances? If she hadn't already agreed to marry him, she'd have been forced to it by now.

"Since sunup," came Honorine's terse answer.

Cordelia cast Sebastian a scathing glance, but he merely chuckled.

"And what prompted this diligence?" he asked, drawing Cordelia to him with a hand about her waist.

"The house is in an uproar, yet no one would disturb Your Grace, and the maid you assigned to Cordelia refused to let anyone disturb her. I, of course, smelled a rat."

"Of course." Sebastian gave her his most ingratiating grin.

"Why is the house in an uproar?" Cordelia asked, almost fearful of hearing the answer. Perhaps she'd been wrong, after all. Perhaps Lord Kent *had* told someone what he'd seen. Merciful heavens, she'd never live down *that* embarrassment.

Honorine planted her hands on her waist. "Lord Kent and Lady Judith have eloped. They left a note saying they were off for Gretna Green."

Sebastian's bark of laughter drew indignant glares from both Cordelia and Honorine. "Got right to it, didn't they?" he announced. "I suppose he decided to make sure the baron didn't make a fuss. Excellent idea. I wish I'd thought of it myself." He grinned wolfishly at Cordelia. "Just think, angel, right now we could be in a comfortable inn somewhere north of London having breakfast served to us in our room."

"Over my dead body," Honorine clipped out, then lifted one eyebrow. "I take it the marriage proposal has at last been made?"

Cordelia glanced quizzically from Sebastian to Honorine.

Sebastian nodded. "Made and accepted. I had to be more persuasive than I'd expected, but . . ." He paused meaningfully before going on, "she came around."

"Of course she did," Honorine retorted. "The girl's not a fool."

"Don't tell me you two have been plotting behind my back," Cordelia said, not sure whether to be outraged, embarrassed, or delighted.

Honorine cast Sebastian a dark look. "Not exactly. When it became obvious that His Grace was overstepping his bounds, I insisted on being let in on his plans, at which time he informed me that no only had he proposed, but that you'd turned him down." She shook her head. "I must say, Cordelia, that was not what I expected of you. His Grace may be a bit overbearing, but he'll make a suitable husband ... after some training, of course."

"I'll make a *perfect* husband for Cordelia," Sebastian asserted. "It just took me some time to convince her."

No, love, she thought, her arm snaking about his waist, *I always knew it.* But she didn't say the words aloud. She was beginning to learn that some things were better left to be discovered.

Sebastian's arm tightened. His words grew clipped as he fixed Honorine with a defiant expression. "Now that you've determined that I mean to do right by Cordelia after all, you must excuse us." He began to pull Cordelia down the hall.

"Not so fast, Your Grace," Honorine called after them. "I expect you both downstairs in fifteen minutes ... *appropriately dressed* ... at which time you will meet with Oswald and make this all official or I *will* tell him *everything*. Is that clear?"

Sebastian groaned and halted. "And she calls *me* overbearing," he muttered under his breath. "I'm beginning to see why your father called her the battle-ax."

Turning to face her, he glared balefully. "I'll be there, Mrs. Beardsley."

"And one more thing."

He gritted his teeth. "Yes?"

She held out an envelope. "This came for Cordelia this morning. It's from Handel."

Sebastian's mouth dropped open, but he recovered quickly enough and stalked back to snatch the envelope from Honorine. He started to tear it open, then apparently realized it wasn't his right to do so. Solemnly he handed it to Cordelia, whose hands were already shaking.

Her heart raced as she stared at the sealed envelope. She held it a moment, almost afraid to find out what it might contain. Sebastian squeezed her shoulder encouragingly, and she sucked in her breath.

And opened the envelope.

Not surprisingly, the script was as dramatic and florid as the composer himself, but what it said came as a shock:

Dear Miss Shalstone,

After reading your notes on my arioso, I am forced to admit that your choral version is an improvement. With your permission, I would like to use it.

In repayment for that use, I shall send Lord Kent an oratorio for publication, as you requested. Since it appears that without my help, Lord Kent will cease publishing your work, and since you stubbornly insist on patronizing Lord Kent, I suppose it is the least I can do. I am reluctant to deprive the world of your intriguing talent.

Please inform Lord Kent that I would like to have him attend me next Tuesday to discuss the particulars, and do come with him. We can discuss the numerous flaws in your choral version.

Respectfully,
    George Frideric Handel

Cordelia had to smile at Handel's closing statement. It must have taken a great deal of humility for the great man to write that first paragraph, so she couldn't blame him for trying to salvage his pride in the last one.

"Well?" Sebastian asked tersely. "What does it say?"

She handed him the note, beaming from ear to ear. As soon as he'd read it, Honorine snatched it back from him and scanned it, trying to suppress a smile as she did so.

"We did it," Sebastian whispered. "Sweet mother of God, we did it!"

Honorine's eyebrows rose. "*We* did nothing, Your Grace. I would say Cordelia was largely responsible for this feat, and don't you forget it." She pursed her lips, apparently attempting to maintain her stern exterior, but Cordelia could see the smile lurking in her eyes as she handed the note back.

"Fifteen minutes," Honorine reminded them. "I shall see you both downstairs in fifteen minutes." Then she marched off.

Cordelia heard her steps quicken on the stairs as soon as she was out of sight, and Sebastian chuckled at the sound of loud humming coming from below. "I believe I must revise my earlier opinion of Mrs. Beardsley."

"She likes you," Cordelia murmured as he enfolded her in his arms. "She simply believes in doing the right thing by me."

Sebastian stared down into her glowing face, his expression suddenly serious. "As do I." He paused, stroking her disheveled hair back from her face. "You know, angel, this changes everything. You truly could be an independent woman now, since Handel—"

She cut him off with one finger to his lips. "Do you intend to forbid me to write music once we're married?"

After planting a kiss on her forehead, he smiled. "I said before that I wouldn't. If Handel refuses to 'deprive the world of your intriguing talent,' who am I to do so?"

She gave a satisfied sigh. "Then I shall merely become an independent woman married to an independent man. With that, I can be content."

He drew her up against his hard body with a growl. "More than content, I hope."

A delighted laugh welled up from her as his lips lowered to hers. "More than content. Much, much more than content." Then she wound her arms about his neck and met his kiss with all the pride and grace and passion of an independent woman.

And the note from Handel fluttered to the floor.

Epilogue

If music be the food of love,
Sing on, till I am fill'd with joy;
For then my list'ning soul you move
To pleasures that can never cloy.
                    —Henry Purcell,
                        "If Music Be the Food of Love"

Sebastian paused on the threshold of the music room, listening to the light air emanating from the harpsichord at the other end. He stared at the back of his wife's head, which bobbed and dipped in time to the music, and he marveled at her talent all over again. To think that he was allowed to partake of this precious sweetness whenever he wished. It was more than any man could want.

Marriage to Cordelia had necessitated some changes in his life, to be sure. For one thing, he'd cut short his remaining time in India, since her association with Handel and his brother would make it difficult for her to live outside England. But his maneuvering had turned out well. She and he had spent only a year in India, enough time for him to tie up loose ends and find sufficient native leadership to take his place. By the time they'd returned to London, his business was on an even keel, and so was Richard's.

He glanced around the lavishly appointed music room, which had become her territory. Here she composed and here she retreated when she wanted solitude. He felt almost like an intruder.

Yet he knew on this day she'd welcome his presence, for it had been three long weeks since he'd last been at home, thanks to business that had taken him to Paris.

As he watched her, still loath to disturb her, her playing grew particularly vigorous, and her cap fell, exposing her gently wound hair, the same hair he loved to draw down at night when all was quiet and still. Less than two years had passed since their majestic wedding at St. Paul's Cathedral, yet he never tired of loosening her hair from its coil, nor of watching her eyes darken in pleasure as her mouth softened under his.

Suddenly the music erupted into crashing dissonance, jarring him from his pleasant thoughts. He frowned. Then a delighted giggle came from the harpsichord as a small head crowned with a few chestnut ringlets emerged above his wife's shoulder.

His frown was transformed into a proud smile at the sight of his little Elizabeth. The child giggled again as more crashing chords sounded.

Cordelia chuckled and squeezed Elizabeth. "You simply can't bear to let me finish the piece, can you?" She smoothed down the baby curls that never stayed tame. "I do so hope you're not going to turn out to be tone-deaf like your grandfather. One of those is quite enough for a family. Of course, your father's side isn't talented either, so it does look as if bloodlines are against you, pet."

"Nonsense," Sebastian said as he began walking toward them. "Her mother has enough talent to make up for all of us."

Cordelia whirled on the bench, a brilliant smile splitting her face. "Sebastian! I thought you weren't returning until tomorrow!"

Elizabeth smiled in delight and held out two chubby hands.

He set down the satchel he held, then caught the baby up in his arms and jiggled her until she laughed. "And how is my musician-to-be? I see Mother has started you on lessons already."

Elizabeth giggled uncomprehendingly, then stuffed her thumb in her mouth.

"Actually, this is the first moment I've had her to myself since Father and Honorine arrived to visit. Fortunately, the girls convinced them to go shopping today and give me some time with her."

Sebastian smiled. "I swear, every time those two visit, my sisters turn them into honorary parents."

He thought of how different Cordelia's father was these days from when Sebastian had first met him. The vicar had apparently finally conquered his problem with liquor by abstaining completely. Sebastian hadn't seen his father-in-law touch a drop since the day Cordelia had threatened to set off for London without him.

"Wait until you see what my father taught Elizabeth to do while you were gone," Cordelia said, her cheeks two excited circles of color. "Put her down on the floor. We've something to show Dada, haven't we, Elizabeth?"

His eyebrows raised, he set Elizabeth on her feet.

"Walk to Dada," Cordelia urged gently. "Go on, pet. Show Dada."

Elizabeth balanced unsteadily for a moment, then took a tentative step forward. She started to teeter, then corrected herself and took another step forward before stopping suddenly too short and falling on her bottom.

He whisked her up, laughing as he cradled her in his arm. "Dada's clever girl," he said. His eyes met Cordelia's. "How lucky I am to have two such clever girls. I only wish I'd been here to see it the first time."

He put Elizabeth down, watching as she crawled off, apparently not quite ready to brave walking again. Then he returned his gaze to Cordelia. "Speaking of clever girls, I've brought you something."

She flashed him a glance of mock reproach. "Something from Paris? Honestly, Sebastian, you don't have to bring me an expensive jewel or gown every time you go off on business. I'm just glad to have you back."

"I didn't get this from Paris." He picked up the

satchel from where he'd left it, then removed a thin quarto with "Kent Publishing" stamped in gold at the top of the first sheet. "I asked Richard to have it ready for my return."

He handed it to her, watching with pleasure as she read the title and then her own name printed in bold black letters immediately below it. Her expression turned from astonishment to delight.

"It's the first, angel," he said, his throat tightening. "Only the first of many pieces to be published under your name. I'm only sorry it took so long, what with our being in India and Richard's struggles to get the company back on its feet."

She laid the music down, then threw herself into his arms, her eyes filling with tears. "It's wonderful!" she choked out, wiping her eyes with the back of her hand. "Truly, Sebastian, 'tis the best gift you could ever have given me."

"I didn't actually have much to do with its production—" he protested laughingly as she covered his cheeks with kisses.

"Of course you did." She drew back to gaze at him with bright eyes and an even brighter smile. "If it weren't for you, I'd still be tending Father in Belham and wishing for something more. If it weren't for you, I'd never have met Handel or your brother or—"

"Ah, but if it weren't for you, my brother's business would have collapsed, and I'd have found myself in an unsatisfying marriage, so I'd say we're even on that score." He thought briefly of how easily it could all have been different, and he stared at her lovingly. "Every day I thank the fates that brought me to you . . . or should I say, the God that saw fit to give me my own special angel."

He lowered his hands to cup her rear, drawing her close enough for her to feel how intensely he'd missed her. After casting a furtive glance at Elizabeth, who was happily spreading all of her mother's sheet music across the floor, he returned his gaze to his wife, his heart pounding at the sight of her warm brown eyes.

Cordelia pressed her ripe young body flush against his. "You thought me a very wicked angel at the time, as I recall."

"Nay," he muttered. "Dangerous, perhaps, but not wicked."

And as he bent her back over his arm and kissed her sweet, familiar mouth with a fervor born of three weeks of abstinence, he thought to himself that a great deal could be said for loving a dangerous angel. A great deal indeed.